THE GRAPHIC NOVEL
William Shakespeare

PLAIN TEXT VERSION

Script Adaptation: John McDonald
Pencils: Neill Cameron
Inks: Bambos
Colouring: Jason Cardy & Kat Nicholson
Lettering: Nigel Dobbyn

Editor in Chief: Clive Bryant

Henry V: The Graphic Novel
Plain Text Version

William Shakespeare

First UK Edition

Published by: Classical Comics Ltd
Copyright ©2007 Classical Comics Ltd.

All enquiries should be addressed to:
Classical Comics Ltd.
PO Box 7280
Litchborough
Towcester
NN12 9AR, UK
Tel: 0845 812 3000

info@classicalcomics.com
www.classicalcomics.com

ISBN: 978-1-906332-01-3

Printed in the UK
by Hampton Printing (Bristol) Ltd

Contents

Dramatis Personæ

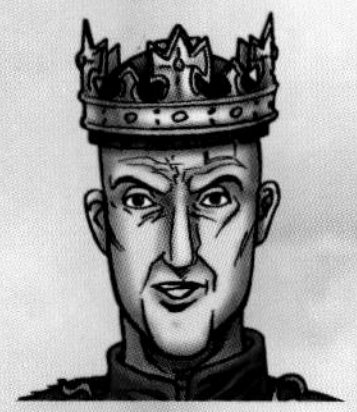

King Henry the Fifth
King of England

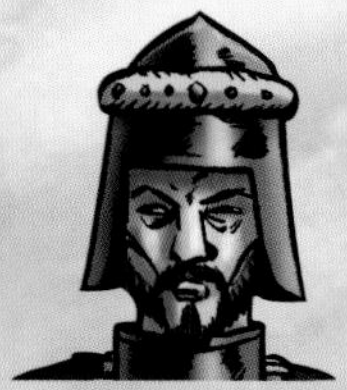

Duke Of Gloucester
Brother to the King

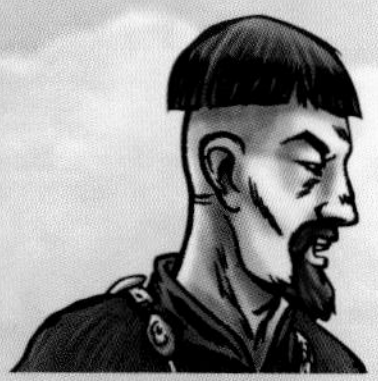

Duke Of Bedford
Brother to the King

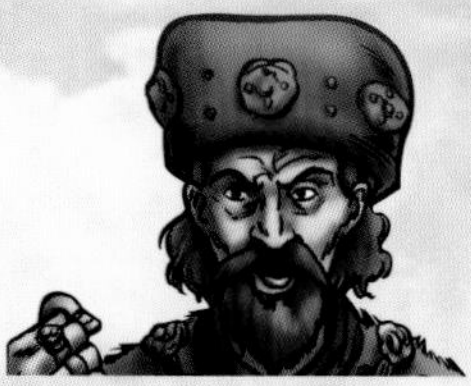

Duke Of Exeter
Uncle to the King

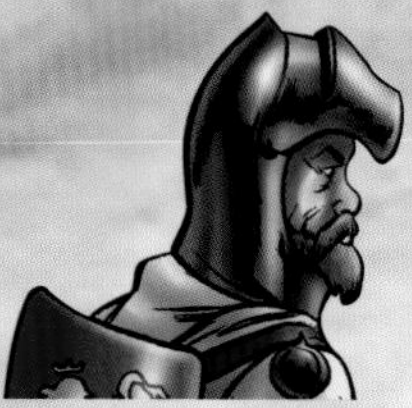

Duke Of York
Cousin to the King

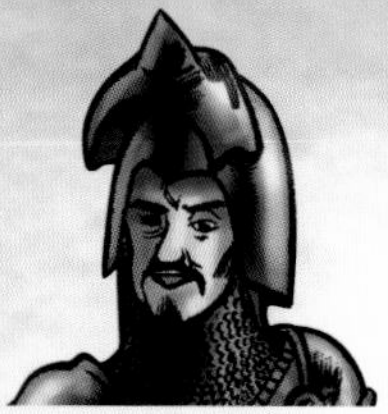

Earl Of Salisbury

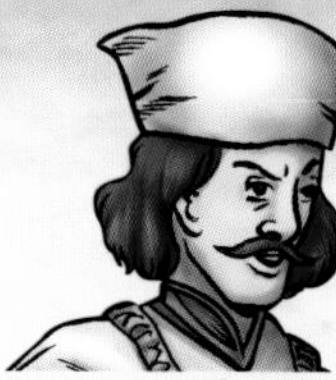

Earl Of Westmoreland

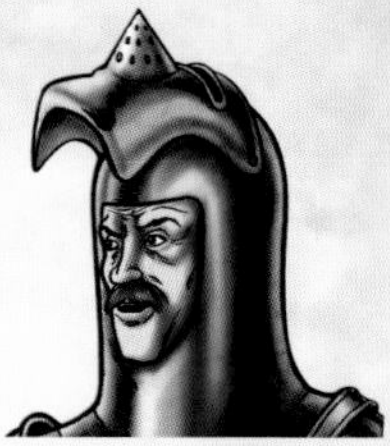

Earl Of Warwick

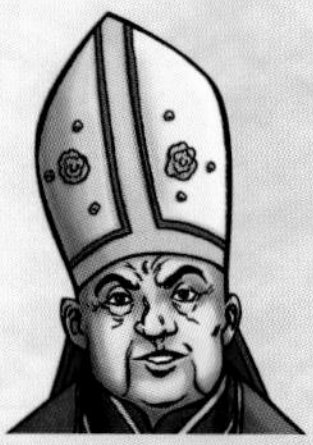

Archbishop Of Canterbury

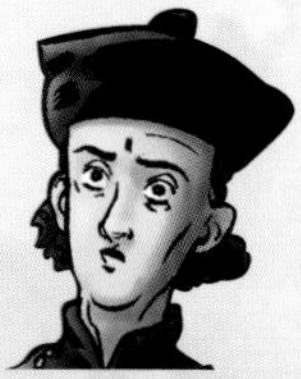

Bishop Of Ely

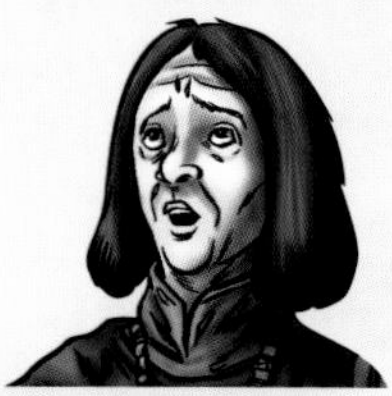

Earl Of Cambridge
Conspirator

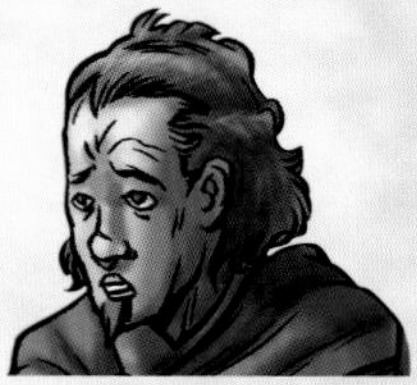

Henry, Lord Scroop of Marsham
Conspirator

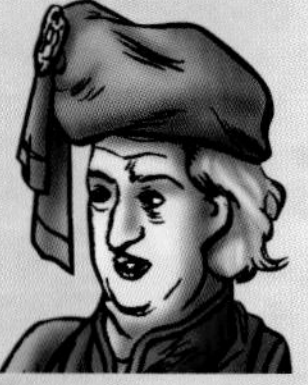

Sir Thomas Grey
Conspirator

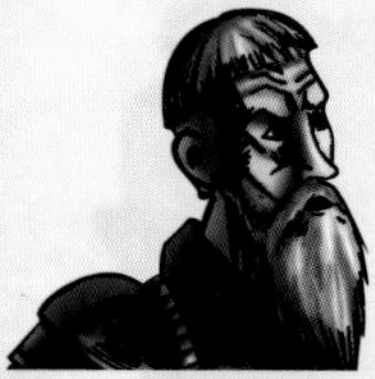

Sir Thomas Erpingham
Officer in King Henry's army

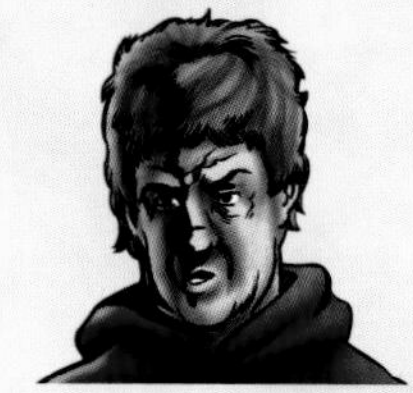

Captain Gower
Officer in King Henry's army

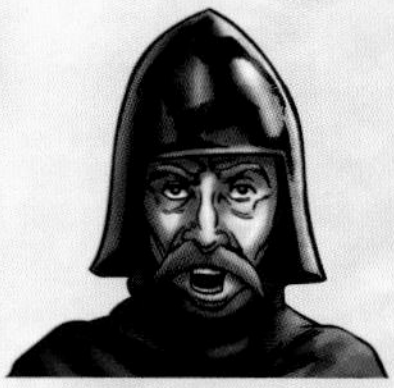

Captain Fluellen
Officer in King Henry's army

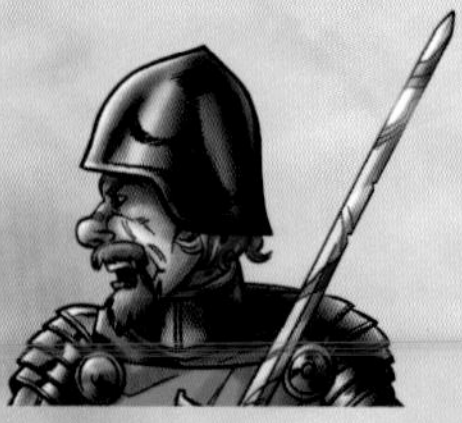

Captain Macmorris
Officer in King Henry's army

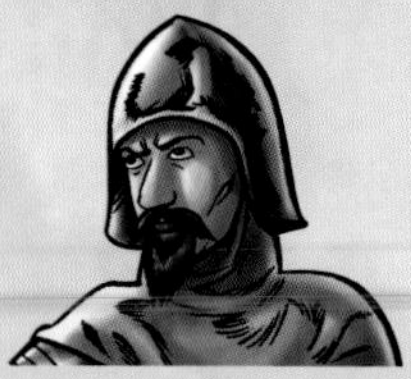

Captain Jamy
Officer in King Henry's army

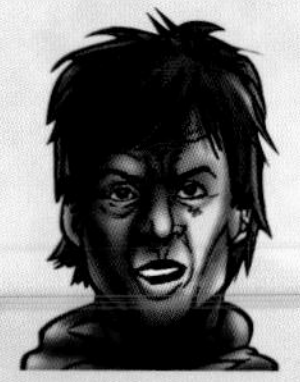

John Bates
Soldier in King Henry's army

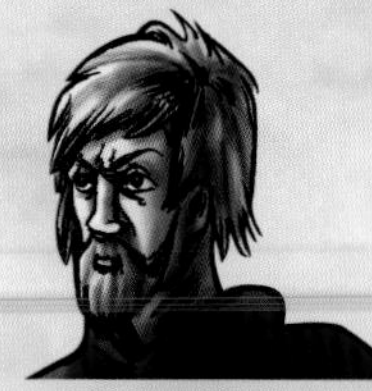

Alexander Court
Soldier in King Henry's army

Dramatis Personæ

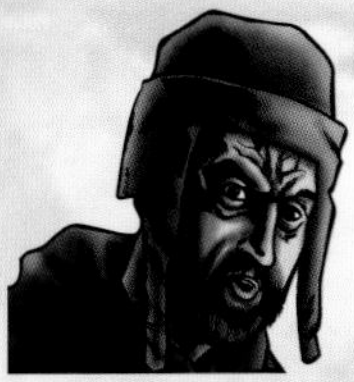

Michael Williams
Soldier in King Henry's army

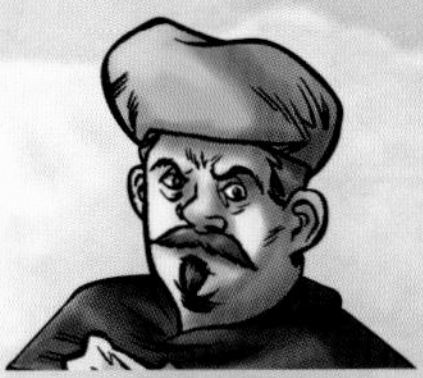

Pistol
Soldier in King Henry's army

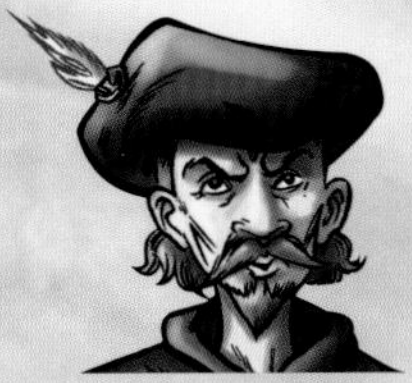

Nym
Soldier in King Henry's army

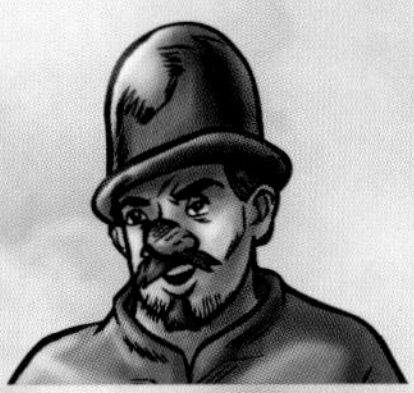

Bardolph
Soldier in King Henry's army

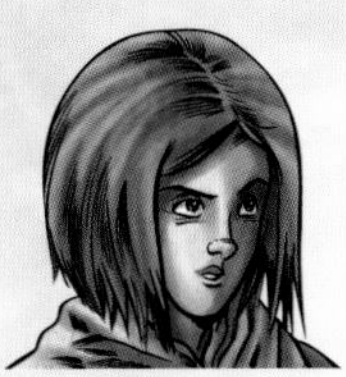

Boy
Servant

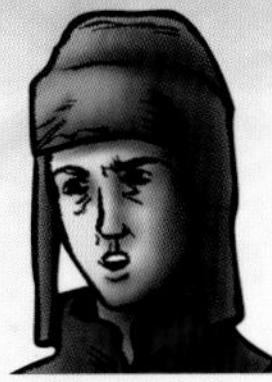

A Herald

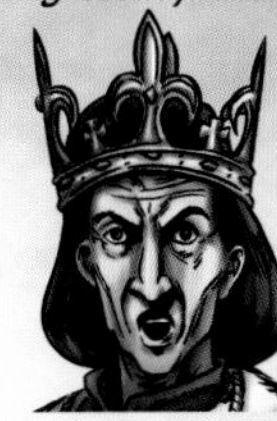

Charles the Sixth
King of France

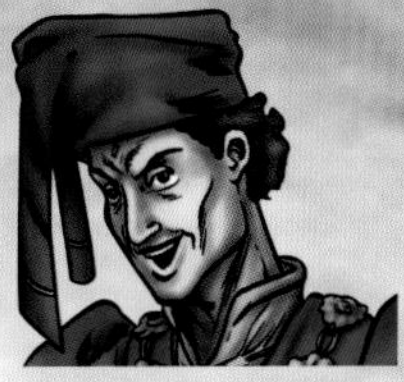

Lewis
The Dauphin

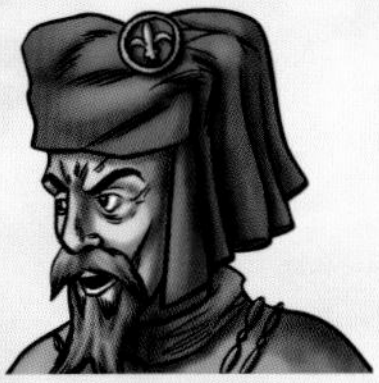

Duke Of Bourbon
French Duke

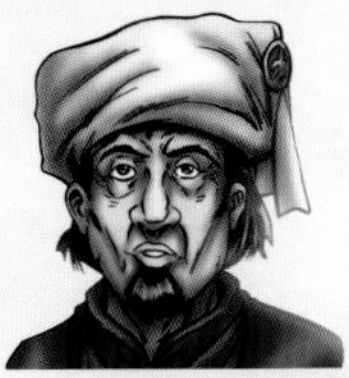

Duke Of Burgundy
French Duke

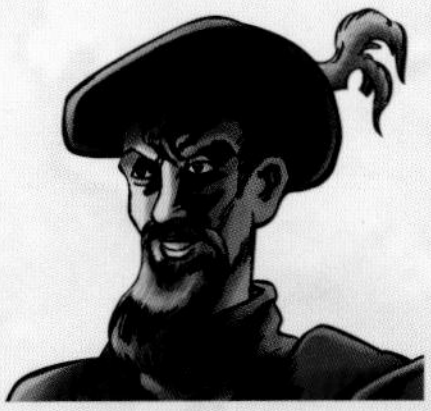

Duke Of Orleans
French Duke

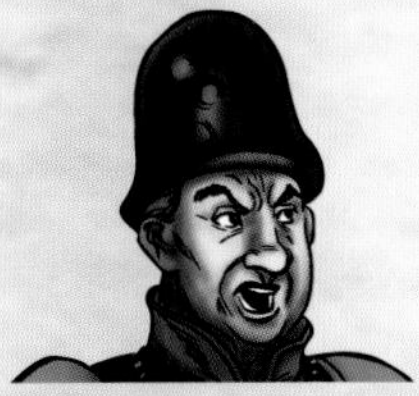

The Constable of France

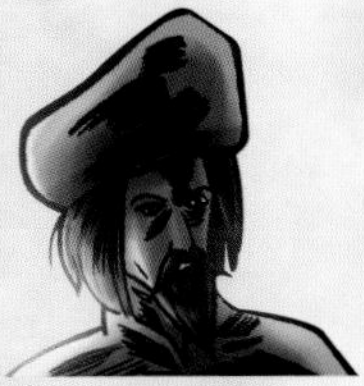

Lord Rambures
French Lord

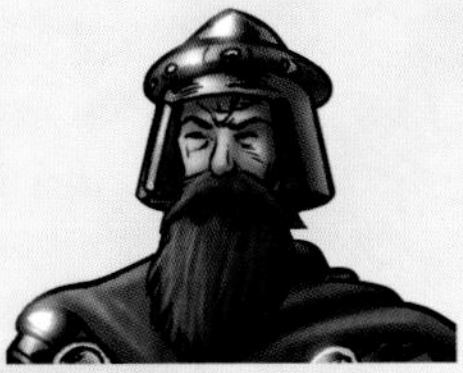

Lord Grandpré
French Lord

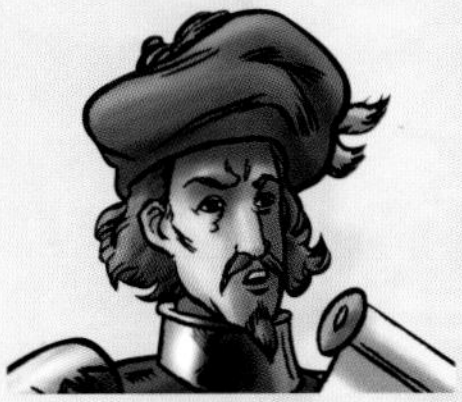

Montjoy
French Herald

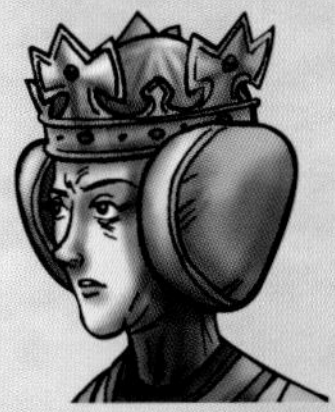

Queen Isabel
Queen of France

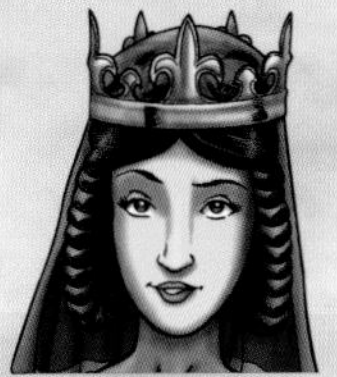

Katherine
Daughter to Charles and Isabel

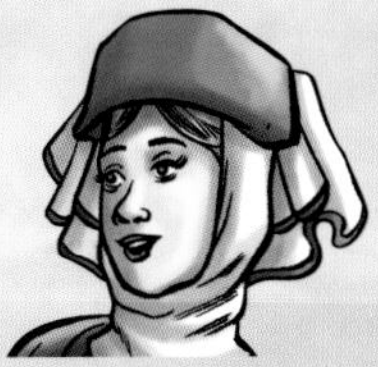

Alice
A lady attending on Katherine

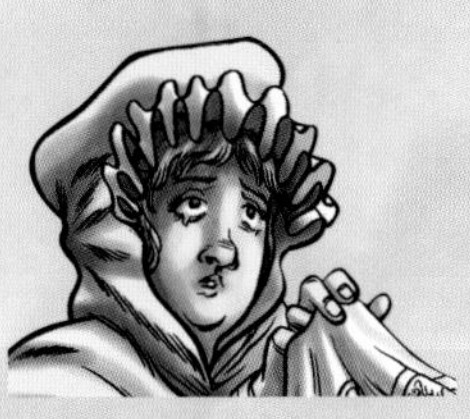

Hostess of a tavern
Formerly Mistress Quickly

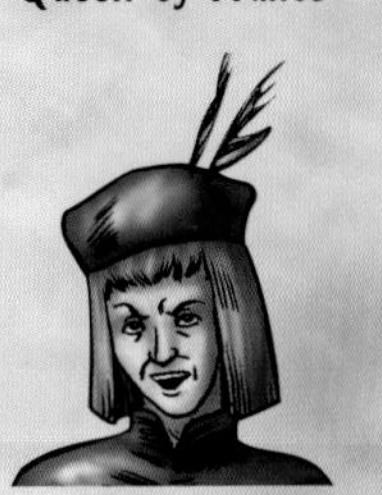

Chorus

Synopsis

It's the 15th century and the Archbishop of Canterbury, worried over impending legislation that would effectively rob the Church in England of its power and wealth, convinces Henry V to forego this pursuit in favour of laying claim to France. Armed with a legal technicality, Henry decides to take the throne of France by whatever means necessary. The Dauphin's insulting response (sending an ambassador with a gift of tennis balls) convinces Henry that the French will only respond to war. He gathers his army to invade France, but he must also make certain that he leaves enough troops in England to quell any potential rebellions. This leaves him with a relatively small invasion force.

Henry must deal with one plot before even crossing the Channel. Lords Cambridge, Scroop and Grey are discovered to be conspiring to assassinate Henry (instigated by the French). Henry makes a very public example of all three, arresting them in person and seeing to their execution. The army then lays siege to Harfleur, capturing it after sustaining heavy losses. Henry wants to take his army out of France before the onset of winter, but the French are certain they can teach the young king a humiliating lesson on the field of battle. This stiffens Henry's resolve and he decides that if the French want a decisive battle, they'll get it!

While in camp, Henry disguises himself as a common soldier and mingles with his troops before the battle. He talks candidly with his men and they with him. The men may be a little wary of their king, but their willingness to fight the French army is undaunted. Next day at Agincourt, Henry makes the stirring St. Crispin's Day speech, knowing his army is outnumbered five to one. But, aided by the longbows of his archers, Henry wins the day. The French sue for peace, which Henry grants on his own terms. These terms are spelled out in the Treaty of Troyes – Henry will marry Princess Katherine of France and will be named as heir to the French throne. England and France will thus be united in peace.

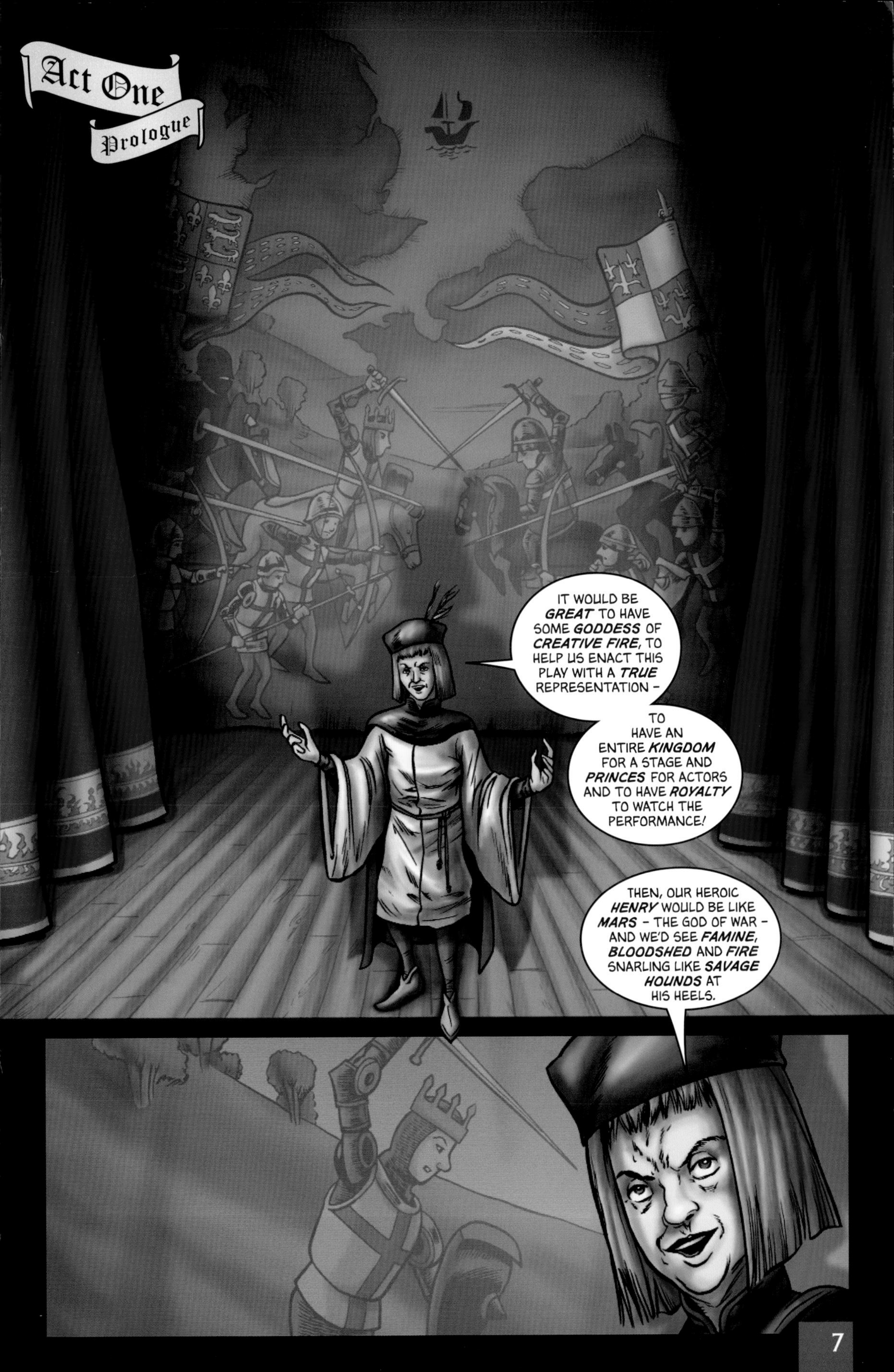
Act One
Prologue
IT WOULD BE GREAT TO HAVE SOME GODDESS OF CREATIVE FIRE, TO HELP US ENACT THIS PLAY WITH A TRUE REPRESENTATION –
TO HAVE AN ENTIRE KINGDOM FOR A STAGE AND PRINCES FOR ACTORS AND TO HAVE ROYALTY TO WATCH THE PERFORMANCE!
THEN, OUR HEROIC HENRY WOULD BE LIKE MARS – THE GOD OF WAR – AND WE'D SEE FAMINE, BLOODSHED AND FIRE SNARLING LIKE SAVAGE HOUNDS AT HIS HEELS.

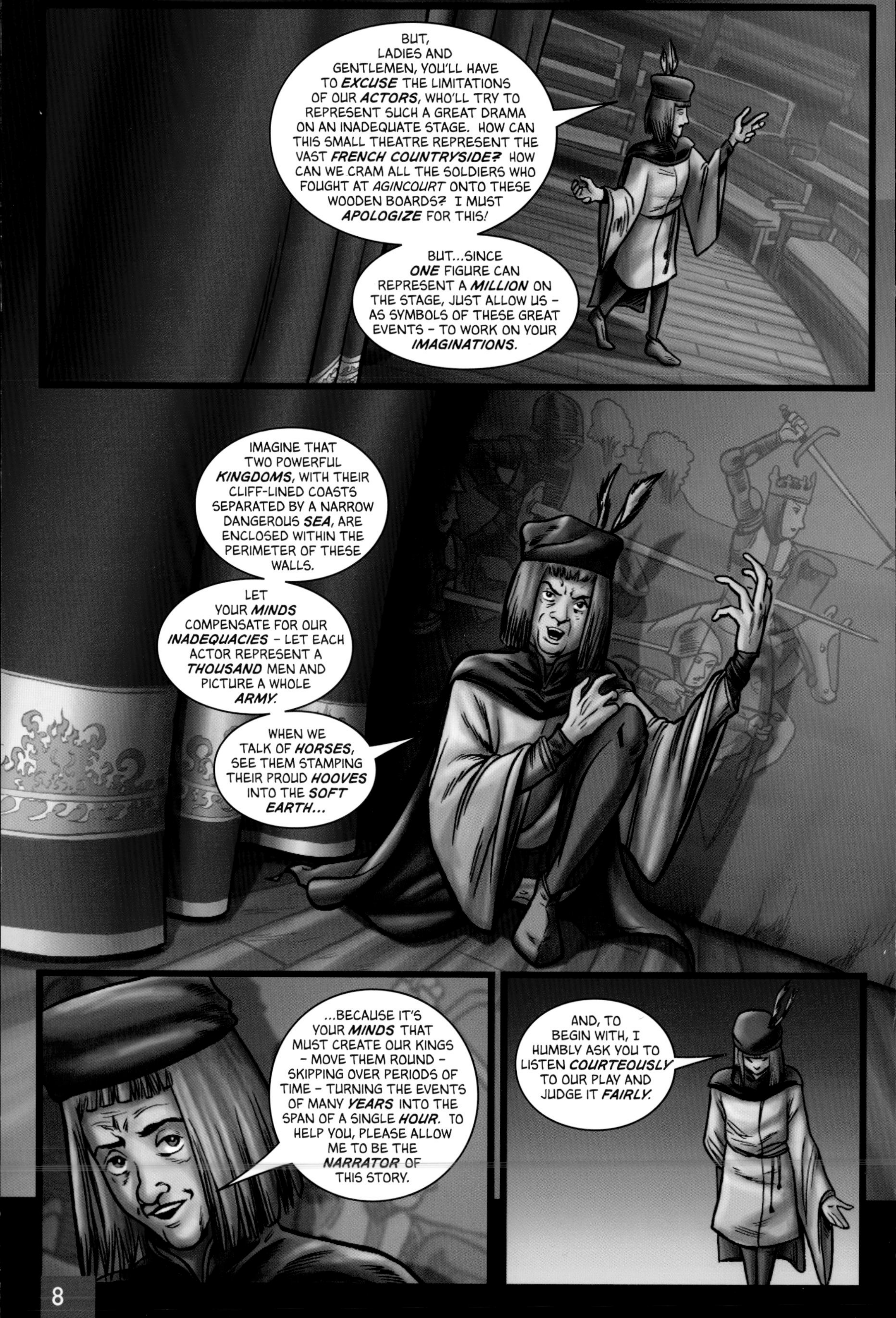
BUT, LADIES AND GENTLEMEN, YOU'LL HAVE TO EXCUSE THE LIMITATIONS OF OUR ACTORS, WHO'LL TRY TO REPRESENT SUCH A GREAT DRAMA ON AN INADEQUATE STAGE. HOW CAN THIS SMALL THEATRE REPRESENT THE VAST FRENCH COUNTRYSIDE? HOW CAN WE CRAM ALL THE SOLDIERS WHO FOUGHT AT AGINCOURT ONTO THESE WOODEN BOARDS? I MUST APOLOGIZE FOR THIS!
BUT...SINCE ONE FIGURE CAN REPRESENT A MILLION ON THE STAGE, JUST ALLOW US – AS SYMBOLS OF THESE GREAT EVENTS – TO WORK ON YOUR IMAGINATIONS.
IMAGINE THAT TWO POWERFUL KINGDOMS, WITH THEIR CLIFF-LINED COASTS SEPARATED BY A NARROW DANGEROUS SEA, ARE ENCLOSED WITHIN THE PERIMETER OF THESE WALLS.
LET YOUR MINDS COMPENSATE FOR OUR INADEQUACIES – LET EACH ACTOR REPRESENT A THOUSAND MEN AND PICTURE A WHOLE ARMY.
WHEN WE TALK OF HORSES, SEE THEM STAMPING THEIR PROUD HOOVES INTO THE SOFT EARTH...
...BECAUSE IT'S YOUR MINDS THAT MUST CREATE OUR KINGS – MOVE THEM ROUND – SKIPPING OVER PERIODS OF TIME – TURNING THE EVENTS OF MANY YEARS INTO THE SPAN OF A SINGLE HOUR. TO HELP YOU, PLEASE ALLOW ME TO BE THE NARRATOR OF THIS STORY.
AND, TO BEGIN WITH, I HUMBLY ASK YOU TO LISTEN COURTEOUSLY TO OUR PLAY AND JUDGE IT FAIRLY.

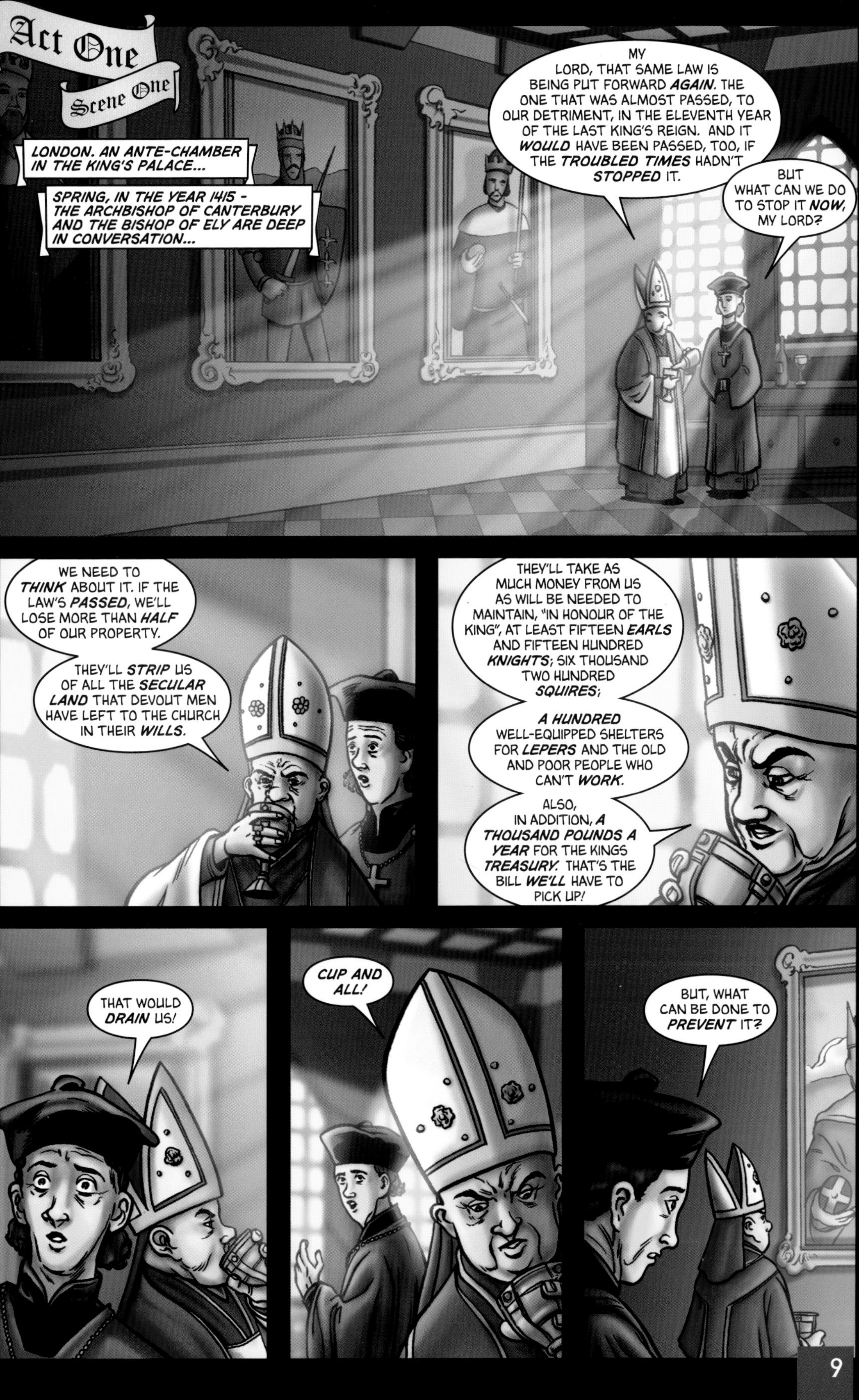
Act One
Scene One
LONDON. AN ANTE-CHAMBER IN THE KING'S PALACE...
SPRING, IN THE YEAR 1415 - THE ARCHBISHOP OF CANTERBURY AND THE BISHOP OF ELY ARE DEEP IN CONVERSATION...
MY LORD, THAT SAME LAW IS BEING PUT FORWARD AGAIN. THE ONE THAT WAS ALMOST PASSED, TO OUR DETRIMENT, IN THE ELEVENTH YEAR OF THE LAST KING'S REIGN. AND IT WOULD HAVE BEEN PASSED, TOO, IF THE TROUBLED TIMES HADN'T STOPPED IT.
BUT WHAT CAN WE DO TO STOP IT NOW, MY LORD?
WE NEED TO THINK ABOUT IT. IF THE LAW'S PASSED, WE'LL LOSE MORE THAN HALF OF OUR PROPERTY.
THEY'LL STRIP US OF ALL THE SECULAR LAND THAT DEVOUT MEN HAVE LEFT TO THE CHURCH IN THEIR WILLS.
THEY'LL TAKE AS MUCH MONEY FROM US AS WILL BE NEEDED TO MAINTAIN, "IN HONOUR OF THE KING", AT LEAST FIFTEEN EARLS AND FIFTEEN HUNDRED KNIGHTS; SIX THOUSAND TWO HUNDRED SQUIRES;
A HUNDRED WELL-EQUIPPED SHELTERS FOR LEPERS AND THE OLD AND POOR PEOPLE WHO CAN'T WORK.
ALSO, IN ADDITION, A THOUSAND POUNDS A YEAR FOR THE KINGS TREASURY. THAT'S THE BILL WE'LL HAVE TO PICK UP!
THAT WOULD DRAIN US!
CUP AND ALL!
BUT, WHAT CAN BE DONE TO PREVENT IT?

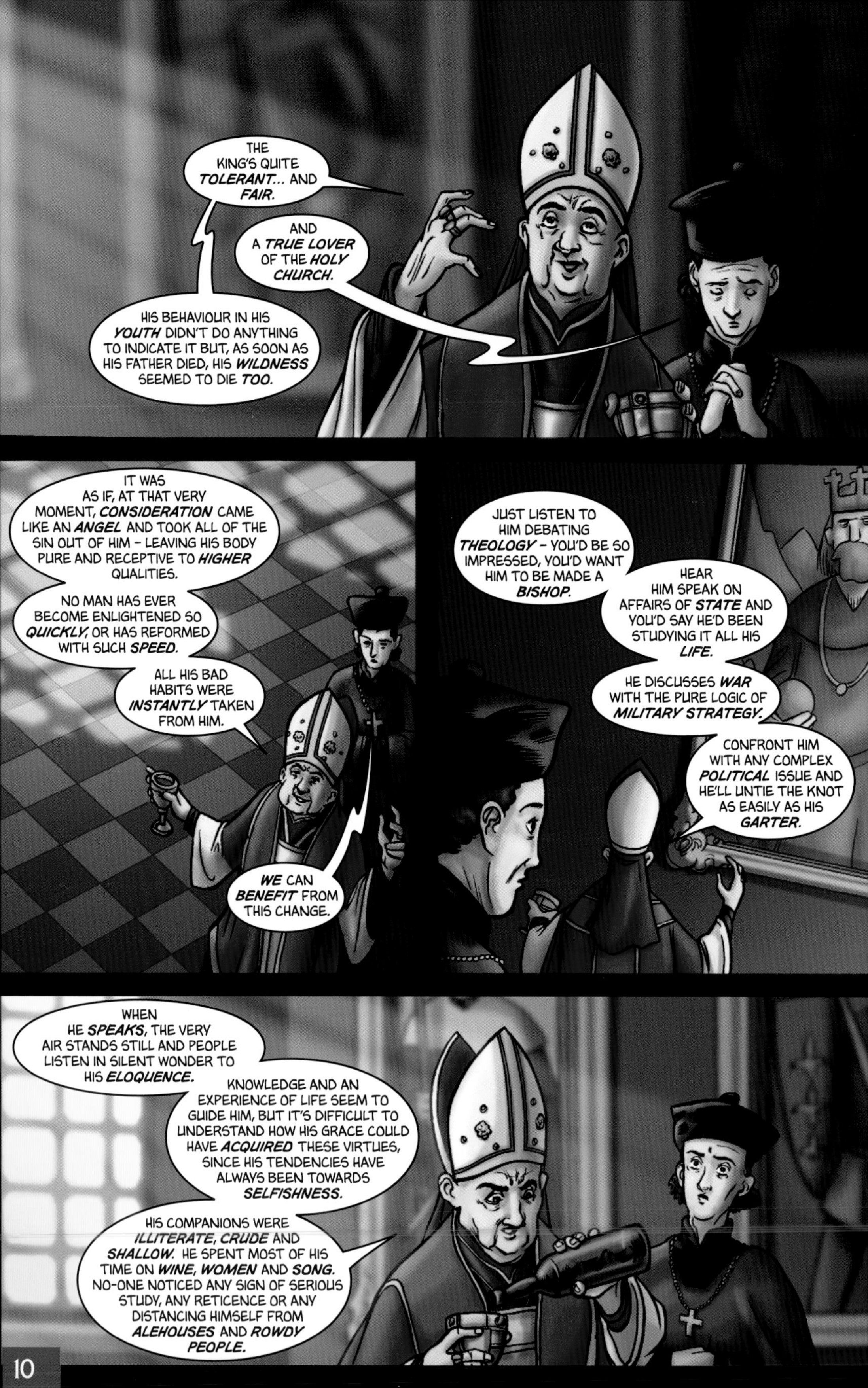
THE KING'S QUITE TOLERANT... AND FAIR.
AND A TRUE LOVER OF THE HOLY CHURCH.
HIS BEHAVIOUR IN HIS YOUTH DIDN'T DO ANYTHING TO INDICATE IT BUT, AS SOON AS HIS FATHER DIED, HIS WILDNESS SEEMED TO DIE TOO.
IT WAS AS IF, AT THAT VERY MOMENT, CONSIDERATION CAME LIKE AN ANGEL AND TOOK ALL OF THE SIN OUT OF HIM – LEAVING HIS BODY PURE AND RECEPTIVE TO HIGHER QUALITIES.
NO MAN HAS EVER BECOME ENLIGHTENED SO QUICKLY, OR HAS REFORMED WITH SUCH SPEED.
ALL HIS BAD HABITS WERE INSTANTLY TAKEN FROM HIM.
WE CAN BENEFIT FROM THIS CHANGE.
JUST LISTEN TO HIM DEBATING THEOLOGY – YOU'D BE SO IMPRESSED, YOU'D WANT HIM TO BE MADE A BISHOP.
HEAR HIM SPEAK ON AFFAIRS OF STATE AND YOU'D SAY HE'D BEEN STUDYING IT ALL HIS LIFE.
HE DISCUSSES WAR WITH THE PURE LOGIC OF MILITARY STRATEGY.
CONFRONT HIM WITH ANY COMPLEX POLITICAL ISSUE AND HE'LL UNTIE THE KNOT AS EASILY AS HIS GARTER.
WHEN HE SPEAKS, THE VERY AIR STANDS STILL AND PEOPLE LISTEN IN SILENT WONDER TO HIS ELOQUENCE.
KNOWLEDGE AND AN EXPERIENCE OF LIFE SEEM TO GUIDE HIM, BUT IT'S DIFFICULT TO UNDERSTAND HOW HIS GRACE COULD HAVE ACQUIRED THESE VIRTUES, SINCE HIS TENDENCIES HAVE ALWAYS BEEN TOWARDS SELFISHNESS.
HIS COMPANIONS WERE ILLITERATE, CRUDE AND SHALLOW. HE SPENT MOST OF HIS TIME ON WINE, WOMEN AND SONG. NO-ONE NOTICED ANY SIGN OF SERIOUS STUDY, ANY RETICENCE OR ANY DISTANCING HIMSELF FROM ALEHOUSES AND ROWDY PEOPLE.

AH YES, BUT THE **STRAWBERRY** GROWS UNDERNEATH THE **NETTLE**. AND HEALTHY BERRIES THRIVE AND RIPEN BEST, BESIDE **COARSER** FRUITS.

IN THE SAME WAY, THE PRINCE HID HIS **SERIOUS** SIDE BEHIND THIS VEIL OF **WILDNESS**. IT DEVELOPED AND GREW UNSEEN IN THE DARK, LIKE **SUMMER GRASS**.

I SUPPOSE... THAT MUST BE IT, BECAUSE THE AGE OF MIRACLES IS **GONE** AND THEREFORE WE NEED TO FIND **ANOTHER** REASON FOR THE WAY THINGS TURN OUT.

BUT, MY GOOD LORD, WHAT ARE WE GOING TO DO ABOUT THIS **BILL** PROPOSED BY THE COMMONS? DOES HIS MAJESTY **SUPPORT** IT OR **NOT?**

HE SEEMS **INDIFFERENT** OR, IF ANYTHING, LEANING MORE TOWARDS **US** THAN THE **PETITIONERS**. I'VE OFFERED HIM A **DONATION**, ON BEHALF OF OUR SYNOD. A DONATION LARGER THAN ANY PREVIOUSLY OFFERED BY THE CLERGY... TO HELP HIM RESOLVE SOME ISSUES WITH **FRANCE...**

HOW DID HE **RESPOND** TO THIS OFFER, MY LORD?

HIS MAJESTY RESPONDED **POSITIVELY.** BUT THERE WASN'T ENOUGH TIME FOR HIM TO HEAR, AS FULLY AS HE'D HAVE WANTED, THE DETAILS OF A VALID CLAIM TO... CERTAIN TERRITORIES AND, MORE OR LESS, TO THE KINGDOM OF **FRANCE** ITSELF. A CLAIM DERIVED FROM HIS GREAT-GRANDFATHER, **EDWARD.**

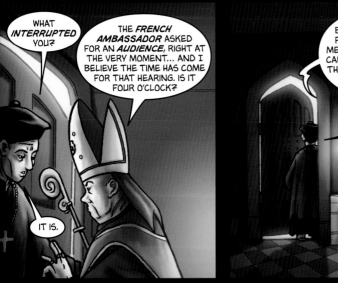

WHAT **INTERRUPTED** YOU?

THE **FRENCH AMBASSADOR** ASKED FOR AN **AUDIENCE**, RIGHT AT THE VERY MOMENT... AND I BELIEVE THE TIME HAS COME FOR THAT HEARING. IS IT FOUR O'CLOCK?

IT IS.

THEN I'D BETTER GO IN AND FIND OUT WHAT HIS MESSAGE IS. THOUGH I CAN **GUESS**... BEFORE THE FRENCHMAN EVEN SPEAKS A **WORD** OF IT.

I'LL GO WITH YOU. **I** WANT TO HEAR IT **TOO.**

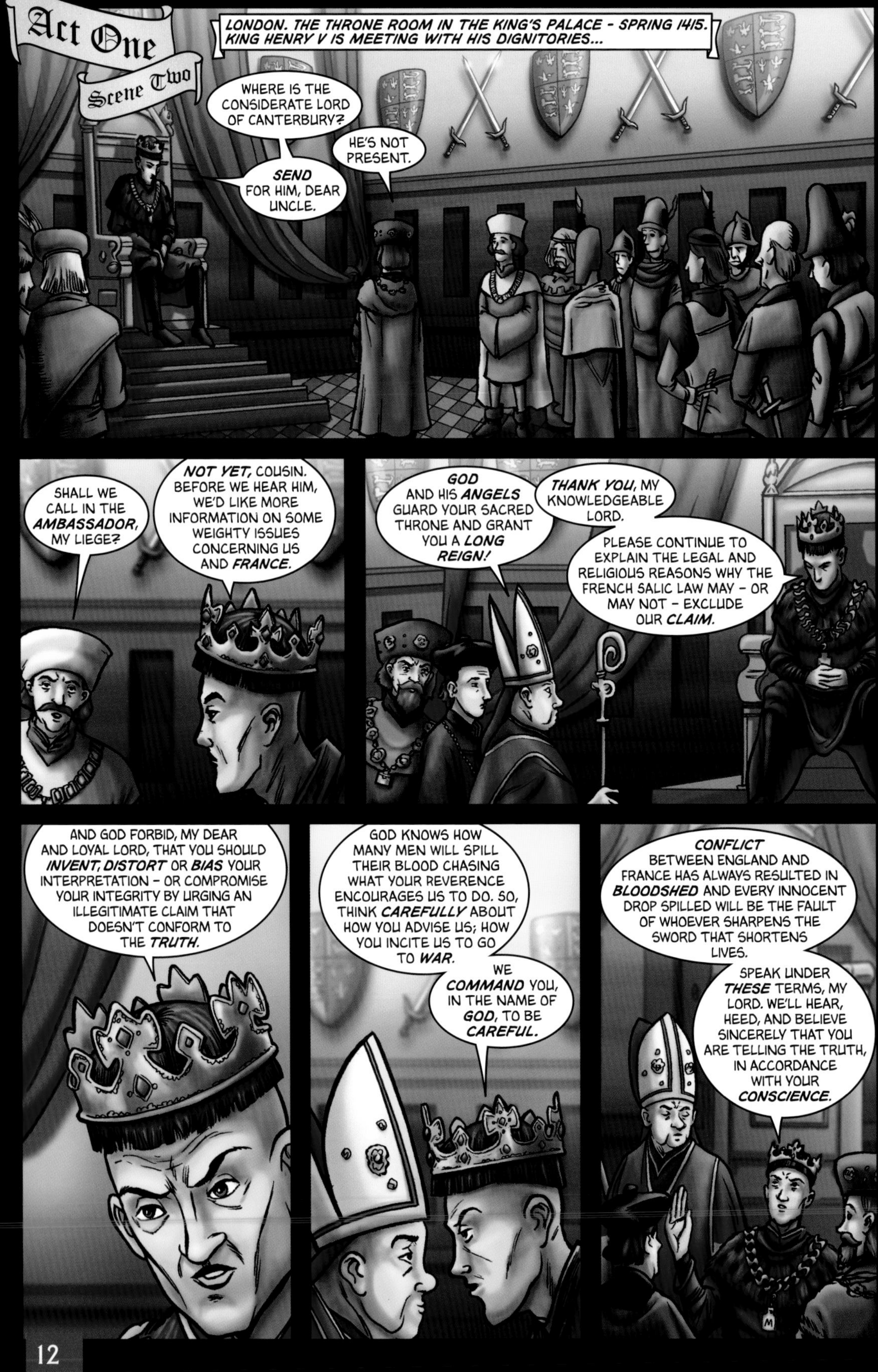
Act One
Scene Two
LONDON. THE THRONE ROOM IN THE KING'S PALACE - SPRING 1415. KING HENRY V IS MEETING WITH HIS DIGNITORIES...
WHERE IS THE CONSIDERATE LORD OF CANTERBURY?
HE'S NOT PRESENT.
SEND FOR HIM, DEAR UNCLE.
SHALL WE CALL IN THE AMBASSADOR, MY LIEGE?
NOT YET, COUSIN. BEFORE WE HEAR HIM, WE'D LIKE MORE INFORMATION ON SOME WEIGHTY ISSUES CONCERNING US AND FRANCE.
GOD AND HIS ANGELS GUARD YOUR SACRED THRONE AND GRANT YOU A LONG REIGN!
THANK YOU, MY KNOWLEDGEABLE LORD.
PLEASE CONTINUE TO EXPLAIN THE LEGAL AND RELIGIOUS REASONS WHY THE FRENCH SALIC LAW MAY - OR MAY NOT - EXCLUDE OUR CLAIM.
AND GOD FORBID, MY DEAR AND LOYAL LORD, THAT YOU SHOULD INVENT, DISTORT OR BIAS YOUR INTERPRETATION - OR COMPROMISE YOUR INTEGRITY BY URGING AN ILLEGITIMATE CLAIM THAT DOESN'T CONFORM TO THE TRUTH.
GOD KNOWS HOW MANY MEN WILL SPILL THEIR BLOOD CHASING WHAT YOUR REVERENCE ENCOURAGES US TO DO. SO, THINK CAREFULLY ABOUT HOW YOU ADVISE US; HOW YOU INCITE US TO GO TO WAR.
WE COMMAND YOU, IN THE NAME OF GOD, TO BE CAREFUL.
CONFLICT BETWEEN ENGLAND AND FRANCE HAS ALWAYS RESULTED IN BLOODSHED AND EVERY INNOCENT DROP SPILLED WILL BE THE FAULT OF WHOEVER SHARPENS THE SWORD THAT SHORTENS LIVES.
SPEAK UNDER THESE TERMS, MY LORD. WE'LL HEAR, HEED, AND BELIEVE SINCERELY THAT YOU ARE TELLING THE TRUTH, IN ACCORDANCE WITH YOUR CONSCIENCE.

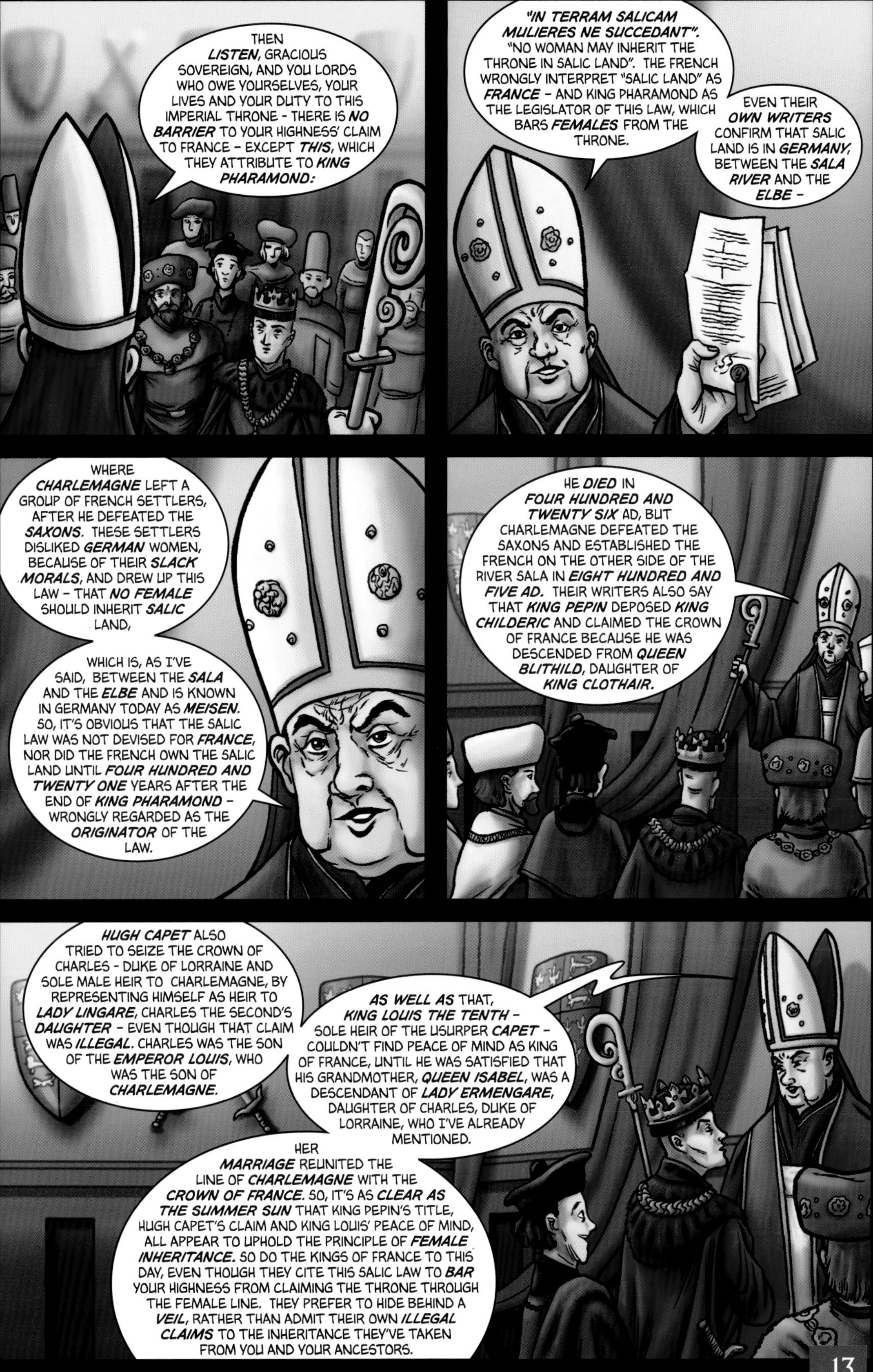
THEN LISTEN, GRACIOUS SOVEREIGN, AND YOU LORDS WHO OWE YOURSELVES, YOUR LIVES AND YOUR DUTY TO THIS IMPERIAL THRONE - THERE IS NO BARRIER TO YOUR HIGHNESS' CLAIM TO FRANCE – EXCEPT THIS, WHICH THEY ATTRIBUTE TO KING PHARAMOND:
"IN TERRAM SALICAM MULIERES NE SUCCEDANT". "NO WOMAN MAY INHERIT THE THRONE IN SALIC LAND". THE FRENCH WRONGLY INTERPRET "SALIC LAND" AS FRANCE – AND KING PHARAMOND AS THE LEGISLATOR OF THIS LAW, WHICH BARS FEMALES FROM THE THRONE.
EVEN THEIR OWN WRITERS CONFIRM THAT SALIC LAND IS IN GERMANY, BETWEEN THE SALA RIVER AND THE ELBE –
WHERE CHARLEMAGNE LEFT A GROUP OF FRENCH SETTLERS, AFTER HE DEFEATED THE SAXONS. THESE SETTLERS DISLIKED GERMAN WOMEN, BECAUSE OF THEIR SLACK MORALS, AND DREW UP THIS LAW – THAT NO FEMALE SHOULD INHERIT SALIC LAND,
WHICH IS, AS I'VE SAID, BETWEEN THE SALA AND THE ELBE AND IS KNOWN IN GERMANY TODAY AS MEISEN. SO, IT'S OBVIOUS THAT THE SALIC LAW WAS NOT DEVISED FOR FRANCE, NOR DID THE FRENCH OWN THE SALIC LAND UNTIL FOUR HUNDRED AND TWENTY ONE YEARS AFTER THE END OF KING PHARAMOND – WRONGLY REGARDED AS THE ORIGINATOR OF THE LAW.
HE DIED IN FOUR HUNDRED AND TWENTY SIX AD, BUT CHARLEMAGNE DEFEATED THE SAXONS AND ESTABLISHED THE FRENCH ON THE OTHER SIDE OF THE RIVER SALA IN EIGHT HUNDRED AND FIVE AD. THEIR WRITERS ALSO SAY THAT KING PEPIN DEPOSED KING CHILDERIC AND CLAIMED THE CROWN OF FRANCE BECAUSE HE WAS DESCENDED FROM QUEEN BLITHILD, DAUGHTER OF KING CLOTHAIR.
HUGH CAPET ALSO TRIED TO SEIZE THE CROWN OF CHARLES - DUKE OF LORRAINE AND SOLE MALE HEIR TO CHARLEMAGNE, BY REPRESENTING HIMSELF AS HEIR TO LADY LINGARE, CHARLES THE SECOND'S DAUGHTER – EVEN THOUGH THAT CLAIM WAS ILLEGAL. CHARLES WAS THE SON OF THE EMPEROR LOUIS, WHO WAS THE SON OF CHARLEMAGNE.
AS WELL AS THAT, KING LOUIS THE TENTH – SOLE HEIR OF THE USURPER CAPET – COULDN'T FIND PEACE OF MIND AS KING OF FRANCE, UNTIL HE WAS SATISFIED THAT HIS GRANDMOTHER, QUEEN ISABEL, WAS A DESCENDANT OF LADY ERMENGARE, DAUGHTER OF CHARLES, DUKE OF LORRAINE, WHO I'VE ALREADY MENTIONED.
HER MARRIAGE REUNITED THE LINE OF CHARLEMAGNE WITH THE CROWN OF FRANCE. SO, IT'S AS CLEAR AS THE SUMMER SUN THAT KING PEPIN'S TITLE, HUGH CAPET'S CLAIM AND KING LOUIS' PEACE OF MIND, ALL APPEAR TO UPHOLD THE PRINCIPLE OF FEMALE INHERITANCE. SO DO THE KINGS OF FRANCE TO THIS DAY, EVEN THOUGH THEY CITE THIS SALIC LAW TO BAR YOUR HIGHNESS FROM CLAIMING THE THRONE THROUGH THE FEMALE LINE. THEY PREFER TO HIDE BEHIND A VEIL, RATHER THAN ADMIT THEIR OWN ILLEGAL CLAIMS TO THE INHERITANCE THEY'VE TAKEN FROM YOU AND YOUR ANCESTORS.

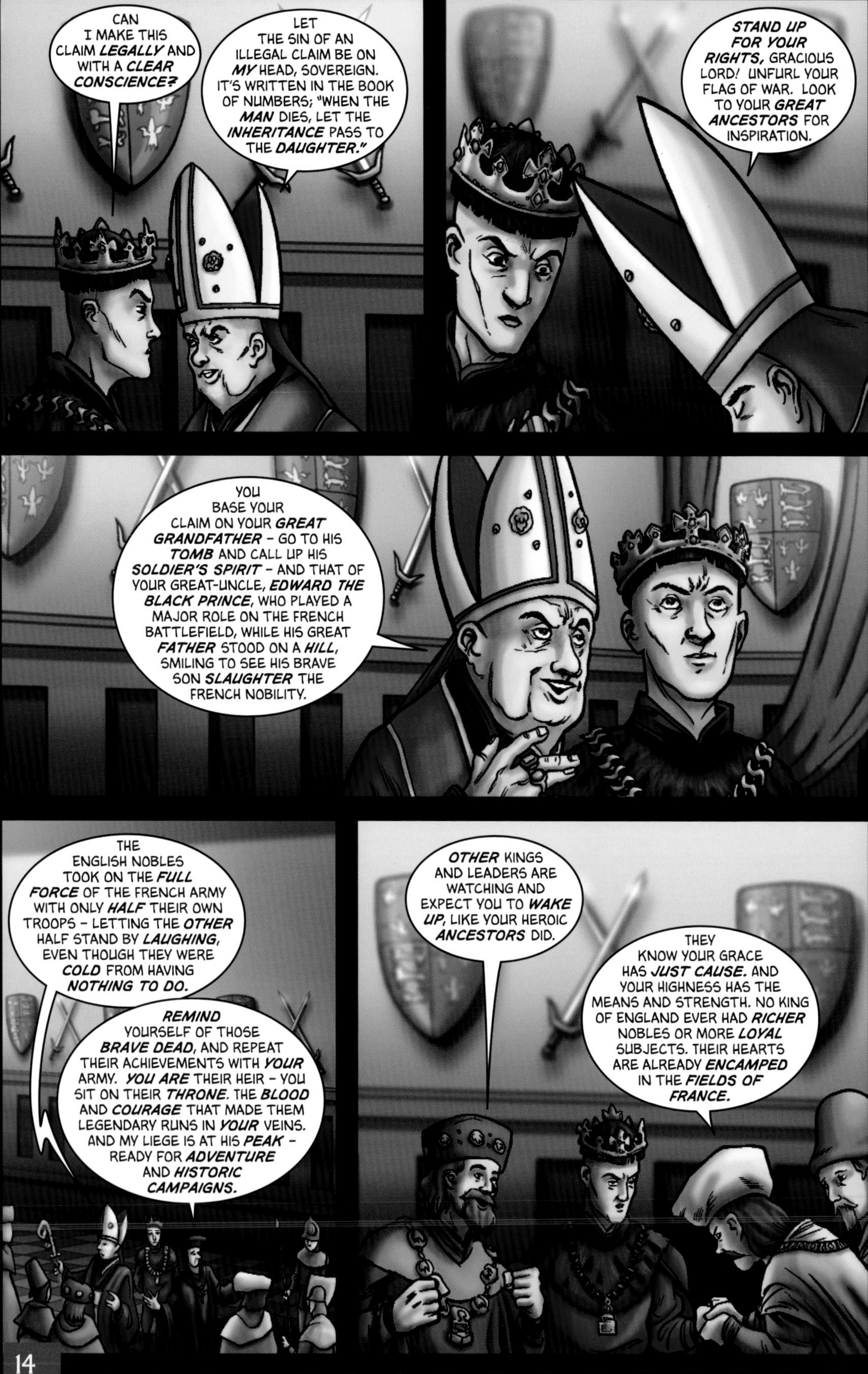
CAN I MAKE THIS CLAIM LEGALLY AND WITH A CLEAR CONSCIENCE?
LET THE SIN OF AN ILLEGAL CLAIM BE ON MY HEAD, SOVEREIGN. IT'S WRITTEN IN THE BOOK OF NUMBERS; "WHEN THE MAN DIES, LET THE INHERITANCE PASS TO THE DAUGHTER."
STAND UP FOR YOUR RIGHTS, GRACIOUS LORD! UNFURL YOUR FLAG OF WAR. LOOK TO YOUR GREAT ANCESTORS FOR INSPIRATION.
YOU BASE YOUR CLAIM ON YOUR GREAT GRANDFATHER – GO TO HIS TOMB AND CALL UP HIS SOLDIER'S SPIRIT – AND THAT OF YOUR GREAT-UNCLE, EDWARD THE BLACK PRINCE, WHO PLAYED A MAJOR ROLE ON THE FRENCH BATTLEFIELD, WHILE HIS GREAT FATHER STOOD ON A HILL, SMILING TO SEE HIS BRAVE SON SLAUGHTER THE FRENCH NOBILITY.
THE ENGLISH NOBLES TOOK ON THE FULL FORCE OF THE FRENCH ARMY WITH ONLY HALF THEIR OWN TROOPS – LETTING THE OTHER HALF STAND BY LAUGHING, EVEN THOUGH THEY WERE COLD FROM HAVING NOTHING TO DO.
REMIND YOURSELF OF THOSE BRAVE DEAD, AND REPEAT THEIR ACHIEVEMENTS WITH YOUR ARMY. YOU ARE THEIR HEIR – YOU SIT ON THEIR THRONE. THE BLOOD AND COURAGE THAT MADE THEM LEGENDARY RUNS IN YOUR VEINS. AND MY LIEGE IS AT HIS PEAK – READY FOR ADVENTURE AND HISTORIC CAMPAIGNS.
OTHER KINGS AND LEADERS ARE WATCHING AND EXPECT YOU TO WAKE UP, LIKE YOUR HEROIC ANCESTORS DID.
THEY KNOW YOUR GRACE HAS JUST CAUSE. AND YOUR HIGHNESS HAS THE MEANS AND STRENGTH. NO KING OF ENGLAND EVER HAD RICHER NOBLES OR MORE LOYAL SUBJECTS. THEIR HEARTS ARE ALREADY ENCAMPED IN THE FIELDS OF FRANCE.

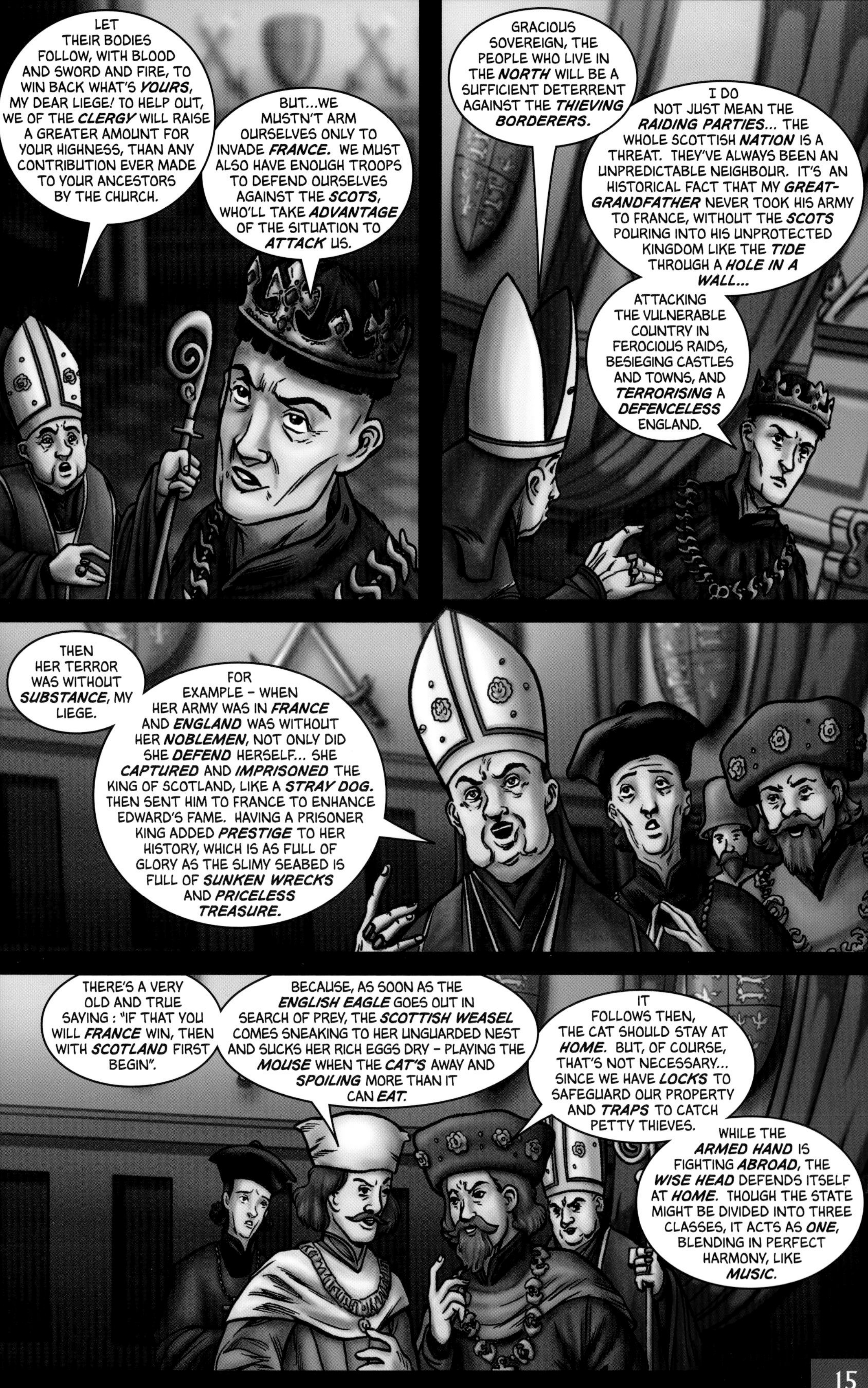
LET THEIR BODIES FOLLOW, WITH BLOOD AND SWORD AND FIRE, TO WIN BACK WHAT'S YOURS, MY DEAR LIEGE! TO HELP OUT, WE OF THE CLERGY WILL RAISE A GREATER AMOUNT FOR YOUR HIGHNESS, THAN ANY CONTRIBUTION EVER MADE TO YOUR ANCESTORS BY THE CHURCH.
BUT...WE MUSTN'T ARM OURSELVES ONLY TO INVADE FRANCE. WE MUST ALSO HAVE ENOUGH TROOPS TO DEFEND OURSELVES AGAINST THE SCOTS, WHO'LL TAKE ADVANTAGE OF THE SITUATION TO ATTACK US.
GRACIOUS SOVEREIGN, THE PEOPLE WHO LIVE IN THE NORTH WILL BE A SUFFICIENT DETERRENT AGAINST THE THIEVING BORDERERS.
I DO NOT JUST MEAN THE RAIDING PARTIES... THE WHOLE SCOTTISH NATION IS A THREAT. THEY'VE ALWAYS BEEN AN UNPREDICTABLE NEIGHBOUR. IT'S AN HISTORICAL FACT THAT MY GREAT-GRANDFATHER NEVER TOOK HIS ARMY TO FRANCE, WITHOUT THE SCOTS POURING INTO HIS UNPROTECTED KINGDOM LIKE THE TIDE THROUGH A HOLE IN A WALL...
ATTACKING THE VULNERABLE COUNTRY IN FEROCIOUS RAIDS, BESIEGING CASTLES AND TOWNS, AND TERRORISING A DEFENCELESS ENGLAND.
THEN HER TERROR WAS WITHOUT SUBSTANCE, MY LIEGE.
FOR EXAMPLE – WHEN HER ARMY WAS IN FRANCE AND ENGLAND WAS WITHOUT HER NOBLEMEN, NOT ONLY DID SHE DEFEND HERSELF... SHE CAPTURED AND IMPRISONED THE KING OF SCOTLAND, LIKE A STRAY DOG. THEN SENT HIM TO FRANCE TO ENHANCE EDWARD'S FAME. HAVING A PRISONER KING ADDED PRESTIGE TO HER HISTORY, WHICH IS AS FULL OF GLORY AS THE SLIMY SEABED IS FULL OF SUNKEN WRECKS AND PRICELESS TREASURE.
THERE'S A VERY OLD AND TRUE SAYING : "IF THAT YOU WILL FRANCE WIN, THEN WITH SCOTLAND FIRST BEGIN".
BECAUSE, AS SOON AS THE ENGLISH EAGLE GOES OUT IN SEARCH OF PREY, THE SCOTTISH WEASEL COMES SNEAKING TO HER UNGUARDED NEST AND SUCKS HER RICH EGGS DRY – PLAYING THE MOUSE WHEN THE CAT'S AWAY AND SPOILING MORE THAN IT CAN EAT.
IT FOLLOWS THEN, THE CAT SHOULD STAY AT HOME. BUT, OF COURSE, THAT'S NOT NECESSARY... SINCE WE HAVE LOCKS TO SAFEGUARD OUR PROPERTY AND TRAPS TO CATCH PETTY THIEVES.
WHILE THE ARMED HAND IS FIGHTING ABROAD, THE WISE HEAD DEFENDS ITSELF AT HOME. THOUGH THE STATE MIGHT BE DIVIDED INTO THREE CLASSES, IT ACTS AS ONE, BLENDING IN PERFECT HARMONY, LIKE MUSIC.

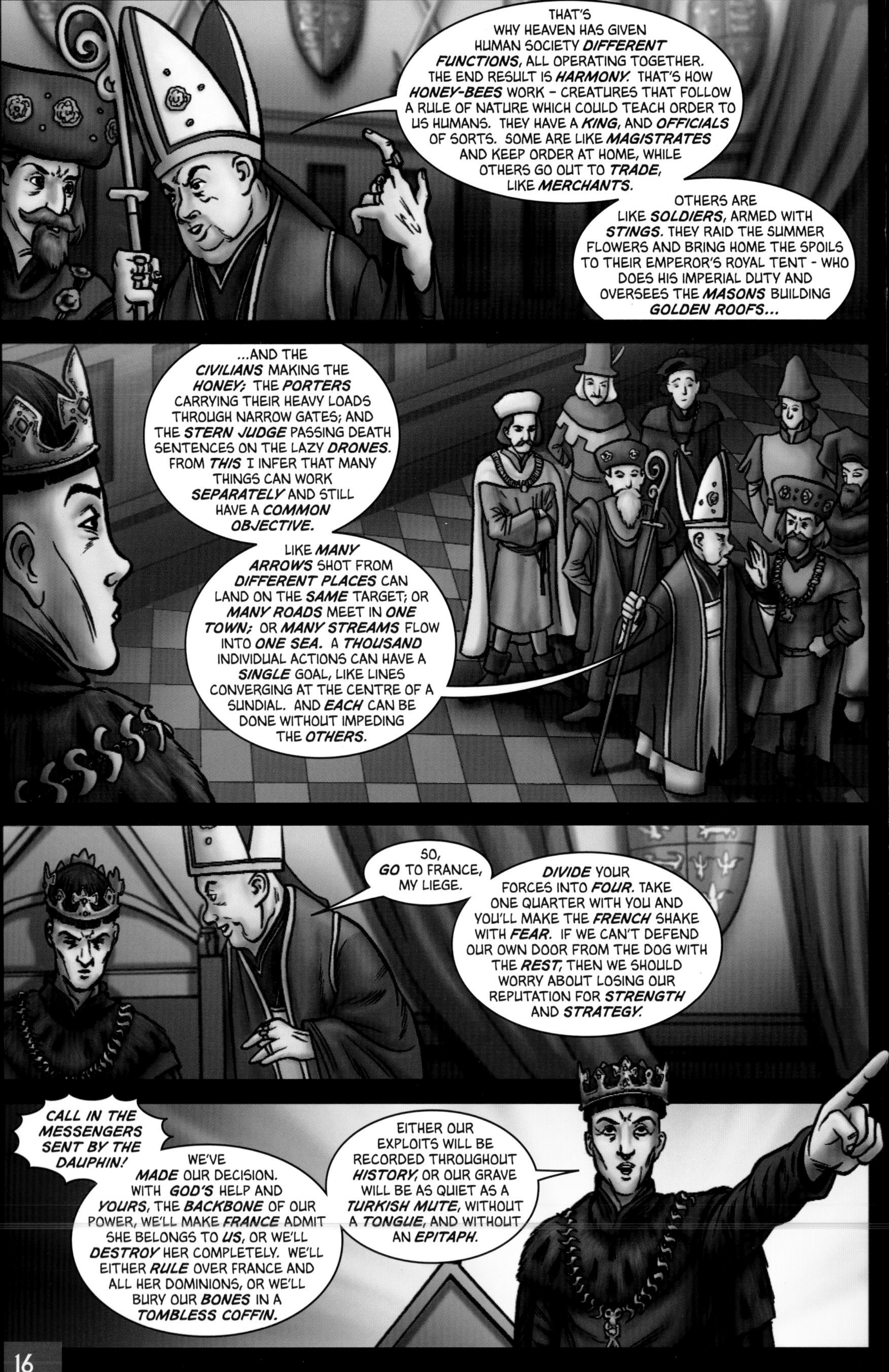
THAT'S WHY HEAVEN HAS GIVEN HUMAN SOCIETY DIFFERENT FUNCTIONS, ALL OPERATING TOGETHER. THE END RESULT IS HARMONY. THAT'S HOW HONEY-BEES WORK – CREATURES THAT FOLLOW A RULE OF NATURE WHICH COULD TEACH ORDER TO US HUMANS. THEY HAVE A KING, AND OFFICIALS OF SORTS. SOME ARE LIKE MAGISTRATES AND KEEP ORDER AT HOME, WHILE OTHERS GO OUT TO TRADE, LIKE MERCHANTS.
OTHERS ARE LIKE SOLDIERS, ARMED WITH STINGS. THEY RAID THE SUMMER FLOWERS AND BRING HOME THE SPOILS TO THEIR EMPEROR'S ROYAL TENT - WHO DOES HIS IMPERIAL DUTY AND OVERSEES THE MASONS BUILDING GOLDEN ROOFS...
...AND THE CIVILIANS MAKING THE HONEY; THE PORTERS CARRYING THEIR HEAVY LOADS THROUGH NARROW GATES; AND THE STERN JUDGE PASSING DEATH SENTENCES ON THE LAZY DRONES. FROM THIS I INFER THAT MANY THINGS CAN WORK SEPARATELY AND STILL HAVE A COMMON OBJECTIVE.
LIKE MANY ARROWS SHOT FROM DIFFERENT PLACES CAN LAND ON THE SAME TARGET; OR MANY ROADS MEET IN ONE TOWN; OR MANY STREAMS FLOW INTO ONE SEA. A THOUSAND INDIVIDUAL ACTIONS CAN HAVE A SINGLE GOAL, LIKE LINES CONVERGING AT THE CENTRE OF A SUNDIAL. AND EACH CAN BE DONE WITHOUT IMPEDING THE OTHERS.
SO, GO TO FRANCE, MY LIEGE.
DIVIDE YOUR FORCES INTO FOUR. TAKE ONE QUARTER WITH YOU AND YOU'LL MAKE THE FRENCH SHAKE WITH FEAR. IF WE CAN'T DEFEND OUR OWN DOOR FROM THE DOG WITH THE REST, THEN WE SHOULD WORRY ABOUT LOSING OUR REPUTATION FOR STRENGTH AND STRATEGY.
CALL IN THE MESSENGERS SENT BY THE DAUPHIN!
WE'VE MADE OUR DECISION. WITH GOD'S HELP AND YOURS, THE BACKBONE OF OUR POWER, WE'LL MAKE FRANCE ADMIT SHE BELONGS TO US, OR WE'LL DESTROY HER COMPLETELY. WE'LL EITHER RULE OVER FRANCE AND ALL HER DOMINIONS, OR WE'LL BURY OUR BONES IN A TOMBLESS COFFIN.
EITHER OUR EXPLOITS WILL BE RECORDED THROUGHOUT HISTORY, OR OUR GRAVE WILL BE AS QUIET AS A TURKISH MUTE, WITHOUT A TONGUE, AND WITHOUT AN EPITAPH.

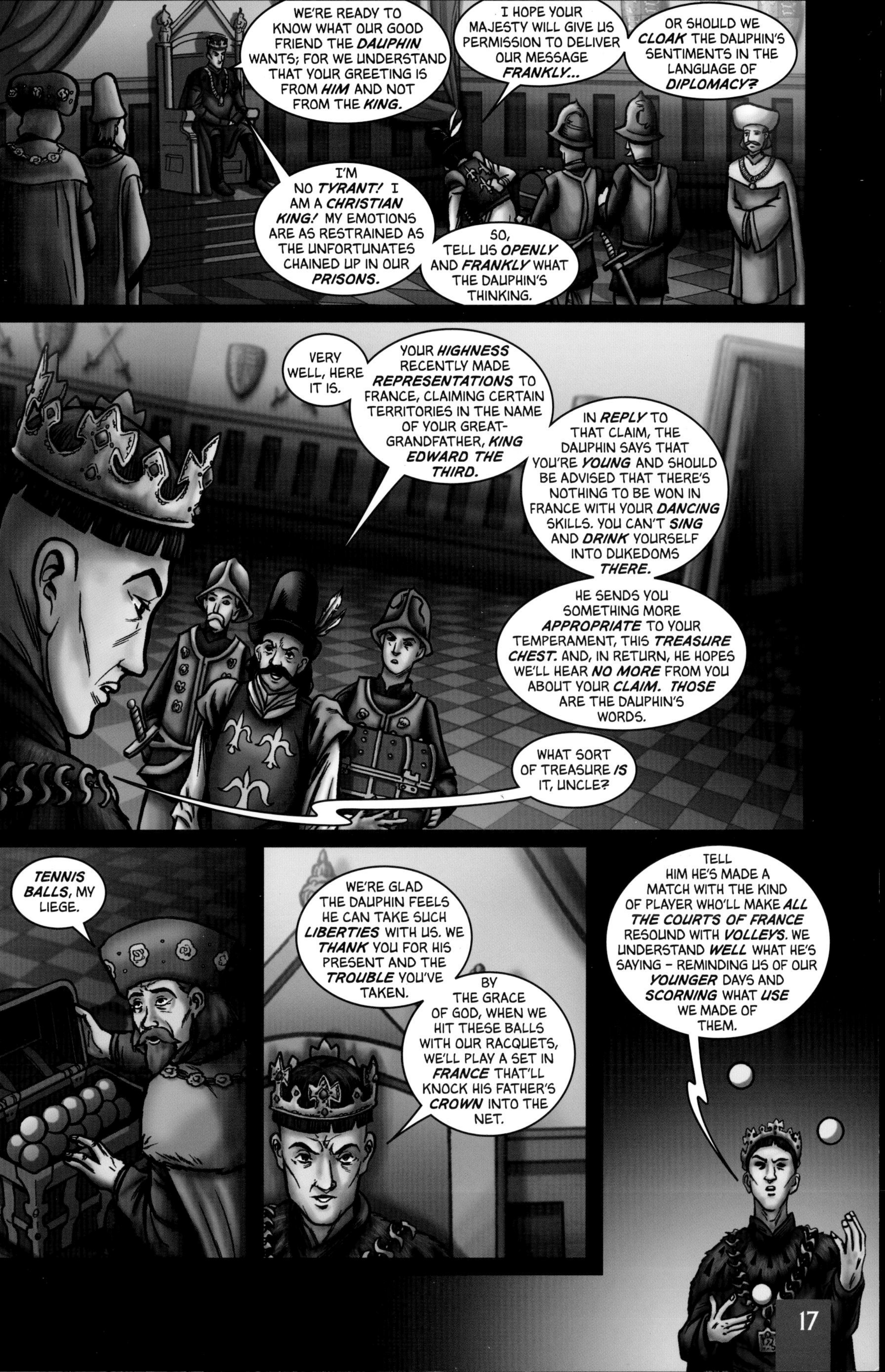
WE'RE READY TO KNOW WHAT OUR GOOD FRIEND THE DAUPHIN WANTS; FOR WE UNDERSTAND THAT YOUR GREETING IS FROM HIM AND NOT FROM THE KING.
I HOPE YOUR MAJESTY WILL GIVE US PERMISSION TO DELIVER OUR MESSAGE FRANKLY...
OR SHOULD WE CLOAK THE DAUPHIN'S SENTIMENTS IN THE LANGUAGE OF DIPLOMACY?
I'M NO TYRANT! I AM A CHRISTIAN KING! MY EMOTIONS ARE AS RESTRAINED AS THE UNFORTUNATES CHAINED UP IN OUR PRISONS.
SO, TELL US OPENLY AND FRANKLY WHAT THE DAUPHIN'S THINKING.
VERY WELL, HERE IT IS.
YOUR HIGHNESS RECENTLY MADE REPRESENTATIONS TO FRANCE, CLAIMING CERTAIN TERRITORIES IN THE NAME OF YOUR GREAT-GRANDFATHER, KING EDWARD THE THIRD.
IN REPLY TO THAT CLAIM, THE DAUPHIN SAYS THAT YOU'RE YOUNG AND SHOULD BE ADVISED THAT THERE'S NOTHING TO BE WON IN FRANCE WITH YOUR DANCING SKILLS. YOU CAN'T SING AND DRINK YOURSELF INTO DUKEDOMS THERE.
HE SENDS YOU SOMETHING MORE APPROPRIATE TO YOUR TEMPERAMENT, THIS TREASURE CHEST. AND, IN RETURN, HE HOPES WE'LL HEAR NO MORE FROM YOU ABOUT YOUR CLAIM. THOSE ARE THE DAUPHIN'S WORDS.
WHAT SORT OF TREASURE IS IT, UNCLE?
TENNIS BALLS, MY LIEGE.
WE'RE GLAD THE DAUPHIN FEELS HE CAN TAKE SUCH LIBERTIES WITH US. WE THANK YOU FOR HIS PRESENT AND THE TROUBLE YOU'VE TAKEN.
BY THE GRACE OF GOD, WHEN WE HIT THESE BALLS WITH OUR RACQUETS, WE'LL PLAY A SET IN FRANCE THAT'LL KNOCK HIS FATHER'S CROWN INTO THE NET.
TELL HIM HE'S MADE A MATCH WITH THE KIND OF PLAYER WHO'LL MAKE ALL THE COURTS OF FRANCE RESOUND WITH VOLLEYS. WE UNDERSTAND WELL WHAT HE'S SAYING – REMINDING US OF OUR YOUNGER DAYS AND SCORNING WHAT USE WE MADE OF THEM.

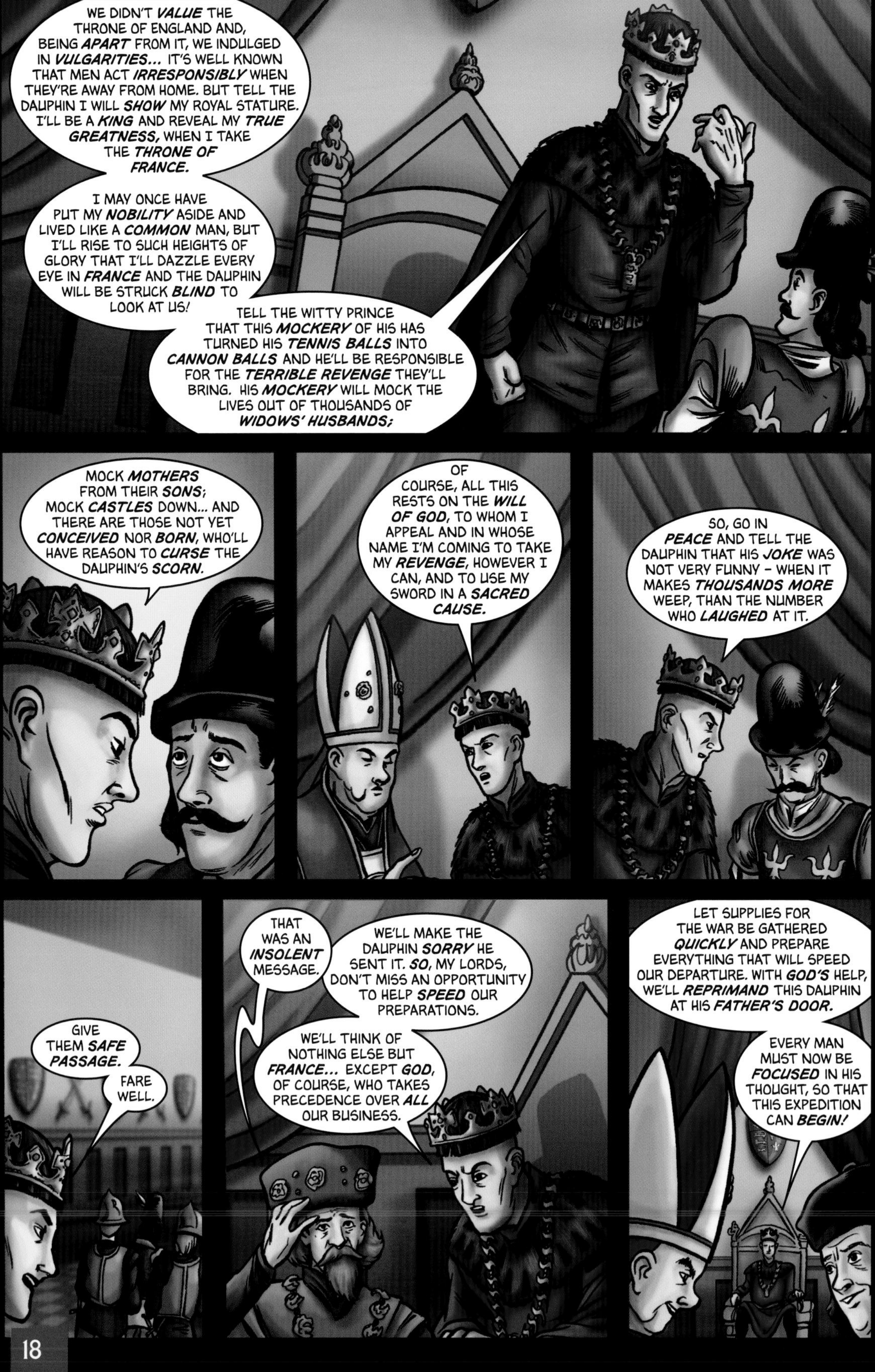

WE DIDN'T VALUE THE THRONE OF ENGLAND AND, BEING APART FROM IT, WE INDULGED IN VULGARITIES... IT'S WELL KNOWN THAT MEN ACT IRRESPONSIBLY WHEN THEY'RE AWAY FROM HOME. BUT TELL THE DAUPHIN I WILL SHOW MY ROYAL STATURE. I'LL BE A KING AND REVEAL MY TRUE GREATNESS, WHEN I TAKE THE THRONE OF FRANCE.
I MAY ONCE HAVE PUT MY NOBILITY ASIDE AND LIVED LIKE A COMMON MAN, BUT I'LL RISE TO SUCH HEIGHTS OF GLORY THAT I'LL DAZZLE EVERY EYE IN FRANCE AND THE DAUPHIN WILL BE STRUCK BLIND TO LOOK AT US!
TELL THE WITTY PRINCE THAT THIS MOCKERY OF HIS HAS TURNED HIS TENNIS BALLS INTO CANNON BALLS AND HE'LL BE RESPONSIBLE FOR THE TERRIBLE REVENGE THEY'LL BRING. HIS MOCKERY WILL MOCK THE LIVES OUT OF THOUSANDS OF WIDOWS' HUSBANDS;
MOCK MOTHERS FROM THEIR SONS; MOCK CASTLES DOWN... AND THERE ARE THOSE NOT YET CONCEIVED NOR BORN, WHO'LL HAVE REASON TO CURSE THE DAUPHIN'S SCORN.
OF COURSE, ALL THIS RESTS ON THE WILL OF GOD, TO WHOM I APPEAL AND IN WHOSE NAME I'M COMING TO TAKE MY REVENGE, HOWEVER I CAN, AND TO USE MY SWORD IN A SACRED CAUSE.
SO, GO IN PEACE AND TELL THE DAUPHIN THAT HIS JOKE WAS NOT VERY FUNNY – WHEN IT MAKES THOUSANDS MORE WEEP, THAN THE NUMBER WHO LAUGHED AT IT.
GIVE THEM SAFE PASSAGE.
FARE WELL.
THAT WAS AN INSOLENT MESSAGE.
WE'LL MAKE THE DAUPHIN SORRY HE SENT IT. SO, MY LORDS, DON'T MISS AN OPPORTUNITY TO HELP SPEED OUR PREPARATIONS.
WE'LL THINK OF NOTHING ELSE BUT FRANCE... EXCEPT GOD, OF COURSE, WHO TAKES PRECEDENCE OVER ALL OUR BUSINESS.
LET SUPPLIES FOR THE WAR BE GATHERED QUICKLY AND PREPARE EVERYTHING THAT WILL SPEED OUR DEPARTURE. WITH GOD'S HELP, WE'LL REPRIMAND THIS DAUPHIN AT HIS FATHER'S DOOR.
EVERY MAN MUST NOW BE FOCUSED IN HIS THOUGHT, SO THAT THIS EXPEDITION CAN BEGIN!

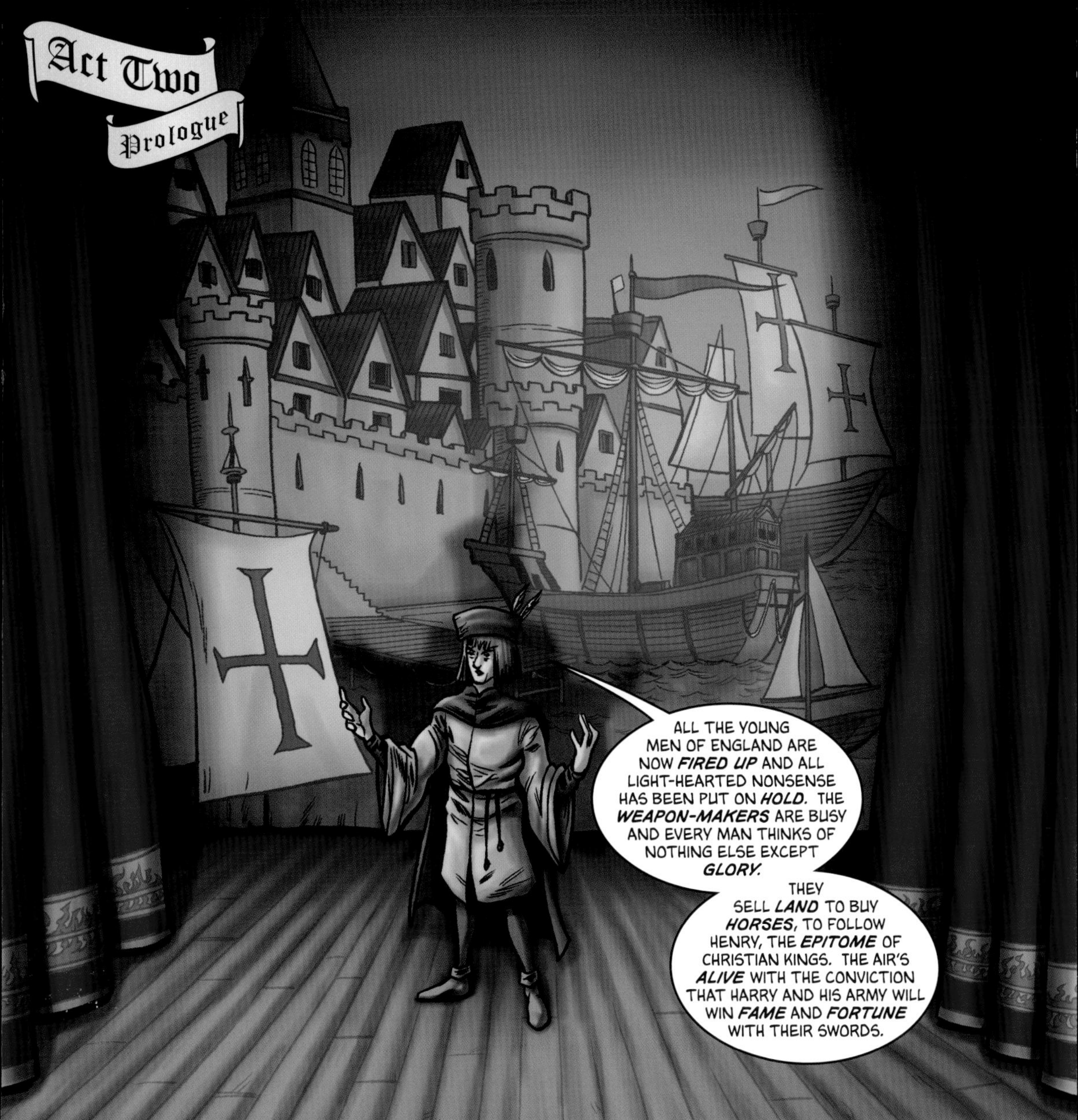
Act Two
Prologue
ALL THE YOUNG MEN OF ENGLAND ARE NOW FIRED UP AND ALL LIGHT-HEARTED NONSENSE HAS BEEN PUT ON HOLD. THE WEAPON-MAKERS ARE BUSY AND EVERY MAN THINKS OF NOTHING ELSE EXCEPT GLORY.
THEY SELL LAND TO BUY HORSES, TO FOLLOW HENRY, THE EPITOME OF CHRISTIAN KINGS. THE AIR'S ALIVE WITH THE CONVICTION THAT HARRY AND HIS ARMY WILL WIN FAME AND FORTUNE WITH THEIR SWORDS.

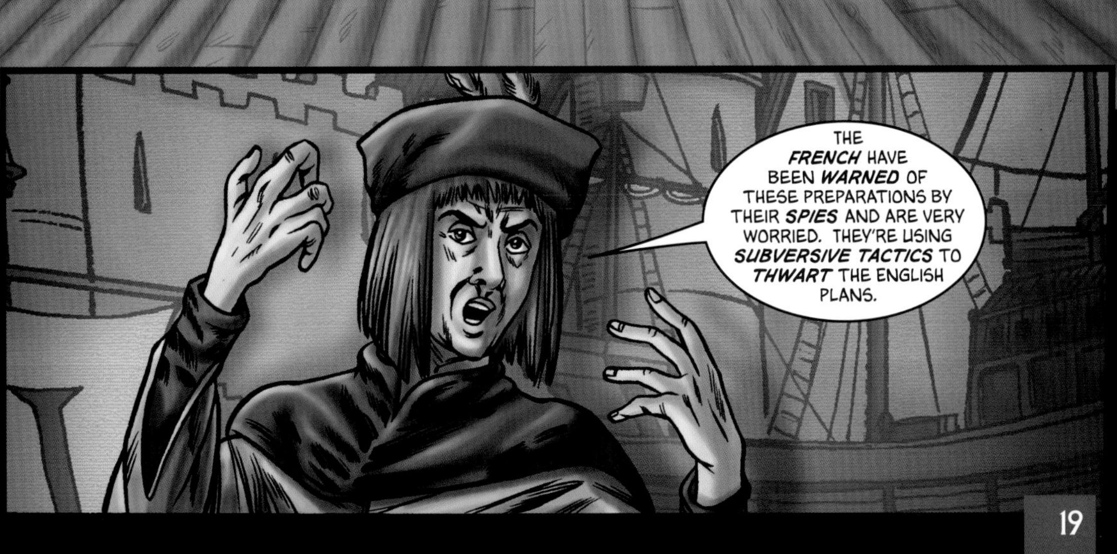
THE FRENCH HAVE BEEN WARNED OF THESE PREPARATIONS BY THEIR SPIES AND ARE VERY WORRIED. THEY'RE USING SUBVERSIVE TACTICS TO THWART THE ENGLISH PLANS.

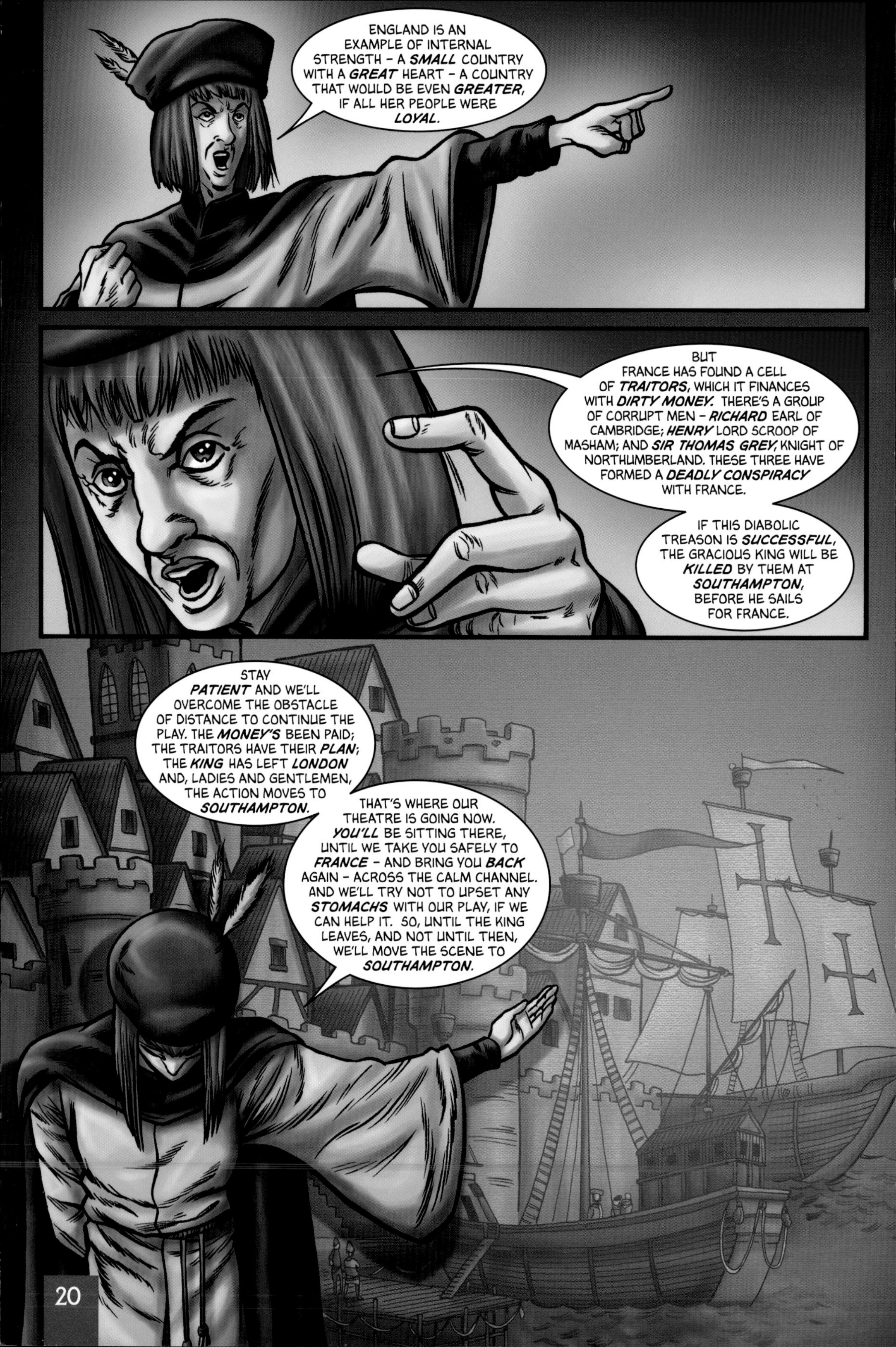

ENGLAND IS AN EXAMPLE OF INTERNAL STRENGTH – A SMALL COUNTRY WITH A GREAT HEART – A COUNTRY THAT WOULD BE EVEN GREATER, IF ALL HER PEOPLE WERE LOYAL.
BUT FRANCE HAS FOUND A CELL OF TRAITORS, WHICH IT FINANCES WITH DIRTY MONEY. THERE'S A GROUP OF CORRUPT MEN – RICHARD EARL OF CAMBRIDGE; HENRY LORD SCROOP OF MASHAM; AND SIR THOMAS GREY, KNIGHT OF NORTHUMBERLAND. THESE THREE HAVE FORMED A DEADLY CONSPIRACY WITH FRANCE.
IF THIS DIABOLIC TREASON IS SUCCESSFUL, THE GRACIOUS KING WILL BE KILLED BY THEM AT SOUTHAMPTON, BEFORE HE SAILS FOR FRANCE.
STAY PATIENT AND WE'LL OVERCOME THE OBSTACLE OF DISTANCE TO CONTINUE THE PLAY. THE MONEY'S BEEN PAID; THE TRAITORS HAVE THEIR PLAN; THE KING HAS LEFT LONDON AND, LADIES AND GENTLEMEN, THE ACTION MOVES TO SOUTHAMPTON.
THAT'S WHERE OUR THEATRE IS GOING NOW. YOU'LL BE SITTING THERE, UNTIL WE TAKE YOU SAFELY TO FRANCE – AND BRING YOU BACK AGAIN – ACROSS THE CALM CHANNEL. AND WE'LL TRY NOT TO UPSET ANY STOMACHS WITH OUR PLAY, IF WE CAN HELP IT. SO, UNTIL THE KING LEAVES, AND NOT UNTIL THEN, WE'LL MOVE THE SCENE TO SOUTHAMPTON.

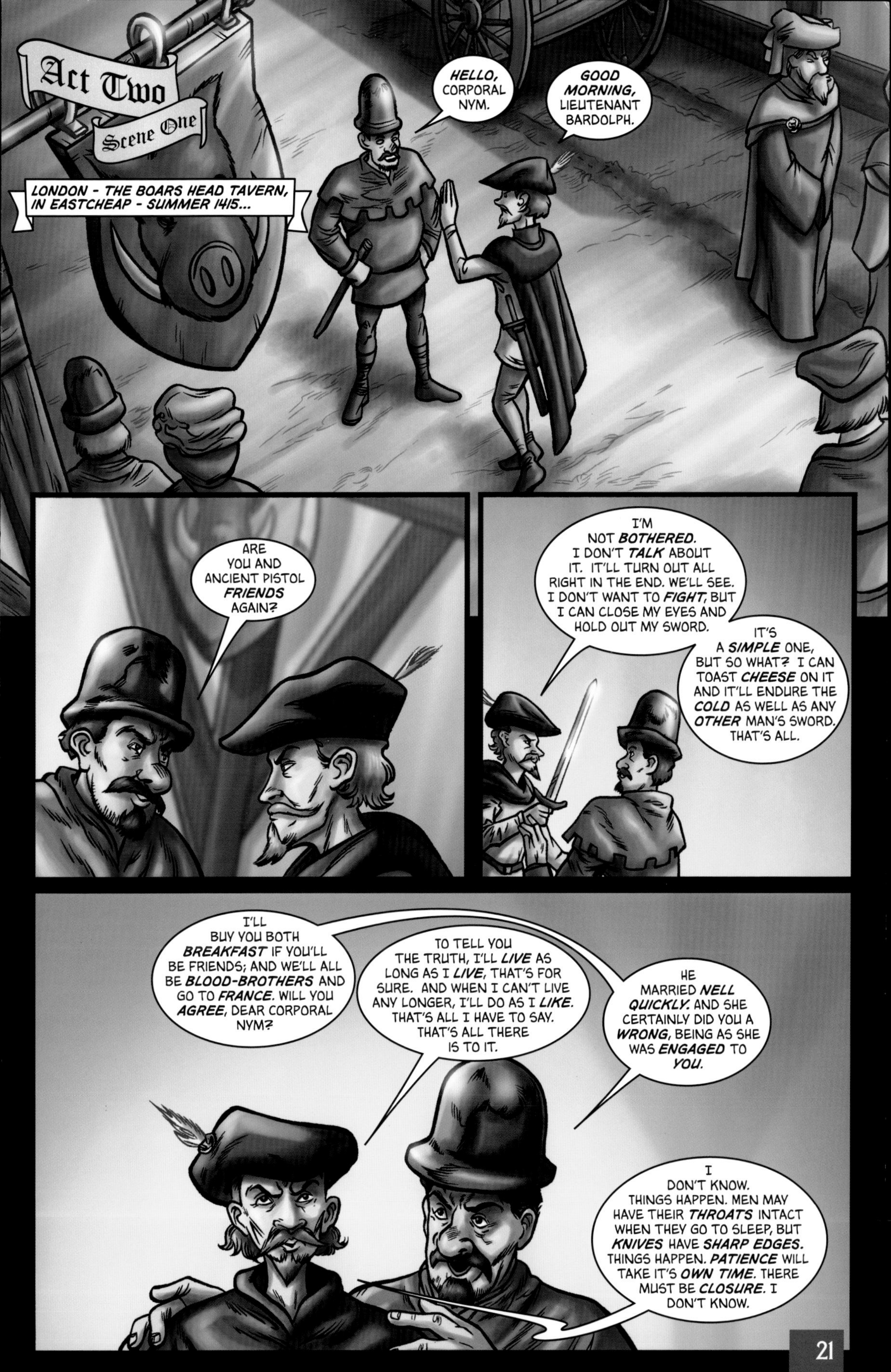

Act Two
Scene One
LONDON - THE BOARS HEAD TAVERN, IN EASTCHEAP - SUMMER 1415...
HELLO, CORPORAL NYM.
GOOD MORNING, LIEUTENANT BARDOLPH.
ARE YOU AND ANCIENT PISTOL FRIENDS AGAIN?
I'M NOT BOTHERED. I DON'T TALK ABOUT IT. IT'LL TURN OUT ALL RIGHT IN THE END. WE'LL SEE. I DON'T WANT TO FIGHT, BUT I CAN CLOSE MY EYES AND HOLD OUT MY SWORD.
IT'S A SIMPLE ONE, BUT SO WHAT? I CAN TOAST CHEESE ON IT AND IT'LL ENDURE THE COLD AS WELL AS ANY OTHER MAN'S SWORD. THAT'S ALL.
I'LL BUY YOU BOTH BREAKFAST IF YOU'LL BE FRIENDS; AND WE'LL ALL BE BLOOD-BROTHERS AND GO TO FRANCE. WILL YOU AGREE, DEAR CORPORAL NYM?
TO TELL YOU THE TRUTH, I'LL LIVE AS LONG AS I LIVE, THAT'S FOR SURE. AND WHEN I CAN'T LIVE ANY LONGER, I'LL DO AS I LIKE. THAT'S ALL I HAVE TO SAY. THAT'S ALL THERE IS TO IT.
HE MARRIED NELL QUICKLY. AND SHE CERTAINLY DID YOU A WRONG, BEING AS SHE WAS ENGAGED TO YOU.
I DON'T KNOW. THINGS HAPPEN. MEN MAY HAVE THEIR THROATS INTACT WHEN THEY GO TO SLEEP, BUT KNIVES HAVE SHARP EDGES. THINGS HAPPEN. PATIENCE WILL TAKE IT'S OWN TIME. THERE MUST BE CLOSURE. I DON'T KNOW.

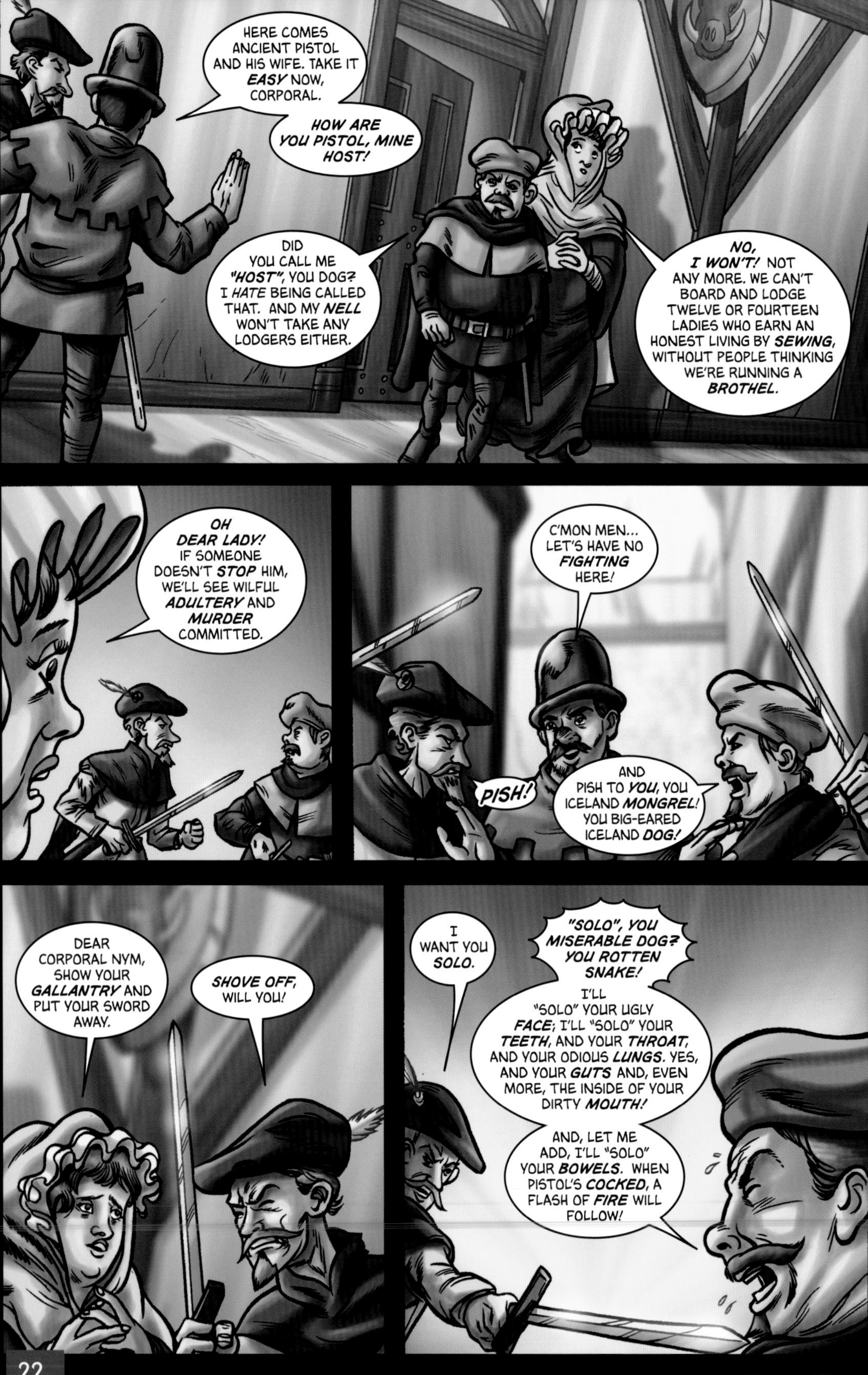
HERE COMES ANCIENT PISTOL AND HIS WIFE. TAKE IT EASY NOW, CORPORAL.
HOW ARE YOU PISTOL, MINE HOST!
DID YOU CALL ME "HOST", YOU DOG? I HATE BEING CALLED THAT. AND MY NELL WON'T TAKE ANY LODGERS EITHER.
NO, I WON'T! NOT ANY MORE. WE CAN'T BOARD AND LODGE TWELVE OR FOURTEEN LADIES WHO EARN AN HONEST LIVING BY SEWING, WITHOUT PEOPLE THINKING WE'RE RUNNING A BROTHEL.
OH DEAR LADY! IF SOMEONE DOESN'T STOP HIM, WE'LL SEE WILFUL ADULTERY AND MURDER COMMITTED.
C'MON MEN... LET'S HAVE NO FIGHTING HERE!
PISH!
AND PISH TO YOU, YOU ICELAND MONGREL! YOU BIG-EARED ICELAND DOG!
DEAR CORPORAL NYM, SHOW YOUR GALLANTRY AND PUT YOUR SWORD AWAY.
SHOVE OFF, WILL YOU!
I WANT YOU SOLO.
"SOLO", YOU MISERABLE DOG? YOU ROTTEN SNAKE!
I'LL "SOLO" YOUR UGLY FACE; I'LL "SOLO" YOUR TEETH, AND YOUR THROAT, AND YOUR ODIOUS LUNGS. YES, AND YOUR GUTS AND, EVEN MORE, THE INSIDE OF YOUR DIRTY MOUTH!
AND, LET ME ADD, I'LL "SOLO" YOUR BOWELS. WHEN PISTOL'S COCKED, A FLASH OF FIRE WILL FOLLOW!

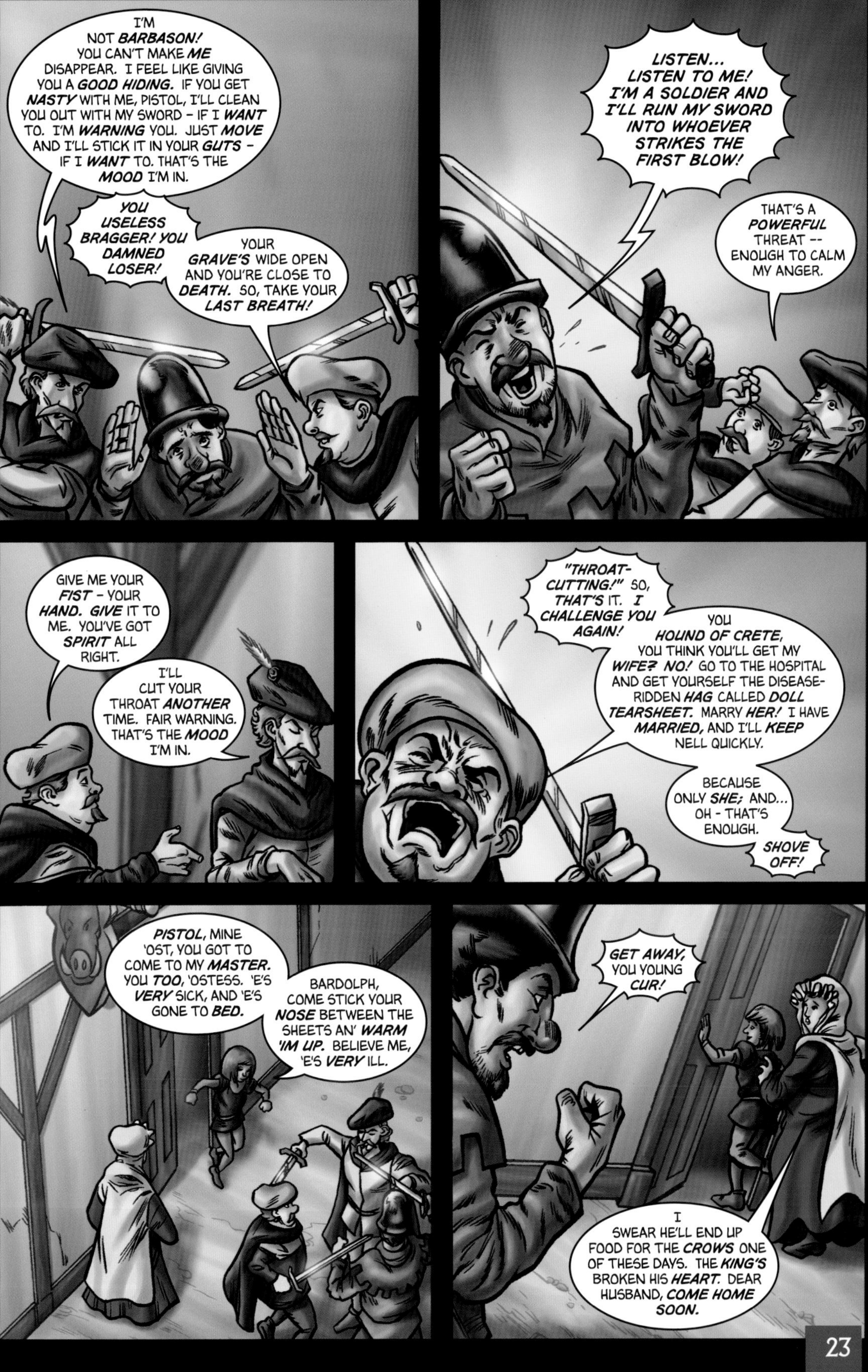
I'M NOT BARBASON! YOU CAN'T MAKE ME DISAPPEAR. I FEEL LIKE GIVING YOU A GOOD HIDING. IF YOU GET NASTY WITH ME, PISTOL, I'LL CLEAN YOU OUT WITH MY SWORD – IF I WANT TO. I'M WARNING YOU. JUST MOVE AND I'LL STICK IT IN YOUR GUTS – IF I WANT TO. THAT'S THE MOOD I'M IN.
YOU USELESS BRAGGER! YOU DAMNED LOSER!
YOUR GRAVE'S WIDE OPEN AND YOU'RE CLOSE TO DEATH. SO, TAKE YOUR LAST BREATH!
LISTEN... LISTEN TO ME! I'M A SOLDIER AND I'LL RUN MY SWORD INTO WHOEVER STRIKES THE FIRST BLOW!
THAT'S A POWERFUL THREAT -- ENOUGH TO CALM MY ANGER.
GIVE ME YOUR FIST – YOUR HAND. GIVE IT TO ME. YOU'VE GOT SPIRIT ALL RIGHT.
I'LL CUT YOUR THROAT ANOTHER TIME. FAIR WARNING. THAT'S THE MOOD I'M IN.
"THROAT-CUTTING!" SO, THAT'S IT. I CHALLENGE YOU AGAIN!
YOU HOUND OF CRETE, YOU THINK YOU'LL GET MY WIFE? NO! GO TO THE HOSPITAL AND GET YOURSELF THE DISEASE-RIDDEN HAG CALLED DOLL TEARSHEET. MARRY HER! I HAVE MARRIED, AND I'LL KEEP NELL QUICKLY.
BECAUSE ONLY SHE; AND... OH - THAT'S ENOUGH.
SHOVE OFF!
PISTOL, MINE 'OST, YOU GOT TO COME TO MY MASTER. YOU TOO, 'OSTESS. 'E'S VERY SICK, AND 'E'S GONE TO BED.
BARDOLPH, COME STICK YOUR NOSE BETWEEN THE SHEETS AN' WARM 'IM UP. BELIEVE ME, 'E'S VERY ILL.
GET AWAY, YOU YOUNG CUR!
I SWEAR HE'LL END UP FOOD FOR THE CROWS ONE OF THESE DAYS. THE KING'S BROKEN HIS HEART. DEAR HUSBAND, COME HOME SOON.

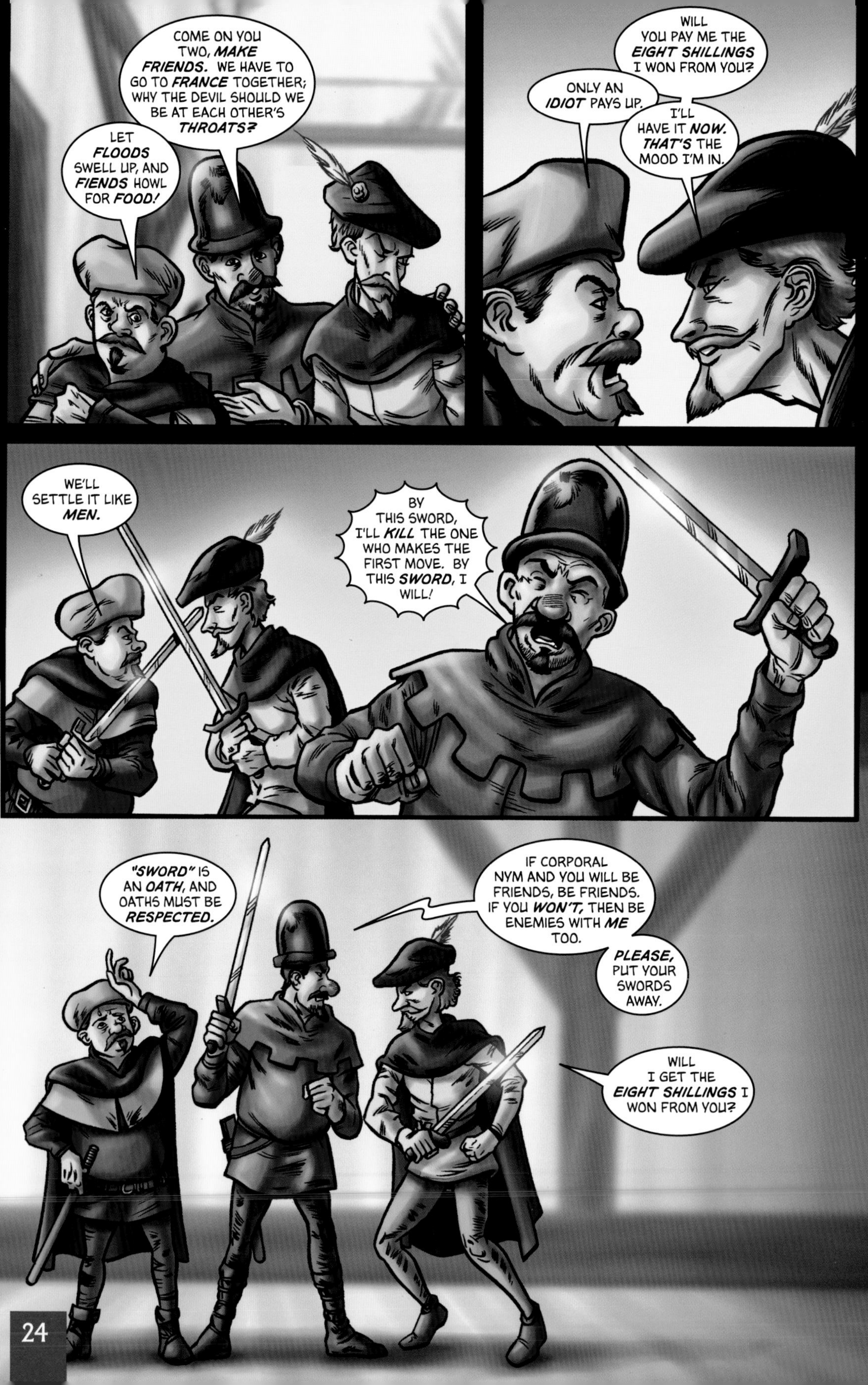
COME ON YOU TWO, MAKE FRIENDS. WE HAVE TO GO TO FRANCE TOGETHER; WHY THE DEVIL SHOULD WE BE AT EACH OTHER'S THROATS?
LET FLOODS SWELL UP, AND FIENDS HOWL FOR FOOD!
WILL YOU PAY ME THE EIGHT SHILLINGS I WON FROM YOU?
ONLY AN IDIOT PAYS UP.
I'LL HAVE IT NOW. THAT'S THE MOOD I'M IN.
WE'LL SETTLE IT LIKE MEN.
BY THIS SWORD, I'LL KILL THE ONE WHO MAKES THE FIRST MOVE. BY THIS SWORD, I WILL!
"SWORD" IS AN OATH, AND OATHS MUST BE RESPECTED.
IF CORPORAL NYM AND YOU WILL BE FRIENDS, BE FRIENDS. IF YOU WON'T, THEN BE ENEMIES WITH ME TOO.
PLEASE, PUT YOUR SWORDS AWAY.
WILL I GET THE EIGHT SHILLINGS I WON FROM YOU?

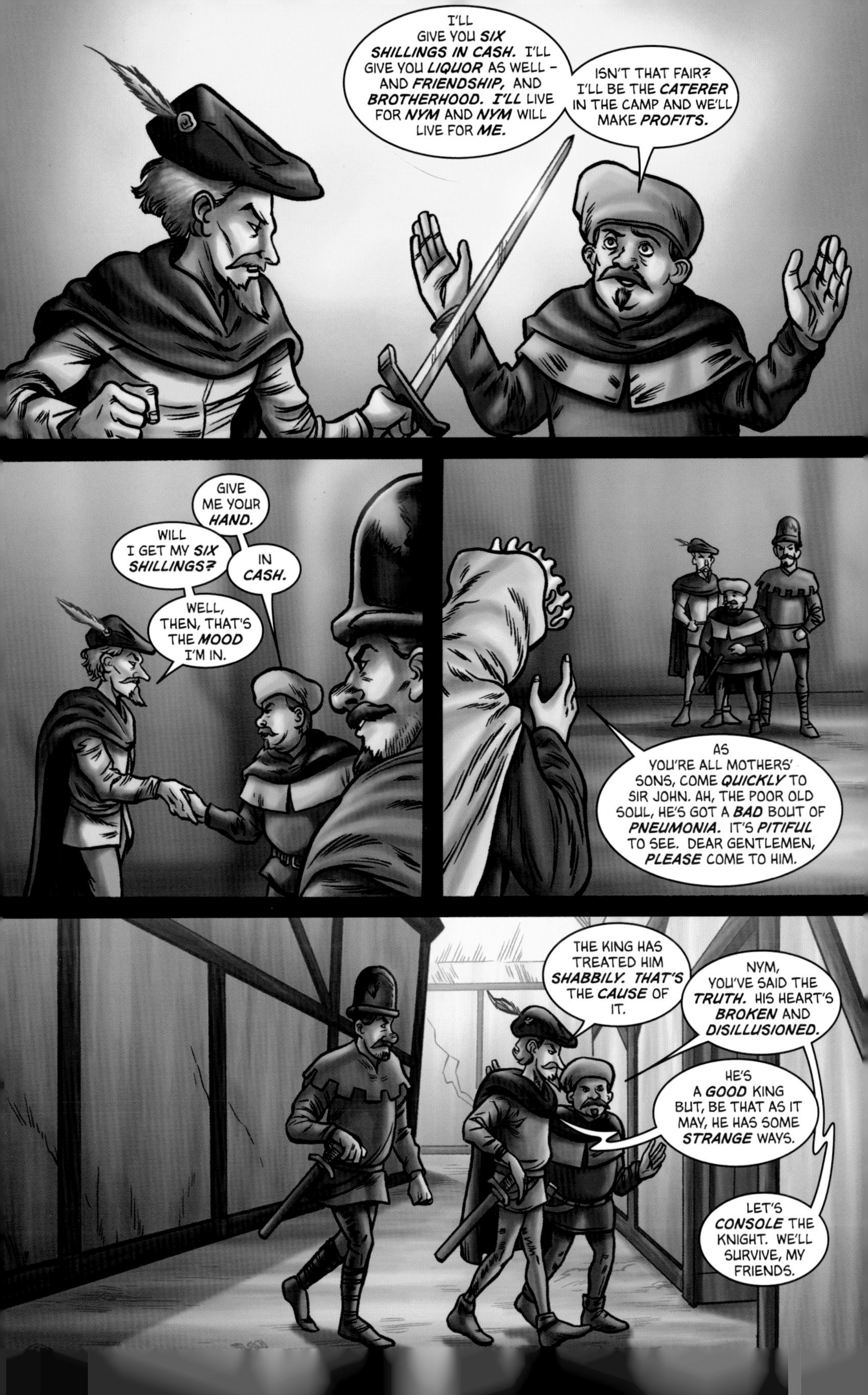
I'LL GIVE YOU SIX SHILLINGS IN CASH. I'LL GIVE YOU LIQUOR AS WELL – AND FRIENDSHIP, AND BROTHERHOOD. I'LL LIVE FOR NYM AND NYM WILL LIVE FOR ME.
ISN'T THAT FAIR? I'LL BE THE CATERER IN THE CAMP AND WE'LL MAKE PROFITS.
WILL I GET MY SIX SHILLINGS?
GIVE ME YOUR HAND.
IN CASH.
WELL, THEN, THAT'S THE MOOD I'M IN.
AS YOU'RE ALL MOTHERS' SONS, COME QUICKLY TO SIR JOHN. AH, THE POOR OLD SOUL, HE'S GOT A BAD BOUT OF PNEUMONIA. IT'S PITIFUL TO SEE. DEAR GENTLEMEN, PLEASE COME TO HIM.
THE KING HAS TREATED HIM SHABBILY. THAT'S THE CAUSE OF IT.
NYM, YOU'VE SAID THE TRUTH. HIS HEART'S BROKEN AND DISILLUSIONED.
HE'S A GOOD KING BUT, BE THAT AS IT MAY, HE HAS SOME STRANGE WAYS.
LET'S CONSOLE THE KNIGHT. WE'LL SURVIVE, MY FRIENDS.

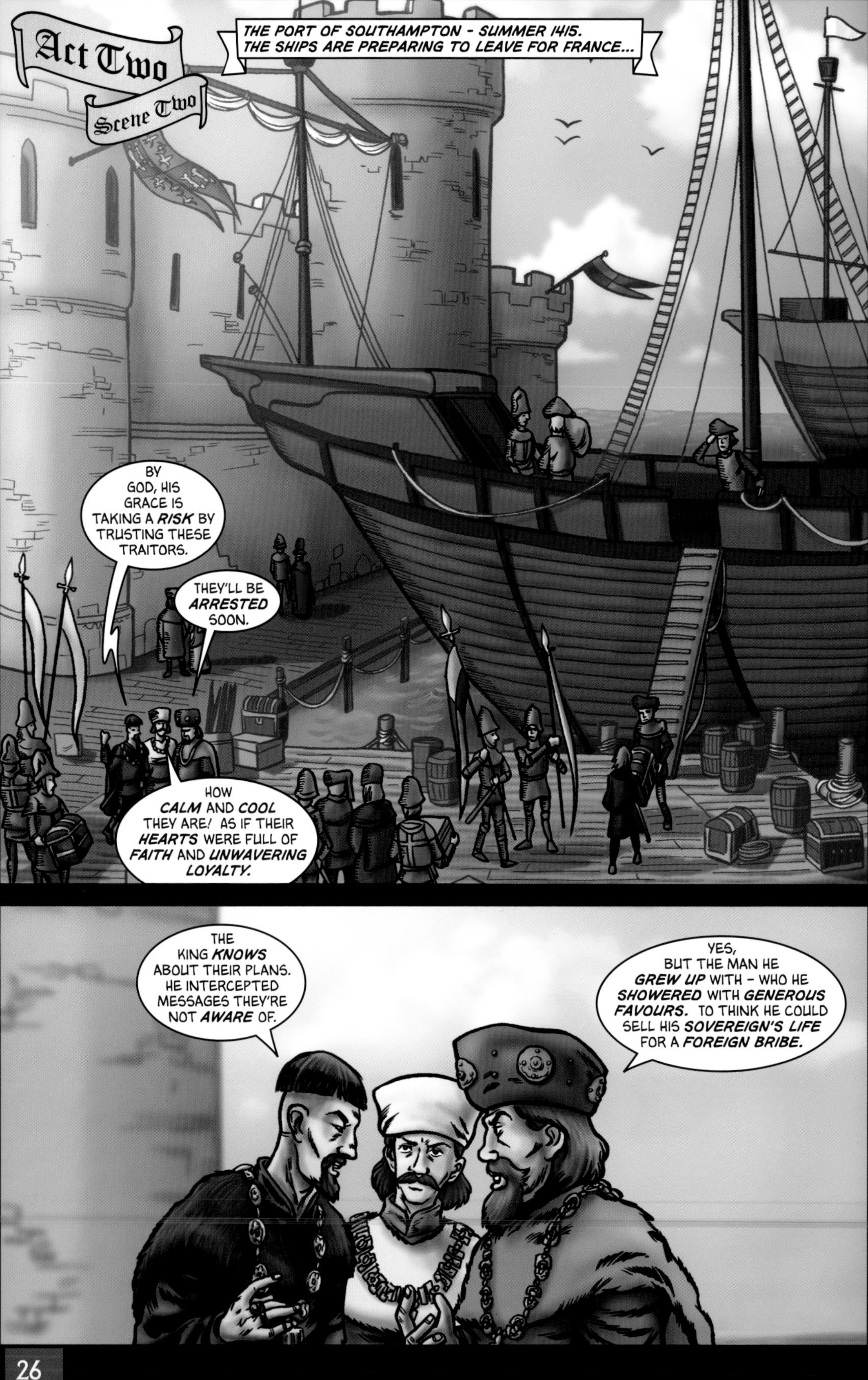
Act Two
Scene Two
THE PORT OF SOUTHAMPTON - SUMMER 1415. THE SHIPS ARE PREPARING TO LEAVE FOR FRANCE...
BY GOD, HIS GRACE IS TAKING A RISK BY TRUSTING THESE TRAITORS.
THEY'LL BE ARRESTED SOON.
HOW CALM AND COOL THEY ARE! AS IF THEIR HEARTS WERE FULL OF FAITH AND UNWAVERING LOYALTY.
THE KING KNOWS ABOUT THEIR PLANS. HE INTERCEPTED MESSAGES THEY'RE NOT AWARE OF.
YES, BUT THE MAN HE GREW UP WITH - WHO HE SHOWERED WITH GENEROUS FAVOURS. TO THINK HE COULD SELL HIS SOVEREIGN'S LIFE FOR A FOREIGN BRIBE.

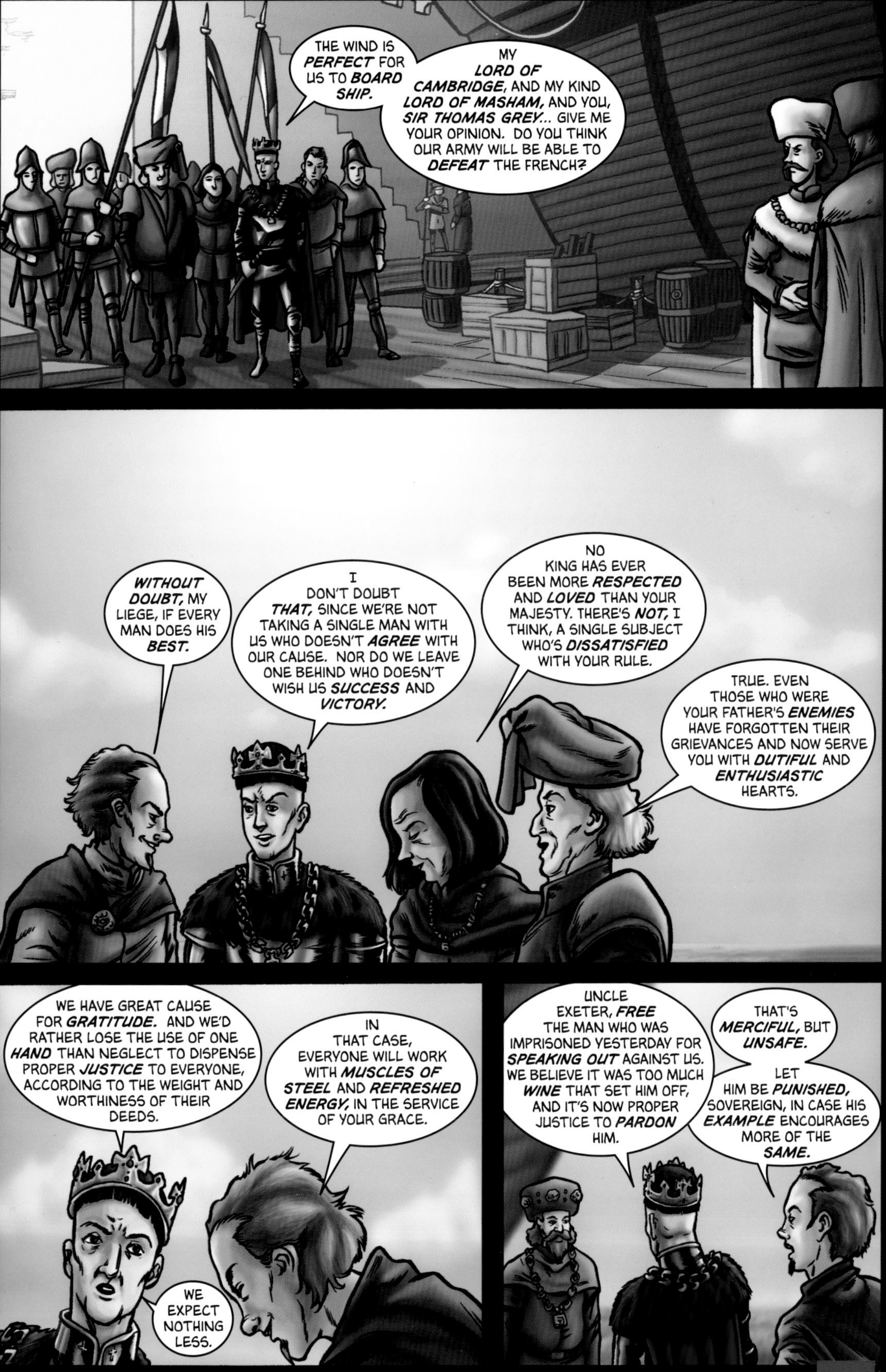
THE WIND IS PERFECT FOR US TO BOARD SHIP.
MY LORD OF CAMBRIDGE, AND MY KIND LORD OF MASHAM, AND YOU, SIR THOMAS GREY... GIVE ME YOUR OPINION. DO YOU THINK OUR ARMY WILL BE ABLE TO DEFEAT THE FRENCH?
WITHOUT DOUBT, MY LIEGE, IF EVERY MAN DOES HIS BEST.
I DON'T DOUBT THAT, SINCE WE'RE NOT TAKING A SINGLE MAN WITH US WHO DOESN'T AGREE WITH OUR CAUSE. NOR DO WE LEAVE ONE BEHIND WHO DOESN'T WISH US SUCCESS AND VICTORY.
NO KING HAS EVER BEEN MORE RESPECTED AND LOVED THAN YOUR MAJESTY. THERE'S NOT, I THINK, A SINGLE SUBJECT WHO'S DISSATISFIED WITH YOUR RULE.
TRUE. EVEN THOSE WHO WERE YOUR FATHER'S ENEMIES HAVE FORGOTTEN THEIR GRIEVANCES AND NOW SERVE YOU WITH DUTIFUL AND ENTHUSIASTIC HEARTS.
WE HAVE GREAT CAUSE FOR GRATITUDE. AND WE'D RATHER LOSE THE USE OF ONE HAND THAN NEGLECT TO DISPENSE PROPER JUSTICE TO EVERYONE, ACCORDING TO THE WEIGHT AND WORTHINESS OF THEIR DEEDS.
IN THAT CASE, EVERYONE WILL WORK WITH MUSCLES OF STEEL AND REFRESHED ENERGY, IN THE SERVICE OF YOUR GRACE.
WE EXPECT NOTHING LESS.
UNCLE EXETER, FREE THE MAN WHO WAS IMPRISONED YESTERDAY FOR SPEAKING OUT AGAINST US. WE BELIEVE IT WAS TOO MUCH WINE THAT SET HIM OFF, AND IT'S NOW PROPER JUSTICE TO PARDON HIM.
THAT'S MERCIFUL, BUT UNSAFE.
LET HIM BE PUNISHED, SOVEREIGN, IN CASE HIS EXAMPLE ENCOURAGES MORE OF THE SAME.

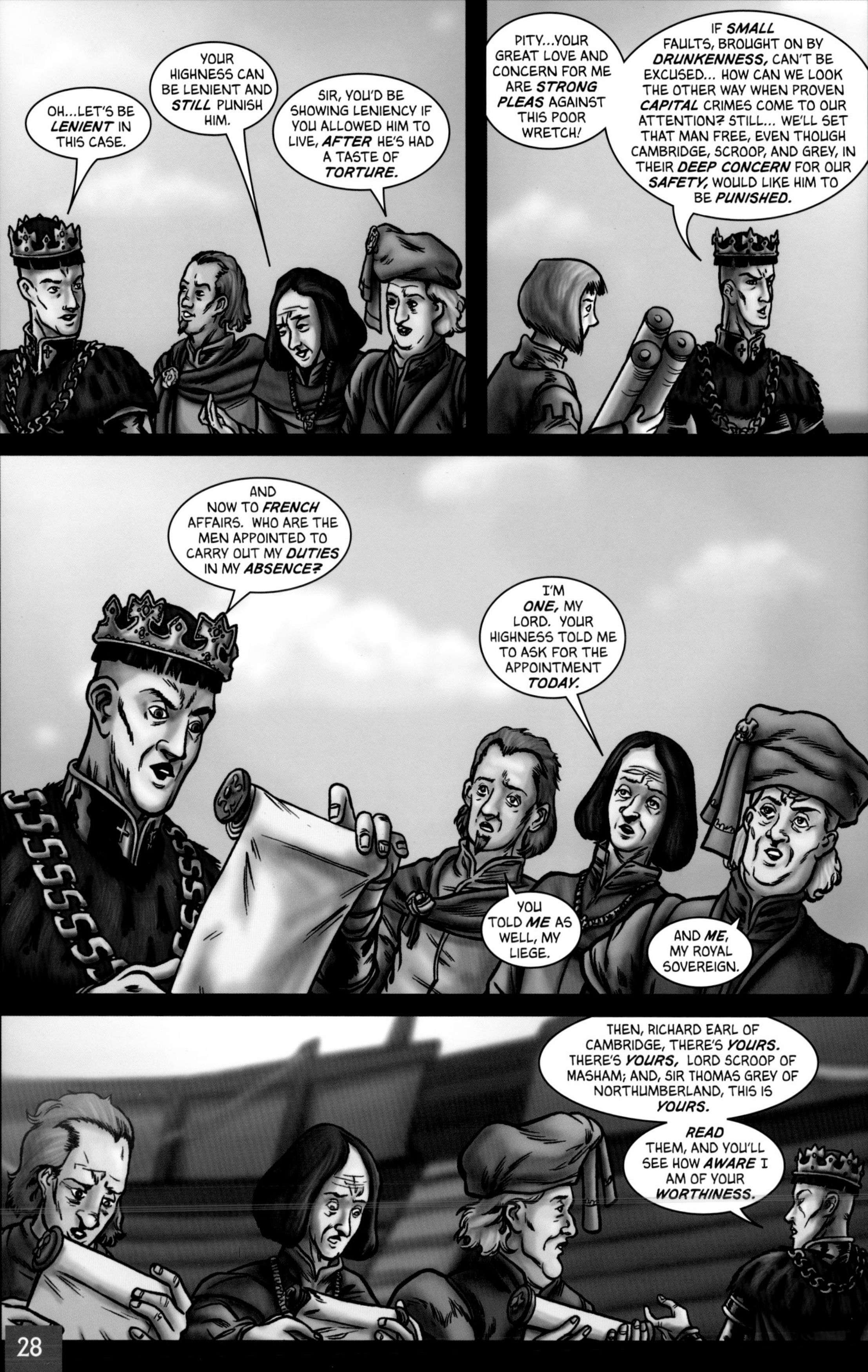

OH...LET'S BE LENIENT IN THIS CASE.
YOUR HIGHNESS CAN BE LENIENT AND STILL PUNISH HIM.
SIR, YOU'D BE SHOWING LENIENCY IF YOU ALLOWED HIM TO LIVE, AFTER HE'S HAD A TASTE OF TORTURE.
PITY...YOUR GREAT LOVE AND CONCERN FOR ME ARE STRONG PLEAS AGAINST THIS POOR WRETCH!
IF SMALL FAULTS, BROUGHT ON BY DRUNKENNESS, CAN'T BE EXCUSED... HOW CAN WE LOOK THE OTHER WAY WHEN PROVEN CAPITAL CRIMES COME TO OUR ATTENTION? STILL... WE'LL SET THAT MAN FREE, EVEN THOUGH CAMBRIDGE, SCROOP, AND GREY, IN THEIR DEEP CONCERN FOR OUR SAFETY, WOULD LIKE HIM TO BE PUNISHED.
AND NOW TO FRENCH AFFAIRS. WHO ARE THE MEN APPOINTED TO CARRY OUT MY DUTIES IN MY ABSENCE?
I'M ONE, MY LORD. YOUR HIGHNESS TOLD ME TO ASK FOR THE APPOINTMENT TODAY.
YOU TOLD ME AS WELL, MY LIEGE.
AND ME, MY ROYAL SOVEREIGN.
THEN, RICHARD EARL OF CAMBRIDGE, THERE'S YOURS. THERE'S YOURS, LORD SCROOP OF MASHAM; AND, SIR THOMAS GREY OF NORTHUMBERLAND, THIS IS YOURS.
READ THEM, AND YOU'LL SEE HOW AWARE I AM OF YOUR WORTHINESS.

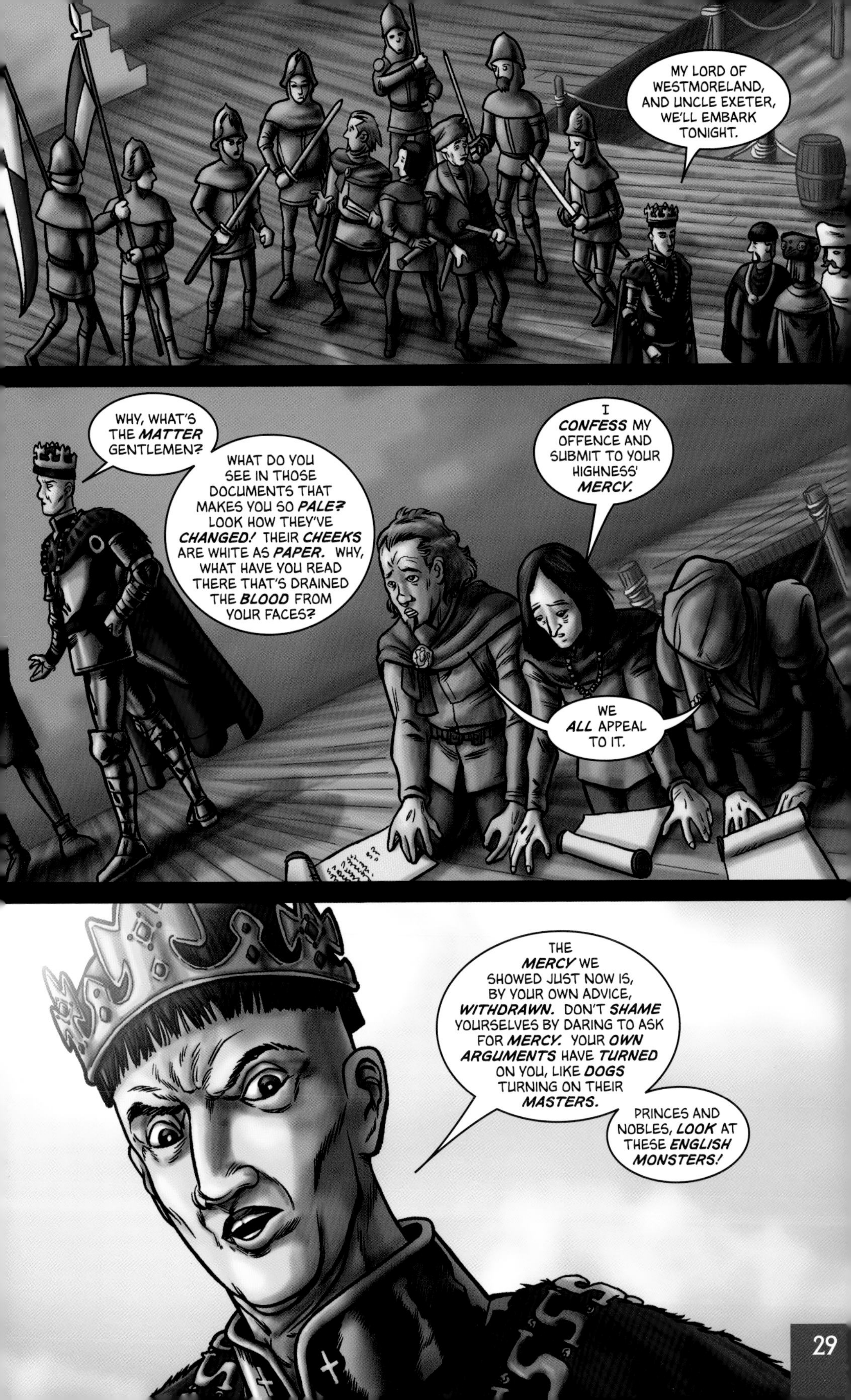
MY LORD OF WESTMORELAND, AND UNCLE EXETER, WE'LL EMBARK TONIGHT.
WHY, WHAT'S THE MATTER GENTLEMEN?
WHAT DO YOU SEE IN THOSE DOCUMENTS THAT MAKES YOU SO PALE? LOOK HOW THEY'VE CHANGED! THEIR CHEEKS ARE WHITE AS PAPER. WHY, WHAT HAVE YOU READ THERE THAT'S DRAINED THE BLOOD FROM YOUR FACES?
I CONFESS MY OFFENCE AND SUBMIT TO YOUR HIGHNESS' MERCY.
WE ALL APPEAL TO IT.
THE MERCY WE SHOWED JUST NOW IS, BY YOUR OWN ADVICE, WITHDRAWN. DON'T SHAME YOURSELVES BY DARING TO ASK FOR MERCY. YOUR OWN ARGUMENTS HAVE TURNED ON YOU, LIKE DOGS TURNING ON THEIR MASTERS.
PRINCES AND NOBLES, LOOK AT THESE ENGLISH MONSTERS!

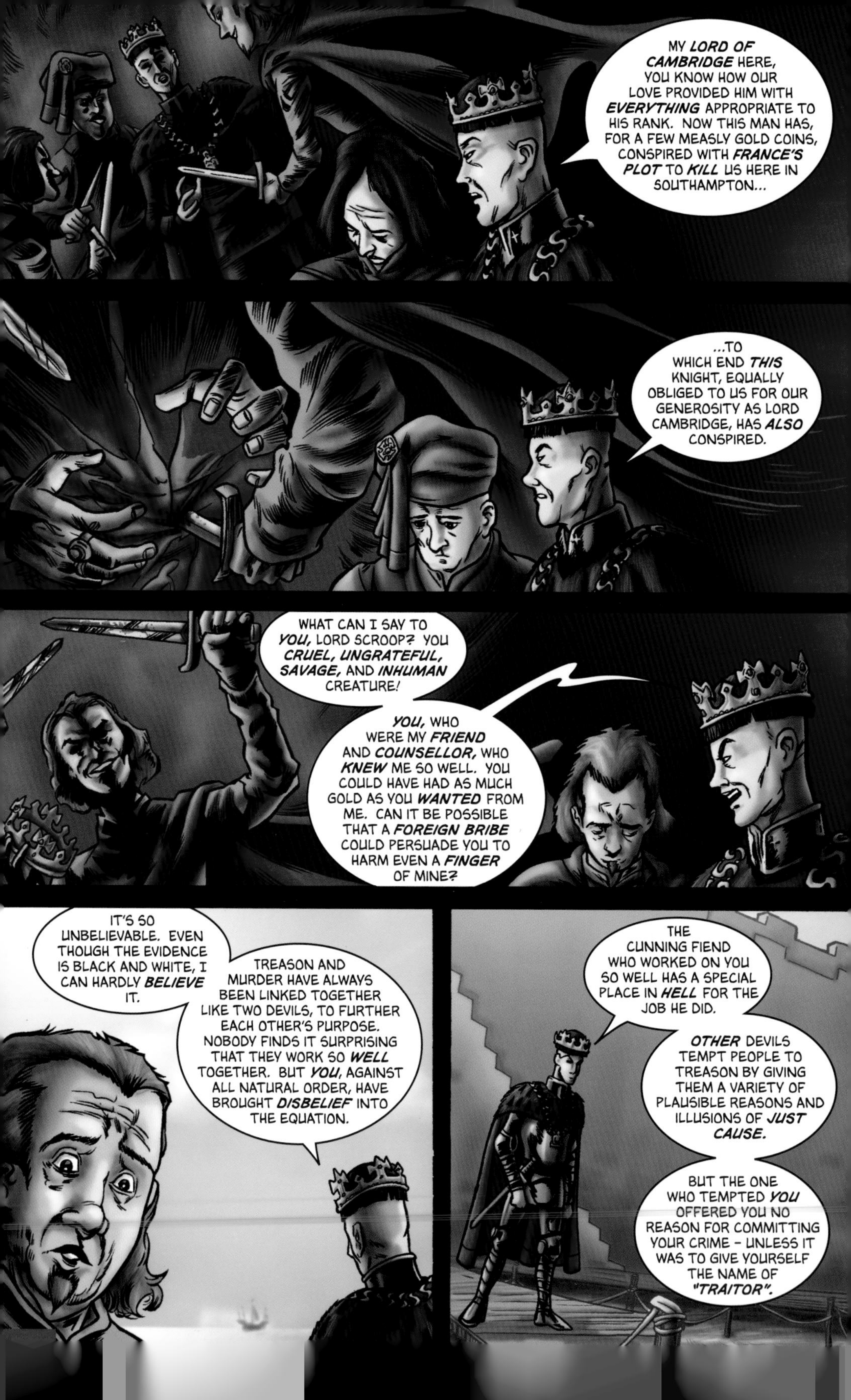
MY LORD OF CAMBRIDGE HERE, YOU KNOW HOW OUR LOVE PROVIDED HIM WITH EVERYTHING APPROPRIATE TO HIS RANK. NOW THIS MAN HAS, FOR A FEW MEASLY GOLD COINS, CONSPIRED WITH FRANCE'S PLOT TO KILL US HERE IN SOUTHAMPTON...
...TO WHICH END THIS KNIGHT, EQUALLY OBLIGED TO US FOR OUR GENEROSITY AS LORD CAMBRIDGE, HAS ALSO CONSPIRED.
WHAT CAN I SAY TO YOU, LORD SCROOP? YOU CRUEL, UNGRATEFUL, SAVAGE, AND INHUMAN CREATURE!
YOU, WHO WERE MY FRIEND AND COUNSELLOR, WHO KNEW ME SO WELL. YOU COULD HAVE HAD AS MUCH GOLD AS YOU WANTED FROM ME. CAN IT BE POSSIBLE THAT A FOREIGN BRIBE COULD PERSUADE YOU TO HARM EVEN A FINGER OF MINE?
IT'S SO UNBELIEVABLE. EVEN THOUGH THE EVIDENCE IS BLACK AND WHITE, I CAN HARDLY BELIEVE IT.
TREASON AND MURDER HAVE ALWAYS BEEN LINKED TOGETHER LIKE TWO DEVILS, TO FURTHER EACH OTHER'S PURPOSE. NOBODY FINDS IT SURPRISING THAT THEY WORK SO WELL TOGETHER. BUT YOU, AGAINST ALL NATURAL ORDER, HAVE BROUGHT DISBELIEF INTO THE EQUATION.
THE CUNNING FIEND WHO WORKED ON YOU SO WELL HAS A SPECIAL PLACE IN HELL FOR THE JOB HE DID.
OTHER DEVILS TEMPT PEOPLE TO TREASON BY GIVING THEM A VARIETY OF PLAUSIBLE REASONS AND ILLUSIONS OF JUST CAUSE.
BUT THE ONE WHO TEMPTED YOU OFFERED YOU NO REASON FOR COMMITTING YOUR CRIME – UNLESS IT WAS TO GIVE YOURSELF THE NAME OF "TRAITOR".

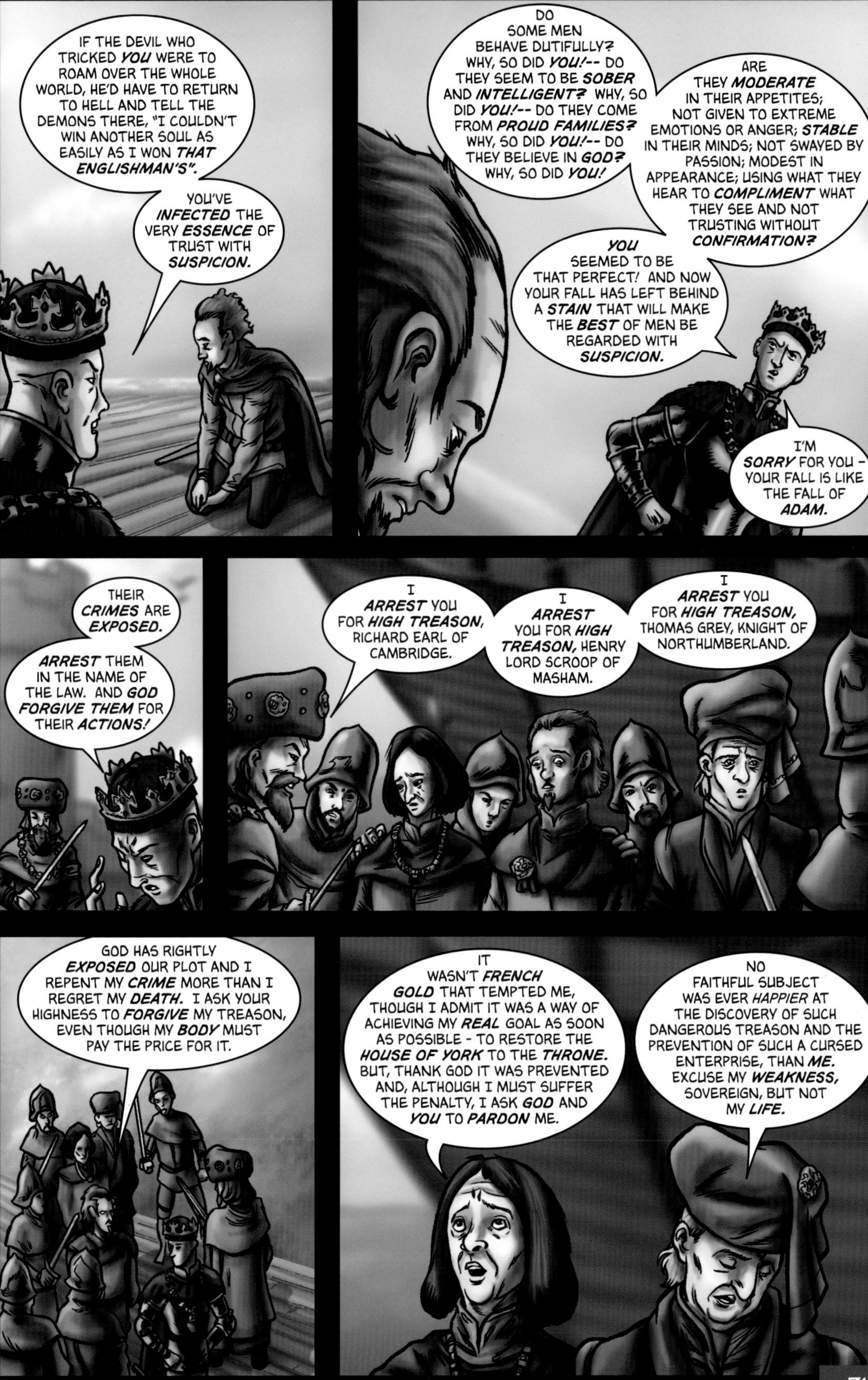
IF THE DEVIL WHO TRICKED YOU WERE TO ROAM OVER THE WHOLE WORLD, HE'D HAVE TO RETURN TO HELL AND TELL THE DEMONS THERE, "I COULDN'T WIN ANOTHER SOUL AS EASILY AS I WON THAT ENGLISHMAN'S".
YOU'VE INFECTED THE VERY ESSENCE OF TRUST WITH SUSPICION.
DO SOME MEN BEHAVE DUTIFULLY? WHY, SO DID YOU!-- DO THEY SEEM TO BE SOBER AND INTELLIGENT? WHY, SO DID YOU!-- DO THEY COME FROM PROUD FAMILIES? WHY, SO DID YOU!-- DO THEY BELIEVE IN GOD? WHY, SO DID YOU!
ARE THEY MODERATE IN THEIR APPETITES; NOT GIVEN TO EXTREME EMOTIONS OR ANGER; STABLE IN THEIR MINDS; NOT SWAYED BY PASSION; MODEST IN APPEARANCE; USING WHAT THEY HEAR TO COMPLIMENT WHAT THEY SEE AND NOT TRUSTING WITHOUT CONFIRMATION?
YOU SEEMED TO BE THAT PERFECT! AND NOW YOUR FALL HAS LEFT BEHIND A STAIN THAT WILL MAKE THE BEST OF MEN BE REGARDED WITH SUSPICION.
I'M SORRY FOR YOU - YOUR FALL IS LIKE THE FALL OF ADAM.
THEIR CRIMES ARE EXPOSED.
ARREST THEM IN THE NAME OF THE LAW. AND GOD FORGIVE THEM FOR THEIR ACTIONS!
I ARREST YOU FOR HIGH TREASON, RICHARD EARL OF CAMBRIDGE.
I ARREST YOU FOR HIGH TREASON, HENRY LORD SCROOP OF MASHAM.
I ARREST YOU FOR HIGH TREASON, THOMAS GREY, KNIGHT OF NORTHUMBERLAND.
GOD HAS RIGHTLY EXPOSED OUR PLOT AND I REPENT MY CRIME MORE THAN I REGRET MY DEATH. I ASK YOUR HIGHNESS TO FORGIVE MY TREASON, EVEN THOUGH MY BODY MUST PAY THE PRICE FOR IT.
IT WASN'T FRENCH GOLD THAT TEMPTED ME, THOUGH I ADMIT IT WAS A WAY OF ACHIEVING MY REAL GOAL AS SOON AS POSSIBLE - TO RESTORE THE HOUSE OF YORK TO THE THRONE. BUT, THANK GOD IT WAS PREVENTED AND, ALTHOUGH I MUST SUFFER THE PENALTY, I ASK GOD AND YOU TO PARDON ME.
NO FAITHFUL SUBJECT WAS EVER HAPPIER AT THE DISCOVERY OF SUCH DANGEROUS TREASON AND THE PREVENTION OF SUCH A CURSED ENTERPRISE, THAN ME. EXCUSE MY WEAKNESS, SOVEREIGN, BUT NOT MY LIFE.

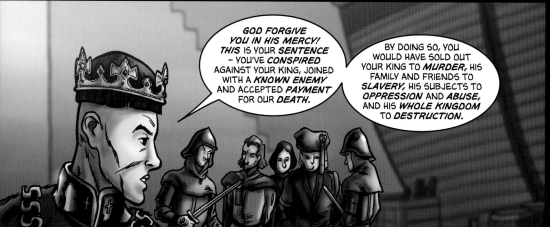

GOD FORGIVE YOU IN HIS MERCY! THIS IS YOUR SENTENCE – YOU'VE CONSPIRED AGAINST YOUR KING, JOINED WITH A KNOWN ENEMY AND ACCEPTED PAYMENT FOR OUR DEATH.

BY DOING SO, YOU WOULD HAVE SOLD OUT YOUR KING TO MURDER, HIS FAMILY AND FRIENDS TO SLAVERY, HIS SUBJECTS TO OPPRESSION AND ABUSE, AND HIS WHOLE KINGDOM TO DESTRUCTION.

WE'RE NOT LOOKING FOR PERSONAL REVENGE, BUT WE MUST CONSIDER OUR KINGDOM'S SAFETY. YOU MUST NOW FACE THE LAWS OF OUR KINGDOM, WHOSE COLLAPSE YOU'VE WORKED FOR. GO FROM HERE, YOU MISERABLE SINNERS, TO YOUR DEATH!

MAY GOD IN HIS MERCY GIVE YOU THE STRENGTH TO FACE IT, AND TO TRULY REPENT FOR YOUR CRIMES!

TAKE THEM AWAY!

NOW, LORDS, LET US GO TO FRANCE – THE MISSION WHICH WILL BRING GLORY TO US ALL.

WE HAVE NO DOUBT THE WAR WILL BE A GOOD AND LUCKY ONE, SINCE GOD HAS SO GENEROUSLY BROUGHT THIS DANGEROUS TREASON TO LIGHT. IT NO LONGER STANDS IN OUR WAY, NOR HAMPERS THE BEGINNING OF OUR CAMPAIGN.

THERE'S NO DOUBT NOW THAT ALL OBSTACLES HAVE BEEN REMOVED. SO, MY COUNTRYMEN, LET'S GO!

LET'S DELIVER OUR ARMY INTO THE HAND OF GOD AND BEGIN OUR EXPEDITION IMMEDIATELY. AWAY TO SEA, WITH OUR WARLIKE ADVANCE!

I WON'T BE KING OF ENGLAND, IF I'M NOT ALSO KING OF FRANCE!

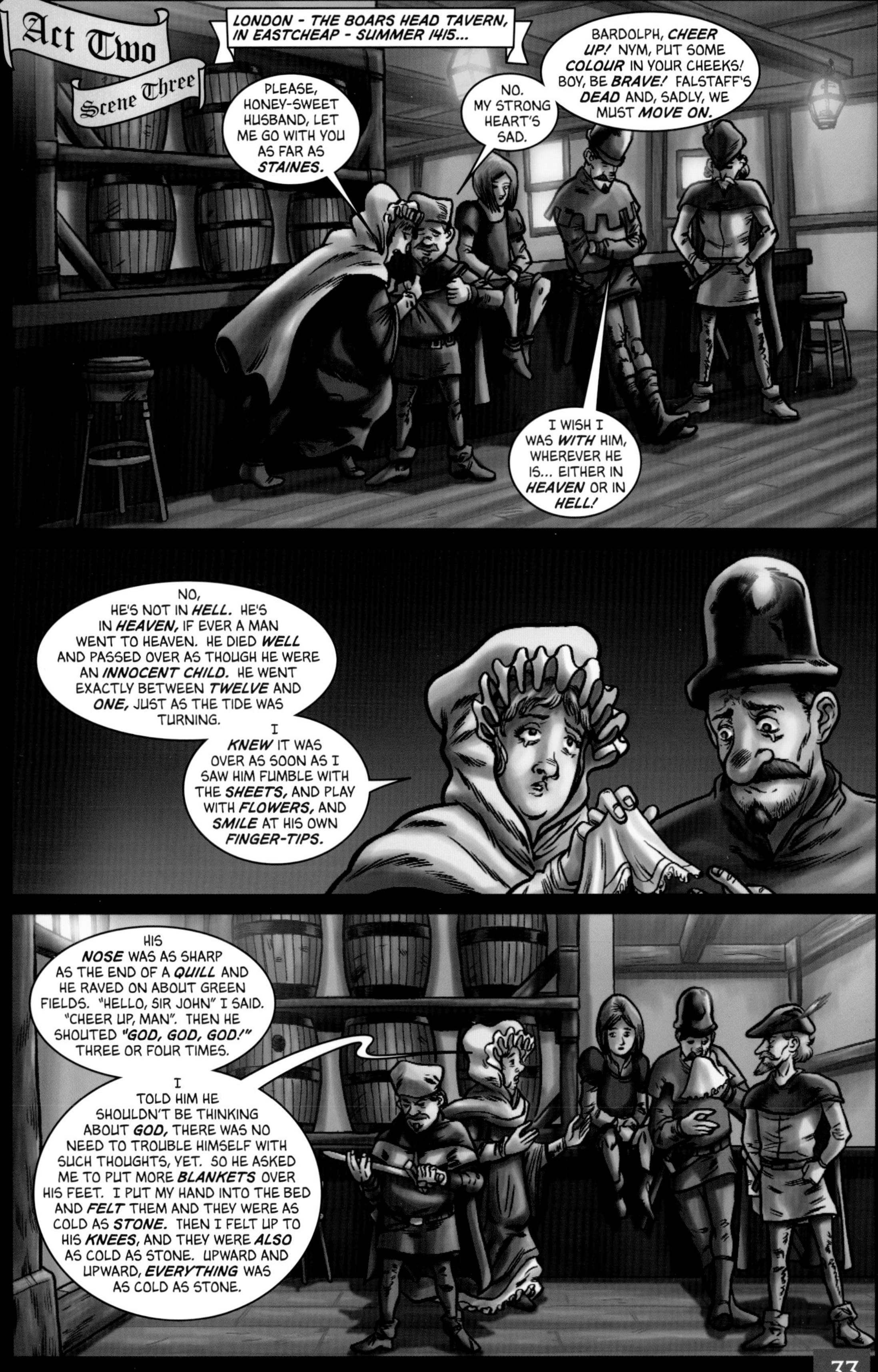
Act Two
Scene Three
LONDON - THE BOARS HEAD TAVERN, IN EASTCHEAP - SUMMER 1415...
PLEASE, HONEY-SWEET HUSBAND, LET ME GO WITH YOU AS FAR AS STAINES.
NO. MY STRONG HEART'S SAD.
BARDOLPH, CHEER UP! NYM, PUT SOME COLOUR IN YOUR CHEEKS! BOY, BE BRAVE! FALSTAFF'S DEAD AND, SADLY, WE MUST MOVE ON.
I WISH I WAS WITH HIM, WHEREVER HE IS... EITHER IN HEAVEN OR IN HELL!
NO, HE'S NOT IN HELL. HE'S IN HEAVEN, IF EVER A MAN WENT TO HEAVEN. HE DIED WELL AND PASSED OVER AS THOUGH HE WERE AN INNOCENT CHILD. HE WENT EXACTLY BETWEEN TWELVE AND ONE, JUST AS THE TIDE WAS TURNING.
I KNEW IT WAS OVER AS SOON AS I SAW HIM FUMBLE WITH THE SHEETS, AND PLAY WITH FLOWERS, AND SMILE AT HIS OWN FINGER-TIPS.
HIS NOSE WAS AS SHARP AS THE END OF A QUILL AND HE RAVED ON ABOUT GREEN FIELDS. "HELLO, SIR JOHN" I SAID. "CHEER UP, MAN". THEN HE SHOUTED "GOD, GOD, GOD!" THREE OR FOUR TIMES.
I TOLD HIM HE SHOULDN'T BE THINKING ABOUT GOD, THERE WAS NO NEED TO TROUBLE HIMSELF WITH SUCH THOUGHTS, YET. SO HE ASKED ME TO PUT MORE BLANKETS OVER HIS FEET. I PUT MY HAND INTO THE BED AND FELT THEM AND THEY WERE AS COLD AS STONE. THEN I FELT UP TO HIS KNEES, AND THEY WERE ALSO AS COLD AS STONE. UPWARD AND UPWARD, EVERYTHING WAS AS COLD AS STONE.

THEY SAY HE BLAMED *WINE* FOR HIS CONDITION.

YES, HE DID.

AND *WOMEN.*

NO, HE DIDN'T.

YES, 'E DID. 'E SAID THEY WAS *DEVILS INCARNATE.*

HE COULDN'T STAND *"CARNATION".* HE *HATED* THE COLOUR.

'E ONCE SAID THE *DEVIL'D* GET 'IM 'CAUSE OF THE *WOMEN.*

ALL RIGHT, MAYBE HE *DID* TALK OF WOMEN; BUT HE WAS *CRAZED* BY THEN AND TALKED ABOUT THE *HAG OF BABYLON.*

D'YOU REMEMBER WHEN 'E SEEN A *FLEA* STUCK ON BARDOLPH'S NOSE AND SAID IT WAS A *BLACK SOUL* BURNING IN 'ELL?

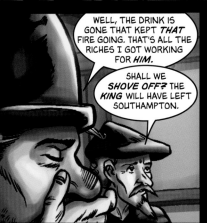

WELL, THE DRINK IS GONE THAT KEPT *THAT* FIRE GOING. THAT'S ALL THE RICHES I GOT WORKING FOR *HIM.*

SHALL WE *SHOVE OFF?* THE *KING* WILL HAVE LEFT SOUTHAMPTON.

RIGHT, LET'S GO. GIVE ME A *KISS,* MY LOVE.

LOOK AFTER MY PROPERTY. BE SENSIBLE; THE RULE IS "CASH AND NO CREDIT" -- TRUST *NO-ONE;* BECAUSE PROMISES ARE WORTHLESS AND MEN'S MORALS ARE *WAFER-THIN.* STANDING YOUR GROUND IS THE ONLY WAY, MY DEAR, AND LET *CAUTION* BE YOUR GUIDE. GO, DRY YOUR EYES.

COMRADES IN ARMS! LET'S GO TO FRANCE LIKE *HORSE-LEECHES,* MY BOYS. WE'LL DRINK THEIR *BLOOD* DRY!

AN' THEY SAY THAT AIN'T VERY GOOD STUFF.

KISS HER AND LET'S *MARCH.*

GOODBYE, HOSTESS.

I *CAN'T* KISS; THAT'S THE *MOOD* I'M IN. BUT GOODBYE.

BE *PRUDENT* AND *CAREFUL* WITH YOUR *MONEY,* I ORDER YOU!

GOODBYE. *ADIEU!*

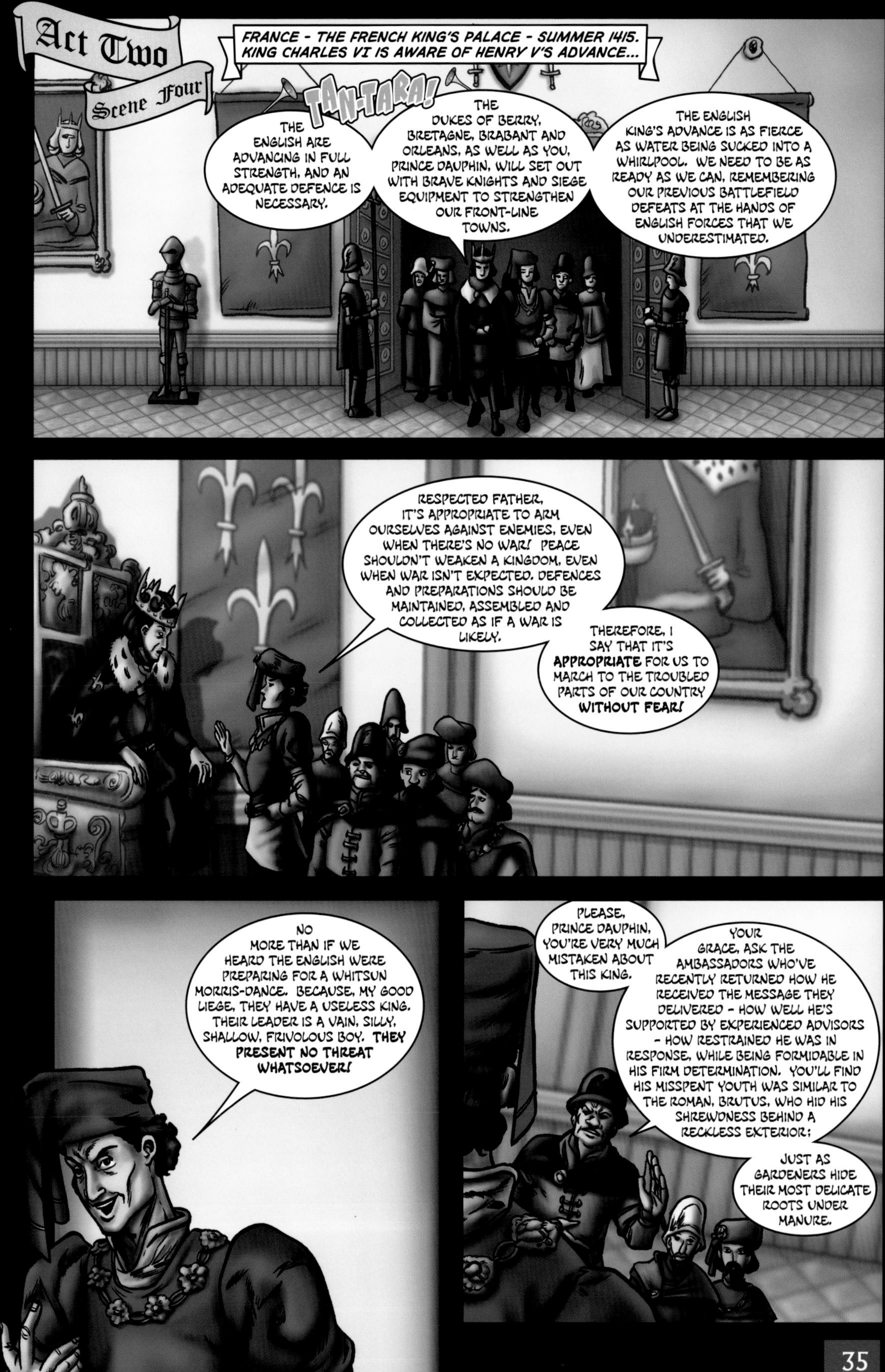

Act Two
Scene Four
FRANCE - THE FRENCH KING'S PALACE - SUMMER 1415. KING CHARLES VI IS AWARE OF HENRY V'S ADVANCE...
TAN-TARA!
THE ENGLISH ARE ADVANCING IN FULL STRENGTH, AND AN ADEQUATE DEFENCE IS NECESSARY.
THE DUKES OF BERRY, BRETAGNE, BRABANT AND ORLEANS, AS WELL AS YOU, PRINCE DAUPHIN, WILL SET OUT WITH BRAVE KNIGHTS AND SIEGE EQUIPMENT TO STRENGTHEN OUR FRONT-LINE TOWNS.
THE ENGLISH KING'S ADVANCE IS AS FIERCE AS WATER BEING SUCKED INTO A WHIRLPOOL. WE NEED TO BE AS READY AS WE CAN, REMEMBERING OUR PREVIOUS BATTLEFIELD DEFEATS AT THE HANDS OF ENGLISH FORCES THAT WE UNDERESTIMATED.
RESPECTED FATHER, IT'S APPROPRIATE TO ARM OURSELVES AGAINST ENEMIES, EVEN WHEN THERE'S NO WAR! PEACE SHOULDN'T WEAKEN A KINGDOM, EVEN WHEN WAR ISN'T EXPECTED. DEFENCES AND PREPARATIONS SHOULD BE MAINTAINED, ASSEMBLED AND COLLECTED AS IF A WAR IS LIKELY.
THEREFORE, I SAY THAT IT'S **APPROPRIATE** FOR US TO MARCH TO THE TROUBLED PARTS OF OUR COUNTRY **WITHOUT FEAR!**
NO MORE THAN IF WE HEARD THE ENGLISH WERE PREPARING FOR A WHITSUN MORRIS-DANCE. BECAUSE, MY GOOD LIEGE, THEY HAVE A USELESS KING. THEIR LEADER IS A VAIN, SILLY, SHALLOW, FRIVOLOUS BOY. **THEY PRESENT NO THREAT WHATSOEVER!**
PLEASE, PRINCE DAUPHIN, YOU'RE VERY MUCH MISTAKEN ABOUT THIS KING.
YOUR GRACE, ASK THE AMBASSADORS WHO'VE RECENTLY RETURNED HOW HE RECEIVED THE MESSAGE THEY DELIVERED - HOW WELL HE'S SUPPORTED BY EXPERIENCED ADVISORS - HOW RESTRAINED HE WAS IN RESPONSE, WHILE BEING FORMIDABLE IN HIS FIRM DETERMINATION. YOU'LL FIND HIS MISSPENT YOUTH WAS SIMILAR TO THE ROMAN, BRUTUS, WHO HID HIS SHREWDNESS BEHIND A RECKLESS EXTERIOR;
JUST AS GARDENERS HIDE THEIR MOST DELICATE ROOTS UNDER MANURE.

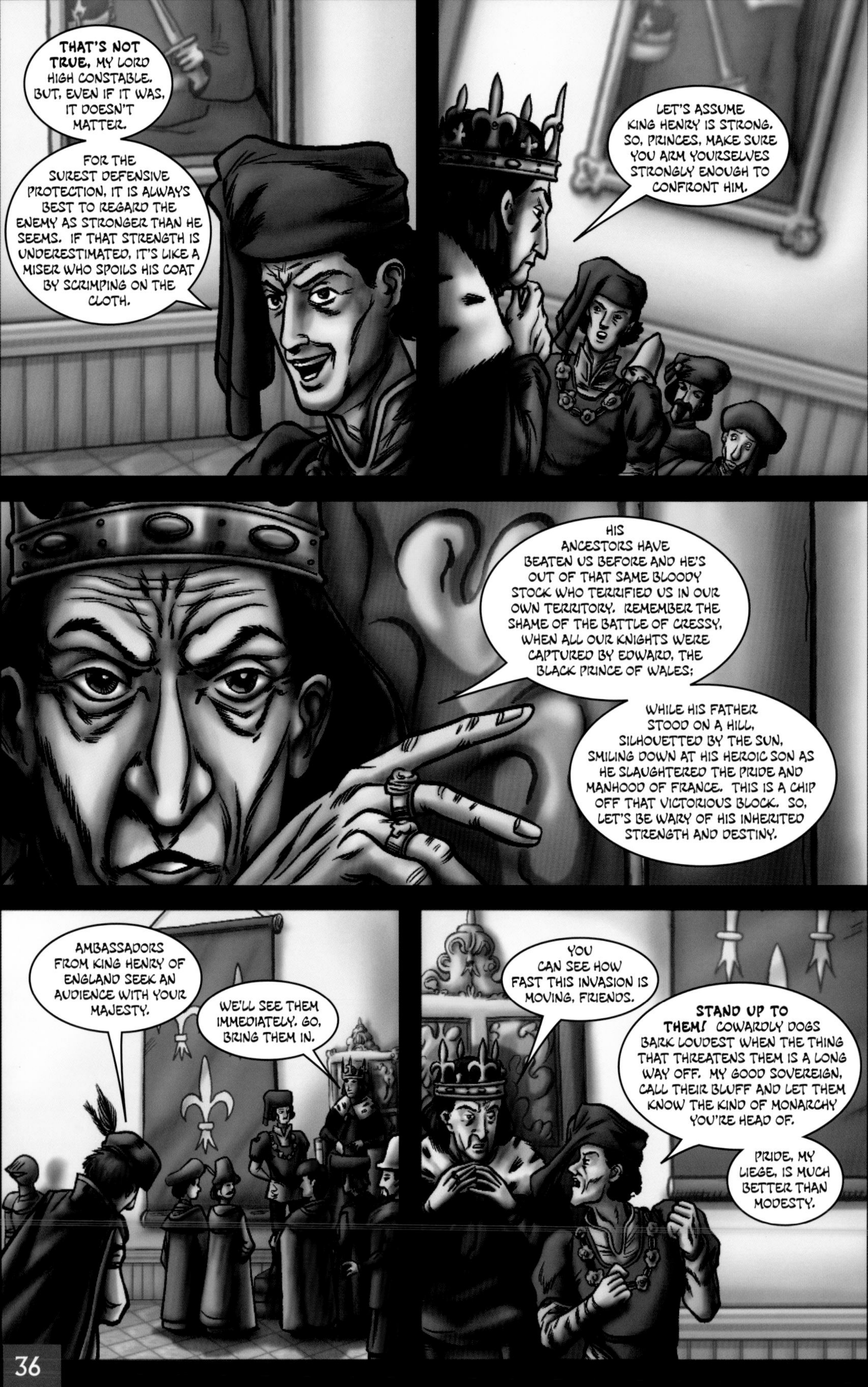
THAT'S NOT TRUE, MY LORD HIGH CONSTABLE. BUT, EVEN IF IT WAS, IT DOESN'T MATTER.
FOR THE SUREST DEFENSIVE PROTECTION, IT IS ALWAYS BEST TO REGARD THE ENEMY AS STRONGER THAN HE SEEMS. IF THAT STRENGTH IS UNDERESTIMATED, IT'S LIKE A MISER WHO SPOILS HIS COAT BY SCRIMPING ON THE CLOTH.
LET'S ASSUME KING HENRY IS STRONG. SO, PRINCES, MAKE SURE YOU ARM YOURSELVES STRONGLY ENOUGH TO CONFRONT HIM.
HIS ANCESTORS HAVE BEATEN US BEFORE AND HE'S OUT OF THAT SAME BLOODY STOCK WHO TERRIFIED US IN OUR OWN TERRITORY. REMEMBER THE SHAME OF THE BATTLE OF CRESSY, WHEN ALL OUR KNIGHTS WERE CAPTURED BY EDWARD, THE BLACK PRINCE OF WALES;
WHILE HIS FATHER STOOD ON A HILL, SILHOUETTED BY THE SUN, SMILING DOWN AT HIS HEROIC SON AS HE SLAUGHTERED THE PRIDE AND MANHOOD OF FRANCE. THIS IS A CHIP OFF THAT VICTORIOUS BLOCK. SO, LET'S BE WARY OF HIS INHERITED STRENGTH AND DESTINY.
AMBASSADORS FROM KING HENRY OF ENGLAND SEEK AN AUDIENCE WITH YOUR MAJESTY.
WE'LL SEE THEM IMMEDIATELY. GO, BRING THEM IN.
YOU CAN SEE HOW FAST THIS INVASION IS MOVING, FRIENDS.
STAND UP TO THEM! COWARDLY DOGS BARK LOUDEST WHEN THE THING THAT THREATENS THEM IS A LONG WAY OFF. MY GOOD SOVEREIGN, CALL THEIR BLUFF AND LET THEM KNOW THE KIND OF MONARCHY YOU'RE HEAD OF.
PRIDE, MY LIEGE, IS MUCH BETTER THAN MODESTY.

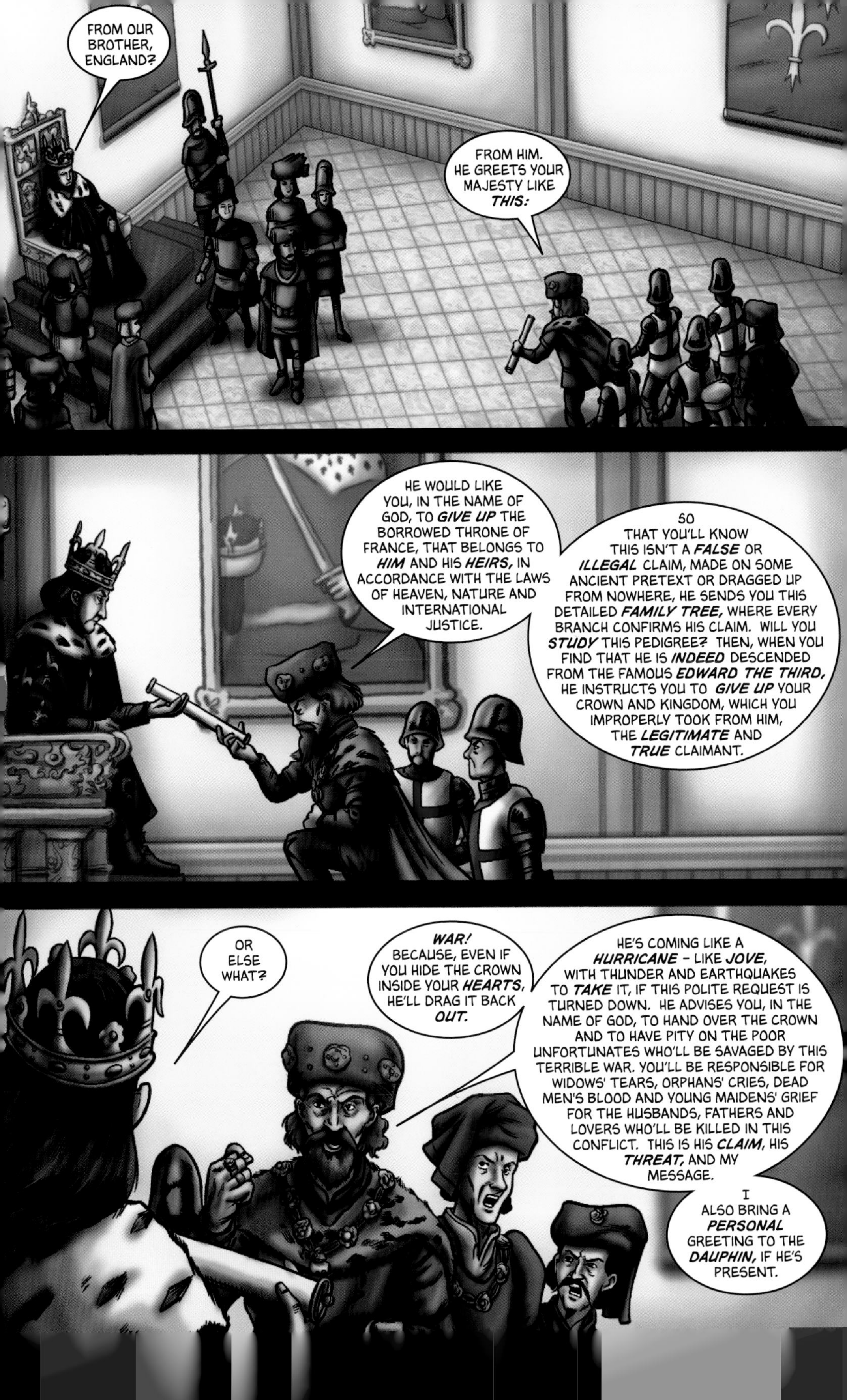
FROM OUR BROTHER, ENGLAND?
FROM HIM. HE GREETS YOUR MAJESTY LIKE THIS:
HE WOULD LIKE YOU, IN THE NAME OF GOD, TO GIVE UP THE BORROWED THRONE OF FRANCE, THAT BELONGS TO HIM AND HIS HEIRS, IN ACCORDANCE WITH THE LAWS OF HEAVEN, NATURE AND INTERNATIONAL JUSTICE.
SO THAT YOU'LL KNOW THIS ISN'T A FALSE OR ILLEGAL CLAIM, MADE ON SOME ANCIENT PRETEXT OR DRAGGED UP FROM NOWHERE, HE SENDS YOU THIS DETAILED FAMILY TREE, WHERE EVERY BRANCH CONFIRMS HIS CLAIM. WILL YOU STUDY THIS PEDIGREE? THEN, WHEN YOU FIND THAT HE IS INDEED DESCENDED FROM THE FAMOUS EDWARD THE THIRD, HE INSTRUCTS YOU TO GIVE UP YOUR CROWN AND KINGDOM, WHICH YOU IMPROPERLY TOOK FROM HIM, THE LEGITIMATE AND TRUE CLAIMANT.
OR ELSE WHAT?
WAR! BECAUSE, EVEN IF YOU HIDE THE CROWN INSIDE YOUR HEARTS, HE'LL DRAG IT BACK OUT.
HE'S COMING LIKE A HURRICANE – LIKE JOVE, WITH THUNDER AND EARTHQUAKES TO TAKE IT, IF THIS POLITE REQUEST IS TURNED DOWN. HE ADVISES YOU, IN THE NAME OF GOD, TO HAND OVER THE CROWN AND TO HAVE PITY ON THE POOR UNFORTUNATES WHO'LL BE SAVAGED BY THIS TERRIBLE WAR. YOU'LL BE RESPONSIBLE FOR WIDOWS' TEARS, ORPHANS' CRIES, DEAD MEN'S BLOOD AND YOUNG MAIDENS' GRIEF FOR THE HUSBANDS, FATHERS AND LOVERS WHO'LL BE KILLED IN THIS CONFLICT. THIS IS HIS CLAIM, HIS THREAT, AND MY MESSAGE.
I ALSO BRING A PERSONAL GREETING TO THE DAUPHIN, IF HE'S PRESENT.

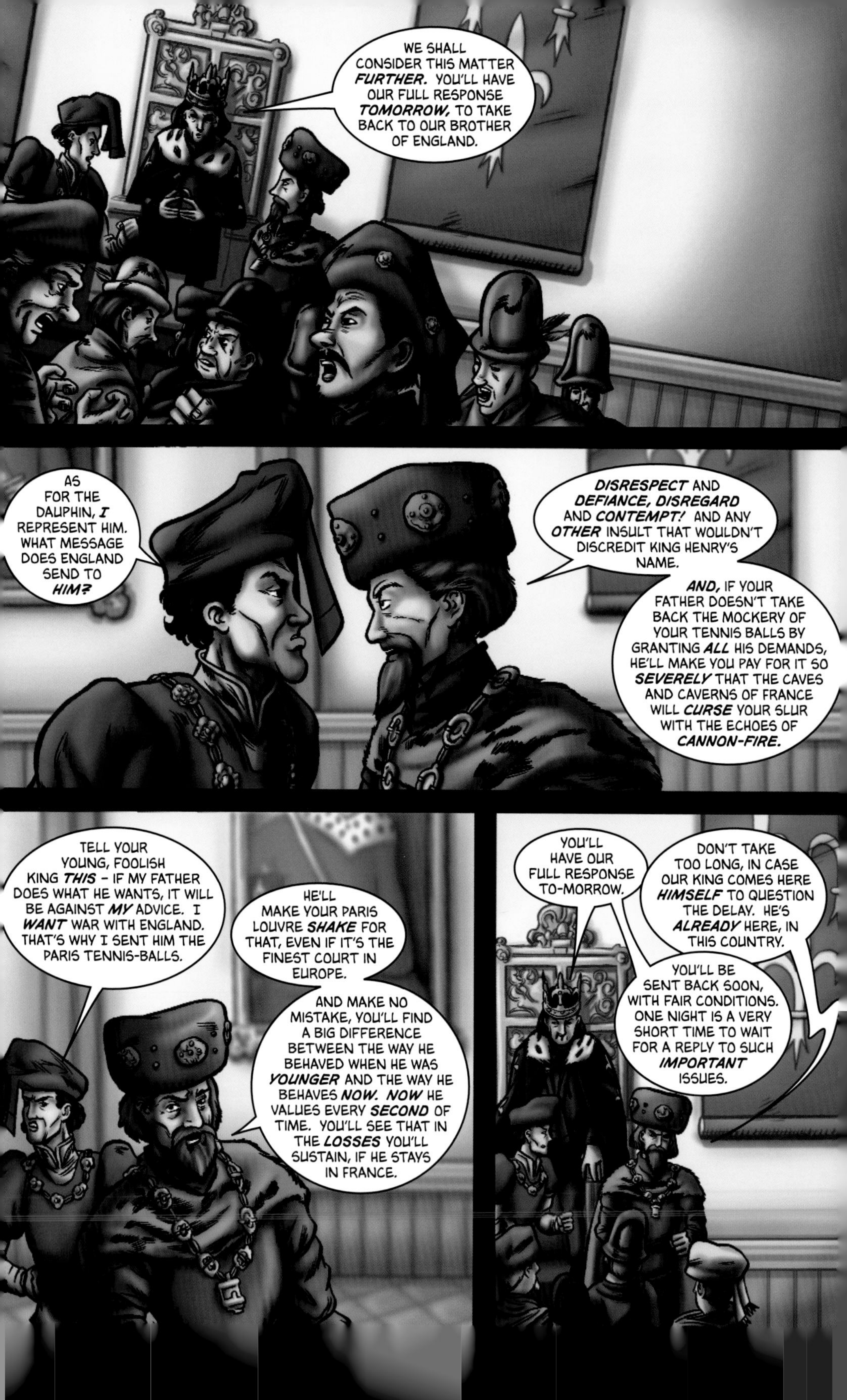

WE SHALL CONSIDER THIS MATTER FURTHER. YOU'LL HAVE OUR FULL RESPONSE TOMORROW, TO TAKE BACK TO OUR BROTHER OF ENGLAND.
AS FOR THE DAUPHIN, I REPRESENT HIM. WHAT MESSAGE DOES ENGLAND SEND TO HIM?
DISRESPECT AND DEFIANCE, DISREGARD AND CONTEMPT! AND ANY OTHER INSULT THAT WOULDN'T DISCREDIT KING HENRY'S NAME.
AND, IF YOUR FATHER DOESN'T TAKE BACK THE MOCKERY OF YOUR TENNIS BALLS BY GRANTING ALL HIS DEMANDS, HE'LL MAKE YOU PAY FOR IT SO SEVERELY THAT THE CAVES AND CAVERNS OF FRANCE WILL CURSE YOUR SLUR WITH THE ECHOES OF CANNON-FIRE.
TELL YOUR YOUNG, FOOLISH KING THIS – IF MY FATHER DOES WHAT HE WANTS, IT WILL BE AGAINST MY ADVICE. I WANT WAR WITH ENGLAND. THAT'S WHY I SENT HIM THE PARIS TENNIS-BALLS.
HE'LL MAKE YOUR PARIS LOUVRE SHAKE FOR THAT, EVEN IF IT'S THE FINEST COURT IN EUROPE.
AND MAKE NO MISTAKE, YOU'LL FIND A BIG DIFFERENCE BETWEEN THE WAY HE BEHAVED WHEN HE WAS YOUNGER AND THE WAY HE BEHAVES NOW. NOW HE VALUES EVERY SECOND OF TIME. YOU'LL SEE THAT IN THE LOSSES YOU'LL SUSTAIN, IF HE STAYS IN FRANCE.
YOU'LL HAVE OUR FULL RESPONSE TO-MORROW.
DON'T TAKE TOO LONG, IN CASE OUR KING COMES HERE HIMSELF TO QUESTION THE DELAY. HE'S ALREADY HERE, IN THIS COUNTRY.
YOU'LL BE SENT BACK SOON, WITH FAIR CONDITIONS. ONE NIGHT IS A VERY SHORT TIME TO WAIT FOR A REPLY TO SUCH IMPORTANT ISSUES.

Act Three
Prologue

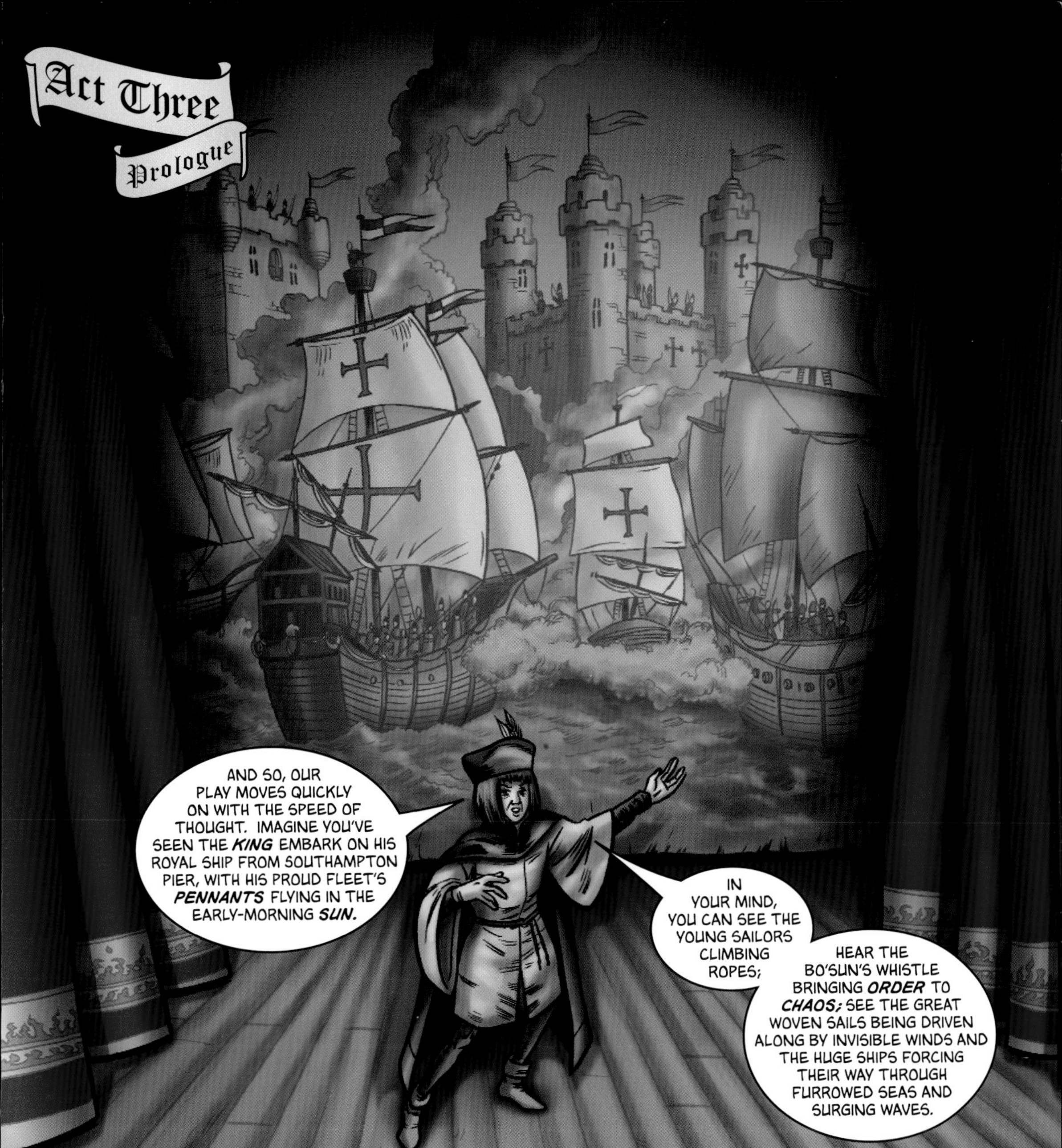
AND SO, OUR PLAY MOVES QUICKLY ON WITH THE SPEED OF THOUGHT. IMAGINE YOU'VE SEEN THE **KING** EMBARK ON HIS ROYAL SHIP FROM SOUTHAMPTON PIER, WITH HIS PROUD FLEET'S ***PENNANTS*** FLYING IN THE EARLY-MORNING ***SUN.***
IN YOUR MIND, YOU CAN SEE THE YOUNG SAILORS CLIMBING ROPES;
HEAR THE BO'SUN'S WHISTLE BRINGING ***ORDER*** TO ***CHAOS;*** SEE THE GREAT WOVEN SAILS BEING DRIVEN ALONG BY INVISIBLE WINDS AND THE HUGE SHIPS FORCING THEIR WAY THROUGH FURROWED SEAS AND SURGING WAVES.

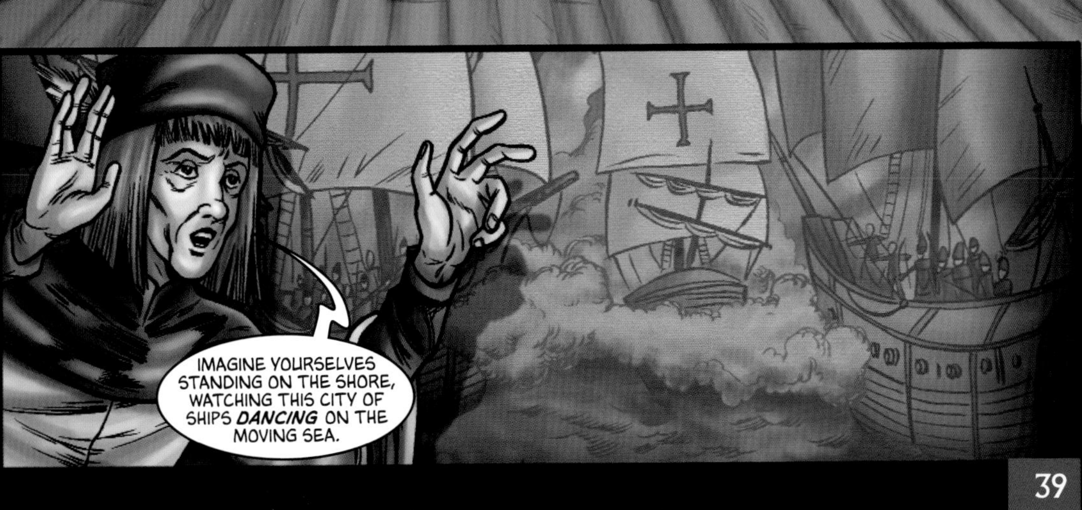
IMAGINE YOURSELVES STANDING ON THE SHORE, WATCHING THIS CITY OF SHIPS ***DANCING*** ON THE MOVING SEA.

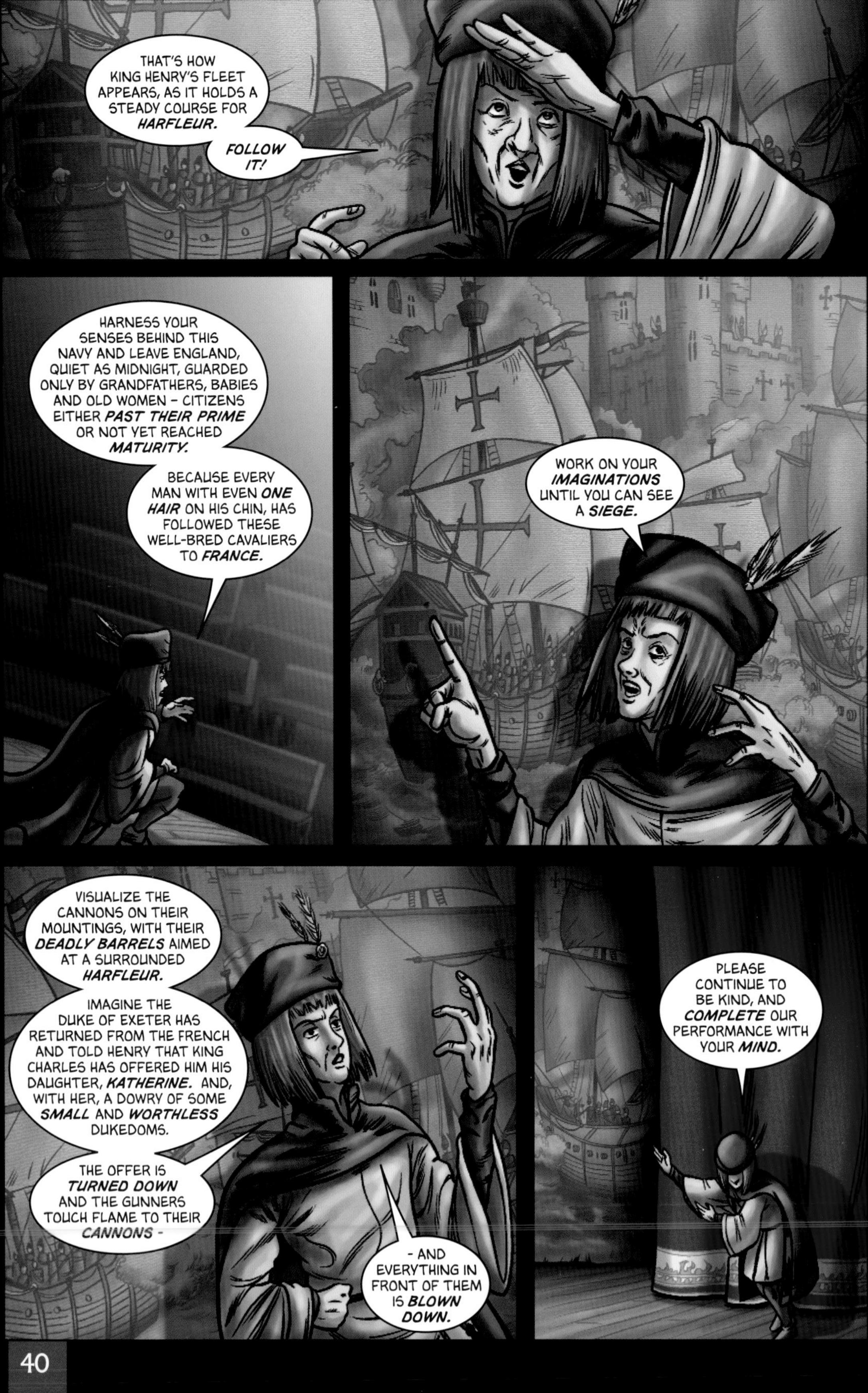
THAT'S HOW KING HENRY'S FLEET APPEARS, AS IT HOLDS A STEADY COURSE FOR HARFLEUR.
FOLLOW IT!
HARNESS YOUR SENSES BEHIND THIS NAVY AND LEAVE ENGLAND, QUIET AS MIDNIGHT, GUARDED ONLY BY GRANDFATHERS, BABIES AND OLD WOMEN - CITIZENS EITHER PAST THEIR PRIME OR NOT YET REACHED MATURITY.
BECAUSE EVERY MAN WITH EVEN ONE HAIR ON HIS CHIN, HAS FOLLOWED THESE WELL-BRED CAVALIERS TO FRANCE.
WORK ON YOUR IMAGINATIONS UNTIL YOU CAN SEE A SIEGE.
VISUALIZE THE CANNONS ON THEIR MOUNTINGS, WITH THEIR DEADLY BARRELS AIMED AT A SURROUNDED HARFLEUR.
IMAGINE THE DUKE OF EXETER HAS RETURNED FROM THE FRENCH AND TOLD HENRY THAT KING CHARLES HAS OFFERED HIM HIS DAUGHTER, KATHERINE. AND, WITH HER, A DOWRY OF SOME SMALL AND WORTHLESS DUKEDOMS.
THE OFFER IS TURNED DOWN AND THE GUNNERS TOUCH FLAME TO THEIR CANNONS -
- AND EVERYTHING IN FRONT OF THEM IS BLOWN DOWN.
PLEASE CONTINUE TO BE KIND, AND COMPLETE OUR PERFORMANCE WITH YOUR MIND.

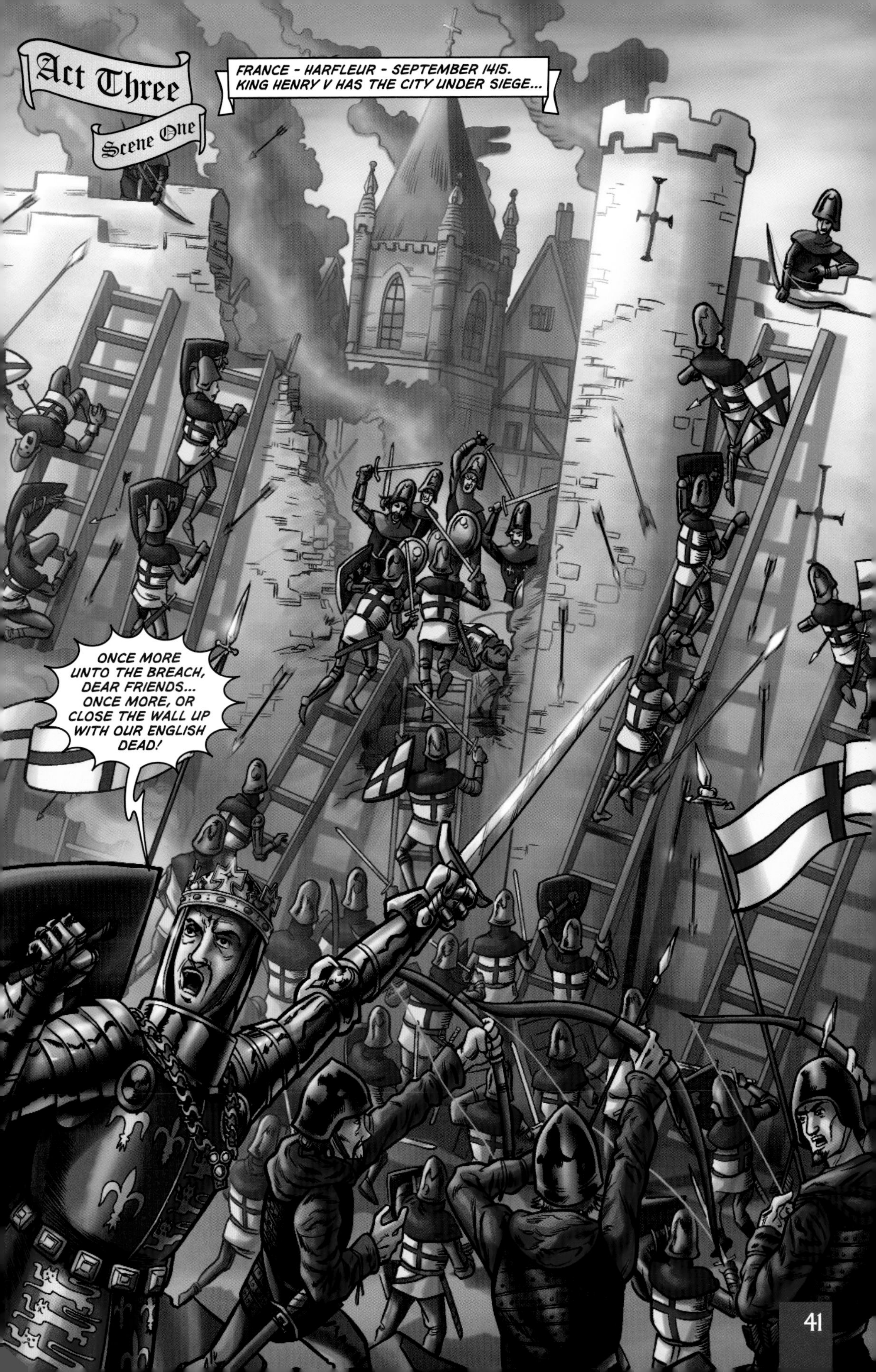
Act Three
Scene One
FRANCE - HARFLEUR - SEPTEMBER 1415. KING HENRY V HAS THE CITY UNDER SIEGE...
ONCE MORE UNTO THE BREACH, DEAR FRIENDS... ONCE MORE, OR CLOSE THE WALL UP WITH OUR ENGLISH DEAD!

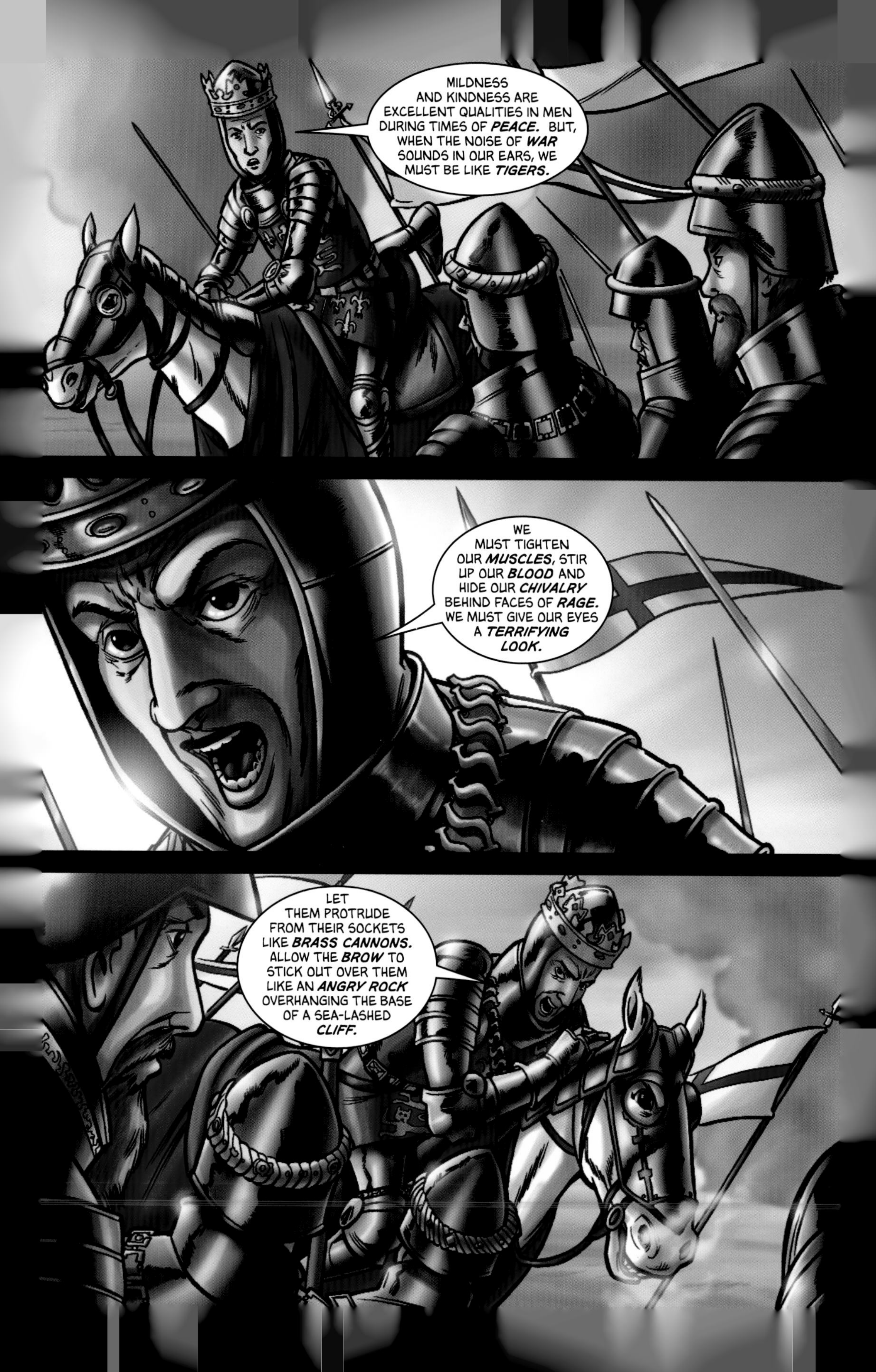
MILDNESS AND KINDNESS ARE EXCELLENT QUALITIES IN MEN DURING TIMES OF PEACE. BUT, WHEN THE NOISE OF WAR SOUNDS IN OUR EARS, WE MUST BE LIKE TIGERS.
WE MUST TIGHTEN OUR MUSCLES, STIR UP OUR BLOOD AND HIDE OUR CHIVALRY BEHIND FACES OF RAGE. WE MUST GIVE OUR EYES A TERRIFYING LOOK.
LET THEM PROTRUDE FROM THEIR SOCKETS LIKE BRASS CANNONS. ALLOW THE BROW TO STICK OUT OVER THEM LIKE AN ANGRY ROCK OVERHANGING THE BASE OF A SEA-LASHED CLIFF.

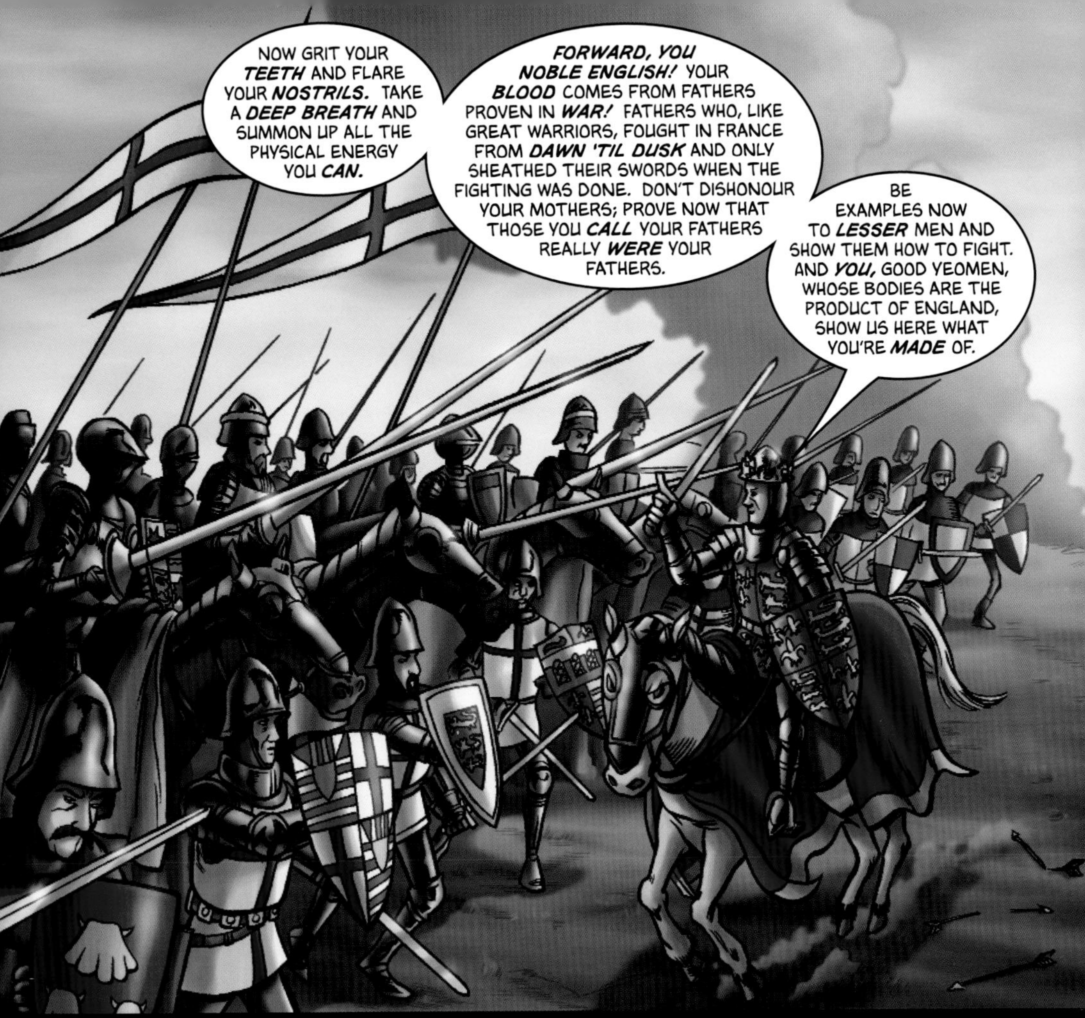
NOW GRIT YOUR TEETH AND FLARE YOUR NOSTRILS. TAKE A DEEP BREATH AND SUMMON UP ALL THE PHYSICAL ENERGY YOU CAN.
FORWARD, YOU NOBLE ENGLISH! YOUR BLOOD COMES FROM FATHERS PROVEN IN WAR! FATHERS WHO, LIKE GREAT WARRIORS, FOUGHT IN FRANCE FROM DAWN 'TIL DUSK AND ONLY SHEATHED THEIR SWORDS WHEN THE FIGHTING WAS DONE. DON'T DISHONOUR YOUR MOTHERS; PROVE NOW THAT THOSE YOU CALL YOUR FATHERS REALLY WERE YOUR FATHERS.
BE EXAMPLES NOW TO LESSER MEN AND SHOW THEM HOW TO FIGHT. AND YOU, GOOD YEOMEN, WHOSE BODIES ARE THE PRODUCT OF ENGLAND, SHOW US HERE WHAT YOU'RE MADE OF.

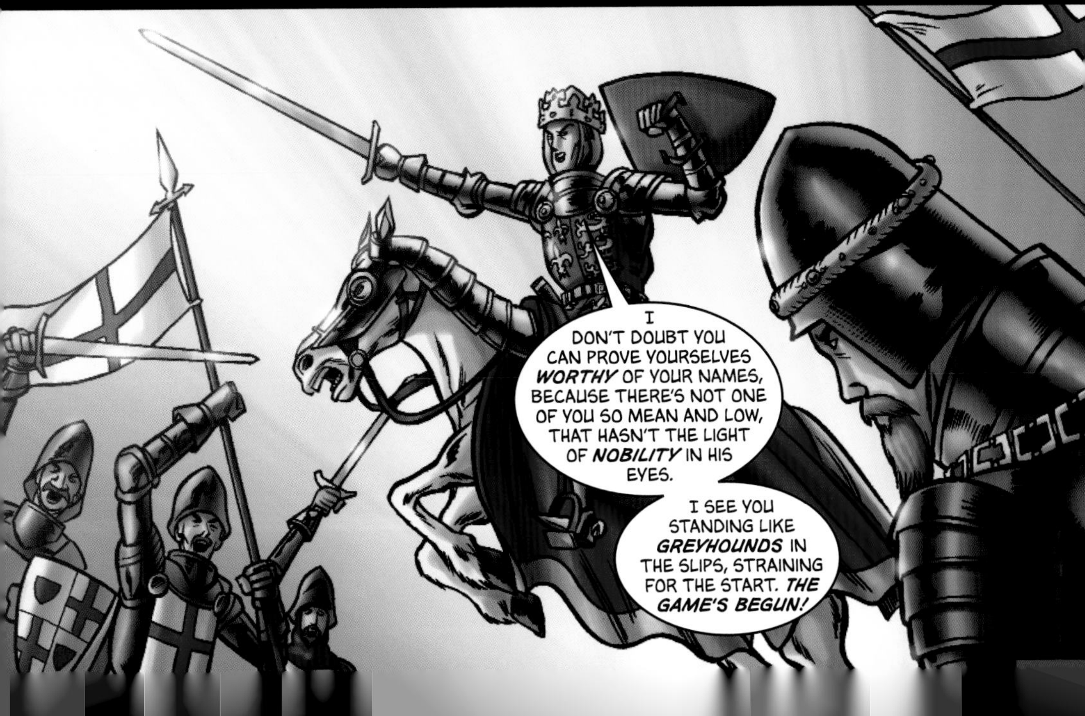
I DON'T DOUBT YOU CAN PROVE YOURSELVES WORTHY OF YOUR NAMES, BECAUSE THERE'S NOT ONE OF YOU SO MEAN AND LOW, THAT HASN'T THE LIGHT OF NOBILITY IN HIS EYES.
I SEE YOU STANDING LIKE GREYHOUNDS IN THE SLIPS, STRAINING FOR THE START. THE GAME'S BEGUN!

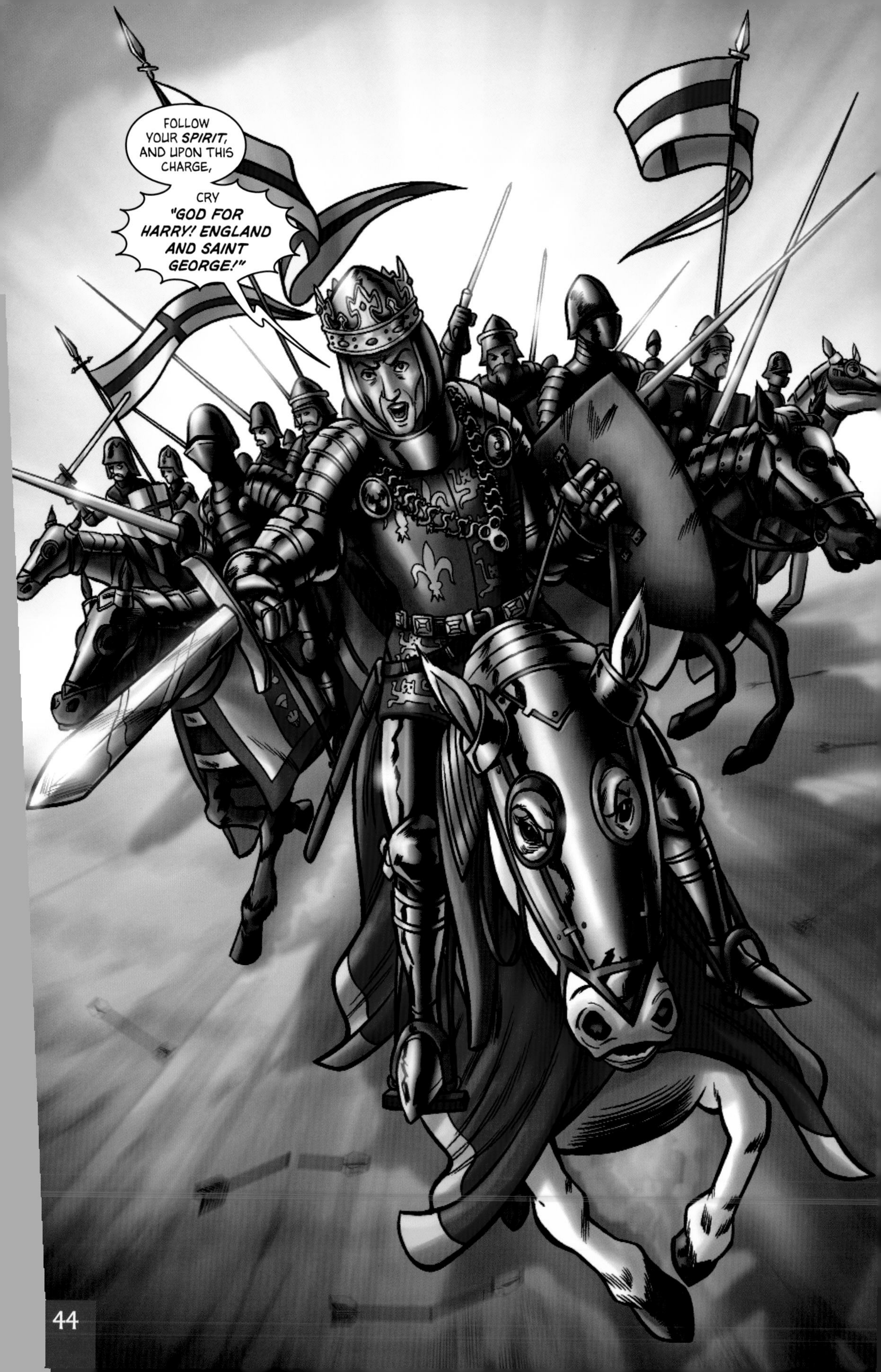
FOLLOW YOUR *SPIRIT*, AND UPON THIS CHARGE,
CRY ***"GOD FOR HARRY! ENGLAND AND SAINT GEORGE!"***

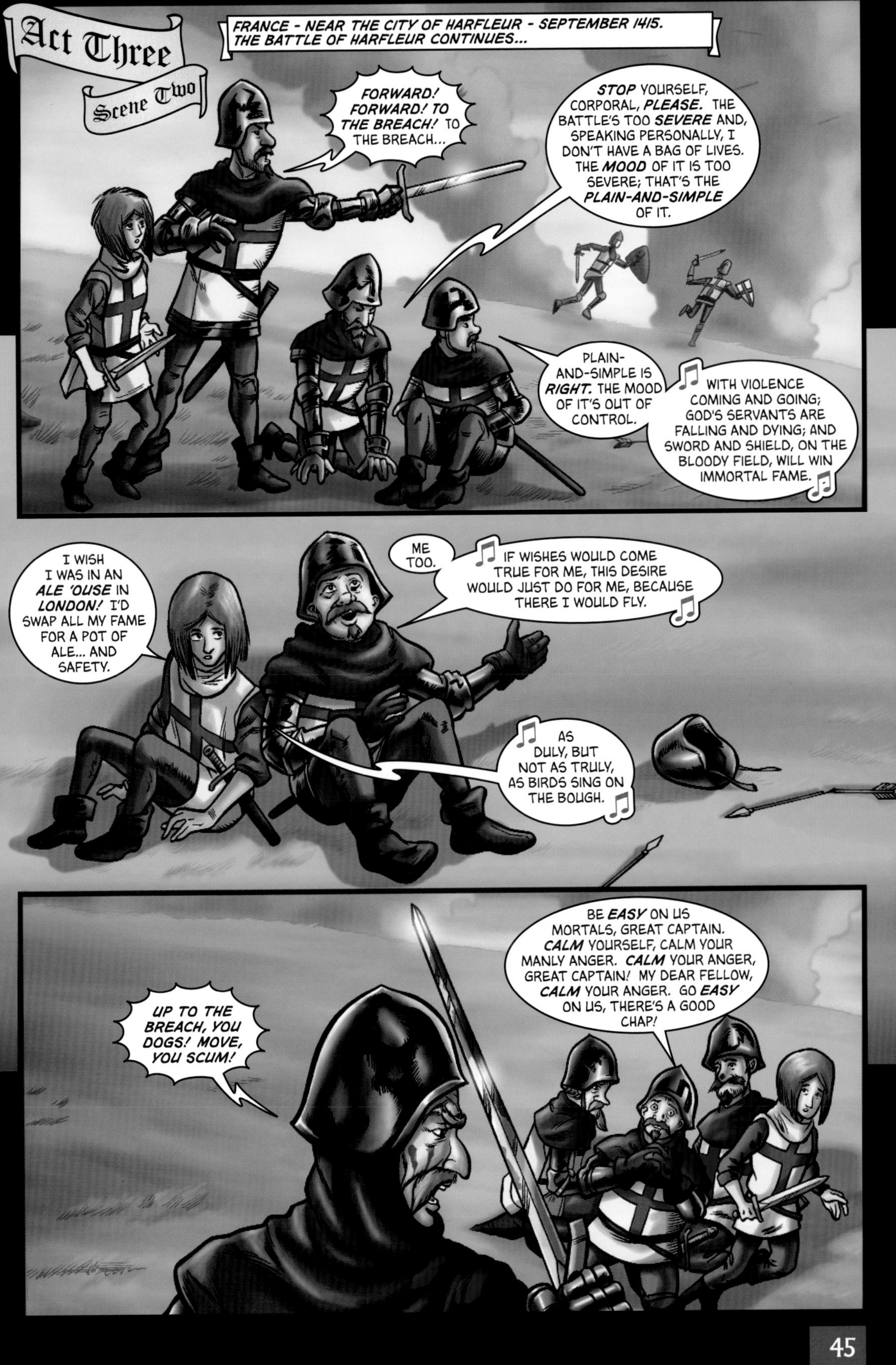

Act Three
Scene Two
FRANCE - NEAR THE CITY OF HARFLEUR - SEPTEMBER 1415. THE BATTLE OF HARFLEUR CONTINUES...
FORWARD! FORWARD! TO THE BREACH! TO THE BREACH...
STOP YOURSELF, CORPORAL, PLEASE. THE BATTLE'S TOO SEVERE AND, SPEAKING PERSONALLY, I DON'T HAVE A BAG OF LIVES. THE MOOD OF IT IS TOO SEVERE; THAT'S THE PLAIN-AND-SIMPLE OF IT.
PLAIN-AND-SIMPLE IS RIGHT. THE MOOD OF IT'S OUT OF CONTROL.
♫ WITH VIOLENCE COMING AND GOING; GOD'S SERVANTS ARE FALLING AND DYING; AND SWORD AND SHIELD, ON THE BLOODY FIELD, WILL WIN IMMORTAL FAME. ♫
I WISH I WAS IN AN ALE 'OUSE IN LONDON! I'D SWAP ALL MY FAME FOR A POT OF ALE... AND SAFETY.
ME TOO.
♫ IF WISHES WOULD COME TRUE FOR ME, THIS DESIRE WOULD JUST DO FOR ME, BECAUSE THERE I WOULD FLY. ♫
♫ AS DULY, BUT NOT AS TRULY, AS BIRDS SING ON THE BOUGH. ♫
UP TO THE BREACH, YOU DOGS! MOVE, YOU SCUM!
BE EASY ON US MORTALS, GREAT CAPTAIN. CALM YOURSELF, CALM YOUR MANLY ANGER. CALM YOUR ANGER, GREAT CAPTAIN! MY DEAR FELLOW, CALM YOUR ANGER. GO EASY ON US, THERE'S A GOOD CHAP!

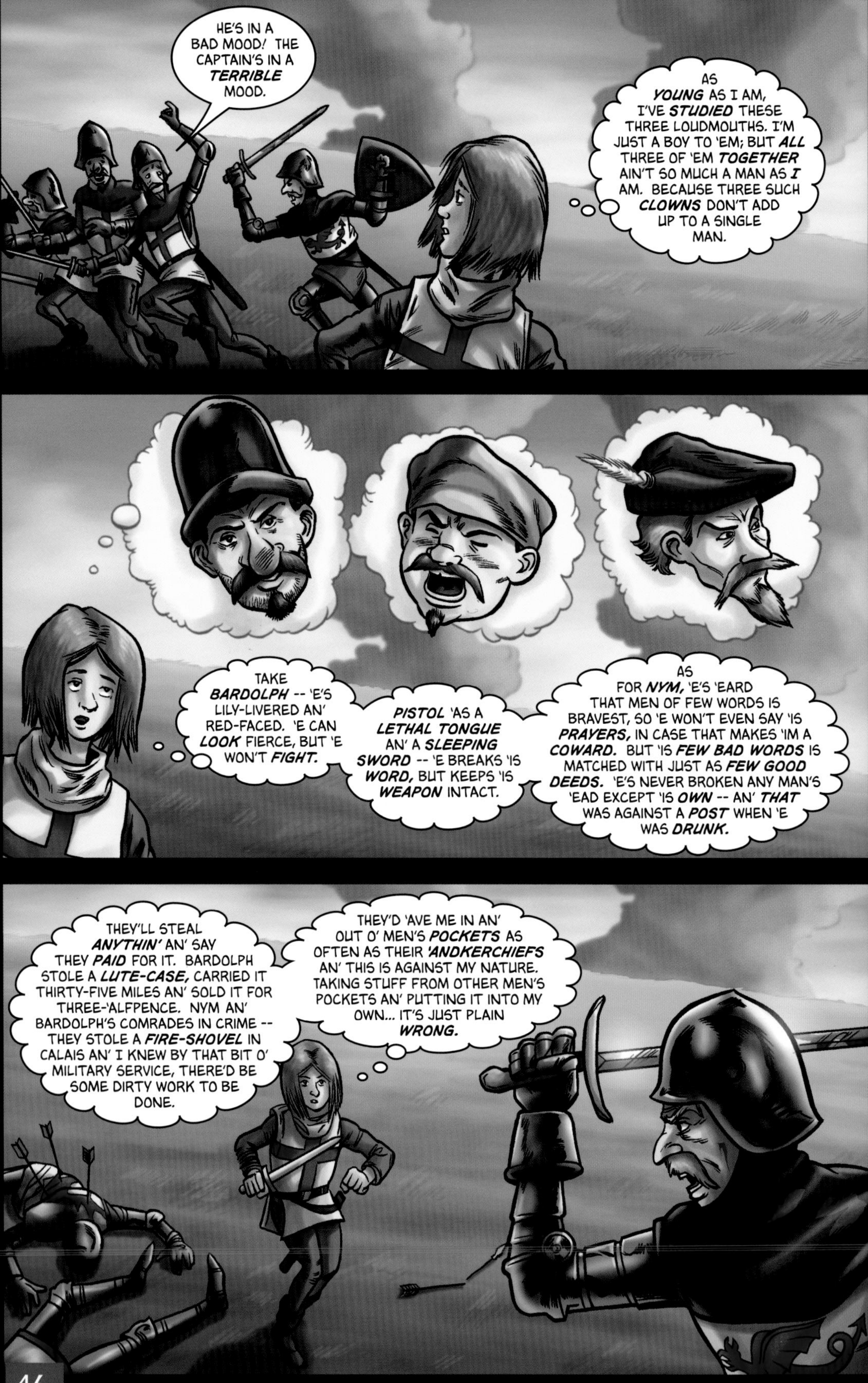
HE'S IN A BAD MOOD! THE CAPTAIN'S IN A *TERRIBLE* MOOD.
AS *YOUNG* AS I AM, I'VE *STUDIED* THESE THREE LOUDMOUTHS. I'M JUST A BOY TO 'EM; BUT *ALL* THREE OF 'EM *TOGETHER* AIN'T SO MUCH A MAN AS *I* AM. BECAUSE THREE SUCH *CLOWNS* DON'T ADD UP TO A SINGLE MAN.
TAKE *BARDOLPH* -- 'E'S LILY-LIVERED AN' RED-FACED. 'E CAN *LOOK* FIERCE, BUT 'E WON'T *FIGHT.*
PISTOL 'AS A *LETHAL TONGUE* AN' A *SLEEPING SWORD* -- 'E BREAKS 'IS *WORD,* BUT KEEPS 'IS *WEAPON* INTACT.
AS FOR *NYM,* 'E'S 'EARD THAT MEN OF FEW WORDS IS BRAVEST, SO 'E WON'T EVEN SAY 'IS *PRAYERS,* IN CASE THAT MAKES 'IM A *COWARD.* BUT 'IS *FEW BAD WORDS* IS MATCHED WITH JUST AS *FEW GOOD DEEDS.* 'E'S NEVER BROKEN ANY MAN'S 'EAD EXCEPT 'IS *OWN* -- AN' *THAT* WAS AGAINST A *POST* WHEN 'E WAS *DRUNK.*
THEY'LL STEAL *ANYTHIN'* AN' SAY THEY *PAID* FOR IT. BARDOLPH STOLE A *LUTE-CASE,* CARRIED IT THIRTY-FIVE MILES AN' SOLD IT FOR THREE-'ALFPENCE. NYM AN' BARDOLPH'S COMRADES IN CRIME -- THEY STOLE A *FIRE-SHOVEL* IN CALAIS AN' I KNEW BY THAT BIT O' MILITARY SERVICE, THERE'D BE SOME DIRTY WORK TO BE DONE.
THEY'D 'AVE ME IN AN' OUT O' MEN'S *POCKETS* AS OFTEN AS THEIR *'ANDKERCHIEFS* AN' THIS IS AGAINST MY NATURE. TAKING STUFF FROM OTHER MEN'S POCKETS AN' PUTTING IT INTO MY OWN... IT'S JUST PLAIN *WRONG.*

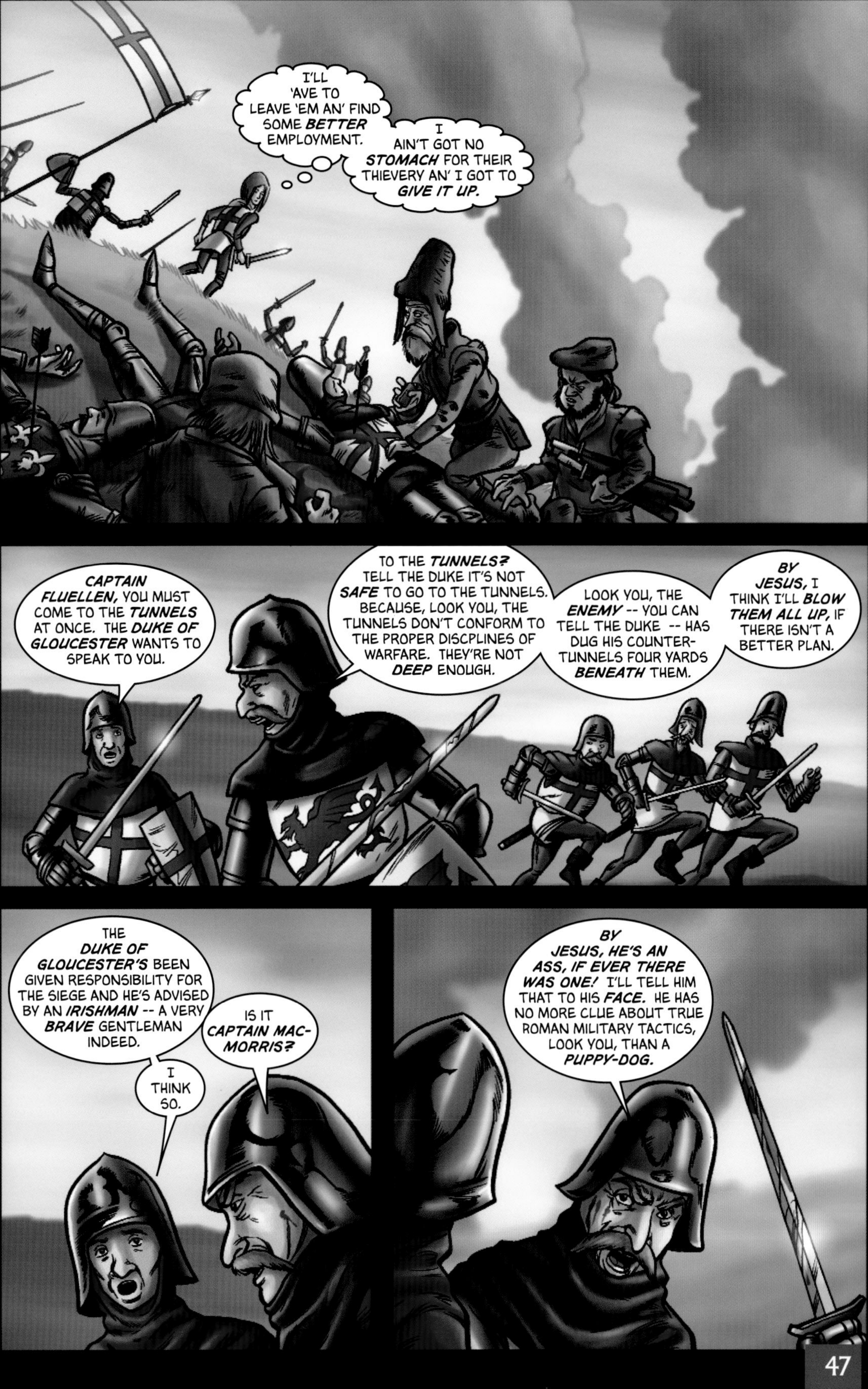

I'LL 'AVE TO LEAVE 'EM AN' FIND SOME BETTER EMPLOYMENT.
I AIN'T GOT NO STOMACH FOR THEIR THIEVERY AN' I GOT TO GIVE IT UP.
CAPTAIN FLUELLEN, YOU MUST COME TO THE TUNNELS AT ONCE. THE DUKE OF GLOUCESTER WANTS TO SPEAK TO YOU.
TO THE TUNNELS? TELL THE DUKE IT'S NOT SAFE TO GO TO THE TUNNELS. BECAUSE, LOOK YOU, THE TUNNELS DON'T CONFORM TO THE PROPER DISCPLINES OF WARFARE. THEY'RE NOT DEEP ENOUGH.
LOOK YOU, THE ENEMY -- YOU CAN TELL THE DUKE -- HAS DUG HIS COUNTER-TUNNELS FOUR YARDS BENEATH THEM.
BY JESUS, I THINK I'LL BLOW THEM ALL UP, IF THERE ISN'T A BETTER PLAN.
THE DUKE OF GLOUCESTER'S BEEN GIVEN RESPONSIBILITY FOR THE SIEGE AND HE'S ADVISED BY AN IRISHMAN -- A VERY BRAVE GENTLEMAN INDEED.
IS IT CAPTAIN MAC-MORRIS?
I THINK SO.
BY JESUS, HE'S AN ASS, IF EVER THERE WAS ONE! I'LL TELL HIM THAT TO HIS FACE. HE HAS NO MORE CLUE ABOUT TRUE ROMAN MILITARY TACTICS, LOOK YOU, THAN A PUPPY-DOG.

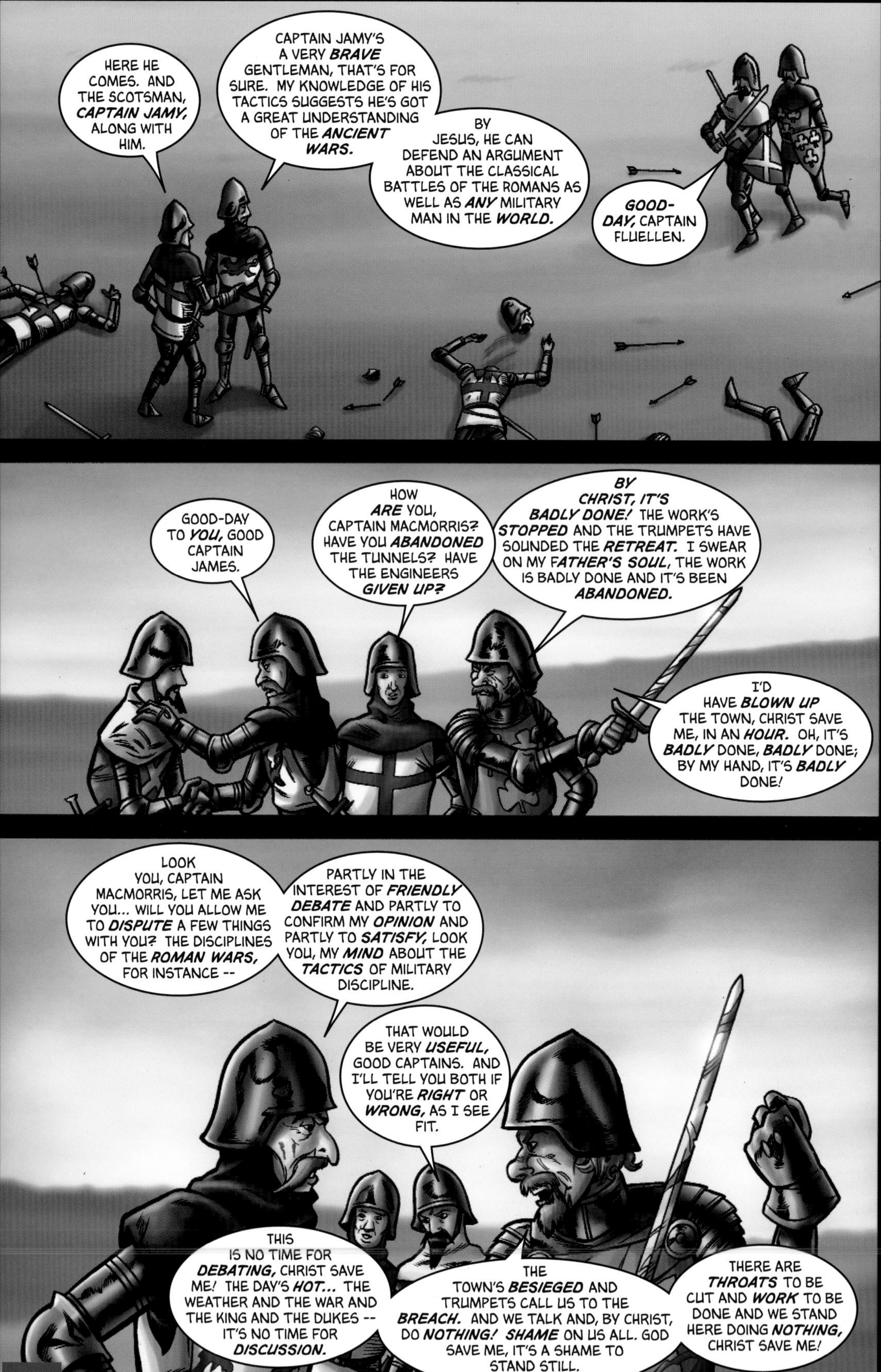
HERE HE COMES. AND THE SCOTSMAN, CAPTAIN JAMY, ALONG WITH HIM.
CAPTAIN JAMY'S A VERY BRAVE GENTLEMAN, THAT'S FOR SURE. MY KNOWLEDGE OF HIS TACTICS SUGGESTS HE'S GOT A GREAT UNDERSTANDING OF THE ANCIENT WARS.
BY JESUS, HE CAN DEFEND AN ARGUMENT ABOUT THE CLASSICAL BATTLES OF THE ROMANS AS WELL AS ANY MILITARY MAN IN THE WORLD.
GOOD-DAY, CAPTAIN FLUELLEN.
GOOD-DAY TO YOU, GOOD CAPTAIN JAMES.
HOW ARE YOU, CAPTAIN MACMORRIS? HAVE YOU ABANDONED THE TUNNELS? HAVE THE ENGINEERS GIVEN UP?
BY CHRIST, IT'S BADLY DONE! THE WORK'S STOPPED AND THE TRUMPETS HAVE SOUNDED THE RETREAT. I SWEAR ON MY FATHER'S SOUL, THE WORK IS BADLY DONE AND IT'S BEEN ABANDONED.
I'D HAVE BLOWN UP THE TOWN, CHRIST SAVE ME, IN AN HOUR. OH, IT'S BADLY DONE, BADLY DONE; BY MY HAND, IT'S BADLY DONE!
LOOK YOU, CAPTAIN MACMORRIS, LET ME ASK YOU... WILL YOU ALLOW ME TO DISPUTE A FEW THINGS WITH YOU? THE DISCIPLINES OF THE ROMAN WARS, FOR INSTANCE --
PARTLY IN THE INTEREST OF FRIENDLY DEBATE AND PARTLY TO CONFIRM MY OPINION AND PARTLY TO SATISFY, LOOK YOU, MY MIND ABOUT THE TACTICS OF MILITARY DISCIPLINE.
THAT WOULD BE VERY USEFUL, GOOD CAPTAINS. AND I'LL TELL YOU BOTH IF YOU'RE RIGHT OR WRONG, AS I SEE FIT.
THIS IS NO TIME FOR DEBATING, CHRIST SAVE ME! THE DAY'S HOT... THE WEATHER AND THE WAR AND THE KING AND THE DUKES -- IT'S NO TIME FOR DISCUSSION.
THE TOWN'S BESIEGED AND TRUMPETS CALL US TO THE BREACH. AND WE TALK AND, BY CHRIST, DO NOTHING! SHAME ON US ALL. GOD SAVE ME, IT'S A SHAME TO STAND STILL.
THERE ARE THROATS TO BE CUT AND WORK TO BE DONE AND WE STAND HERE DOING NOTHING, CHRIST SAVE ME!

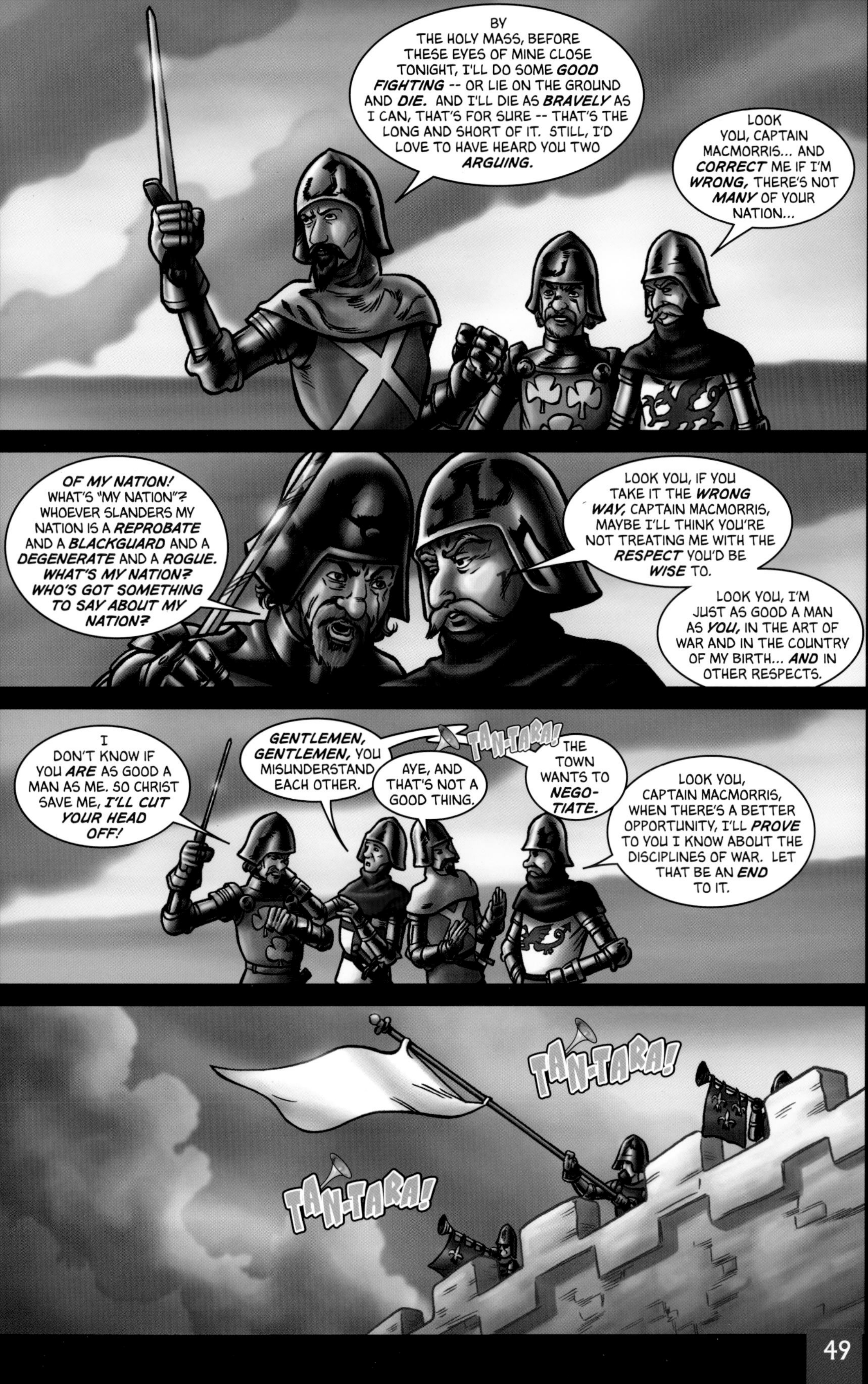
BY THE HOLY MASS, BEFORE THESE EYES OF MINE CLOSE TONIGHT, I'LL DO SOME GOOD FIGHTING -- OR LIE ON THE GROUND AND DIE. AND I'LL DIE AS BRAVELY AS I CAN, THAT'S FOR SURE -- THAT'S THE LONG AND SHORT OF IT. STILL, I'D LOVE TO HAVE HEARD YOU TWO ARGUING.
LOOK YOU, CAPTAIN MACMORRIS... AND CORRECT ME IF I'M WRONG, THERE'S NOT MANY OF YOUR NATION...
OF MY NATION! WHAT'S "MY NATION"? WHOEVER SLANDERS MY NATION IS A REPROBATE AND A BLACKGUARD AND A DEGENERATE AND A ROGUE. WHAT'S MY NATION? WHO'S GOT SOMETHING TO SAY ABOUT MY NATION?
LOOK YOU, IF YOU TAKE IT THE WRONG WAY, CAPTAIN MACMORRIS, MAYBE I'LL THINK YOU'RE NOT TREATING ME WITH THE RESPECT YOU'D BE WISE TO.
LOOK YOU, I'M JUST AS GOOD A MAN AS YOU, IN THE ART OF WAR AND IN THE COUNTRY OF MY BIRTH... AND IN OTHER RESPECTS.
I DON'T KNOW IF YOU ARE AS GOOD A MAN AS ME. SO CHRIST SAVE ME, I'LL CUT YOUR HEAD OFF!
GENTLEMEN, GENTLEMEN, YOU MISUNDERSTAND EACH OTHER.
AYE, AND THAT'S NOT A GOOD THING.
TAN-TARA!
THE TOWN WANTS TO NEGO-TIATE.
LOOK YOU, CAPTAIN MACMORRIS, WHEN THERE'S A BETTER OPPORTUNITY, I'LL PROVE TO YOU I KNOW ABOUT THE DISCIPLINES OF WAR. LET THAT BE AN END TO IT.
TAN-TARA!
TAN-TARA!

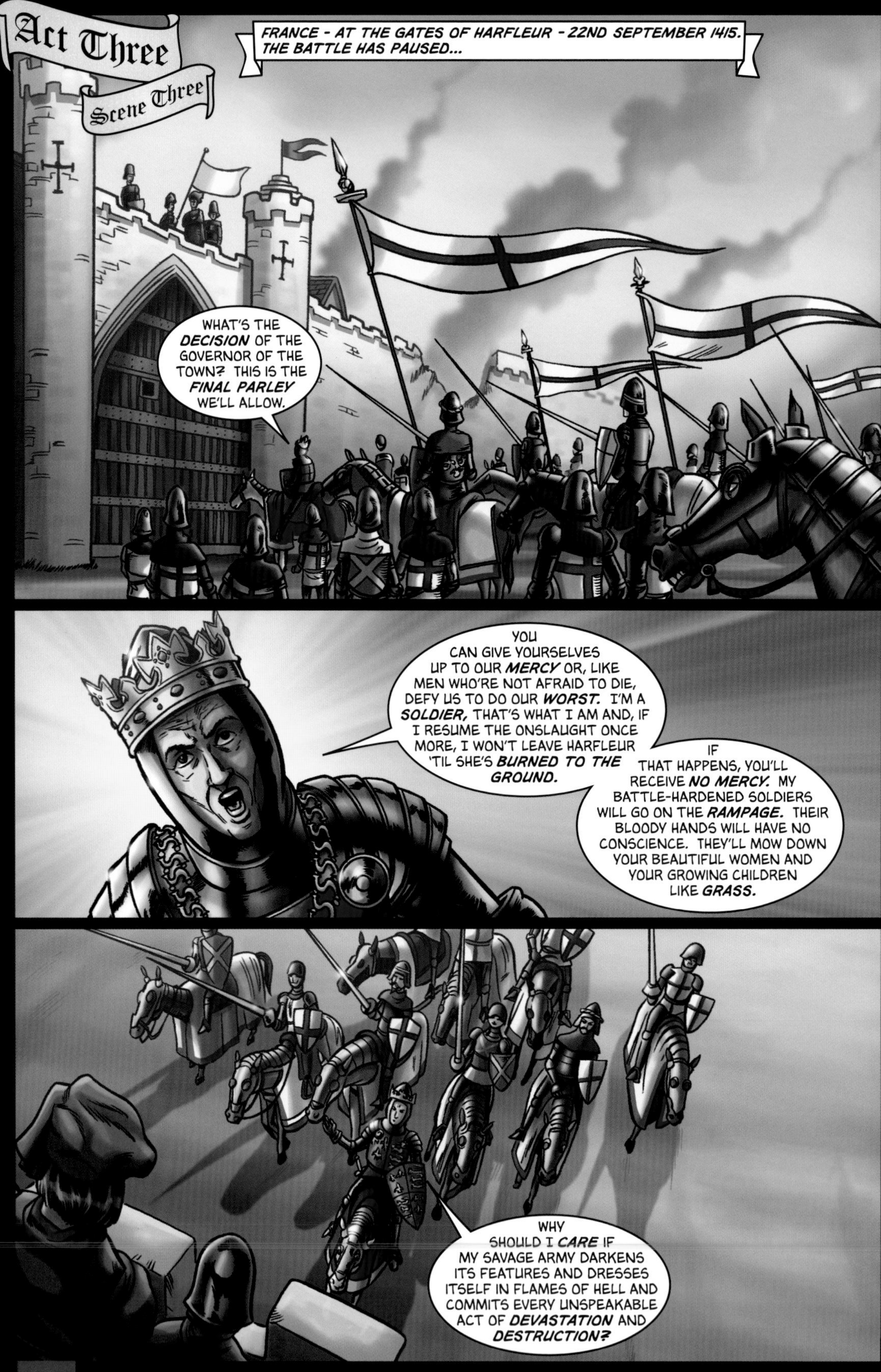

Act Three
Scene Three
FRANCE - AT THE GATES OF HARFLEUR - 22ND SEPTEMBER 1415. THE BATTLE HAS PAUSED...
WHAT'S THE DECISION OF THE GOVERNOR OF THE TOWN? THIS IS THE FINAL PARLEY WE'LL ALLOW.
YOU CAN GIVE YOURSELVES UP TO OUR MERCY OR, LIKE MEN WHO'RE NOT AFRAID TO DIE, DEFY US TO DO OUR WORST. I'M A SOLDIER, THAT'S WHAT I AM AND, IF I RESUME THE ONSLAUGHT ONCE MORE, I WON'T LEAVE HARFLEUR 'TIL SHE'S BURNED TO THE GROUND.
IF THAT HAPPENS, YOU'LL RECEIVE NO MERCY. MY BATTLE-HARDENED SOLDIERS WILL GO ON THE RAMPAGE. THEIR BLOODY HANDS WILL HAVE NO CONSCIENCE. THEY'LL MOW DOWN YOUR BEAUTIFUL WOMEN AND YOUR GROWING CHILDREN LIKE GRASS.
WHY SHOULD I CARE IF MY SAVAGE ARMY DARKENS ITS FEATURES AND DRESSES ITSELF IN FLAMES OF HELL AND COMMITS EVERY UNSPEAKABLE ACT OF DEVASTATION AND DESTRUCTION?

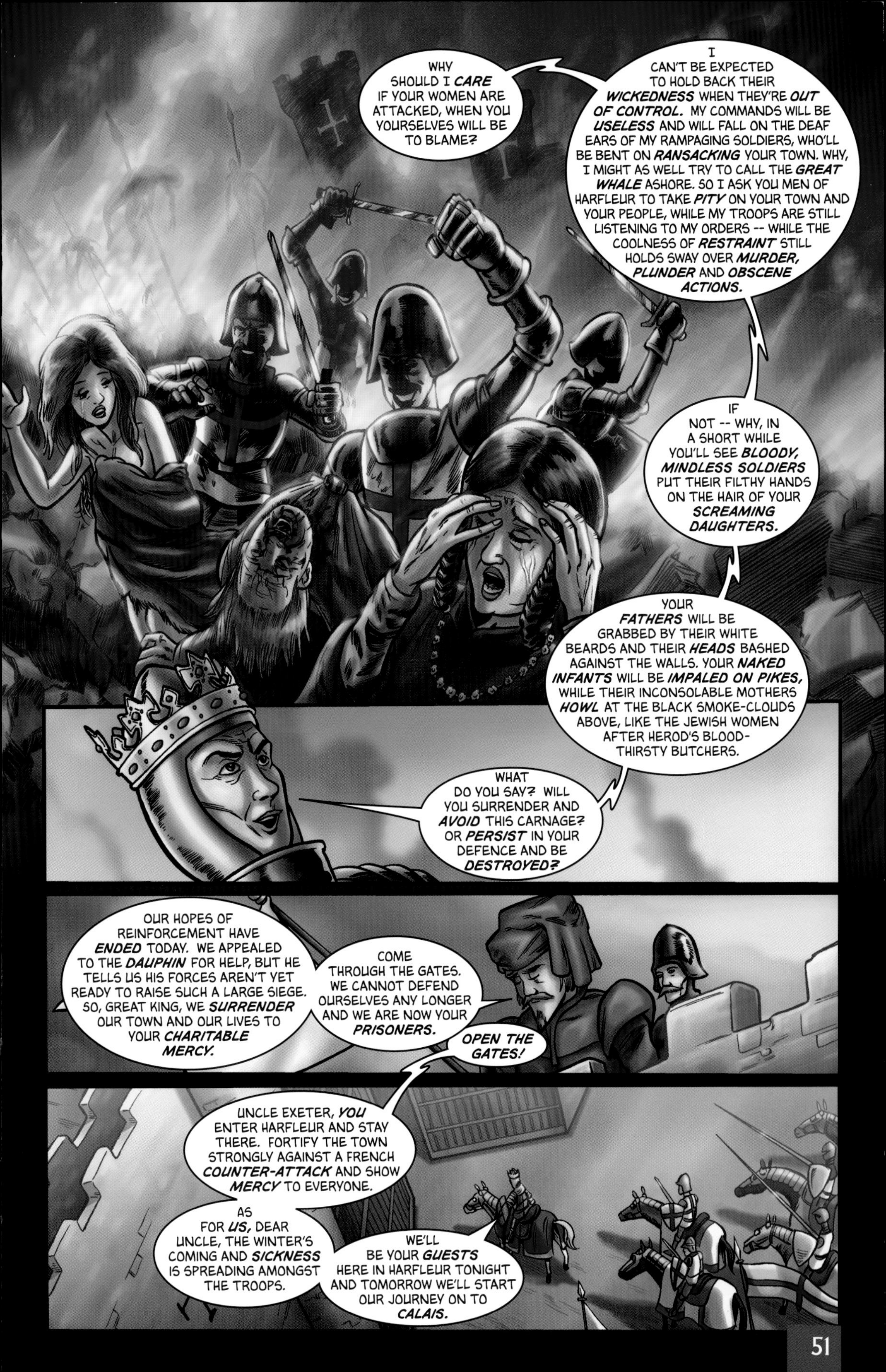

WHY SHOULD I *CARE* IF YOUR WOMEN ARE ATTACKED, WHEN YOU YOURSELVES WILL BE TO BLAME?
I CAN'T BE EXPECTED TO HOLD BACK THEIR *WICKEDNESS* WHEN THEY'RE *OUT OF CONTROL.* MY COMMANDS WILL BE *USELESS* AND WILL FALL ON THE DEAF EARS OF MY RAMPAGING SOLDIERS, WHO'LL BE BENT ON *RANSACKING* YOUR TOWN. WHY, I MIGHT AS WELL TRY TO CALL THE *GREAT WHALE* ASHORE. SO I ASK YOU MEN OF HARFLEUR TO TAKE *PITY* ON YOUR TOWN AND YOUR PEOPLE, WHILE MY TROOPS ARE STILL LISTENING TO MY ORDERS -- WHILE THE COOLNESS OF *RESTRAINT* STILL HOLDS SWAY OVER *MURDER, PLUNDER* AND *OBSCENE ACTIONS.*
IF NOT -- WHY, IN A SHORT WHILE YOU'LL SEE *BLOODY, MINDLESS SOLDIERS* PUT THEIR FILTHY HANDS ON THE HAIR OF YOUR *SCREAMING DAUGHTERS.*
YOUR *FATHERS* WILL BE GRABBED BY THEIR WHITE BEARDS AND THEIR *HEADS* BASHED AGAINST THE WALLS. YOUR *NAKED INFANTS* WILL BE *IMPALED ON PIKES,* WHILE THEIR INCONSOLABLE MOTHERS *HOWL* AT THE BLACK SMOKE-CLOUDS ABOVE, LIKE THE JEWISH WOMEN AFTER HEROD'S BLOOD-THIRSTY BUTCHERS.
WHAT DO YOU SAY? WILL YOU SURRENDER AND *AVOID* THIS CARNAGE? OR *PERSIST* IN YOUR DEFENCE AND BE *DESTROYED?*
OUR HOPES OF REINFORCEMENT HAVE *ENDED* TODAY. WE APPEALED TO THE *DAUPHIN* FOR HELP, BUT HE TELLS US HIS FORCES AREN'T YET READY TO RAISE SUCH A LARGE SIEGE. SO, GREAT KING, WE *SURRENDER* OUR TOWN AND OUR LIVES TO YOUR *CHARITABLE MERCY.*
COME THROUGH THE GATES. WE CANNOT DEFEND OURSELVES ANY LONGER AND WE ARE NOW YOUR *PRISONERS.*
OPEN THE GATES!
UNCLE EXETER, *YOU* ENTER HARFLEUR AND STAY THERE. FORTIFY THE TOWN STRONGLY AGAINST A FRENCH *COUNTER-ATTACK* AND SHOW *MERCY* TO EVERYONE.
AS FOR *US,* DEAR UNCLE, THE WINTER'S COMING AND *SICKNESS* IS SPREADING AMONGST THE TROOPS.
WE'LL BE YOUR *GUESTS* HERE IN HARFLEUR TONIGHT AND TOMORROW WE'LL START OUR JOURNEY ON TO *CALAIS.*

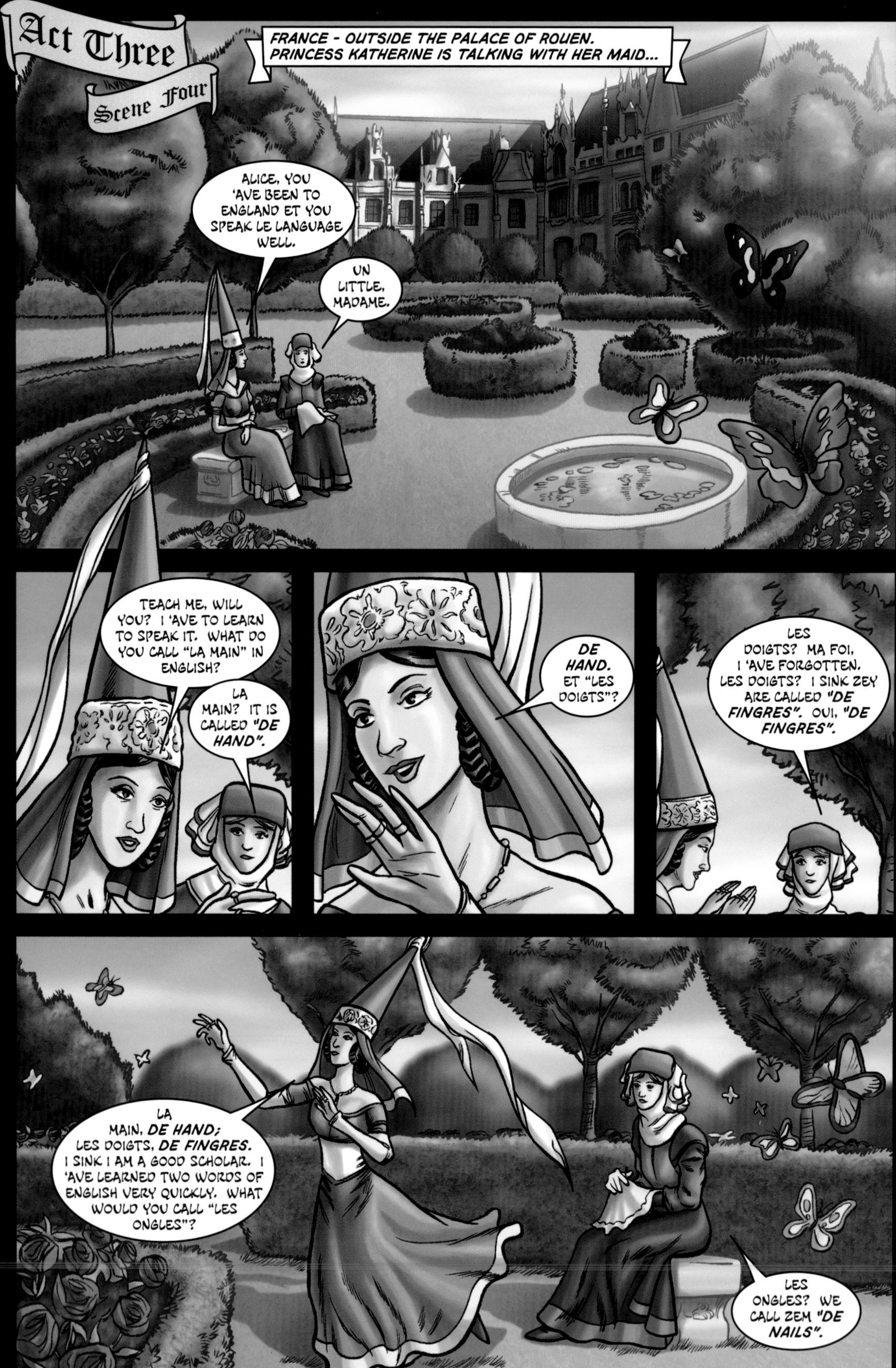
Act Three
Scene Four
FRANCE - OUTSIDE THE PALACE OF ROUEN. PRINCESS KATHERINE IS TALKING WITH HER MAID...
ALICE, YOU 'AVE BEEN TO ENGLAND ET YOU SPEAK LE LANGUAGE WELL.
UN LITTLE, MADAME.
TEACH ME, WILL YOU? I 'AVE TO LEARN TO SPEAK IT. WHAT DO YOU CALL "LA MAIN" IN ENGLISH?
LA MAIN? IT IS CALLED "DE HAND".
DE HAND. ET "LES DOIGTS"?
LES DOIGTS? MA FOI, I 'AVE FORGOTTEN. LES DOIGTS? I SINK ZEY ARE CALLED "DE FINGRES". OUI, "DE FINGRES".
LA MAIN, DE HAND; LES DOIGTS, DE FINGRES. I SINK I AM A GOOD SCHOLAR. I 'AVE LEARNED TWO WORDS OF ENGLISH VERY QUICKLY. WHAT WOULD YOU CALL "LES ONGLES"?
LES ONGLES? WE CALL ZEM "DE NAILS".

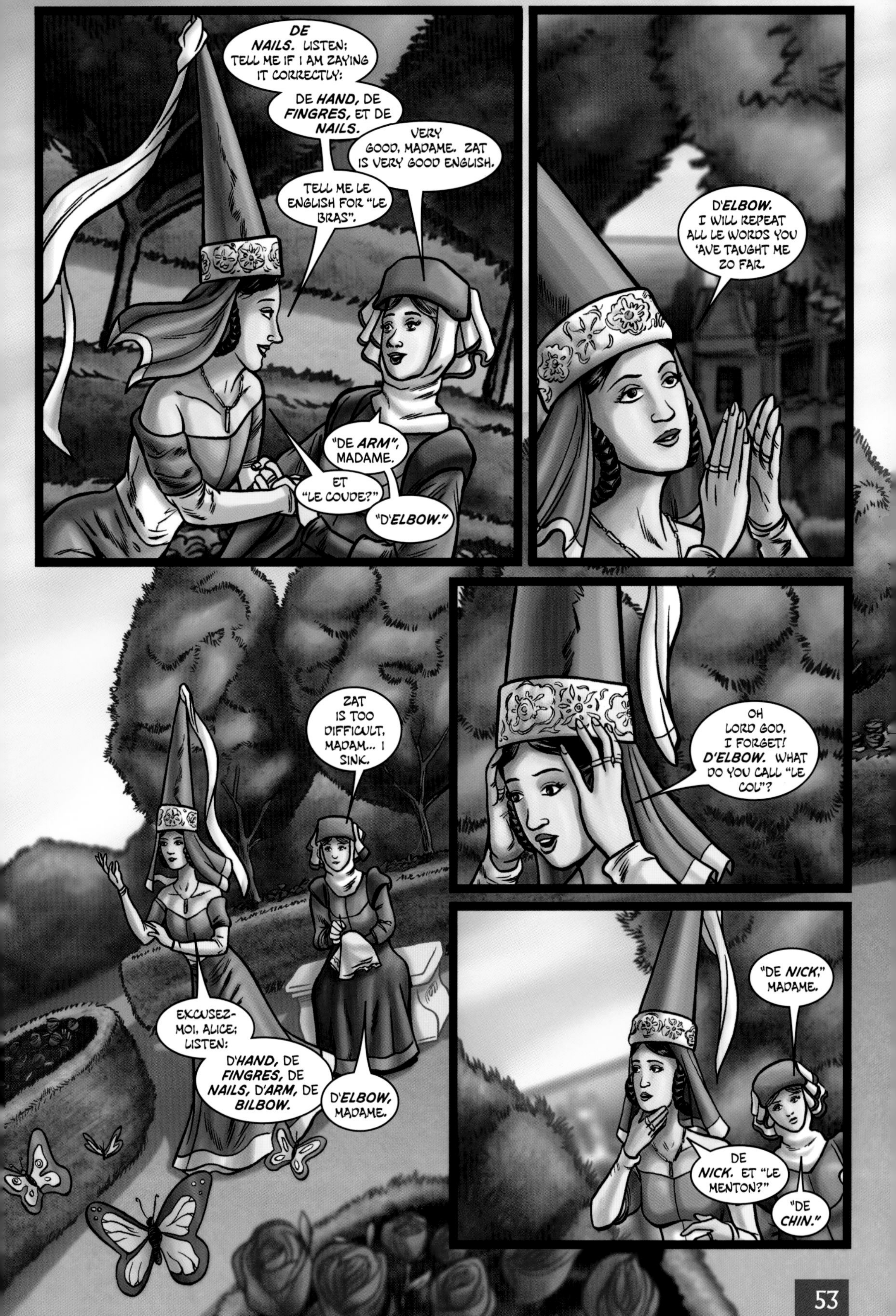
DE NAILS. LISTEN; TELL ME IF I AM ZAYING IT CORRECTLY:
DE HAND, DE FINGRES, ET DE NAILS.
VERY GOOD, MADAME. ZAT IS VERY GOOD ENGLISH.
TELL ME LE ENGLISH FOR "LE BRAS".
"DE ARM", MADAME.
ET "LE COUDE?"
"D'ELBOW."
D'ELBOW. I WILL REPEAT ALL LE WORDS YOU 'AVE TAUGHT ME ZO FAR.
ZAT IS TOO DIFFICULT, MADAM... I SINK.
EXCUSEZ-MOI, ALICE; LISTEN:
D'HAND, DE FINGRES, DE NAILS, D'ARM, DE BILBOW.
D'ELBOW, MADAME.
OH LORD GOD, I FORGET! D'ELBOW. WHAT DO YOU CALL "LE COL"?
"DE NICK," MADAME.
DE NICK. ET "LE MENTON?"
"DE CHIN."

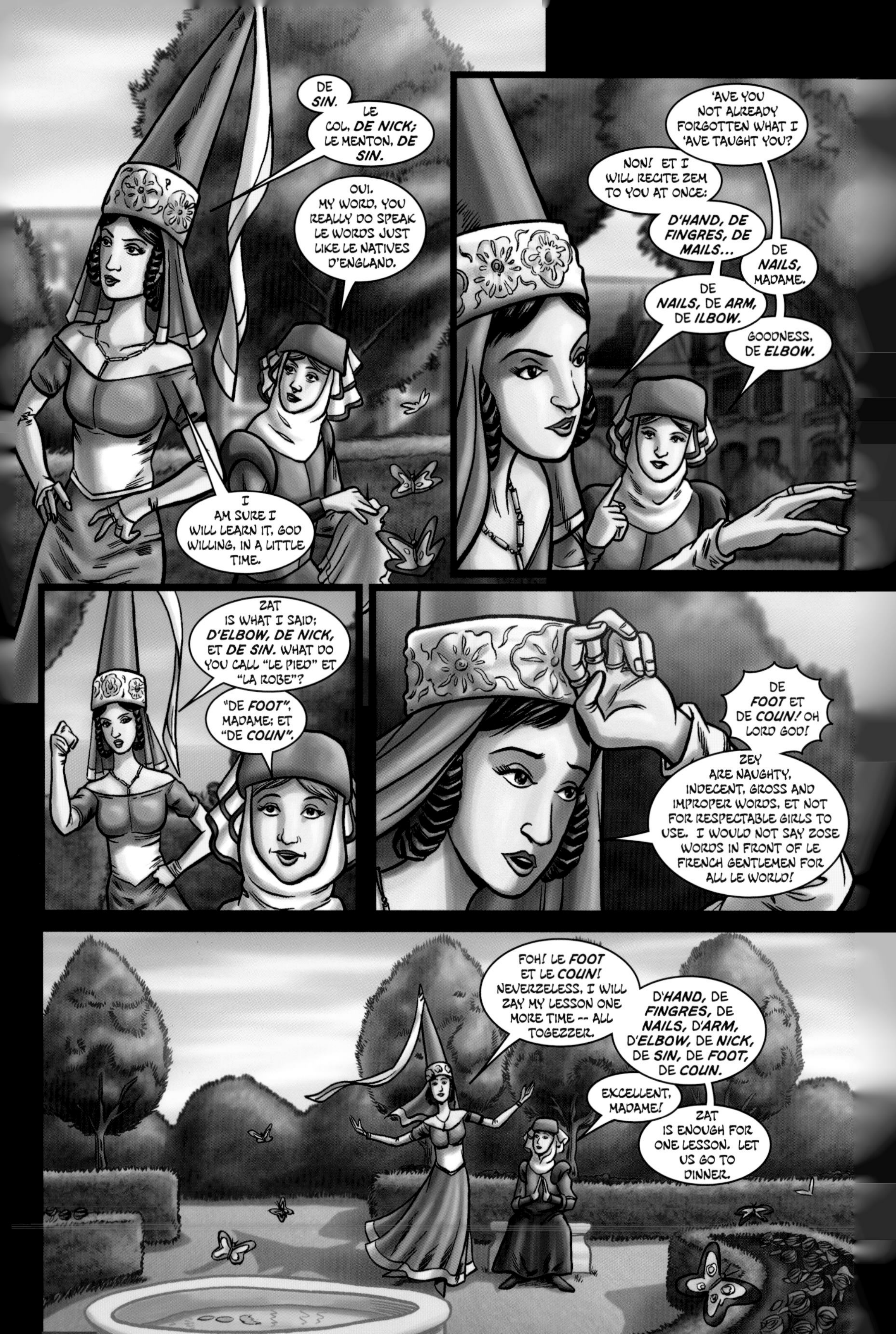
DE SIN.
LE COL, DE NICK; LE MENTON, DE SIN.
OUI. MY WORD, YOU REALLY DO SPEAK LE WORDS JUST LIKE LE NATIVES D'ENGLAND.
I AM SURE I WILL LEARN IT, GOD WILLING, IN A LITTLE TIME.
'AVE YOU NOT ALREADY FORGOTTEN WHAT I 'AVE TAUGHT YOU?
NON! ET I WILL RECITE ZEM TO YOU AT ONCE:
D'HAND, DE FINGRES, DE MAILS...
DE NAILS, MADAME.
DE NAILS, DE ARM, DE ILBOW.
GOODNESS, DE ELBOW.
ZAT IS WHAT I SAID; D'ELBOW, DE NICK, ET DE SIN. WHAT DO YOU CALL "LE PIED" ET "LA ROBE"?
"DE FOOT", MADAME; ET "DE COUN".
DE FOOT ET DE COUN! OH LORD GOD!
ZEY ARE NAUGHTY, INDECENT, GROSS AND IMPROPER WORDS, ET NOT FOR RESPECTABLE GIRLS TO USE. I WOULD NOT SAY ZOSE WORDS IN FRONT OF LE FRENCH GENTLEMEN FOR ALL LE WORLD!
FOH! LE FOOT ET LE COUN! NEVERZELESS, I WILL ZAY MY LESSON ONE MORE TIME -- ALL TOGEZZER.
D'HAND, DE FINGRES, DE NAILS, D'ARM, D'ELBOW, DE NICK, DE SIN, DE FOOT, DE COUN.
EXCELLENT, MADAME!
ZAT IS ENOUGH FOR ONE LESSON. LET US GO TO DINNER.

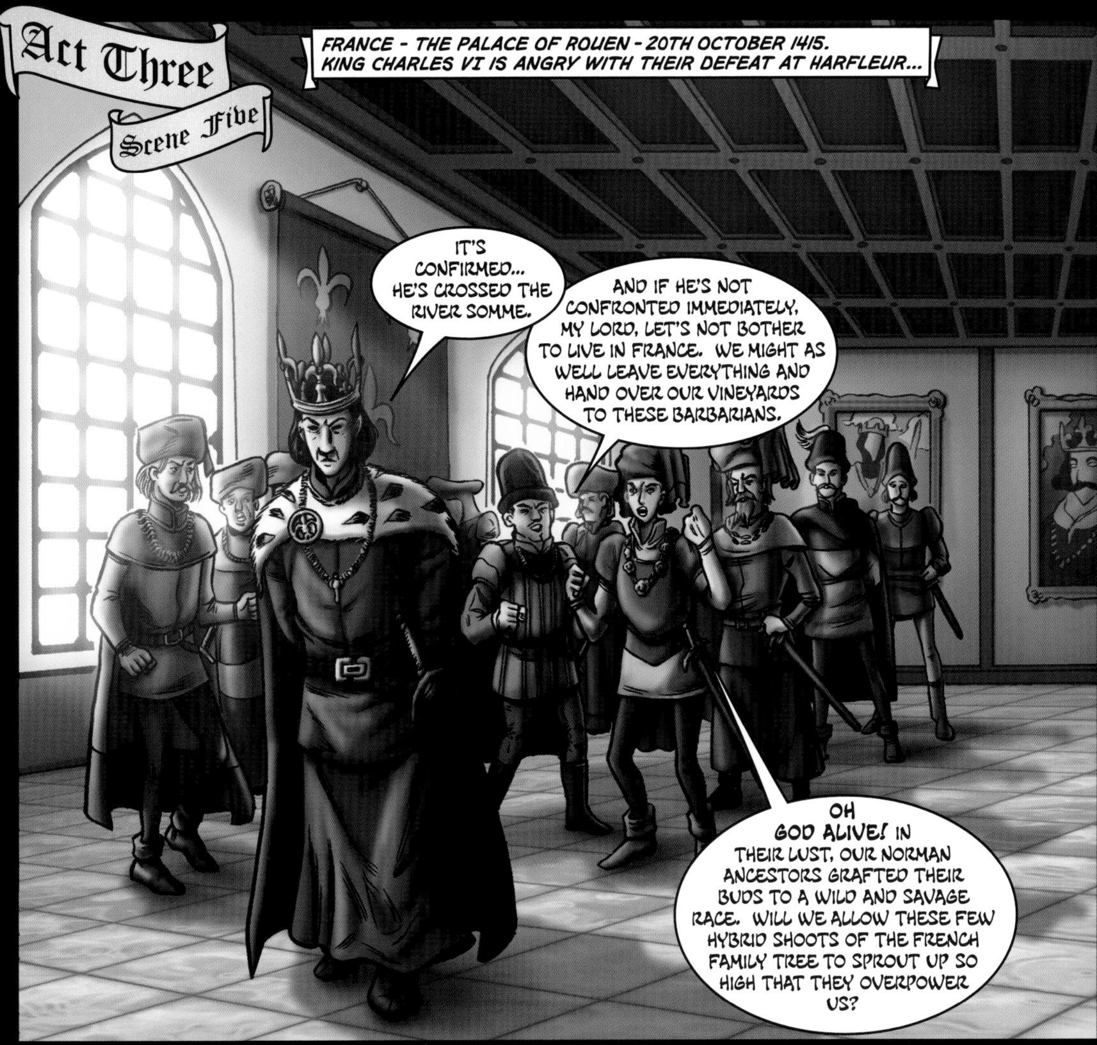
Act Three
Scene Five
FRANCE - THE PALACE OF ROUEN - 20TH OCTOBER 1415. KING CHARLES VI IS ANGRY WITH THEIR DEFEAT AT HARFLEUR...
IT'S CONFIRMED... HE'S CROSSED THE RIVER SOMME.
AND IF HE'S NOT CONFRONTED IMMEDIATELY, MY LORD, LET'S NOT BOTHER TO LIVE IN FRANCE. WE MIGHT AS WELL LEAVE EVERYTHING AND HAND OVER OUR VINEYARDS TO THESE BARBARIANS.
OH GOD ALIVE! IN THEIR LUST, OUR NORMAN ANCESTORS GRAFTED THEIR BUDS TO A WILD AND SAVAGE RACE. WILL WE ALLOW THESE FEW HYBRID SHOOTS OF THE FRENCH FAMILY TREE TO SPROUT UP SO HIGH THAT THEY OVERPOWER US?

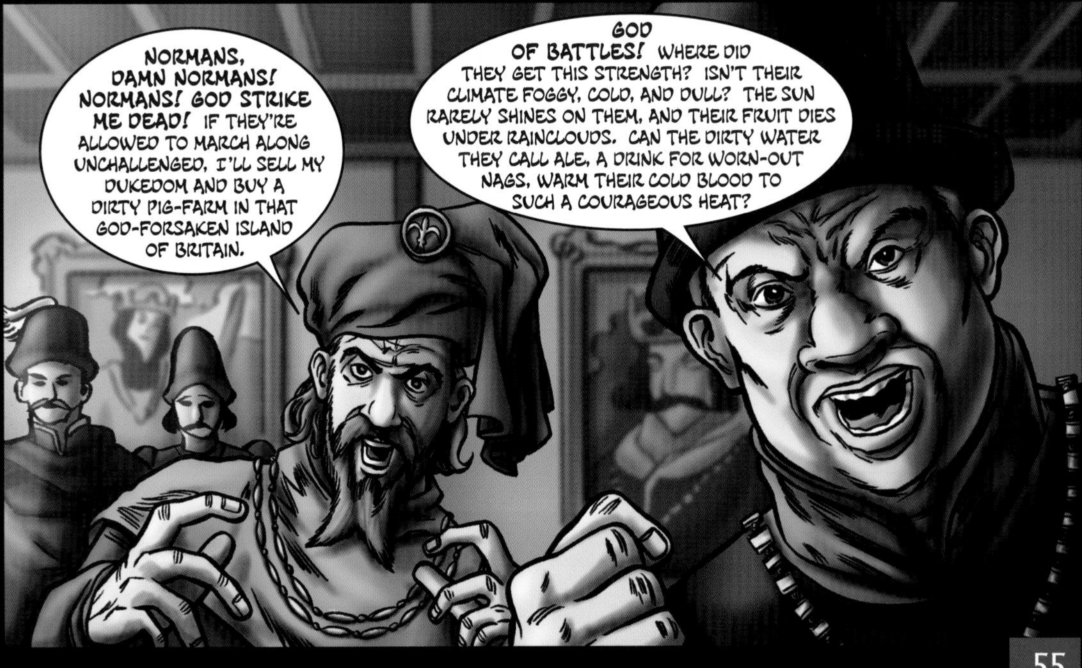
NORMANS, DAMN NORMANS! NORMANS! GOD STRIKE ME DEAD! IF THEY'RE ALLOWED TO MARCH ALONG UNCHALLENGED, I'LL SELL MY DUKEDOM AND BUY A DIRTY PIG-FARM IN THAT GOD-FORSAKEN ISLAND OF BRITAIN.
GOD OF BATTLES! WHERE DID THEY GET THIS STRENGTH? ISN'T THEIR CLIMATE FOGGY, COLD, AND DULL? THE SUN RARELY SHINES ON THEM, AND THEIR FRUIT DIES UNDER RAINCLOUDS. CAN THE DIRTY WATER THEY CALL ALE, A DRINK FOR WORN-OUT NAGS, WARM THEIR COLD BLOOD TO SUCH A COURAGEOUS HEAT?

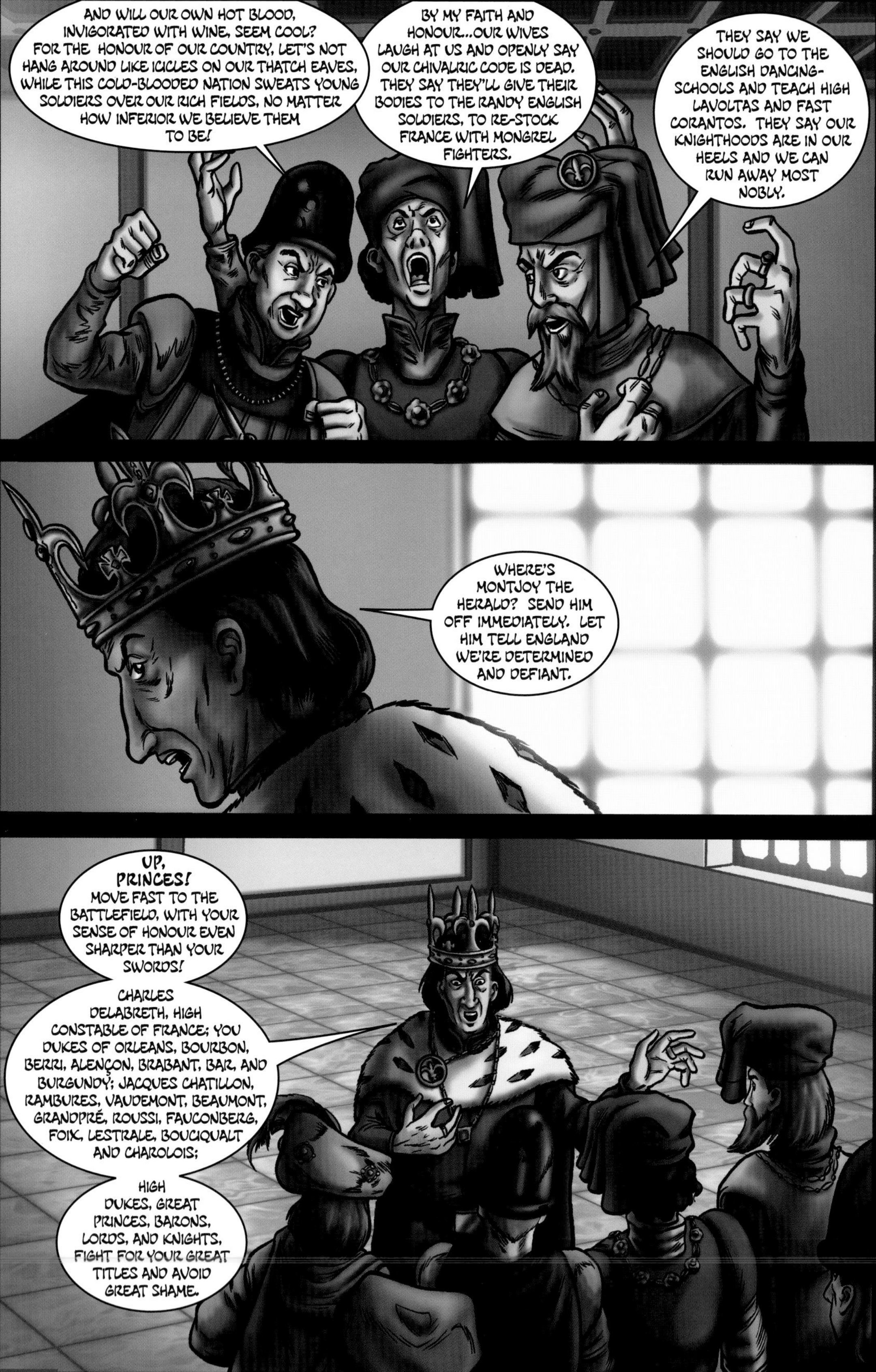
AND WILL OUR OWN HOT BLOOD, INVIGORATED WITH WINE, SEEM COOL? FOR THE HONOUR OF OUR COUNTRY, LET'S NOT HANG AROUND LIKE ICICLES ON OUR THATCH EAVES, WHILE THIS COLD-BLOODED NATION SWEATS YOUNG SOLDIERS OVER OUR RICH FIELDS, NO MATTER HOW INFERIOR WE BELIEVE THEM TO BE!
BY MY FAITH AND HONOUR...OUR WIVES LAUGH AT US AND OPENLY SAY OUR CHIVALRIC CODE IS DEAD. THEY SAY THEY'LL GIVE THEIR BODIES TO THE RANDY ENGLISH SOLDIERS, TO RE-STOCK FRANCE WITH MONGREL FIGHTERS.
THEY SAY WE SHOULD GO TO THE ENGLISH DANCING-SCHOOLS AND TEACH HIGH LAVOLTAS AND FAST CORANTOS. THEY SAY OUR KNIGHTHOODS ARE IN OUR HEELS AND WE CAN RUN AWAY MOST NOBLY.
WHERE'S MONTJOY THE HERALD? SEND HIM OFF IMMEDIATELY. LET HIM TELL ENGLAND WE'RE DETERMINED AND DEFIANT.
UP, PRINCES! MOVE FAST TO THE BATTLEFIELD, WITH YOUR SENSE OF HONOUR EVEN SHARPER THAN YOUR SWORDS!
CHARLES DELABRETH, HIGH CONSTABLE OF FRANCE; YOU DUKES OF ORLEANS, BOURBON, BERRI, ALENÇON, BRABANT, BAR, AND BURGUNDY; JACQUES CHATILLON, RAMBURES, VAUDEMONT, BEAUMONT, GRANDPRÉ, ROUSSI, FAUCONBERG, FOIX, LESTRALE, BOUCIQUALT AND CHAROLOIS;
HIGH DUKES, GREAT PRINCES, BARONS, LORDS, AND KNIGHTS, FIGHT FOR YOUR GREAT TITLES AND AVOID GREAT SHAME.

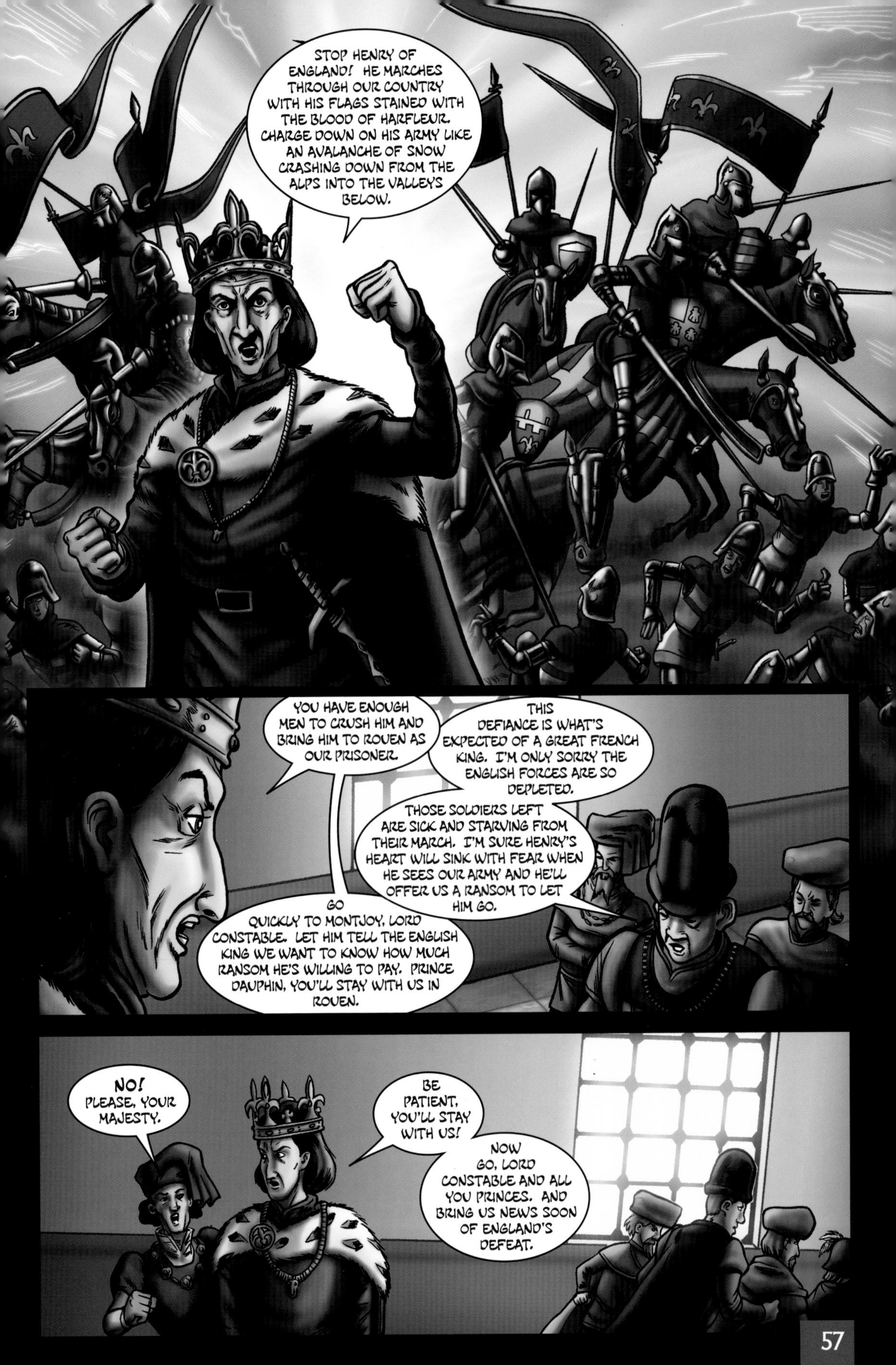
STOP HENRY OF ENGLAND! HE MARCHES THROUGH OUR COUNTRY WITH HIS FLAGS STAINED WITH THE BLOOD OF HARFLEUR. CHARGE DOWN ON HIS ARMY LIKE AN AVALANCHE OF SNOW CRASHING DOWN FROM THE ALPS INTO THE VALLEYS BELOW.
YOU HAVE ENOUGH MEN TO CRUSH HIM AND BRING HIM TO ROUEN AS OUR PRISONER.
THIS DEFIANCE IS WHAT'S EXPECTED OF A GREAT FRENCH KING. I'M ONLY SORRY THE ENGLISH FORCES ARE SO DEPLETED.
THOSE SOLDIERS LEFT ARE SICK AND STARVING FROM THEIR MARCH. I'M SURE HENRY'S HEART WILL SINK WITH FEAR WHEN HE SEES OUR ARMY AND HE'LL OFFER US A RANSOM TO LET HIM GO.
GO QUICKLY TO MONTJOY, LORD CONSTABLE. LET HIM TELL THE ENGLISH KING WE WANT TO KNOW HOW MUCH RANSOM HE'S WILLING TO PAY. PRINCE DAUPHIN, YOU'LL STAY WITH US IN ROUEN.
NO! PLEASE, YOUR MAJESTY.
BE PATIENT, YOU'LL STAY WITH US!
NOW GO, LORD CONSTABLE AND ALL YOU PRINCES. AND BRING US NEWS SOON OF ENGLAND'S DEFEAT.

FRANCE - THE ENGLISH CAMP OF PICARDY - 23RD OCTOBER 1415. NEAR THE BRIDGE OVER THE RIVER TERNOISE...

HOW ARE YOU, CAPTAIN FLUELLEN? HAVE YOU COME FROM THE *BRIDGE?*

LET ME TELL YOU, THERE'S BEEN *HEROIC DEEDS* DONE AT THE BRIDGE.

IS THE *DUKE OF EXETER* SAFE?

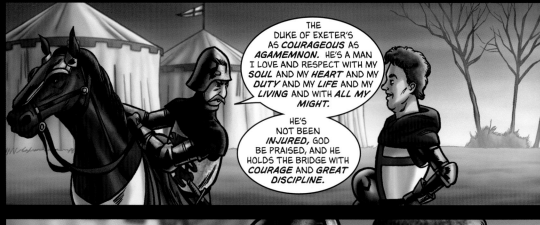

THE DUKE OF EXETER'S AS *COURAGEOUS* AS *AGAMEMNON.* HE'S A MAN I LOVE AND RESPECT WITH MY *SOUL* AND MY *HEART* AND MY *DUTY* AND MY *LIFE* AND MY *LIVING* AND WITH *ALL MY MIGHT.*

HE'S NOT BEEN *INJURED,* GOD BE PRAISED, AND HE HOLDS THE BRIDGE WITH *COURAGE* AND *GREAT DISCIPLINE.*

THERE'S AN ANCIENT *LIEUTENANT* AT THE BRIDGE. I CONSIDER HIM TO BE AS *BRAVE* A MAN AS *MARK ANTONY;* EVEN IF HE'S SOMEONE OF NO GREAT RANK. BUT I DID SEE HIM PERFORM GALLANTLY.

WHAT'S HIS NAME?

HE'S CALLED *ANCIENT PISTOL.*

I DON'T KNOW HIM.

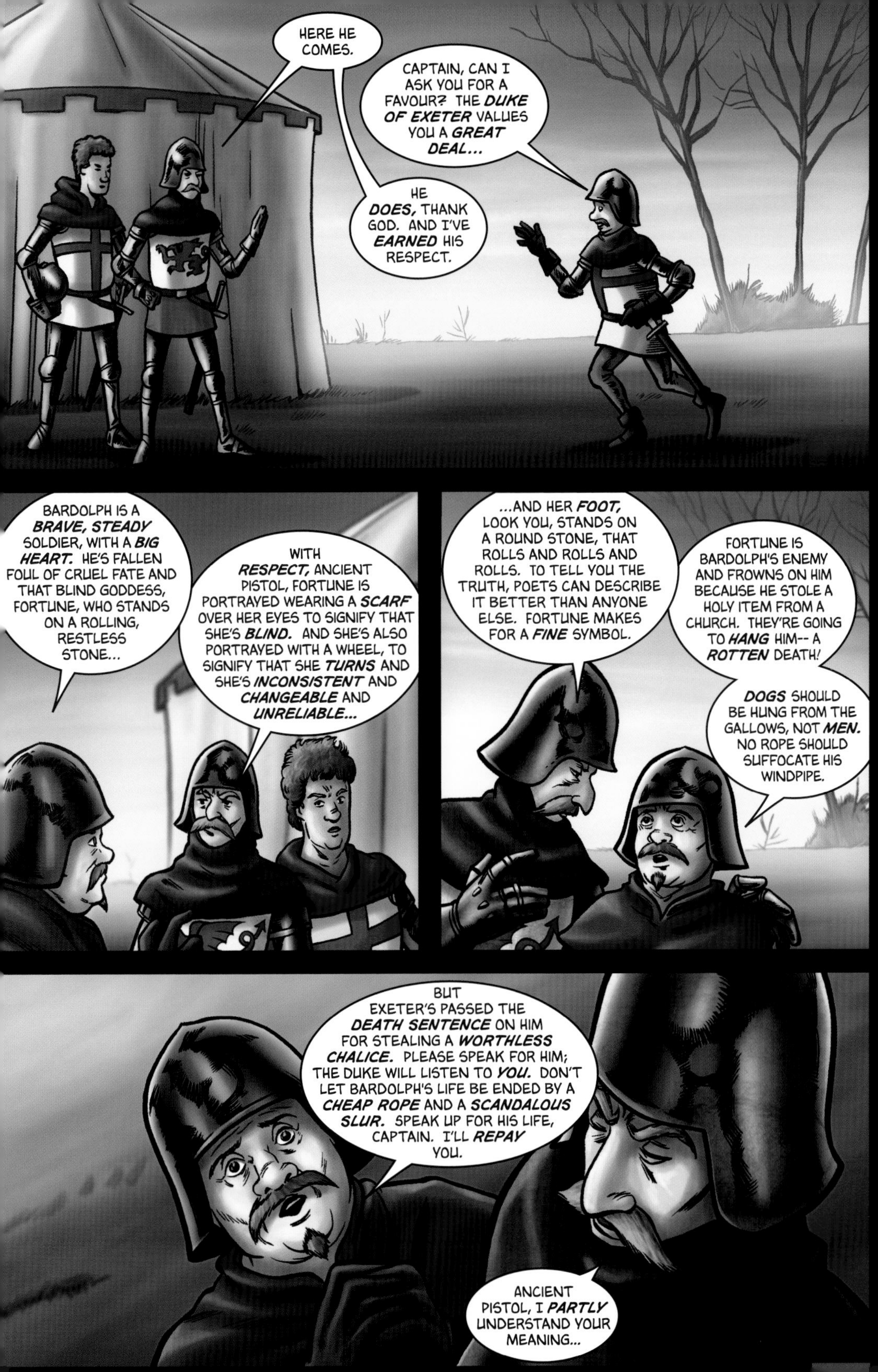
HERE HE COMES.
CAPTAIN, CAN I ASK YOU FOR A FAVOUR? THE DUKE OF EXETER VALUES YOU A GREAT DEAL...
HE DOES, THANK GOD. AND I'VE EARNED HIS RESPECT.
BARDOLPH IS A BRAVE, STEADY SOLDIER, WITH A BIG HEART. HE'S FALLEN FOUL OF CRUEL FATE AND THAT BLIND GODDESS, FORTUNE, WHO STANDS ON A ROLLING, RESTLESS STONE...
WITH RESPECT, ANCIENT PISTOL, FORTUNE IS PORTRAYED WEARING A SCARF OVER HER EYES TO SIGNIFY THAT SHE'S BLIND. AND SHE'S ALSO PORTRAYED WITH A WHEEL, TO SIGNIFY THAT SHE TURNS AND SHE'S INCONSISTENT AND CHANGEABLE AND UNRELIABLE...
...AND HER FOOT, LOOK YOU, STANDS ON A ROUND STONE, THAT ROLLS AND ROLLS AND ROLLS. TO TELL YOU THE TRUTH, POETS CAN DESCRIBE IT BETTER THAN ANYONE ELSE. FORTUNE MAKES FOR A FINE SYMBOL.
FORTUNE IS BARDOLPH'S ENEMY AND FROWNS ON HIM BECAUSE HE STOLE A HOLY ITEM FROM A CHURCH. THEY'RE GOING TO HANG HIM-- A ROTTEN DEATH!
DOGS SHOULD BE HUNG FROM THE GALLOWS, NOT MEN. NO ROPE SHOULD SUFFOCATE HIS WINDPIPE.
BUT EXETER'S PASSED THE DEATH SENTENCE ON HIM FOR STEALING A WORTHLESS CHALICE. PLEASE SPEAK FOR HIM; THE DUKE WILL LISTEN TO YOU. DON'T LET BARDOLPH'S LIFE BE ENDED BY A CHEAP ROPE AND A SCANDALOUS SLUR. SPEAK UP FOR HIS LIFE, CAPTAIN. I'LL REPAY YOU.
ANCIENT PISTOL, I PARTLY UNDERSTAND YOUR MEANING...

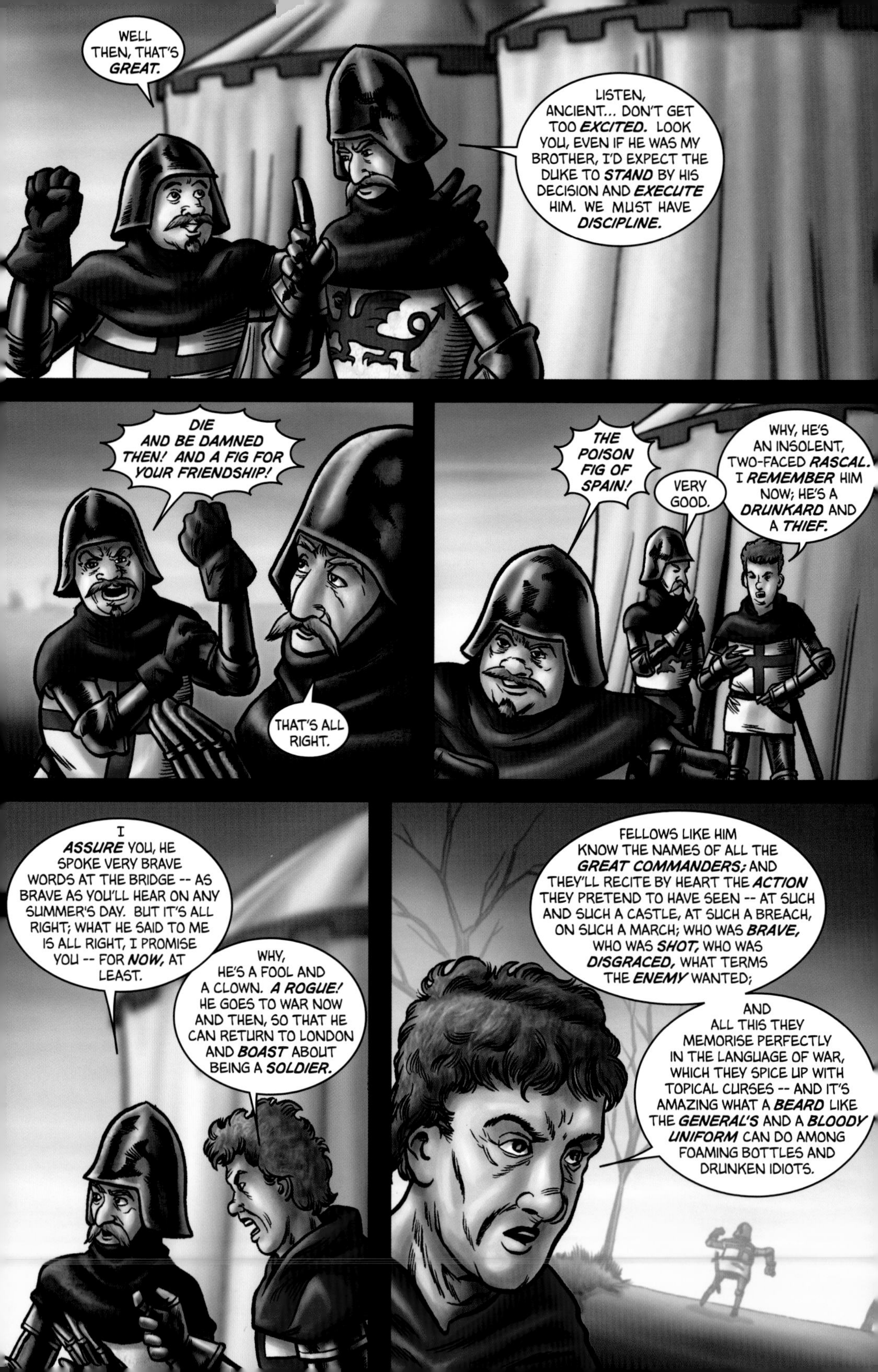
WELL THEN, THAT'S GREAT.
LISTEN, ANCIENT... DON'T GET TOO EXCITED. LOOK YOU, EVEN IF HE WAS MY BROTHER, I'D EXPECT THE DUKE TO STAND BY HIS DECISION AND EXECUTE HIM. WE MUST HAVE DISCIPLINE.
DIE AND BE DAMNED THEN! AND A FIG FOR YOUR FRIENDSHIP!
THAT'S ALL RIGHT.
THE POISON FIG OF SPAIN!
VERY GOOD.
WHY, HE'S AN INSOLENT, TWO-FACED RASCAL. I REMEMBER HIM NOW; HE'S A DRUNKARD AND A THIEF.
I ASSURE YOU, HE SPOKE VERY BRAVE WORDS AT THE BRIDGE -- AS BRAVE AS YOU'LL HEAR ON ANY SUMMER'S DAY. BUT IT'S ALL RIGHT; WHAT HE SAID TO ME IS ALL RIGHT, I PROMISE YOU -- FOR NOW, AT LEAST.
WHY, HE'S A FOOL AND A CLOWN. A ROGUE! HE GOES TO WAR NOW AND THEN, SO THAT HE CAN RETURN TO LONDON AND BOAST ABOUT BEING A SOLDIER.
FELLOWS LIKE HIM KNOW THE NAMES OF ALL THE GREAT COMMANDERS; AND THEY'LL RECITE BY HEART THE ACTION THEY PRETEND TO HAVE SEEN -- AT SUCH AND SUCH A CASTLE, AT SUCH A BREACH, ON SUCH A MARCH; WHO WAS BRAVE, WHO WAS SHOT, WHO WAS DISGRACED, WHAT TERMS THE ENEMY WANTED;
AND ALL THIS THEY MEMORISE PERFECTLY IN THE LANGUAGE OF WAR, WHICH THEY SPICE UP WITH TOPICAL CURSES -- AND IT'S AMAZING WHAT A BEARD LIKE THE GENERAL'S AND A BLOODY UNIFORM CAN DO AMONG FOAMING BOTTLES AND DRUNKEN IDIOTS.

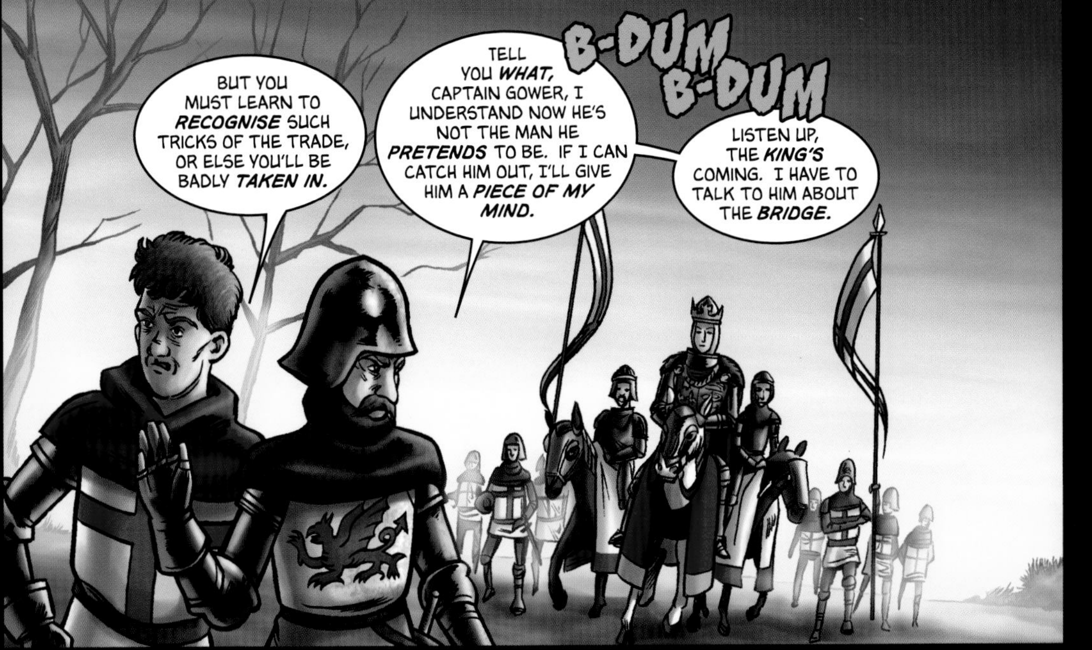
BUT YOU MUST LEARN TO *RECOGNISE* SUCH TRICKS OF THE TRADE, OR ELSE YOU'LL BE BADLY *TAKEN IN.*
TELL YOU *WHAT,* CAPTAIN GOWER, I UNDERSTAND NOW HE'S NOT THE MAN HE *PRETENDS* TO BE. IF I CAN CATCH HIM OUT, I'LL GIVE HIM A *PIECE OF MY MIND.*
B-DUM B-DUM
LISTEN UP, THE *KING'S* COMING. I HAVE TO TALK TO HIM ABOUT THE *BRIDGE.*

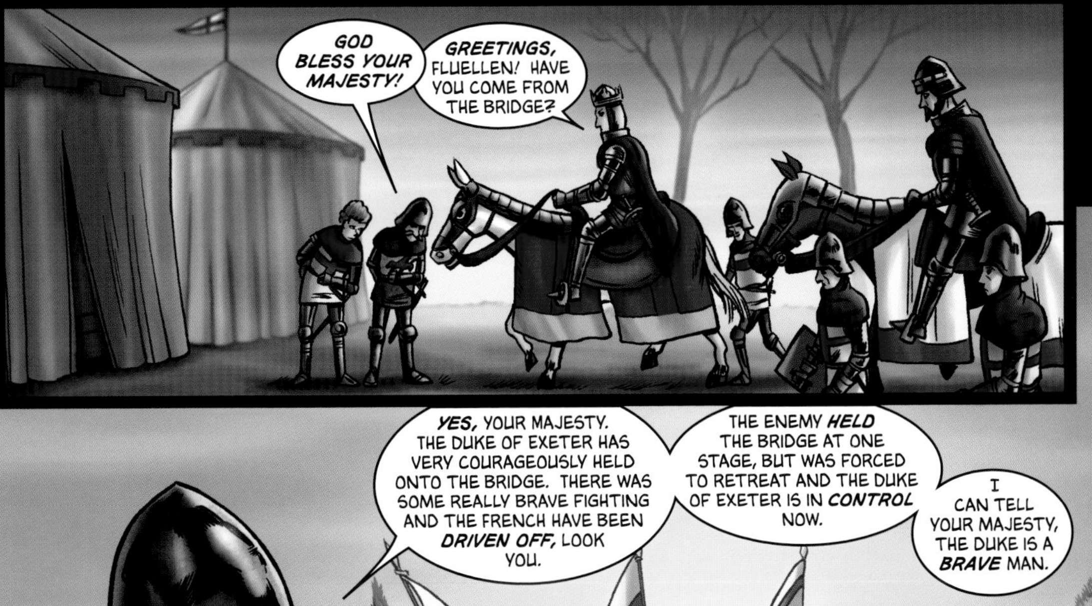
GOD BLESS YOUR MAJESTY!
GREETINGS, FLUELLEN! HAVE YOU COME FROM THE BRIDGE?

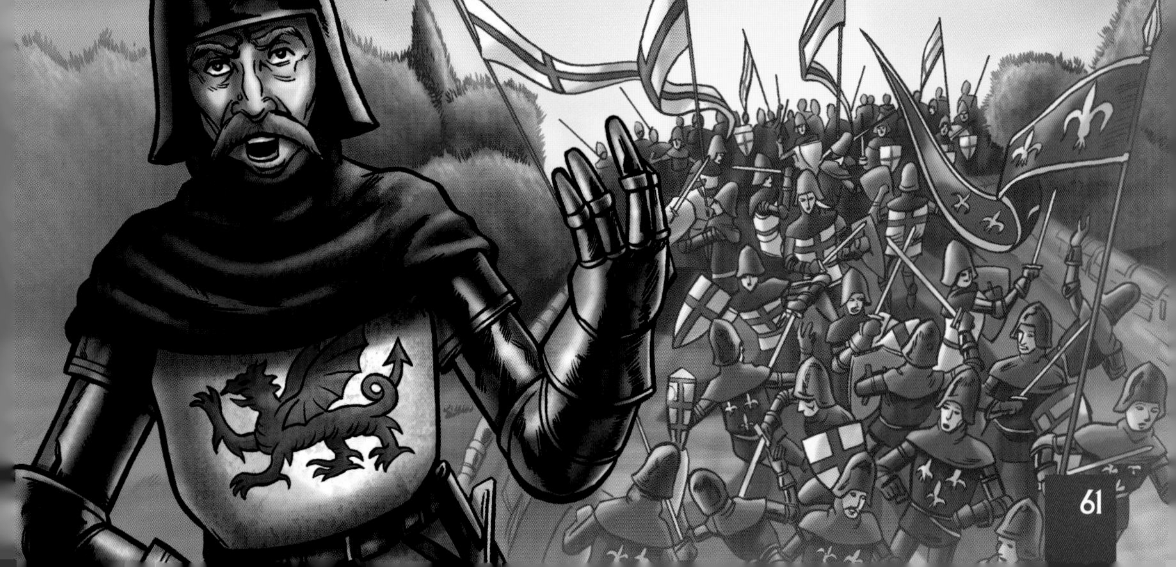
YES, YOUR MAJESTY. THE DUKE OF EXETER HAS VERY COURAGEOUSLY HELD ONTO THE BRIDGE. THERE WAS SOME REALLY BRAVE FIGHTING AND THE FRENCH HAVE BEEN *DRIVEN OFF,* LOOK YOU.
THE ENEMY *HELD* THE BRIDGE AT ONE STAGE, BUT WAS FORCED TO RETREAT AND THE DUKE OF EXETER IS IN *CONTROL* NOW.
I CAN TELL YOUR MAJESTY, THE DUKE IS A *BRAVE* MAN.

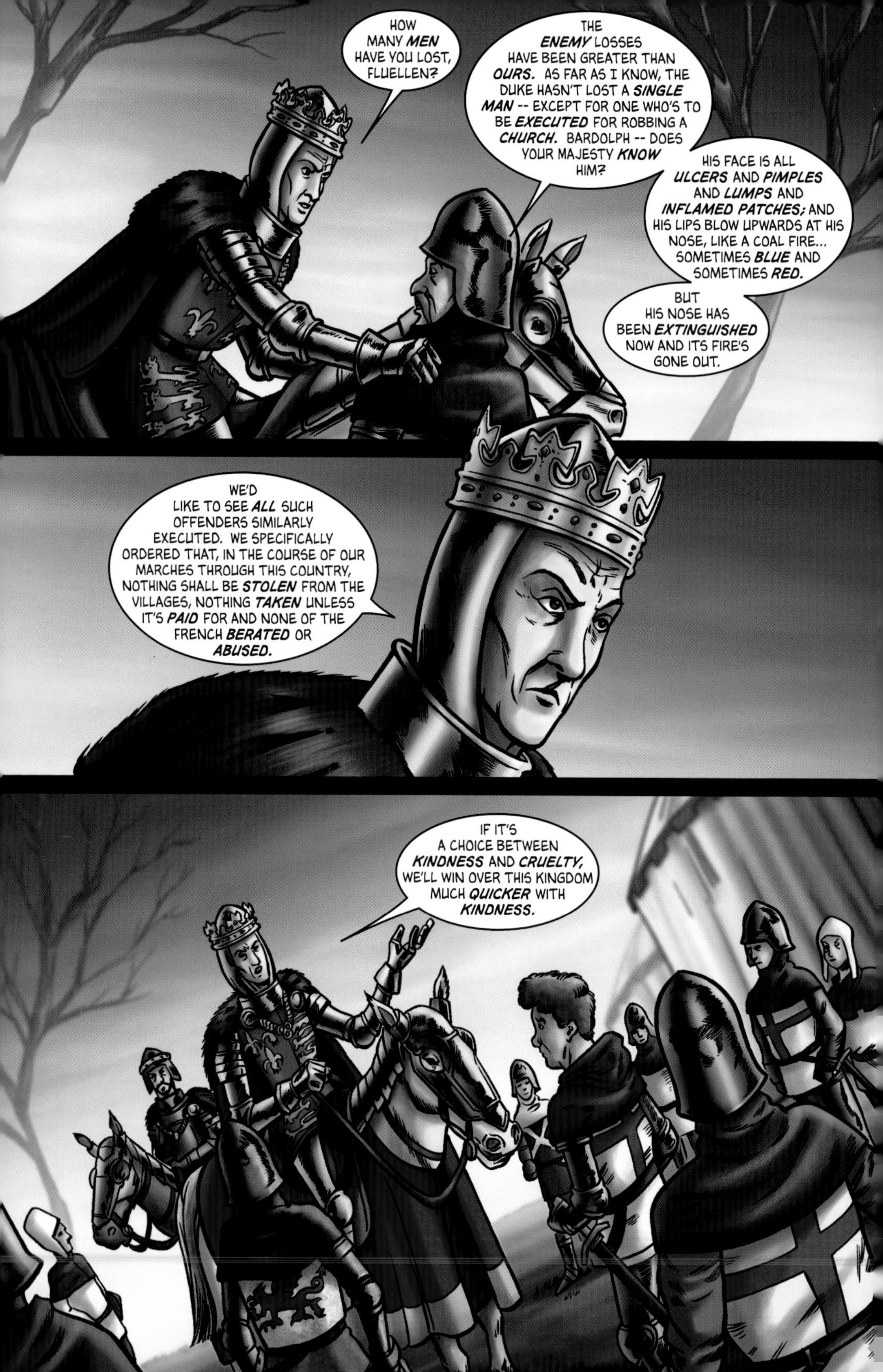
HOW MANY MEN HAVE YOU LOST, FLUELLEN?
THE ENEMY LOSSES HAVE BEEN GREATER THAN OURS. AS FAR AS I KNOW, THE DUKE HASN'T LOST A SINGLE MAN -- EXCEPT FOR ONE WHO'S TO BE EXECUTED FOR ROBBING A CHURCH. BARDOLPH -- DOES YOUR MAJESTY KNOW HIM?
HIS FACE IS ALL ULCERS AND PIMPLES AND LUMPS AND INFLAMED PATCHES; AND HIS LIPS BLOW UPWARDS AT HIS NOSE, LIKE A COAL FIRE... SOMETIMES BLUE AND SOMETIMES RED.
BUT HIS NOSE HAS BEEN EXTINGUISHED NOW AND ITS FIRE'S GONE OUT.
WE'D LIKE TO SEE ALL SUCH OFFENDERS SIMILARLY EXECUTED. WE SPECIFICALLY ORDERED THAT, IN THE COURSE OF OUR MARCHES THROUGH THIS COUNTRY, NOTHING SHALL BE STOLEN FROM THE VILLAGES, NOTHING TAKEN UNLESS IT'S PAID FOR AND NONE OF THE FRENCH BERATED OR ABUSED.
IF IT'S A CHOICE BETWEEN KINDNESS AND CRUELTY, WE'LL WIN OVER THIS KINGDOM MUCH QUICKER WITH KINDNESS.

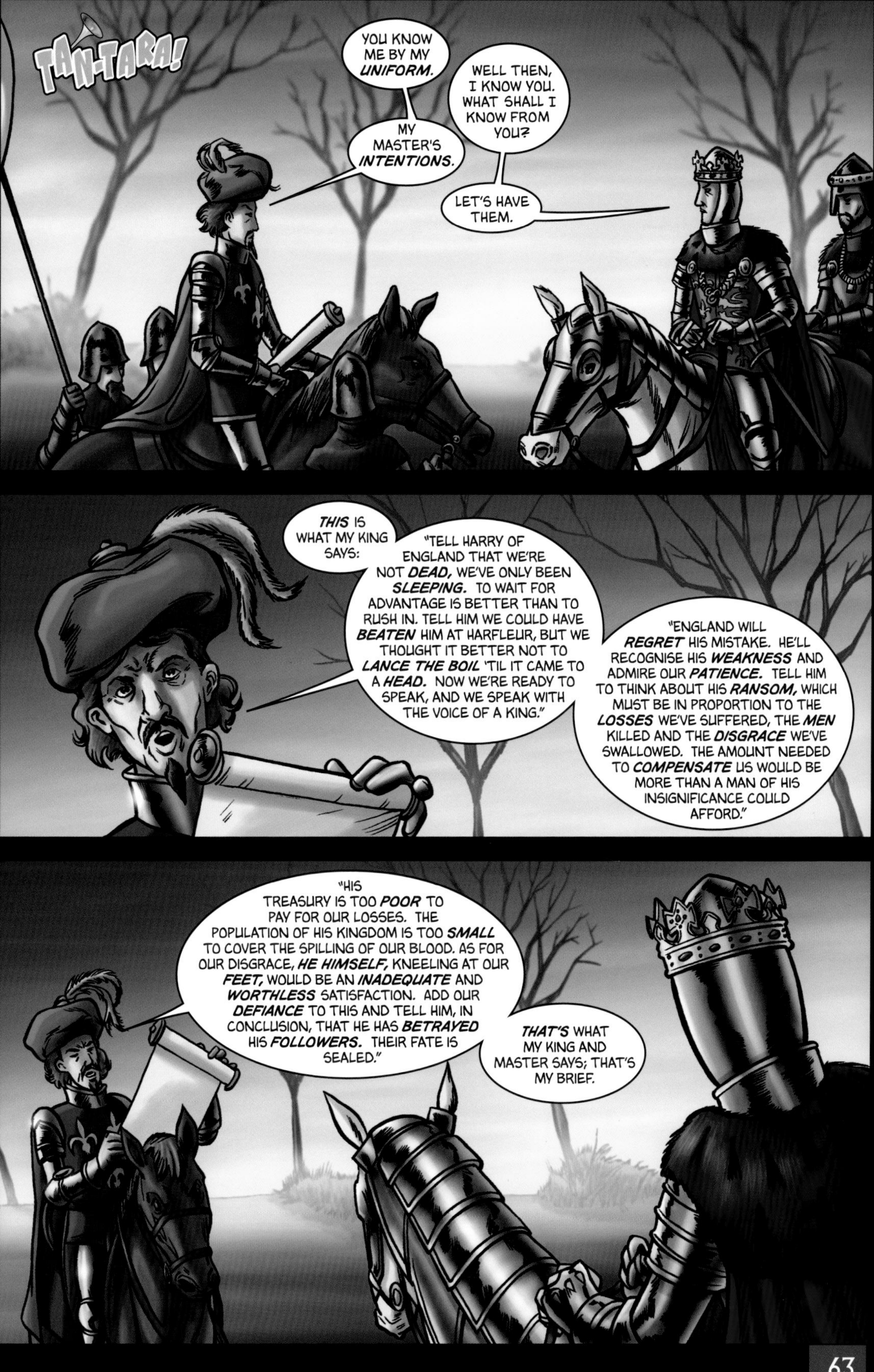
TAN-TARA!
YOU KNOW ME BY MY UNIFORM.
MY MASTER'S INTENTIONS.
WELL THEN, I KNOW YOU. WHAT SHALL I KNOW FROM YOU?
LET'S HAVE THEM.
THIS IS WHAT MY KING SAYS:
"TELL HARRY OF ENGLAND THAT WE'RE NOT DEAD, WE'VE ONLY BEEN SLEEPING. TO WAIT FOR ADVANTAGE IS BETTER THAN TO RUSH IN. TELL HIM WE COULD HAVE BEATEN HIM AT HARFLEUR, BUT WE THOUGHT IT BETTER NOT TO LANCE THE BOIL 'TIL IT CAME TO A HEAD. NOW WE'RE READY TO SPEAK, AND WE SPEAK WITH THE VOICE OF A KING."
"ENGLAND WILL REGRET HIS MISTAKE. HE'LL RECOGNISE HIS WEAKNESS AND ADMIRE OUR PATIENCE. TELL HIM TO THINK ABOUT HIS RANSOM, WHICH MUST BE IN PROPORTION TO THE LOSSES WE'VE SUFFERED, THE MEN KILLED AND THE DISGRACE WE'VE SWALLOWED. THE AMOUNT NEEDED TO COMPENSATE US WOULD BE MORE THAN A MAN OF HIS INSIGNIFICANCE COULD AFFORD."
"HIS TREASURY IS TOO POOR TO PAY FOR OUR LOSSES. THE POPULATION OF HIS KINGDOM IS TOO SMALL TO COVER THE SPILLING OF OUR BLOOD. AS FOR OUR DISGRACE, HE HIMSELF, KNEELING AT OUR FEET, WOULD BE AN INADEQUATE AND WORTHLESS SATISFACTION. ADD OUR DEFIANCE TO THIS AND TELL HIM, IN CONCLUSION, THAT HE HAS BETRAYED HIS FOLLOWERS. THEIR FATE IS SEALED."
THAT'S WHAT MY KING AND MASTER SAYS; THAT'S MY BRIEF.

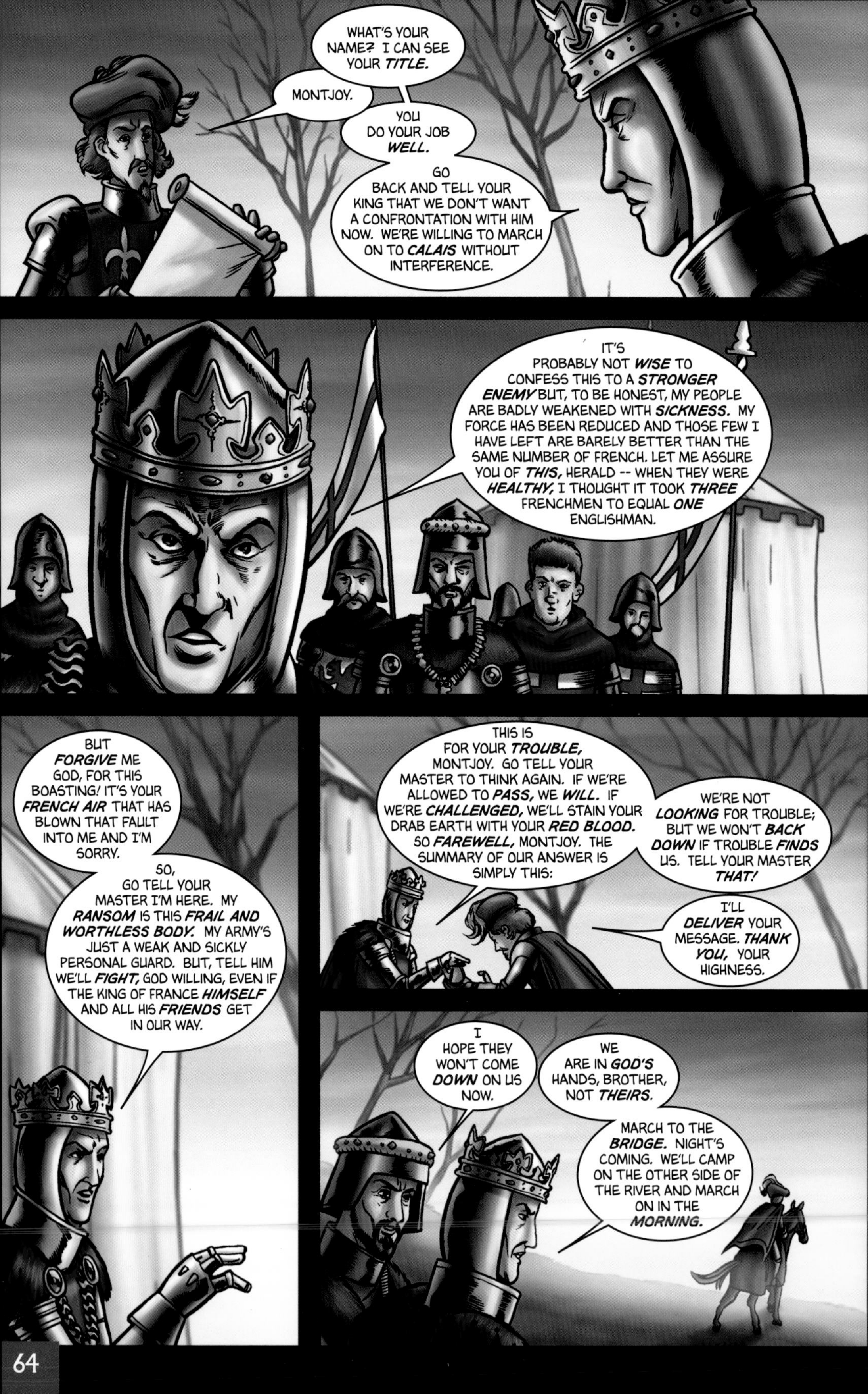
WHAT'S YOUR NAME? I CAN SEE YOUR TITLE.
MONTJOY.
YOU DO YOUR JOB WELL.
GO BACK AND TELL YOUR KING THAT WE DON'T WANT A CONFRONTATION WITH HIM NOW. WE'RE WILLING TO MARCH ON TO CALAIS WITHOUT INTERFERENCE.
IT'S PROBABLY NOT WISE TO CONFESS THIS TO A STRONGER ENEMY BUT, TO BE HONEST, MY PEOPLE ARE BADLY WEAKENED WITH SICKNESS. MY FORCE HAS BEEN REDUCED AND THOSE FEW I HAVE LEFT ARE BARELY BETTER THAN THE SAME NUMBER OF FRENCH. LET ME ASSURE YOU OF THIS, HERALD -- WHEN THEY WERE HEALTHY, I THOUGHT IT TOOK THREE FRENCHMEN TO EQUAL ONE ENGLISHMAN.
BUT FORGIVE ME GOD, FOR THIS BOASTING! IT'S YOUR FRENCH AIR THAT HAS BLOWN THAT FAULT INTO ME AND I'M SORRY.
SO, GO TELL YOUR MASTER I'M HERE. MY RANSOM IS THIS FRAIL AND WORTHLESS BODY. MY ARMY'S JUST A WEAK AND SICKLY PERSONAL GUARD. BUT, TELL HIM WE'LL FIGHT, GOD WILLING, EVEN IF THE KING OF FRANCE HIMSELF AND ALL HIS FRIENDS GET IN OUR WAY.
THIS IS FOR YOUR TROUBLE, MONTJOY. GO TELL YOUR MASTER TO THINK AGAIN. IF WE'RE ALLOWED TO PASS, WE WILL. IF WE'RE CHALLENGED, WE'LL STAIN YOUR DRAB EARTH WITH YOUR RED BLOOD. SO FAREWELL, MONTJOY. THE SUMMARY OF OUR ANSWER IS SIMPLY THIS:
WE'RE NOT LOOKING FOR TROUBLE; BUT WE WON'T BACK DOWN IF TROUBLE FINDS US. TELL YOUR MASTER THAT!
I'LL DELIVER YOUR MESSAGE. THANK YOU, YOUR HIGHNESS.
I HOPE THEY WON'T COME DOWN ON US NOW.
WE ARE IN GOD'S HANDS, BROTHER, NOT THEIRS.
MARCH TO THE BRIDGE. NIGHT'S COMING. WE'LL CAMP ON THE OTHER SIDE OF THE RIVER AND MARCH ON IN THE MORNING.

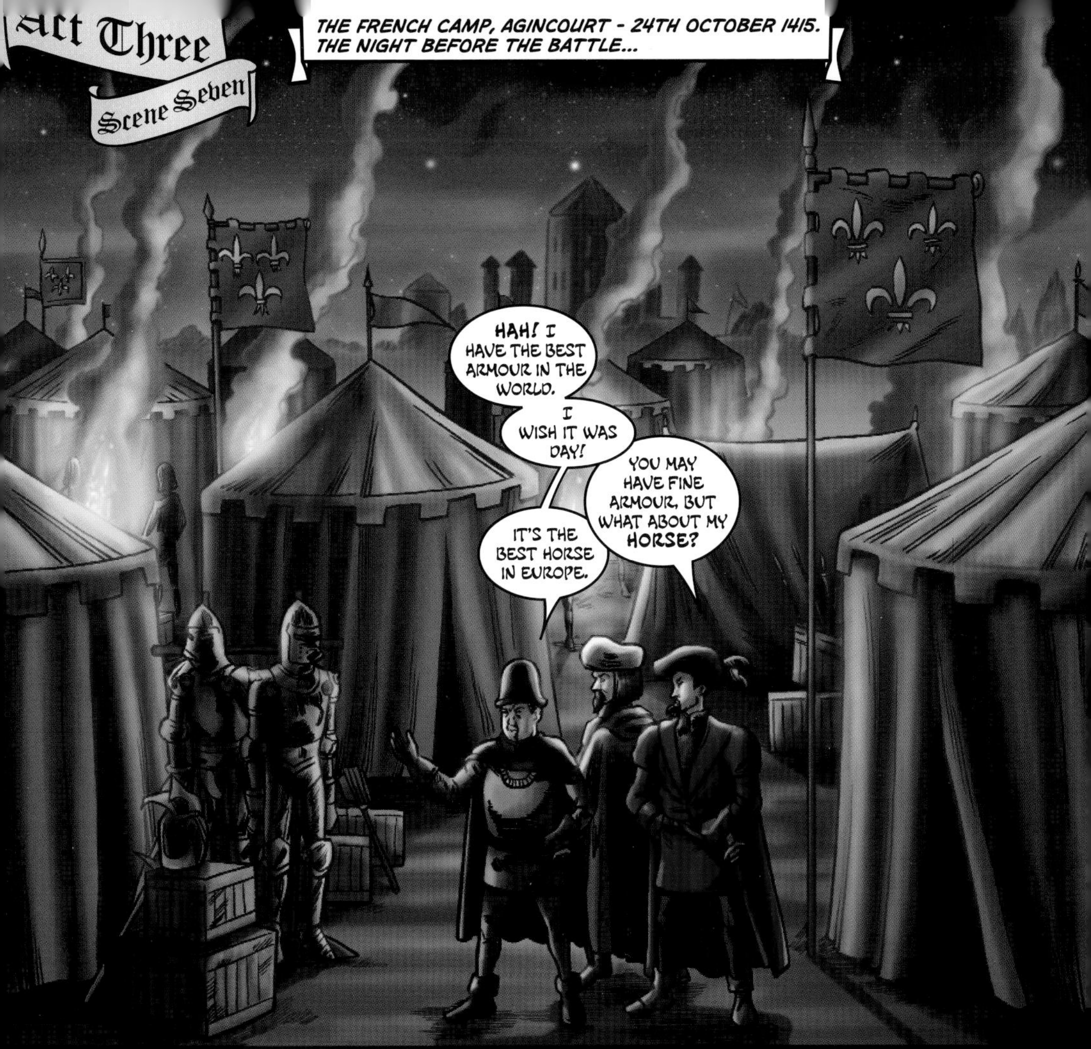
Act Three
Scene Seven
THE FRENCH CAMP, AGINCOURT - 24TH OCTOBER 1415. THE NIGHT BEFORE THE BATTLE...
HAH! I HAVE THE BEST ARMOUR IN THE WORLD.
I WISH IT WAS DAY!
YOU MAY HAVE FINE ARMOUR, BUT WHAT ABOUT MY HORSE?
IT'S THE BEST HORSE IN EUROPE.

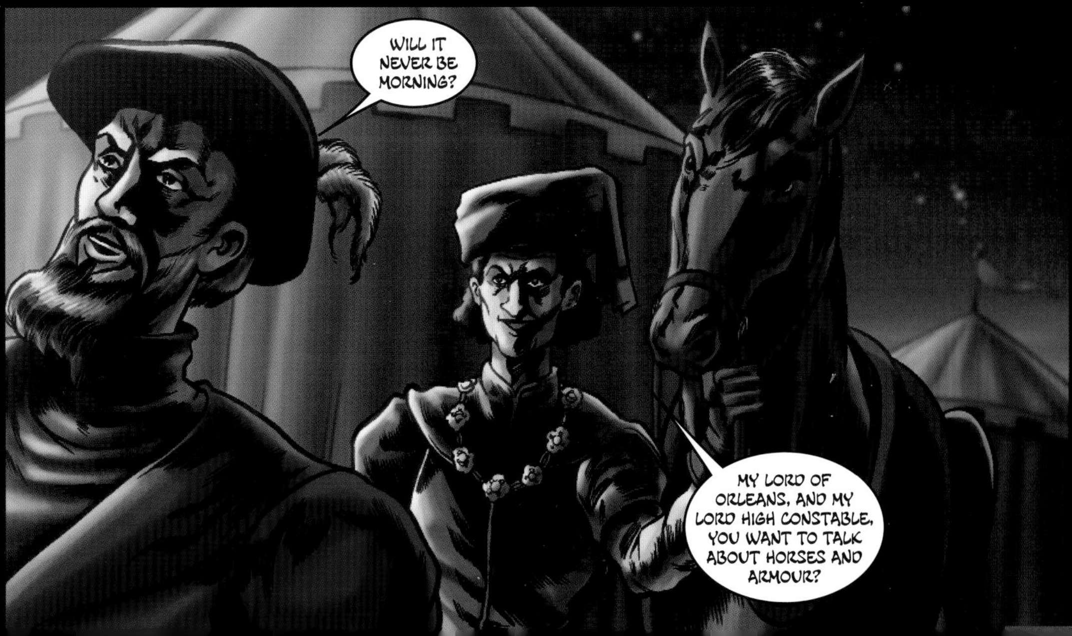
WILL IT NEVER BE MORNING?
MY LORD OF ORLEANS, AND MY LORD HIGH CONSTABLE, YOU WANT TO TALK ABOUT HORSES AND ARMOUR?

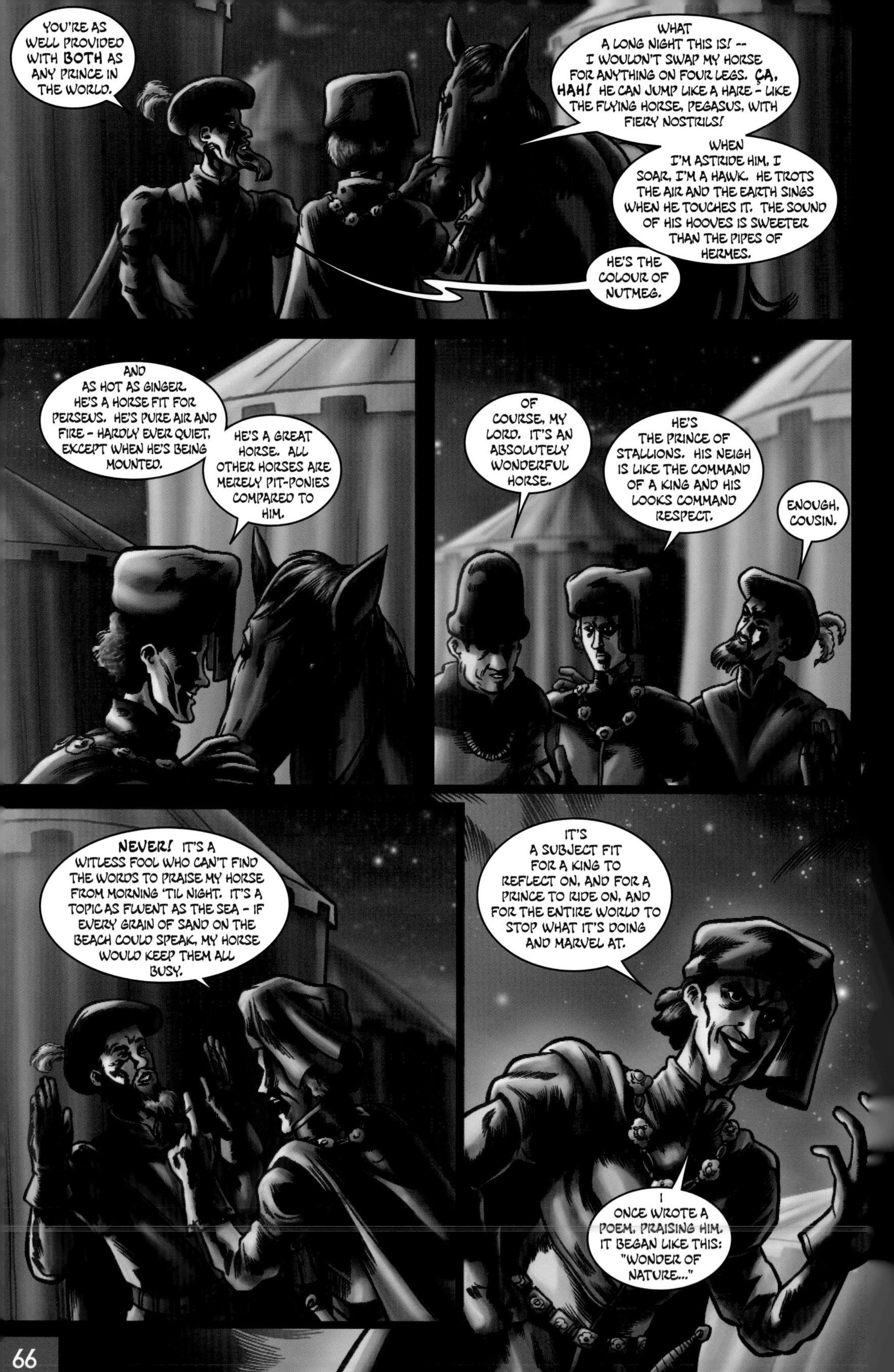

YOU'RE AS WELL PROVIDED WITH BOTH AS ANY PRINCE IN THE WORLD.
WHAT A LONG NIGHT THIS IS! -- I WOULDN'T SWAP MY HORSE FOR ANYTHING ON FOUR LEGS. ÇA, HAH! HE CAN JUMP LIKE A HARE - LIKE THE FLYING HORSE, PEGASUS, WITH FIERY NOSTRILS!
WHEN I'M ASTRIDE HIM, I SOAR, I'M A HAWK. HE TROTS THE AIR AND THE EARTH SINGS WHEN HE TOUCHES IT. THE SOUND OF HIS HOOVES IS SWEETER THAN THE PIPES OF HERMES.
HE'S THE COLOUR OF NUTMEG.
AND AS HOT AS GINGER. HE'S A HORSE FIT FOR PERSEUS. HE'S PURE AIR AND FIRE - HARDLY EVER QUIET, EXCEPT WHEN HE'S BEING MOUNTED.
HE'S A GREAT HORSE. ALL OTHER HORSES ARE MERELY PIT-PONIES COMPARED TO HIM.
OF COURSE, MY LORD. IT'S AN ABSOLUTELY WONDERFUL HORSE.
HE'S THE PRINCE OF STALLIONS. HIS NEIGH IS LIKE THE COMMAND OF A KING AND HIS LOOKS COMMAND RESPECT.
ENOUGH, COUSIN.
NEVER! IT'S A WITLESS FOOL WHO CAN'T FIND THE WORDS TO PRAISE MY HORSE FROM MORNING 'TIL NIGHT. IT'S A TOPIC AS FLUENT AS THE SEA - IF EVERY GRAIN OF SAND ON THE BEACH COULD SPEAK, MY HORSE WOULD KEEP THEM ALL BUSY.
IT'S A SUBJECT FIT FOR A KING TO REFLECT ON, AND FOR A PRINCE TO RIDE ON, AND FOR THE ENTIRE WORLD TO STOP WHAT IT'S DOING AND MARVEL AT.
I ONCE WROTE A POEM, PRAISING HIM. IT BEGAN LIKE THIS: "WONDER OF NATURE..."

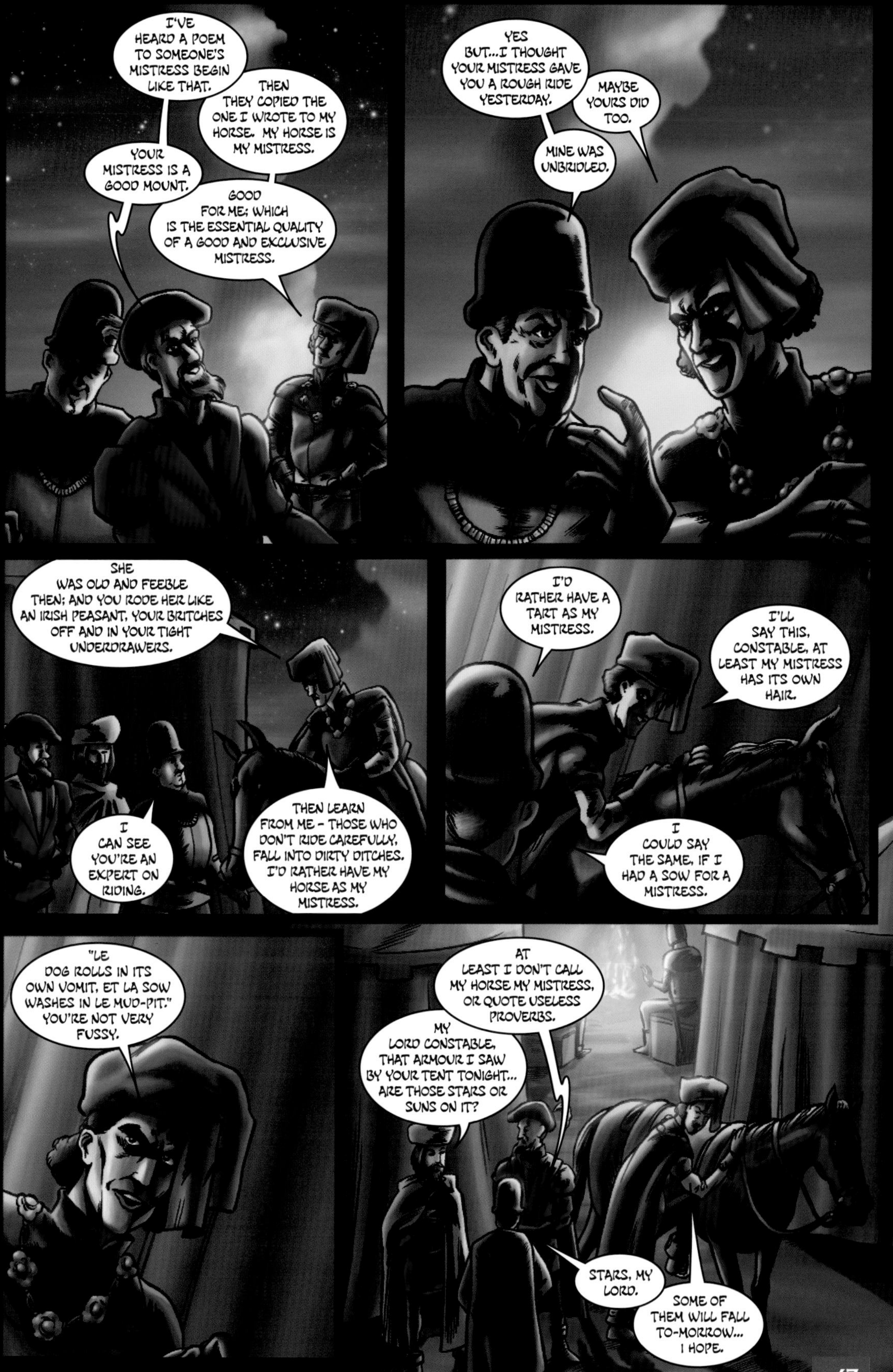
I'VE HEARD A POEM TO SOMEONE'S MISTRESS BEGIN LIKE THAT.
THEN THEY COPIED THE ONE I WROTE TO MY HORSE. MY HORSE IS MY MISTRESS.
YOUR MISTRESS IS A GOOD MOUNT.
GOOD FOR ME; WHICH IS THE ESSENTIAL QUALITY OF A GOOD AND EXCLUSIVE MISTRESS.
YES BUT...I THOUGHT YOUR MISTRESS GAVE YOU A ROUGH RIDE YESTERDAY.
MAYBE YOURS DID TOO.
MINE WAS UNBRIDLED.
SHE WAS OLD AND FEEBLE THEN; AND YOU RODE HER LIKE AN IRISH PEASANT, YOUR BRITCHES OFF AND IN YOUR TIGHT UNDERDRAWERS.
I CAN SEE YOU'RE AN EXPERT ON RIDING.
THEN LEARN FROM ME – THOSE WHO DON'T RIDE CAREFULLY, FALL INTO DIRTY DITCHES. I'D RATHER HAVE MY HORSE AS MY MISTRESS.
I'D RATHER HAVE A TART AS MY MISTRESS.
I'LL SAY THIS, CONSTABLE, AT LEAST MY MISTRESS HAS ITS OWN HAIR.
I COULD SAY THE SAME, IF I HAD A SOW FOR A MISTRESS.
"LE DOG ROLLS IN ITS OWN VOMIT, ET LA SOW WASHES IN LE MUD-PIT." YOU'RE NOT VERY FUSSY.
AT LEAST I DON'T CALL MY HORSE MY MISTRESS, OR QUOTE USELESS PROVERBS.
MY LORD CONSTABLE, THAT ARMOUR I SAW BY YOUR TENT TONIGHT... ARE THOSE STARS OR SUNS ON IT?
STARS, MY LORD.
SOME OF THEM WILL FALL TO-MORROW... I HOPE.

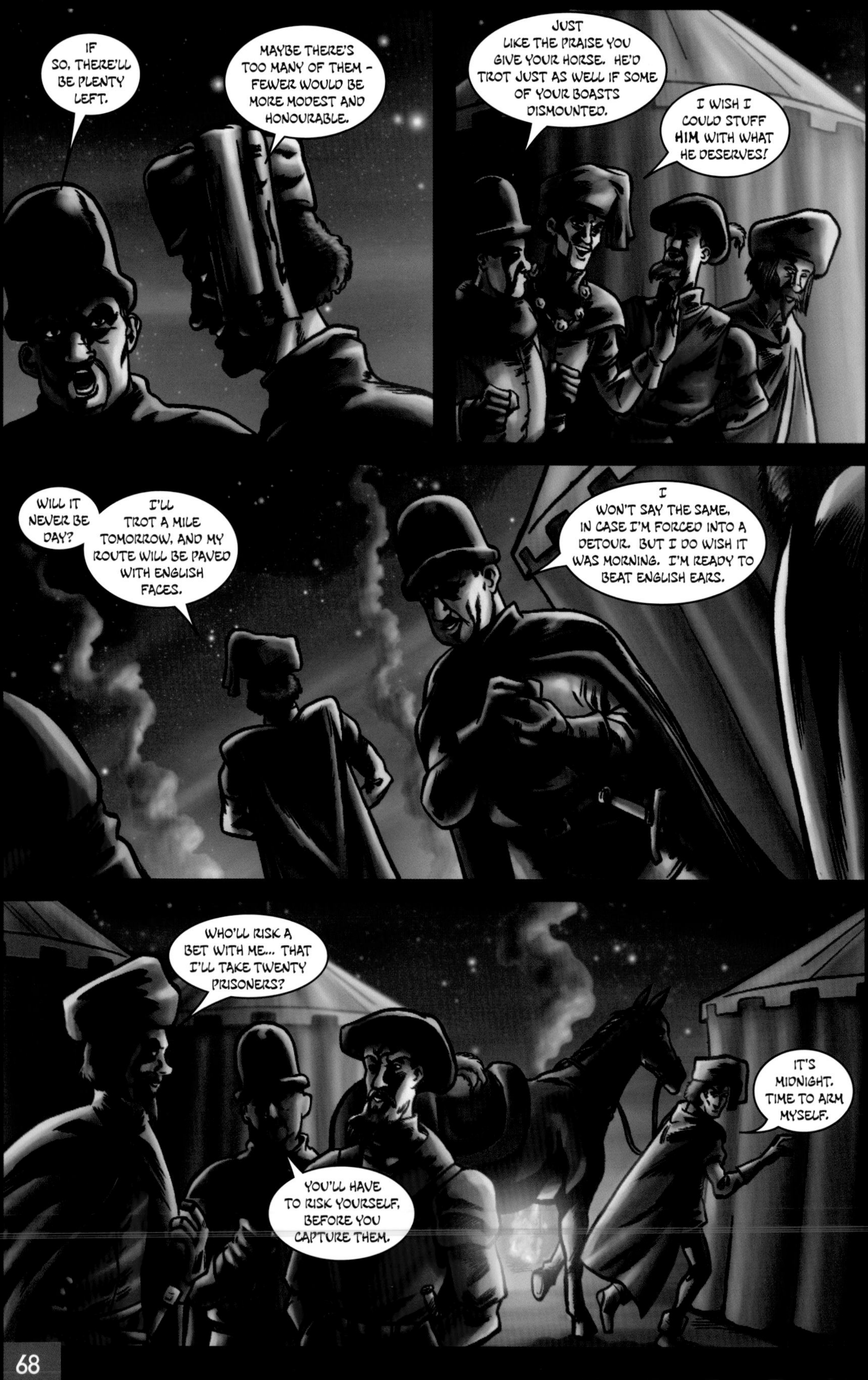
IF SO, THERE'LL BE PLENTY LEFT.
MAYBE THERE'S TOO MANY OF THEM - FEWER WOULD BE MORE MODEST AND HONOURABLE.
JUST LIKE THE PRAISE YOU GIVE YOUR HORSE. HE'D TROT JUST AS WELL IF SOME OF YOUR BOASTS DISMOUNTED.
I WISH I COULD STUFF **HIM** WITH WHAT HE DESERVES!
WILL IT NEVER BE DAY?
I'LL TROT A MILE TOMORROW, AND MY ROUTE WILL BE PAVED WITH ENGLISH FACES.
I WON'T SAY THE SAME, IN CASE I'M FORCED INTO A DETOUR. BUT I DO WISH IT WAS MORNING. I'M READY TO BEAT ENGLISH EARS.
WHO'LL RISK A BET WITH ME... THAT I'LL TAKE TWENTY PRISONERS?
YOU'LL HAVE TO RISK YOURSELF, BEFORE YOU CAPTURE THEM.
IT'S MIDNIGHT. TIME TO ARM MYSELF.

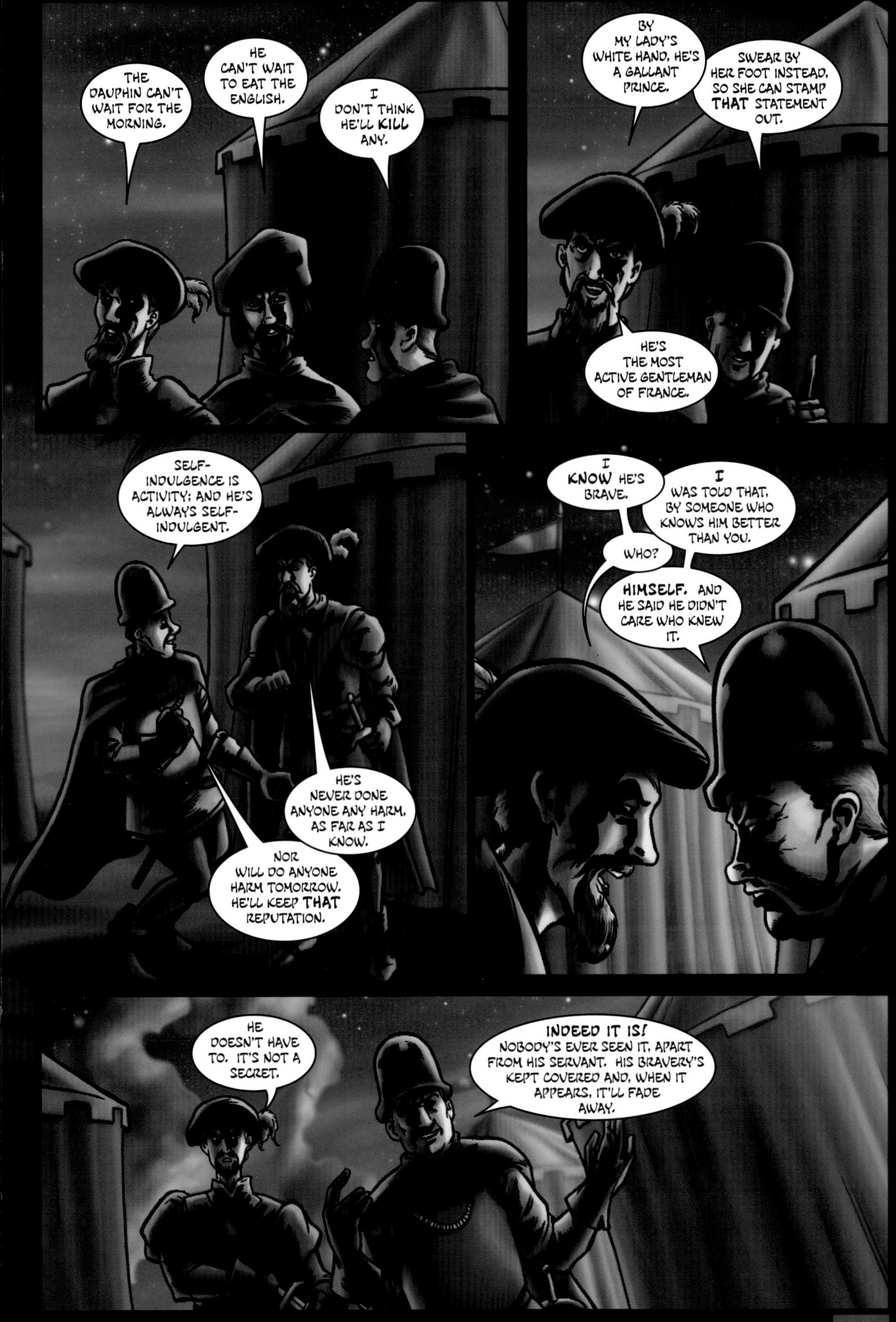
THE DAUPHIN CAN'T WAIT FOR THE MORNING.
HE CAN'T WAIT TO EAT THE ENGLISH.
I DON'T THINK HE'LL KILL ANY.
BY MY LADY'S WHITE HAND, HE'S A GALLANT PRINCE.
SWEAR BY HER FOOT INSTEAD, SO SHE CAN STAMP THAT STATEMENT OUT.
HE'S THE MOST ACTIVE GENTLEMAN OF FRANCE.
SELF-INDULGENCE IS ACTIVITY; AND HE'S ALWAYS SELF-INDULGENT.
HE'S NEVER DONE ANYONE ANY HARM, AS FAR AS I KNOW.
NOR WILL DO ANYONE HARM TOMORROW. HE'LL KEEP THAT REPUTATION.
I KNOW HE'S BRAVE.
I WAS TOLD THAT, BY SOMEONE WHO KNOWS HIM BETTER THAN YOU.
WHO?
HIMSELF. AND HE SAID HE DIDN'T CARE WHO KNEW IT.
HE DOESN'T HAVE TO. IT'S NOT A SECRET.
INDEED IT IS! NOBODY'S EVER SEEN IT, APART FROM HIS SERVANT. HIS BRAVERY'S KEPT COVERED AND, WHEN IT APPEARS, IT'LL FADE AWAY.

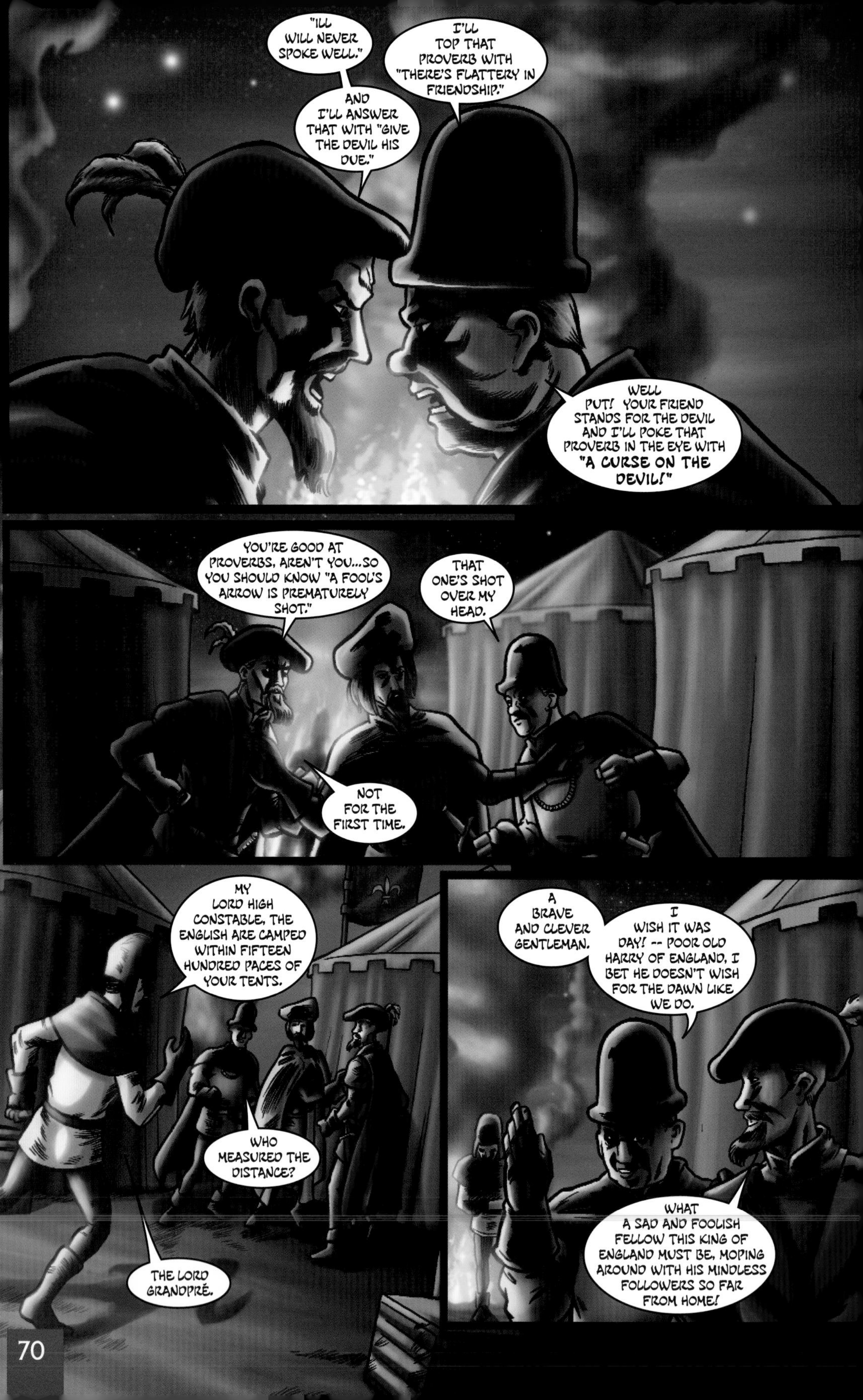
"ILL WILL NEVER SPOKE WELL."
I'LL TOP THAT PROVERB WITH "THERE'S FLATTERY IN FRIENDSHIP."
AND I'LL ANSWER THAT WITH "GIVE THE DEVIL HIS DUE."
WELL PUT! YOUR FRIEND STANDS FOR THE DEVIL AND I'LL POKE THAT PROVERB IN THE EYE WITH "A CURSE ON THE DEVIL!"
YOU'RE GOOD AT PROVERBS, AREN'T YOU...SO YOU SHOULD KNOW "A FOOL'S ARROW IS PREMATURELY SHOT."
THAT ONE'S SHOT OVER MY HEAD.
NOT FOR THE FIRST TIME.
MY LORD HIGH CONSTABLE, THE ENGLISH ARE CAMPED WITHIN FIFTEEN HUNDRED PACES OF YOUR TENTS.
WHO MEASURED THE DISTANCE?
THE LORD GRANDPRÉ.
A BRAVE AND CLEVER GENTLEMAN.
I WISH IT WAS DAY! -- POOR OLD HARRY OF ENGLAND, I BET HE DOESN'T WISH FOR THE DAWN LIKE WE DO.
WHAT A SAD AND FOOLISH FELLOW THIS KING OF ENGLAND MUST BE, MOPING AROUND WITH HIS MINDLESS FOLLOWERS SO FAR FROM HOME!

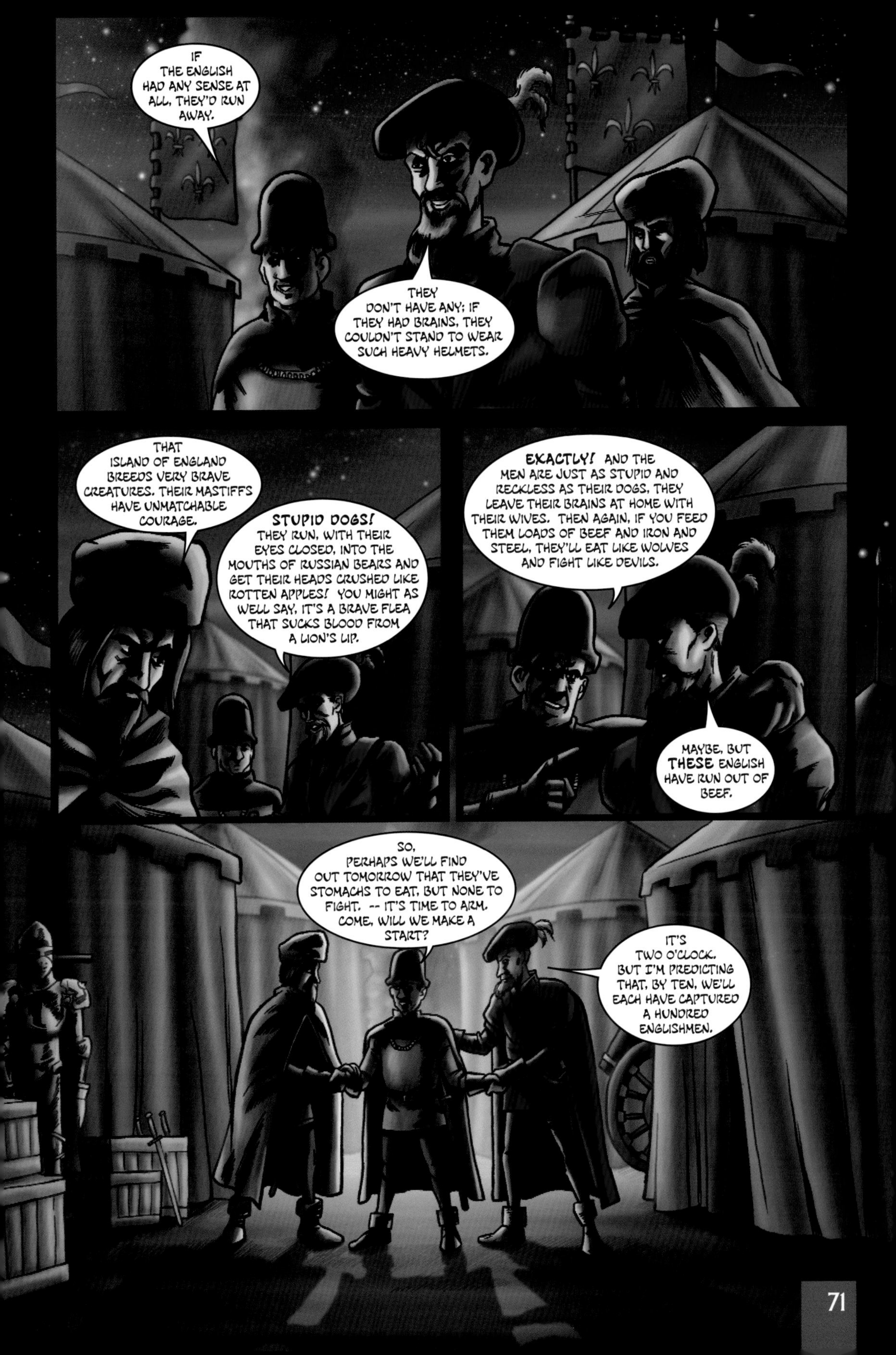
IF THE ENGLISH HAD ANY SENSE AT ALL, THEY'D RUN AWAY.
THEY DON'T HAVE ANY; IF THEY HAD BRAINS, THEY COULDN'T STAND TO WEAR SUCH HEAVY HELMETS.
THAT ISLAND OF ENGLAND BREEDS VERY BRAVE CREATURES. THEIR MASTIFFS HAVE UNMATCHABLE COURAGE.
STUPID DOGS! THEY RUN, WITH THEIR EYES CLOSED, INTO THE MOUTHS OF RUSSIAN BEARS AND GET THEIR HEADS CRUSHED LIKE ROTTEN APPLES! YOU MIGHT AS WELL SAY, IT'S A BRAVE FLEA THAT SUCKS BLOOD FROM A LION'S LIP.
EXACTLY! AND THE MEN ARE JUST AS STUPID AND RECKLESS AS THEIR DOGS, THEY LEAVE THEIR BRAINS AT HOME WITH THEIR WIVES. THEN AGAIN, IF YOU FEED THEM LOADS OF BEEF AND IRON AND STEEL, THEY'LL EAT LIKE WOLVES AND FIGHT LIKE DEVILS.
MAYBE, BUT THESE ENGLISH HAVE RUN OUT OF BEEF.
SO, PERHAPS WE'LL FIND OUT TOMORROW THAT THEY'VE STOMACHS TO EAT, BUT NONE TO FIGHT. -- IT'S TIME TO ARM. COME, WILL WE MAKE A START?
IT'S TWO O'CLOCK. BUT I'M PREDICTING THAT, BY TEN, WE'LL EACH HAVE CAPTURED A HUNDRED ENGLISHMEN.

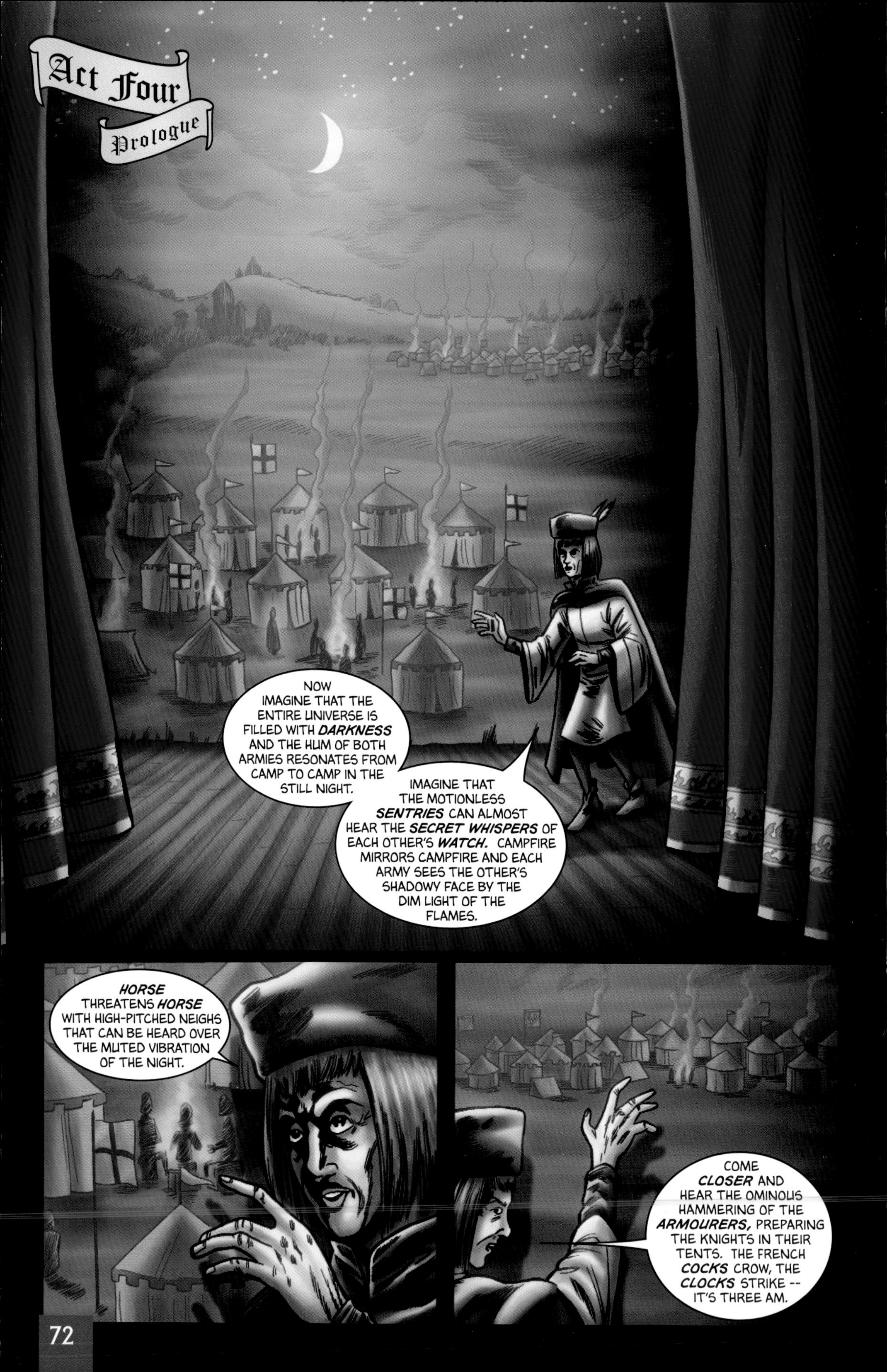
Act Four
Prologue
NOW IMAGINE THAT THE ENTIRE UNIVERSE IS FILLED WITH DARKNESS AND THE HUM OF BOTH ARMIES RESONATES FROM CAMP TO CAMP IN THE STILL NIGHT.
IMAGINE THAT THE MOTIONLESS SENTRIES CAN ALMOST HEAR THE SECRET WHISPERS OF EACH OTHER'S WATCH. CAMPFIRE MIRRORS CAMPFIRE AND EACH ARMY SEES THE OTHER'S SHADOWY FACE BY THE DIM LIGHT OF THE FLAMES.
HORSE THREATENS HORSE WITH HIGH-PITCHED NEIGHS THAT CAN BE HEARD OVER THE MUTED VIBRATION OF THE NIGHT.
COME CLOSER AND HEAR THE OMINOUS HAMMERING OF THE ARMOURERS, PREPARING THE KNIGHTS IN THEIR TENTS. THE FRENCH COCKS CROW, THE CLOCKS STRIKE -- IT'S THREE AM.

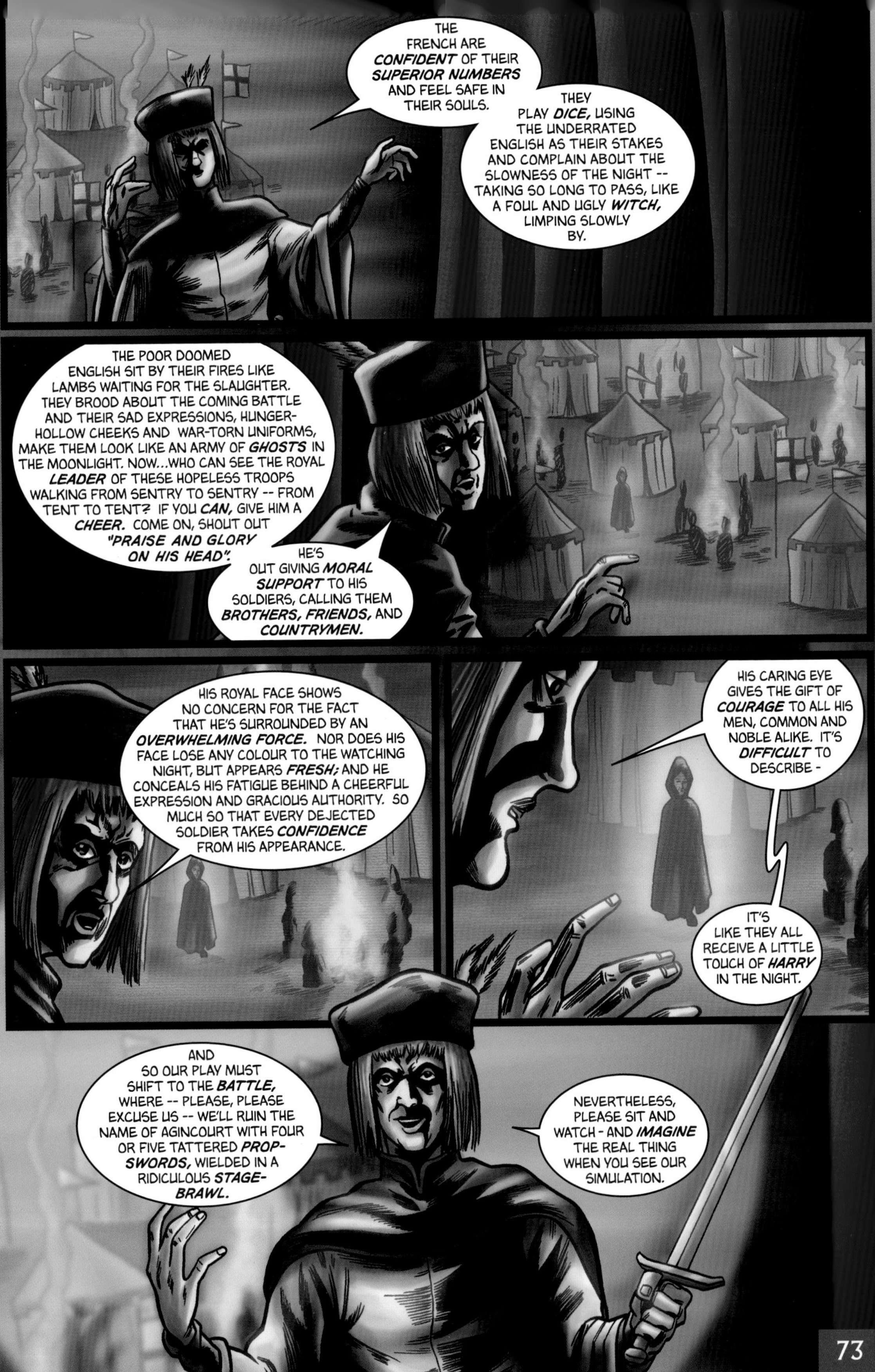
THE FRENCH ARE CONFIDENT OF THEIR SUPERIOR NUMBERS AND FEEL SAFE IN THEIR SOULS.
THEY PLAY DICE, USING THE UNDERRATED ENGLISH AS THEIR STAKES AND COMPLAIN ABOUT THE SLOWNESS OF THE NIGHT -- TAKING SO LONG TO PASS, LIKE A FOUL AND UGLY WITCH, LIMPING SLOWLY BY.
THE POOR DOOMED ENGLISH SIT BY THEIR FIRES LIKE LAMBS WAITING FOR THE SLAUGHTER. THEY BROOD ABOUT THE COMING BATTLE AND THEIR SAD EXPRESSIONS, HUNGER-HOLLOW CHEEKS AND WAR-TORN UNIFORMS, MAKE THEM LOOK LIKE AN ARMY OF GHOSTS IN THE MOONLIGHT. NOW...WHO CAN SEE THE ROYAL LEADER OF THESE HOPELESS TROOPS WALKING FROM SENTRY TO SENTRY -- FROM TENT TO TENT? IF YOU CAN, GIVE HIM A CHEER. COME ON, SHOUT OUT "PRAISE AND GLORY ON HIS HEAD".
HE'S OUT GIVING MORAL SUPPORT TO HIS SOLDIERS, CALLING THEM BROTHERS, FRIENDS, AND COUNTRYMEN.
HIS ROYAL FACE SHOWS NO CONCERN FOR THE FACT THAT HE'S SURROUNDED BY AN OVERWHELMING FORCE. NOR DOES HIS FACE LOSE ANY COLOUR TO THE WATCHING NIGHT, BUT APPEARS FRESH; AND HE CONCEALS HIS FATIGUE BEHIND A CHEERFUL EXPRESSION AND GRACIOUS AUTHORITY. SO MUCH SO THAT EVERY DEJECTED SOLDIER TAKES CONFIDENCE FROM HIS APPEARANCE.
HIS CARING EYE GIVES THE GIFT OF COURAGE TO ALL HIS MEN, COMMON AND NOBLE ALIKE. IT'S DIFFICULT TO DESCRIBE -
IT'S LIKE THEY ALL RECEIVE A LITTLE TOUCH OF HARRY IN THE NIGHT.
AND SO OUR PLAY MUST SHIFT TO THE BATTLE, WHERE -- PLEASE, PLEASE EXCUSE US -- WE'LL RUIN THE NAME OF AGINCOURT WITH FOUR OR FIVE TATTERED PROP-SWORDS, WIELDED IN A RIDICULOUS STAGE-BRAWL.
NEVERTHELESS, PLEASE SIT AND WATCH - AND IMAGINE THE REAL THING WHEN YOU SEE OUR SIMULATION.

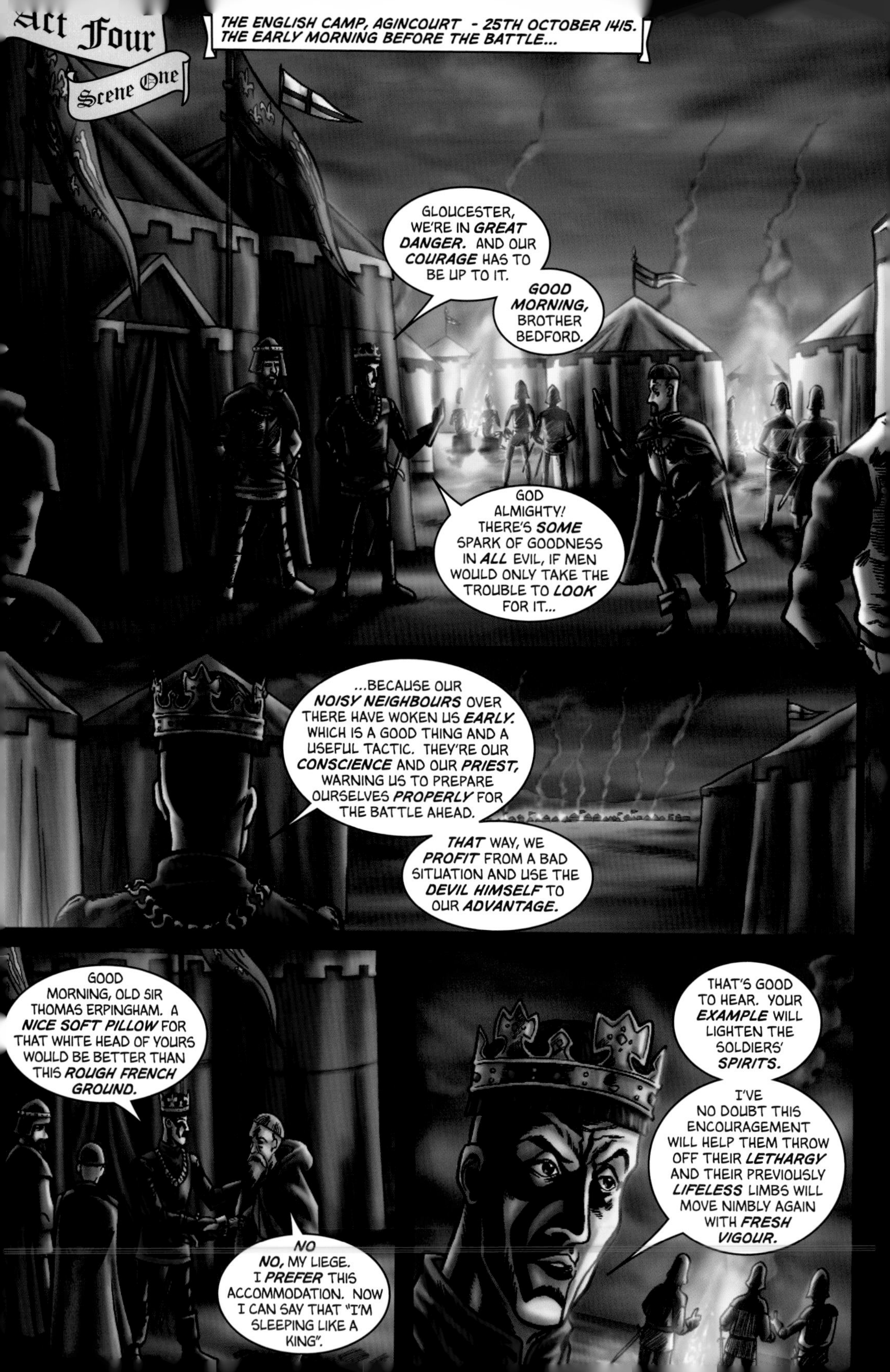
Act Four
Scene One
THE ENGLISH CAMP, AGINCOURT - 25TH OCTOBER 1415. THE EARLY MORNING BEFORE THE BATTLE...
GLOUCESTER, WE'RE IN GREAT DANGER. AND OUR COURAGE HAS TO BE UP TO IT.
GOOD MORNING, BROTHER BEDFORD.
GOD ALMIGHTY! THERE'S SOME SPARK OF GOODNESS IN ALL EVIL, IF MEN WOULD ONLY TAKE THE TROUBLE TO LOOK FOR IT...
...BECAUSE OUR NOISY NEIGHBOURS OVER THERE HAVE WOKEN US EARLY. WHICH IS A GOOD THING AND A USEFUL TACTIC. THEY'RE OUR CONSCIENCE AND OUR PRIEST, WARNING US TO PREPARE OURSELVES PROPERLY FOR THE BATTLE AHEAD.
THAT WAY, WE PROFIT FROM A BAD SITUATION AND USE THE DEVIL HIMSELF TO OUR ADVANTAGE.
GOOD MORNING, OLD SIR THOMAS ERPINGHAM. A NICE SOFT PILLOW FOR THAT WHITE HEAD OF YOURS WOULD BE BETTER THAN THIS ROUGH FRENCH GROUND.
NO NO, MY LIEGE. I PREFER THIS ACCOMMODATION. NOW I CAN SAY THAT "I'M SLEEPING LIKE A KING".
THAT'S GOOD TO HEAR. YOUR EXAMPLE WILL LIGHTEN THE SOLDIERS' SPIRITS.
I'VE NO DOUBT THIS ENCOURAGEMENT WILL HELP THEM THROW OFF THEIR LETHARGY AND THEIR PREVIOUSLY LIFELESS LIMBS WILL MOVE NIMBLY AGAIN WITH FRESH VIGOUR.

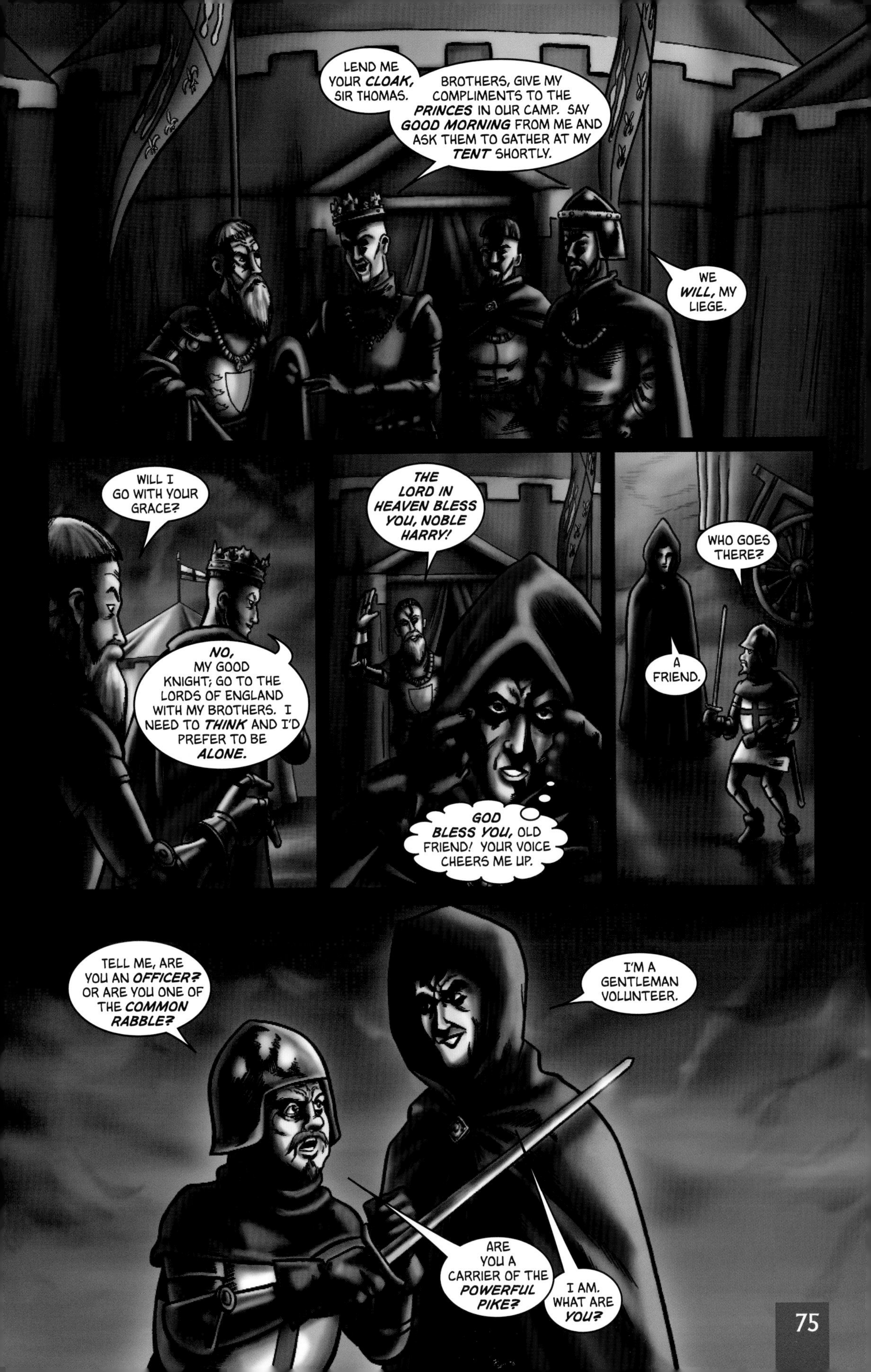
LEND ME YOUR CLOAK, SIR THOMAS.
BROTHERS, GIVE MY COMPLIMENTS TO THE PRINCES IN OUR CAMP. SAY GOOD MORNING FROM ME AND ASK THEM TO GATHER AT MY TENT SHORTLY.
WE WILL, MY LIEGE.
WILL I GO WITH YOUR GRACE?
NO, MY GOOD KNIGHT; GO TO THE LORDS OF ENGLAND WITH MY BROTHERS. I NEED TO THINK AND I'D PREFER TO BE ALONE.
THE LORD IN HEAVEN BLESS YOU, NOBLE HARRY!
GOD BLESS YOU, OLD FRIEND! YOUR VOICE CHEERS ME UP.
WHO GOES THERE?
A FRIEND.
TELL ME, ARE YOU AN OFFICER? OR ARE YOU ONE OF THE COMMON RABBLE?
I'M A GENTLEMAN VOLUNTEER.
ARE YOU A CARRIER OF THE POWERFUL PIKE?
I AM. WHAT ARE YOU?

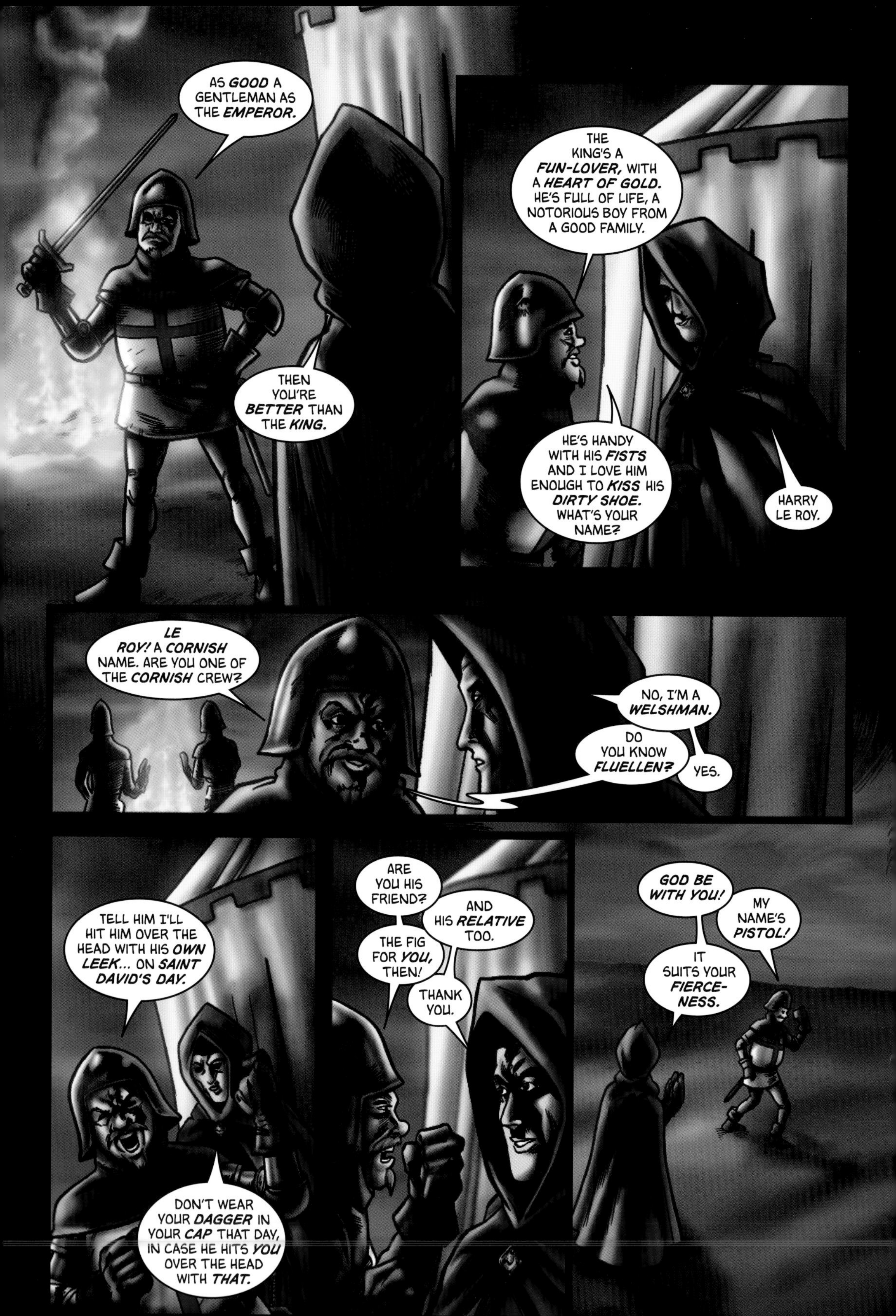
AS GOOD A GENTLEMAN AS THE EMPEROR.
THEN YOU'RE BETTER THAN THE KING.
THE KING'S A FUN-LOVER, WITH A HEART OF GOLD. HE'S FULL OF LIFE, A NOTORIOUS BOY FROM A GOOD FAMILY.
HE'S HANDY WITH HIS FISTS AND I LOVE HIM ENOUGH TO KISS HIS DIRTY SHOE. WHAT'S YOUR NAME?
HARRY LE ROY.
LE ROY! A CORNISH NAME. ARE YOU ONE OF THE CORNISH CREW?
NO, I'M A WELSHMAN.
DO YOU KNOW FLUELLEN?
YES.
TELL HIM I'LL HIT HIM OVER THE HEAD WITH HIS OWN LEEK... ON SAINT DAVID'S DAY.
DON'T WEAR YOUR DAGGER IN YOUR CAP THAT DAY, IN CASE HE HITS YOU OVER THE HEAD WITH THAT.
ARE YOU HIS FRIEND?
AND HIS RELATIVE TOO.
THE FIG FOR YOU, THEN!
THANK YOU.
GOD BE WITH YOU!
MY NAME'S PISTOL!
IT SUITS YOUR FIERCE-NESS.

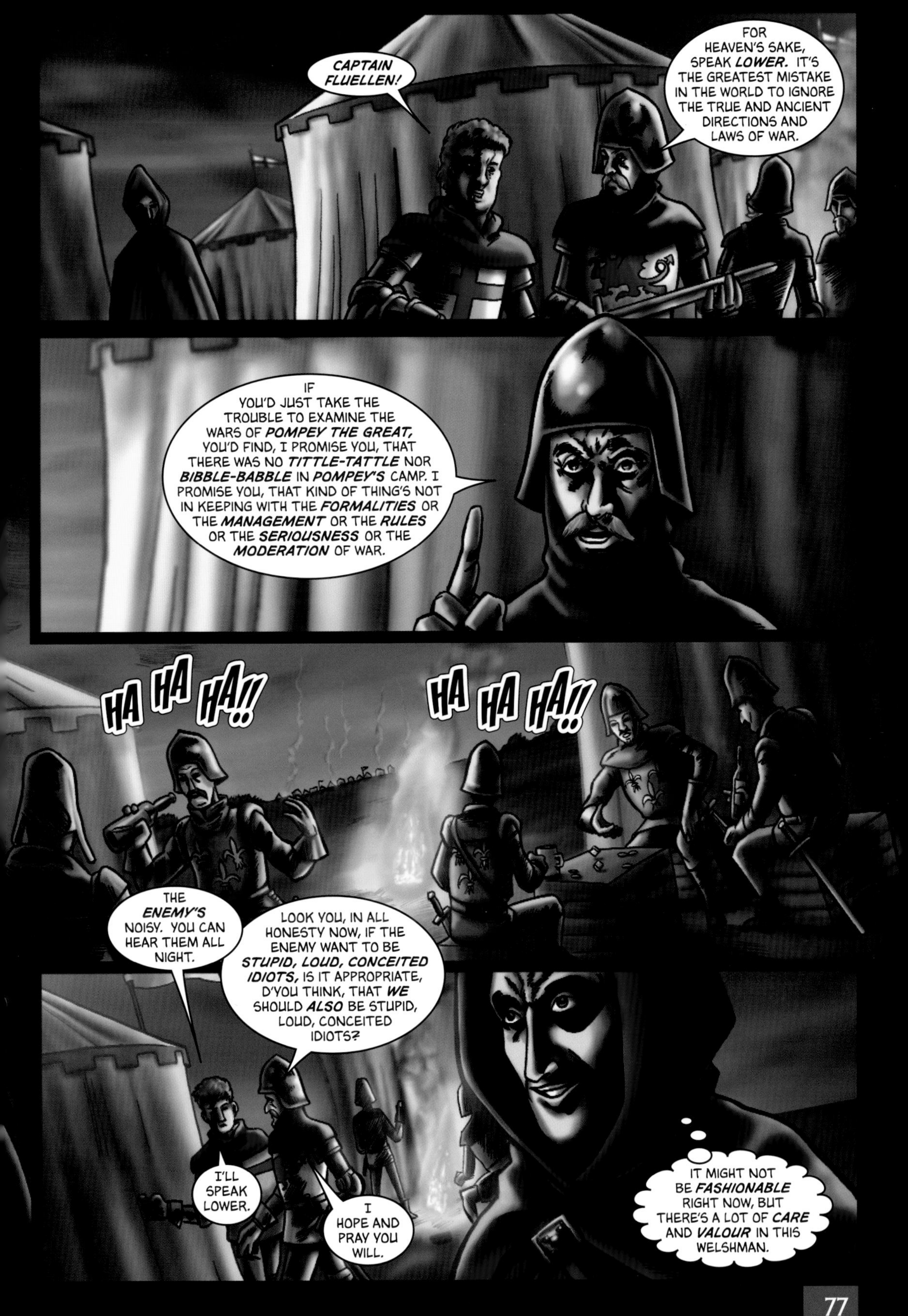
CAPTAIN FLUELLEN!
FOR HEAVEN'S SAKE, SPEAK LOWER. IT'S THE GREATEST MISTAKE IN THE WORLD TO IGNORE THE TRUE AND ANCIENT DIRECTIONS AND LAWS OF WAR.
IF YOU'D JUST TAKE THE TROUBLE TO EXAMINE THE WARS OF POMPEY THE GREAT, YOU'D FIND, I PROMISE YOU, THAT THERE WAS NO TITTLE-TATTLE NOR BIBBLE-BABBLE IN POMPEY'S CAMP. I PROMISE YOU, THAT KIND OF THING'S NOT IN KEEPING WITH THE FORMALITIES OR THE MANAGEMENT OR THE RULES OR THE SERIOUSNESS OR THE MODERATION OF WAR.
HA HA HA!!
HA HA HA!!
THE ENEMY'S NOISY. YOU CAN HEAR THEM ALL NIGHT.
LOOK YOU, IN ALL HONESTY NOW, IF THE ENEMY WANT TO BE STUPID, LOUD, CONCEITED IDIOTS, IS IT APPROPRIATE, D'YOU THINK, THAT WE SHOULD ALSO BE STUPID, LOUD, CONCEITED IDIOTS?
I'LL SPEAK LOWER.
I HOPE AND PRAY YOU WILL.
IT MIGHT NOT BE FASHIONABLE RIGHT NOW, BUT THERE'S A LOT OF CARE AND VALOUR IN THIS WELSHMAN.

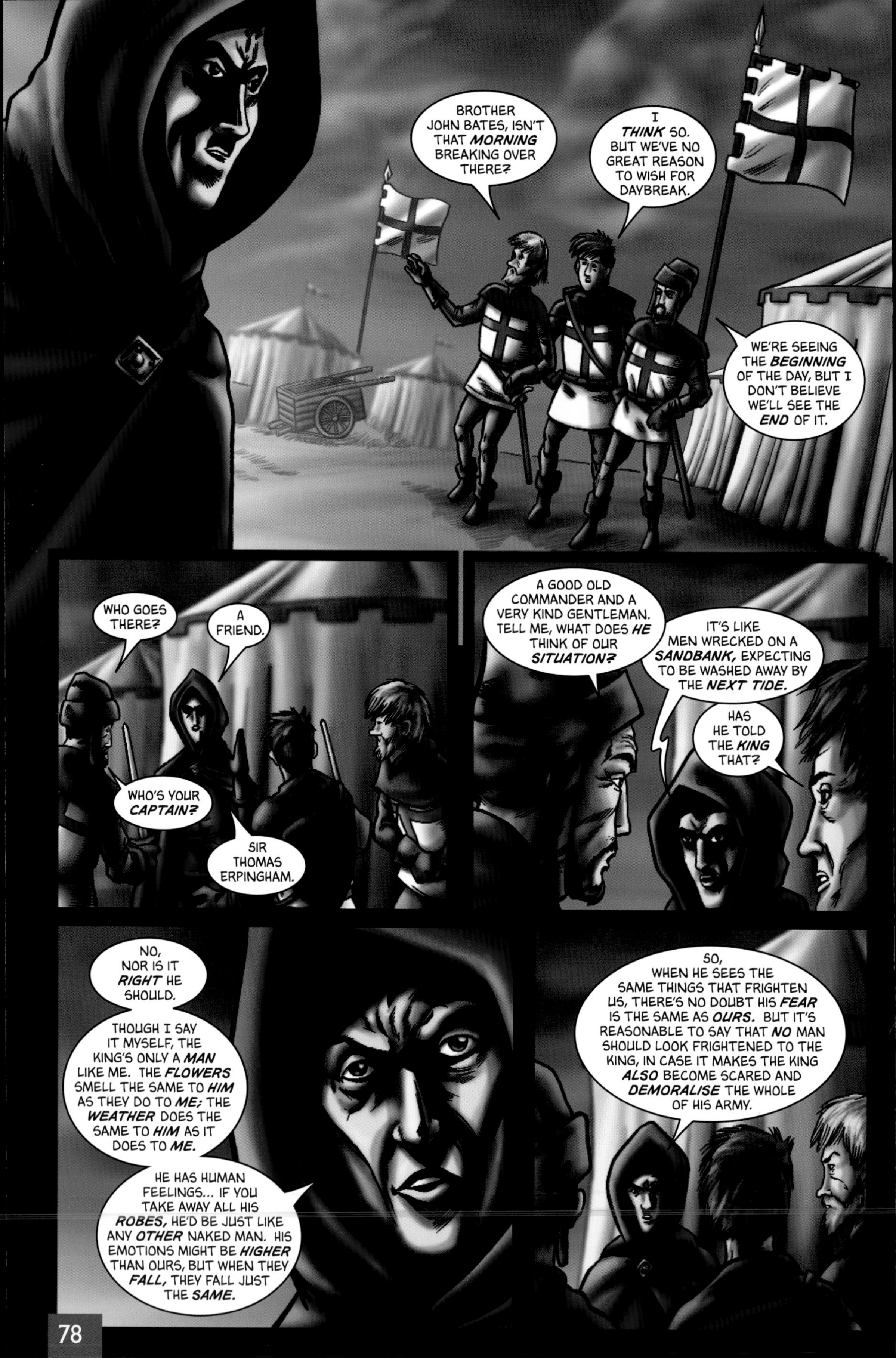
BROTHER JOHN BATES, ISN'T THAT MORNING BREAKING OVER THERE?
I THINK SO. BUT WE'VE NO GREAT REASON TO WISH FOR DAYBREAK.
WE'RE SEEING THE BEGINNING OF THE DAY, BUT I DON'T BELIEVE WE'LL SEE THE END OF IT.
WHO GOES THERE?
A FRIEND.
WHO'S YOUR CAPTAIN?
SIR THOMAS ERPINGHAM.
A GOOD OLD COMMANDER AND A VERY KIND GENTLEMAN. TELL ME, WHAT DOES HE THINK OF OUR SITUATION?
IT'S LIKE MEN WRECKED ON A SANDBANK, EXPECTING TO BE WASHED AWAY BY THE NEXT TIDE.
HAS HE TOLD THE KING THAT?
NO, NOR IS IT RIGHT HE SHOULD.
THOUGH I SAY IT MYSELF, THE KING'S ONLY A MAN LIKE ME. THE FLOWERS SMELL THE SAME TO HIM AS THEY DO TO ME; THE WEATHER DOES THE SAME TO HIM AS IT DOES TO ME.
HE HAS HUMAN FEELINGS... IF YOU TAKE AWAY ALL HIS ROBES, HE'D BE JUST LIKE ANY OTHER NAKED MAN. HIS EMOTIONS MIGHT BE HIGHER THAN OURS, BUT WHEN THEY FALL, THEY FALL JUST THE SAME.
SO, WHEN HE SEES THE SAME THINGS THAT FRIGHTEN US, THERE'S NO DOUBT HIS FEAR IS THE SAME AS OURS. BUT IT'S REASONABLE TO SAY THAT NO MAN SHOULD LOOK FRIGHTENED TO THE KING, IN CASE IT MAKES THE KING ALSO BECOME SCARED AND DEMORALISE THE WHOLE OF HIS ARMY.

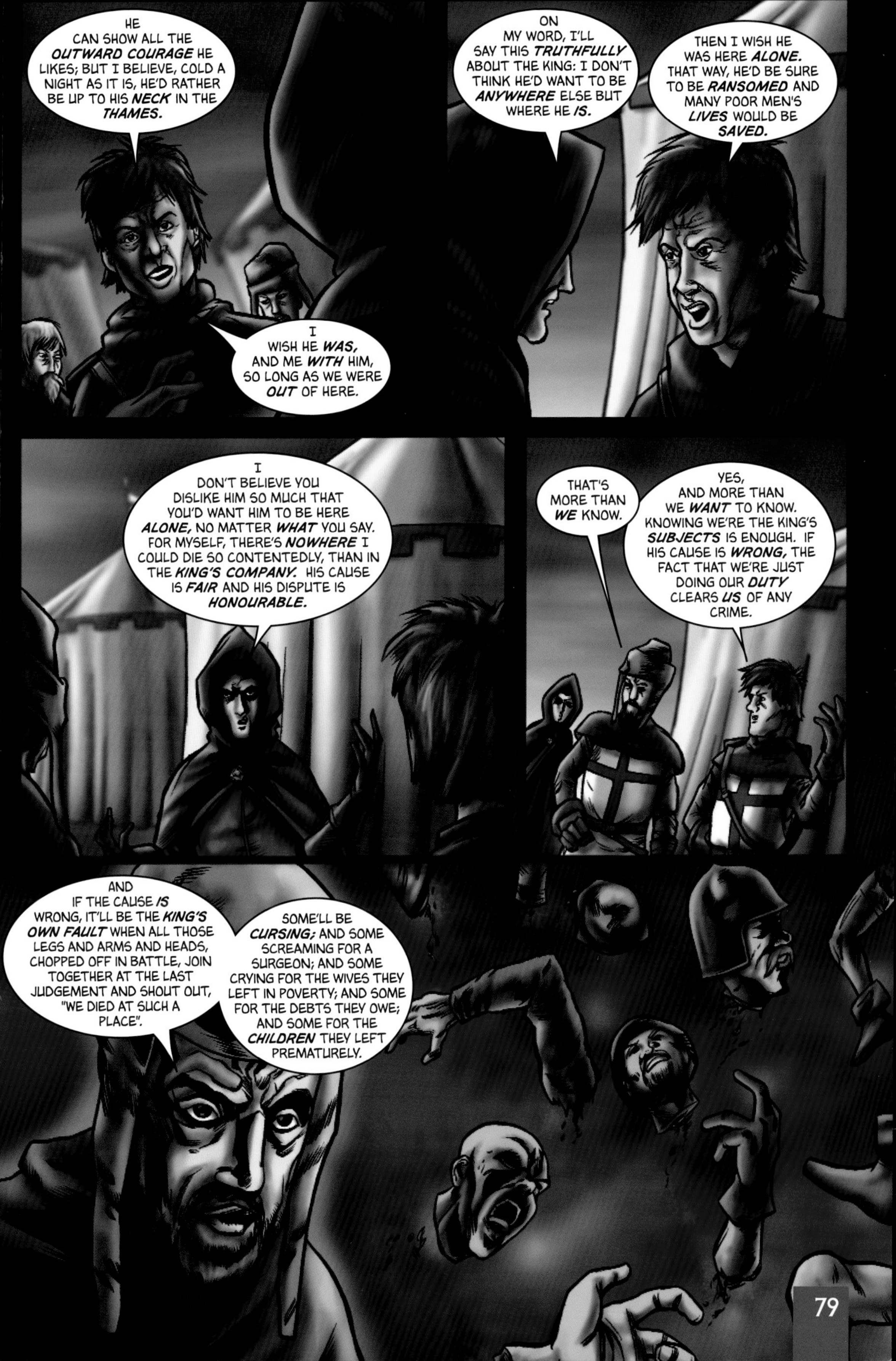

HE CAN SHOW ALL THE OUTWARD COURAGE HE LIKES; BUT I BELIEVE, COLD A NIGHT AS IT IS, HE'D RATHER BE UP TO HIS NECK IN THE THAMES.
I WISH HE WAS, AND ME WITH HIM, SO LONG AS WE WERE OUT OF HERE.
ON MY WORD, I'LL SAY THIS TRUTHFULLY ABOUT THE KING: I DON'T THINK HE'D WANT TO BE ANYWHERE ELSE BUT WHERE HE IS.
THEN I WISH HE WAS HERE ALONE. THAT WAY, HE'D BE SURE TO BE RANSOMED AND MANY POOR MEN'S LIVES WOULD BE SAVED.
I DON'T BELIEVE YOU DISLIKE HIM SO MUCH THAT YOU'D WANT HIM TO BE HERE ALONE, NO MATTER WHAT YOU SAY. FOR MYSELF, THERE'S NOWHERE I COULD DIE SO CONTENTEDLY, THAN IN THE KING'S COMPANY. HIS CAUSE IS FAIR AND HIS DISPUTE IS HONOURABLE.
THAT'S MORE THAN WE KNOW.
YES, AND MORE THAN WE WANT TO KNOW. KNOWING WE'RE THE KING'S SUBJECTS IS ENOUGH. IF HIS CAUSE IS WRONG, THE FACT THAT WE'RE JUST DOING OUR DUTY CLEARS US OF ANY CRIME.
AND IF THE CAUSE IS WRONG, IT'LL BE THE KING'S OWN FAULT WHEN ALL THOSE LEGS AND ARMS AND HEADS, CHOPPED OFF IN BATTLE, JOIN TOGETHER AT THE LAST JUDGEMENT AND SHOUT OUT, "WE DIED AT SUCH A PLACE".
SOME'LL BE CURSING; AND SOME SCREAMING FOR A SURGEON; AND SOME CRYING FOR THE WIVES THEY LEFT IN POVERTY; AND SOME FOR THE DEBTS THEY OWE; AND SOME FOR THE CHILDREN THEY LEFT PREMATURELY.

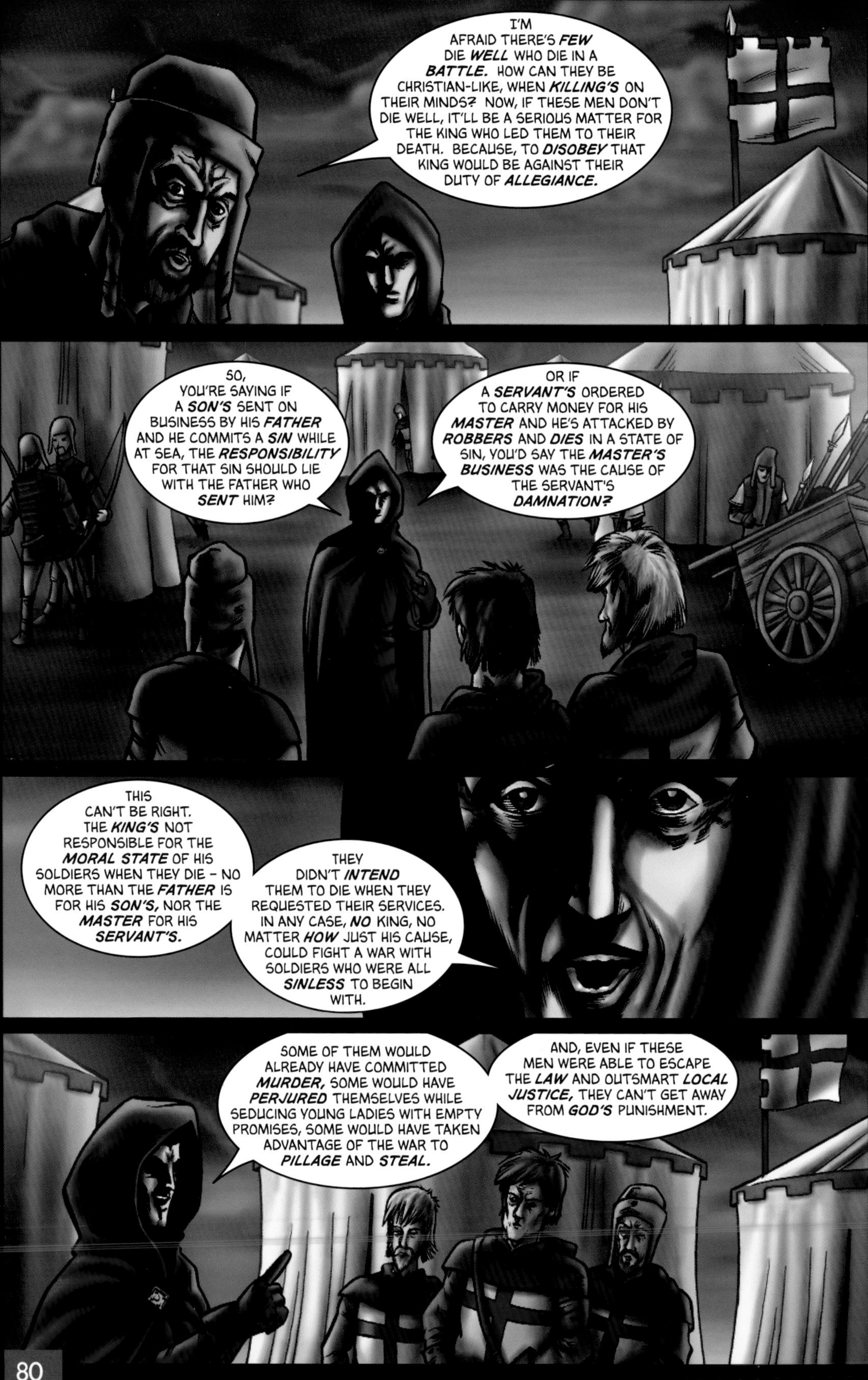
I'M AFRAID THERE'S *FEW* DIE *WELL* WHO DIE IN A *BATTLE.* HOW CAN THEY BE CHRISTIAN-LIKE, WHEN *KILLING'S* ON THEIR MINDS? NOW, IF THESE MEN DON'T DIE WELL, IT'LL BE A SERIOUS MATTER FOR THE KING WHO LED THEM TO THEIR DEATH. BECAUSE, TO *DISOBEY* THAT KING WOULD BE AGAINST THEIR DUTY OF *ALLEGIANCE.*
SO, YOU'RE SAYING IF A *SON'S* SENT ON BUSINESS BY HIS *FATHER* AND HE COMMITS A *SIN* WHILE AT SEA, THE *RESPONSIBILITY* FOR THAT SIN SHOULD LIE WITH THE FATHER WHO *SENT* HIM?
OR IF A *SERVANT'S* ORDERED TO CARRY MONEY FOR HIS *MASTER* AND HE'S ATTACKED BY *ROBBERS* AND *DIES* IN A STATE OF SIN, YOU'D SAY THE *MASTER'S BUSINESS* WAS THE CAUSE OF THE SERVANT'S *DAMNATION?*
THIS CAN'T BE RIGHT. THE *KING'S* NOT RESPONSIBLE FOR THE *MORAL STATE* OF HIS SOLDIERS WHEN THEY DIE – NO MORE THAN THE *FATHER* IS FOR HIS *SON'S,* NOR THE *MASTER* FOR HIS *SERVANT'S.*
THEY DIDN'T *INTEND* THEM TO DIE WHEN THEY REQUESTED THEIR SERVICES. IN ANY CASE, *NO* KING, NO MATTER *HOW* JUST HIS CAUSE, COULD FIGHT A WAR WITH SOLDIERS WHO WERE ALL *SINLESS* TO BEGIN WITH.
SOME OF THEM WOULD ALREADY HAVE COMMITTED *MURDER,* SOME WOULD HAVE *PERJURED* THEMSELVES WHILE SEDUCING YOUNG LADIES WITH EMPTY PROMISES, SOME WOULD HAVE TAKEN ADVANTAGE OF THE WAR TO *PILLAGE* AND *STEAL.*
AND, EVEN IF THESE MEN WERE ABLE TO ESCAPE THE *LAW* AND OUTSMART *LOCAL JUSTICE,* THEY CAN'T GET AWAY FROM *GOD'S* PUNISHMENT.

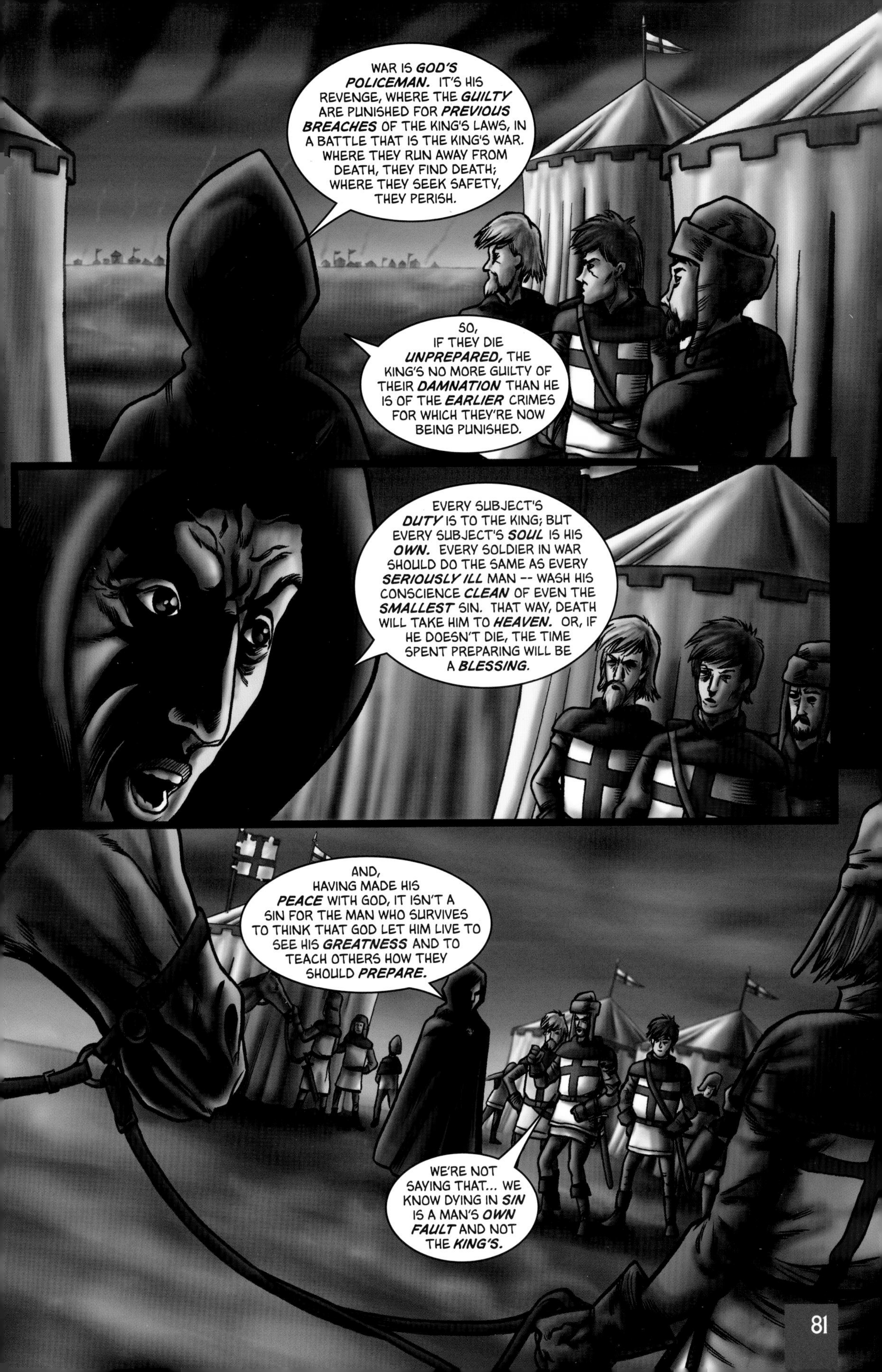
WAR IS GOD'S POLICEMAN. IT'S HIS REVENGE, WHERE THE GUILTY ARE PUNISHED FOR PREVIOUS BREACHES OF THE KING'S LAWS, IN A BATTLE THAT IS THE KING'S WAR. WHERE THEY RUN AWAY FROM DEATH, THEY FIND DEATH; WHERE THEY SEEK SAFETY, THEY PERISH.
SO, IF THEY DIE UNPREPARED, THE KING'S NO MORE GUILTY OF THEIR DAMNATION THAN HE IS OF THE EARLIER CRIMES FOR WHICH THEY'RE NOW BEING PUNISHED.
EVERY SUBJECT'S DUTY IS TO THE KING; BUT EVERY SUBJECT'S SOUL IS HIS OWN. EVERY SOLDIER IN WAR SHOULD DO THE SAME AS EVERY SERIOUSLY ILL MAN -- WASH HIS CONSCIENCE CLEAN OF EVEN THE SMALLEST SIN. THAT WAY, DEATH WILL TAKE HIM TO HEAVEN. OR, IF HE DOESN'T DIE, THE TIME SPENT PREPARING WILL BE A BLESSING.
AND, HAVING MADE HIS PEACE WITH GOD, IT ISN'T A SIN FOR THE MAN WHO SURVIVES TO THINK THAT GOD LET HIM LIVE TO SEE HIS GREATNESS AND TO TEACH OTHERS HOW THEY SHOULD PREPARE.
WE'RE NOT SAYING THAT... WE KNOW DYING IN SIN IS A MAN'S OWN FAULT AND NOT THE KING'S.

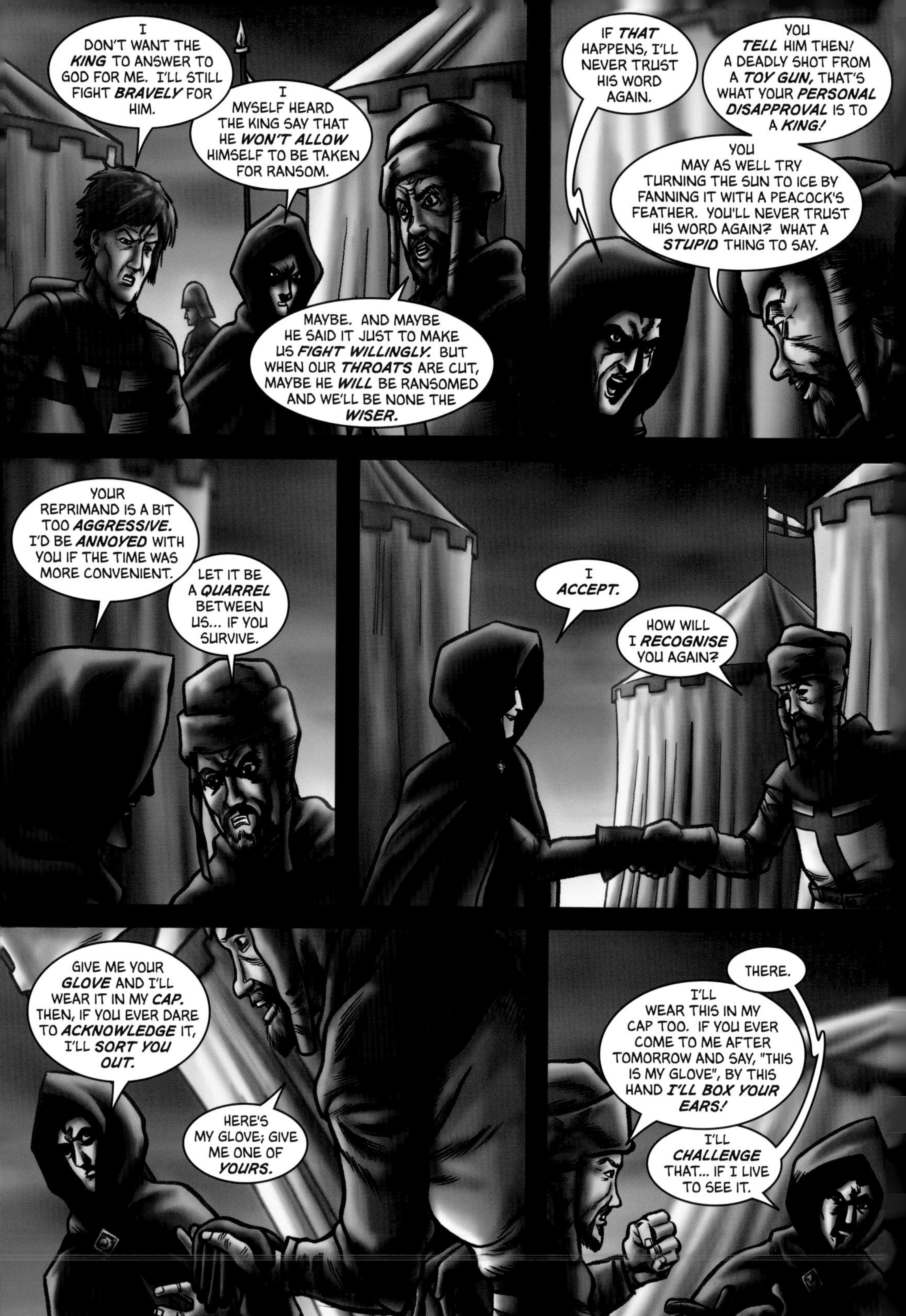
I DON'T WANT THE KING TO ANSWER TO GOD FOR ME. I'LL STILL FIGHT BRAVELY FOR HIM.
I MYSELF HEARD THE KING SAY THAT HE WON'T ALLOW HIMSELF TO BE TAKEN FOR RANSOM.
MAYBE. AND MAYBE HE SAID IT JUST TO MAKE US FIGHT WILLINGLY. BUT WHEN OUR THROATS ARE CUT, MAYBE HE WILL BE RANSOMED AND WE'LL BE NONE THE WISER.
IF THAT HAPPENS, I'LL NEVER TRUST HIS WORD AGAIN.
YOU TELL HIM THEN! A DEADLY SHOT FROM A TOY GUN, THAT'S WHAT YOUR PERSONAL DISAPPROVAL IS TO A KING!
YOU MAY AS WELL TRY TURNING THE SUN TO ICE BY FANNING IT WITH A PEACOCK'S FEATHER. YOU'LL NEVER TRUST HIS WORD AGAIN? WHAT A STUPID THING TO SAY.
YOUR REPRIMAND IS A BIT TOO AGGRESSIVE. I'D BE ANNOYED WITH YOU IF THE TIME WAS MORE CONVENIENT.
LET IT BE A QUARREL BETWEEN US... IF YOU SURVIVE.
I ACCEPT.
HOW WILL I RECOGNISE YOU AGAIN?
GIVE ME YOUR GLOVE AND I'LL WEAR IT IN MY CAP. THEN, IF YOU EVER DARE TO ACKNOWLEDGE IT, I'LL SORT YOU OUT.
HERE'S MY GLOVE; GIVE ME ONE OF YOURS.
THERE.
I'LL WEAR THIS IN MY CAP TOO. IF YOU EVER COME TO ME AFTER TOMORROW AND SAY, "THIS IS MY GLOVE", BY THIS HAND I'LL BOX YOUR EARS!
I'LL CHALLENGE THAT... IF I LIVE TO SEE IT.

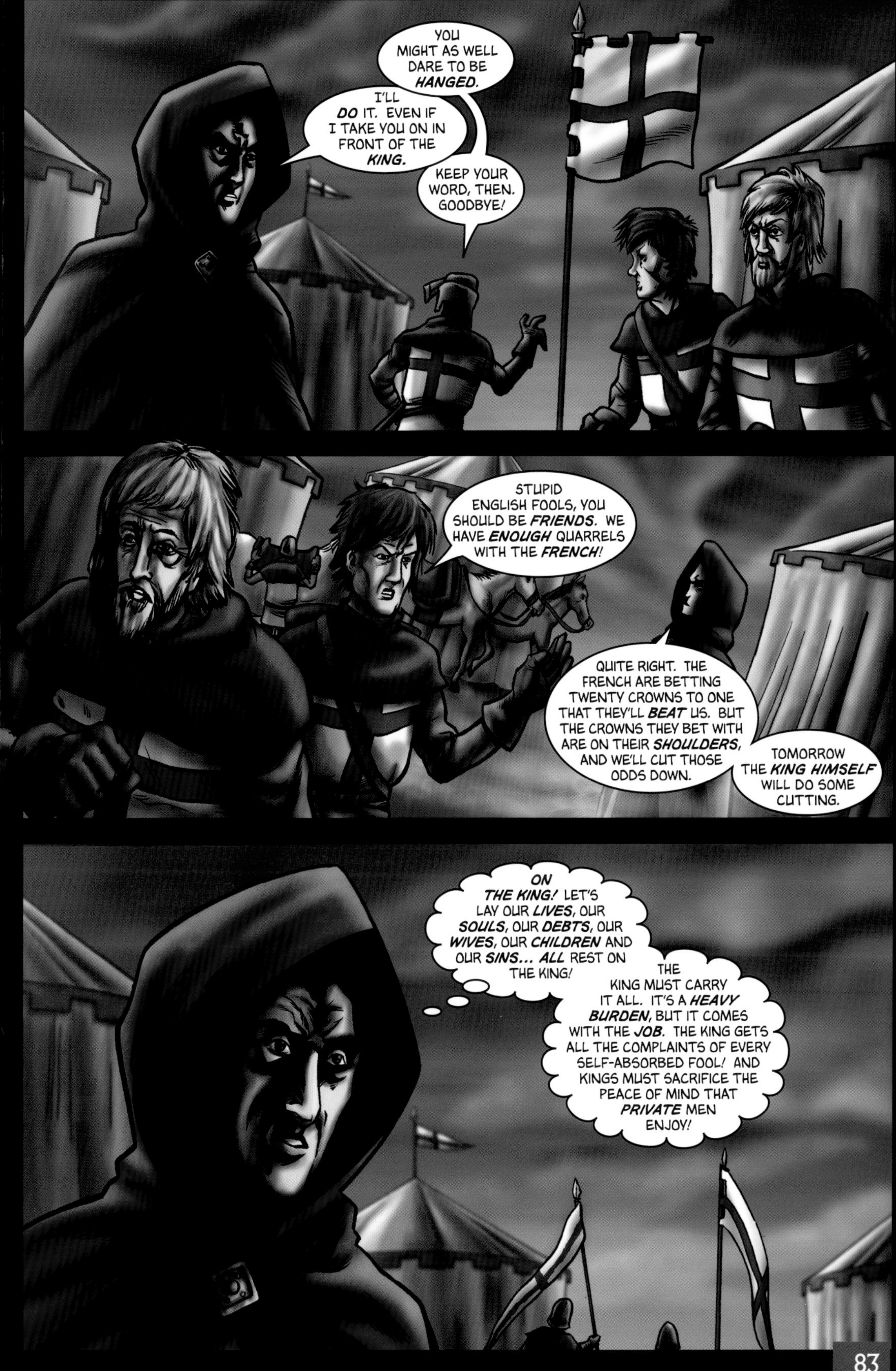
YOU MIGHT AS WELL DARE TO BE HANGED.
I'LL DO IT. EVEN IF I TAKE YOU ON IN FRONT OF THE KING.
KEEP YOUR WORD, THEN. GOODBYE!
STUPID ENGLISH FOOLS, YOU SHOULD BE FRIENDS. WE HAVE ENOUGH QUARRELS WITH THE FRENCH!
QUITE RIGHT. THE FRENCH ARE BETTING TWENTY CROWNS TO ONE THAT THEY'LL BEAT US. BUT THE CROWNS THEY BET WITH ARE ON THEIR SHOULDERS, AND WE'LL CUT THOSE ODDS DOWN.
TOMORROW THE KING HIMSELF WILL DO SOME CUTTING.
ON THE KING! LET'S LAY OUR LIVES, OUR SOULS, OUR DEBTS, OUR WIVES, OUR CHILDREN AND OUR SINS... ALL REST ON THE KING!
THE KING MUST CARRY IT ALL. IT'S A HEAVY BURDEN, BUT IT COMES WITH THE JOB. THE KING GETS ALL THE COMPLAINTS OF EVERY SELF-ABSORBED FOOL! AND KINGS MUST SACRIFICE THE PEACE OF MIND THAT PRIVATE MEN ENJOY!

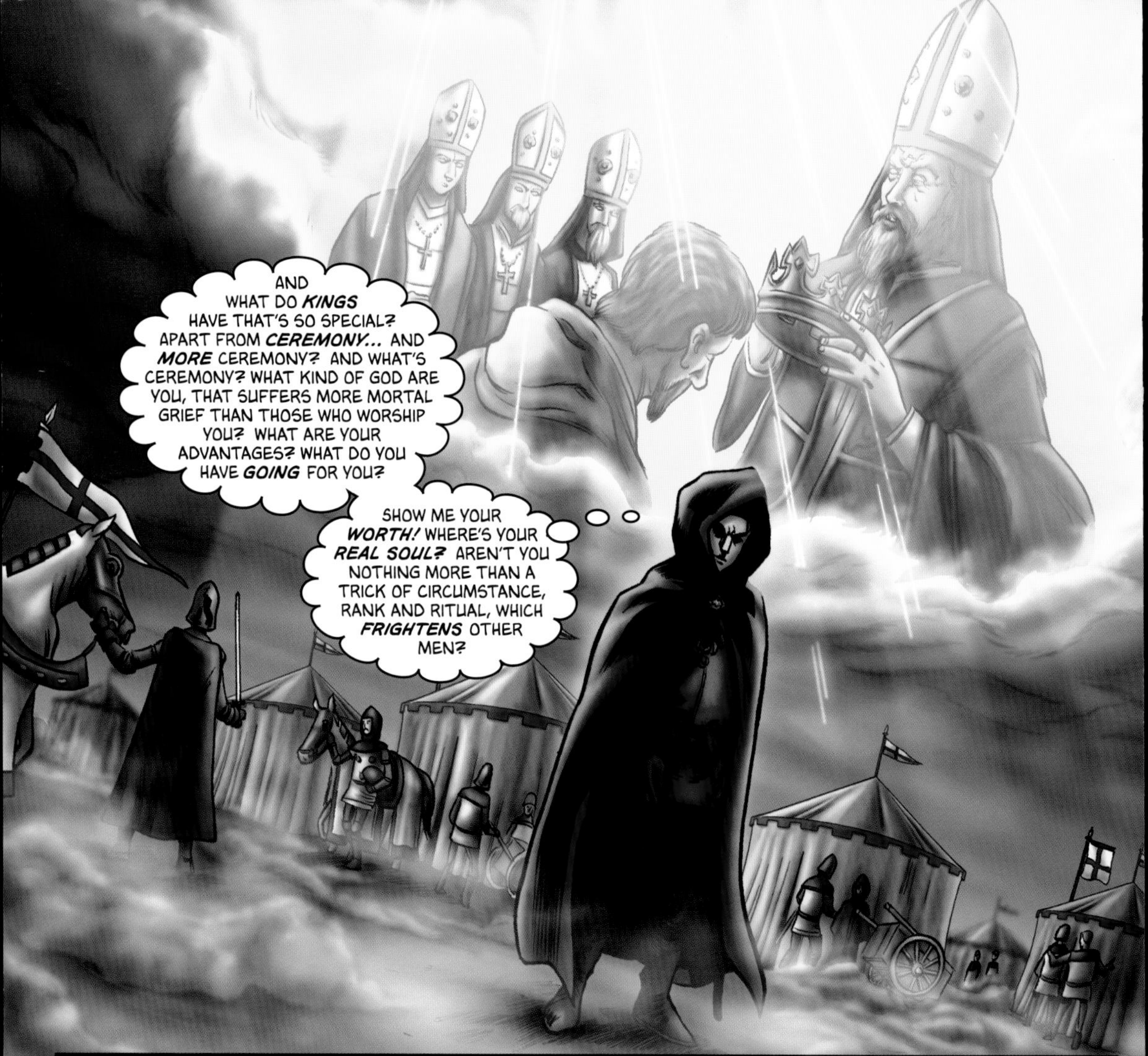
AND WHAT DO KINGS HAVE THAT'S SO SPECIAL? APART FROM CEREMONY... AND MORE CEREMONY? AND WHAT'S CEREMONY? WHAT KIND OF GOD ARE YOU, THAT SUFFERS MORE MORTAL GRIEF THAN THOSE WHO WORSHIP YOU? WHAT ARE YOUR ADVANTAGES? WHAT DO YOU HAVE GOING FOR YOU?
SHOW ME YOUR WORTH! WHERE'S YOUR REAL SOUL? AREN'T YOU NOTHING MORE THAN A TRICK OF CIRCUMSTANCE, RANK AND RITUAL, WHICH FRIGHTENS OTHER MEN?

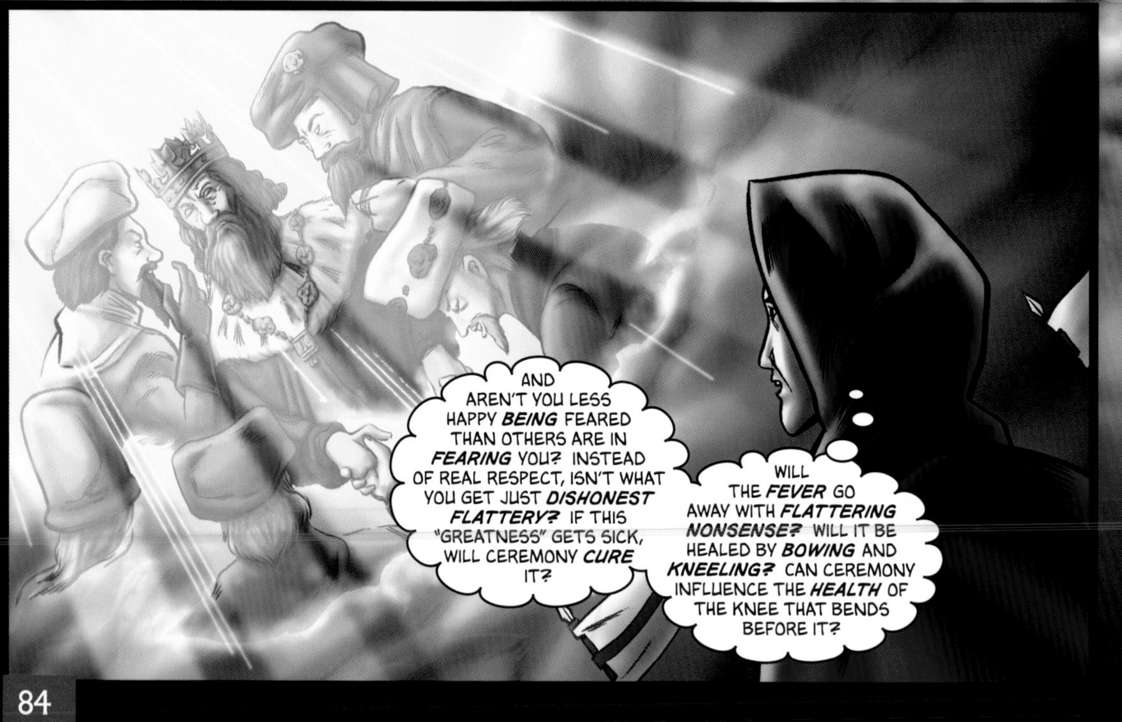
AND AREN'T YOU LESS HAPPY BEING FEARED THAN OTHERS ARE IN FEARING YOU? INSTEAD OF REAL RESPECT, ISN'T WHAT YOU GET JUST DISHONEST FLATTERY? IF THIS "GREATNESS" GETS SICK, WILL CEREMONY CURE IT?
WILL THE FEVER GO AWAY WITH FLATTERING NONSENSE? WILL IT BE HEALED BY BOWING AND KNEELING? CAN CEREMONY INFLUENCE THE HEALTH OF THE KNEE THAT BENDS BEFORE IT?

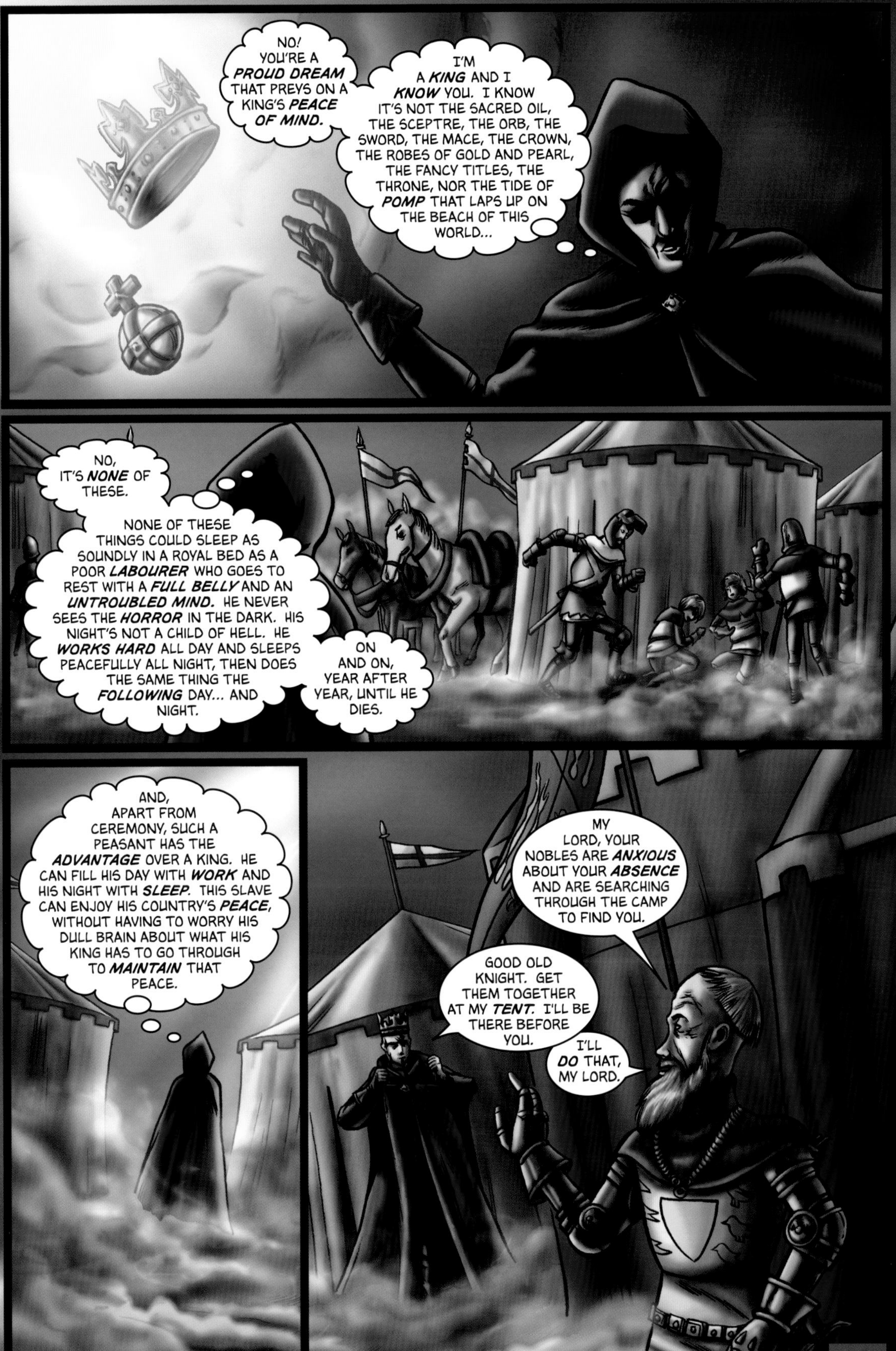
NO! YOU'RE A PROUD DREAM THAT PREYS ON A KING'S PEACE OF MIND.
I'M A KING AND I KNOW YOU. I KNOW IT'S NOT THE SACRED OIL, THE SCEPTRE, THE ORB, THE SWORD, THE MACE, THE CROWN, THE ROBES OF GOLD AND PEARL, THE FANCY TITLES, THE THRONE, NOR THE TIDE OF POMP THAT LAPS UP ON THE BEACH OF THIS WORLD...
NO, IT'S NONE OF THESE.
NONE OF THESE THINGS COULD SLEEP AS SOUNDLY IN A ROYAL BED AS A POOR LABOURER WHO GOES TO REST WITH A FULL BELLY AND AN UNTROUBLED MIND. HE NEVER SEES THE HORROR IN THE DARK. HIS NIGHT'S NOT A CHILD OF HELL. HE WORKS HARD ALL DAY AND SLEEPS PEACEFULLY ALL NIGHT, THEN DOES THE SAME THING THE FOLLOWING DAY... AND NIGHT.
ON AND ON, YEAR AFTER YEAR, UNTIL HE DIES.
AND, APART FROM CEREMONY, SUCH A PEASANT HAS THE ADVANTAGE OVER A KING. HE CAN FILL HIS DAY WITH WORK AND HIS NIGHT WITH SLEEP. THIS SLAVE CAN ENJOY HIS COUNTRY'S PEACE, WITHOUT HAVING TO WORRY HIS DULL BRAIN ABOUT WHAT HIS KING HAS TO GO THROUGH TO MAINTAIN THAT PEACE.
MY LORD, YOUR NOBLES ARE ANXIOUS ABOUT YOUR ABSENCE AND ARE SEARCHING THROUGH THE CAMP TO FIND YOU.
GOOD OLD KNIGHT. GET THEM TOGETHER AT MY TENT. I'LL BE THERE BEFORE YOU.
I'LL DO THAT, MY LORD.

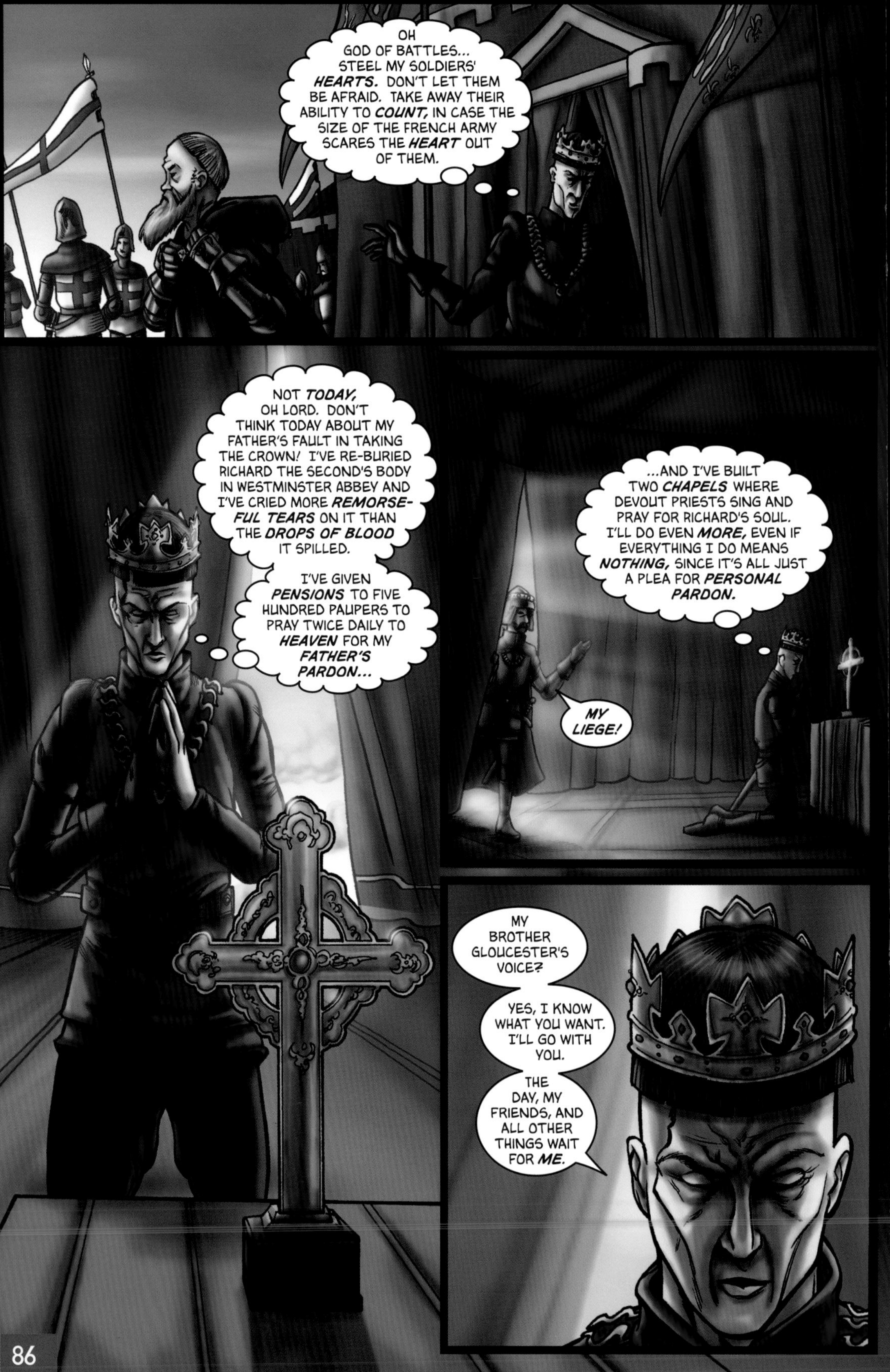
OH GOD OF BATTLES... STEEL MY SOLDIERS' **HEARTS.** DON'T LET THEM BE AFRAID. TAKE AWAY THEIR ABILITY TO **COUNT,** IN CASE THE SIZE OF THE FRENCH ARMY SCARES THE **HEART** OUT OF THEM.
NOT **TODAY,** OH LORD. DON'T THINK TODAY ABOUT MY FATHER'S FAULT IN TAKING THE CROWN! I'VE RE-BURIED RICHARD THE SECOND'S BODY IN WESTMINSTER ABBEY AND I'VE CRIED MORE **REMORSEFUL TEARS** ON IT THAN THE **DROPS OF BLOOD** IT SPILLED.
I'VE GIVEN **PENSIONS** TO FIVE HUNDRED PAUPERS TO PRAY TWICE DAILY TO **HEAVEN** FOR MY **FATHER'S PARDON...**
...AND I'VE BUILT TWO **CHAPELS** WHERE DEVOUT PRIESTS SING AND PRAY FOR RICHARD'S SOUL. I'LL DO EVEN **MORE,** EVEN IF EVERYTHING I DO MEANS **NOTHING,** SINCE IT'S ALL JUST A PLEA FOR **PERSONAL PARDON.**
MY LIEGE!
MY BROTHER GLOUCESTER'S VOICE?
YES, I KNOW WHAT YOU WANT. I'LL GO WITH YOU.
THE DAY, MY FRIENDS, AND ALL OTHER THINGS WAIT FOR **ME.**

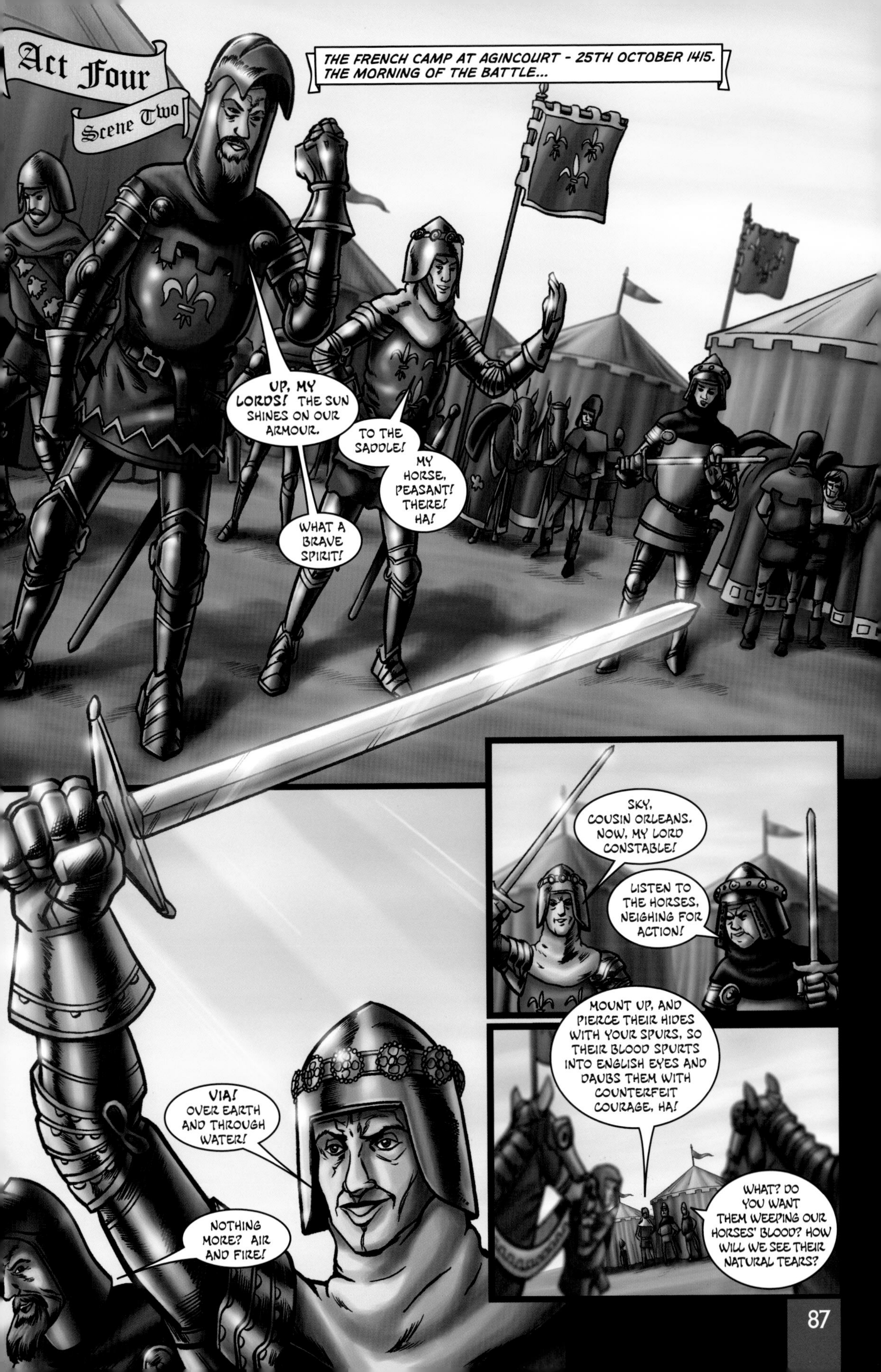

Act Four
Scene Two
THE FRENCH CAMP AT AGINCOURT - 25TH OCTOBER 1415. THE MORNING OF THE BATTLE...
UP, MY LORDS! THE SUN SHINES ON OUR ARMOUR.
WHAT A BRAVE SPIRIT!
TO THE SADDLE!
MY HORSE, PEASANT! THERE! HA!
VIA! OVER EARTH AND THROUGH WATER!
NOTHING MORE? AIR AND FIRE!
SKY, COUSIN ORLEANS. NOW, MY LORD CONSTABLE!
LISTEN TO THE HORSES, NEIGHING FOR ACTION!
MOUNT UP, AND PIERCE THEIR HIDES WITH YOUR SPURS, SO THEIR BLOOD SPURTS INTO ENGLISH EYES AND DAUBS THEM WITH COUNTERFEIT COURAGE, HA!
WHAT? DO YOU WANT THEM WEEPING OUR HORSES' BLOOD? HOW WILL WE SEE THEIR NATURAL TEARS?

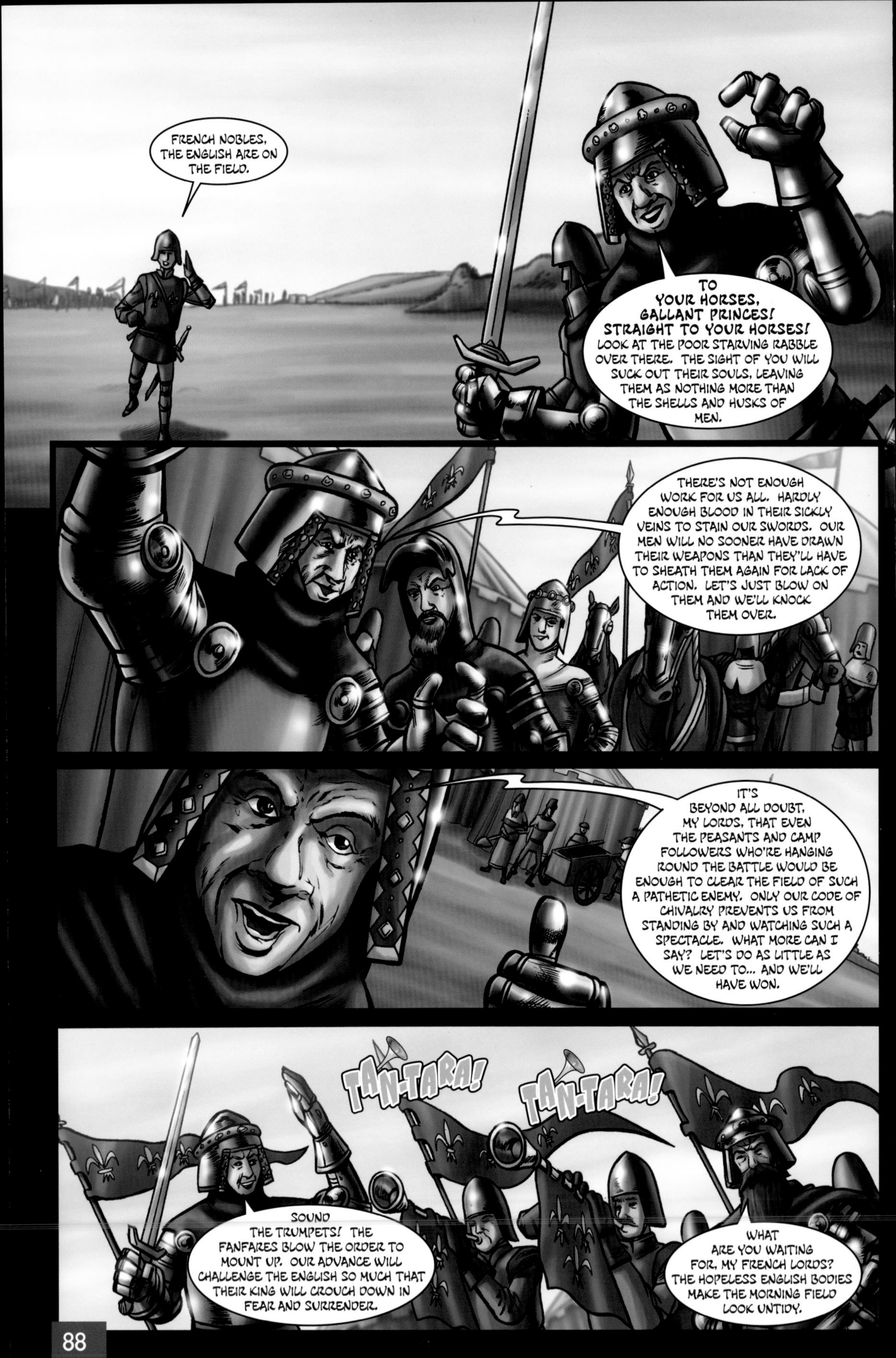

FRENCH NOBLES, THE ENGLISH ARE ON THE FIELD.
TO YOUR HORSES, GALLANT PRINCES! STRAIGHT TO YOUR HORSES! LOOK AT THE POOR STARVING RABBLE OVER THERE. THE SIGHT OF YOU WILL SUCK OUT THEIR SOULS, LEAVING THEM AS NOTHING MORE THAN THE SHELLS AND HUSKS OF MEN.
THERE'S NOT ENOUGH WORK FOR US ALL. HARDLY ENOUGH BLOOD IN THEIR SICKLY VEINS TO STAIN OUR SWORDS. OUR MEN WILL NO SOONER HAVE DRAWN THEIR WEAPONS THAN THEY'LL HAVE TO SHEATH THEM AGAIN FOR LACK OF ACTION. LET'S JUST BLOW ON THEM AND WE'LL KNOCK THEM OVER.
IT'S BEYOND ALL DOUBT, MY LORDS, THAT EVEN THE PEASANTS AND CAMP FOLLOWERS WHO'RE HANGING ROUND THE BATTLE WOULD BE ENOUGH TO CLEAR THE FIELD OF SUCH A PATHETIC ENEMY. ONLY OUR CODE OF CHIVALRY PREVENTS US FROM STANDING BY AND WATCHING SUCH A SPECTACLE. WHAT MORE CAN I SAY? LET'S DO AS LITTLE AS WE NEED TO... AND WE'LL HAVE WON.
TAN-TARA!
TAN-TARA!
SOUND THE TRUMPETS! THE FANFARES BLOW THE ORDER TO MOUNT UP. OUR ADVANCE WILL CHALLENGE THE ENGLISH SO MUCH THAT THEIR KING WILL CROUCH DOWN IN FEAR AND SURRENDER.
WHAT ARE YOU WAITING FOR, MY FRENCH LORDS? THE HOPELESS ENGLISH BODIES MAKE THE MORNING FIELD LOOK UNTIDY.

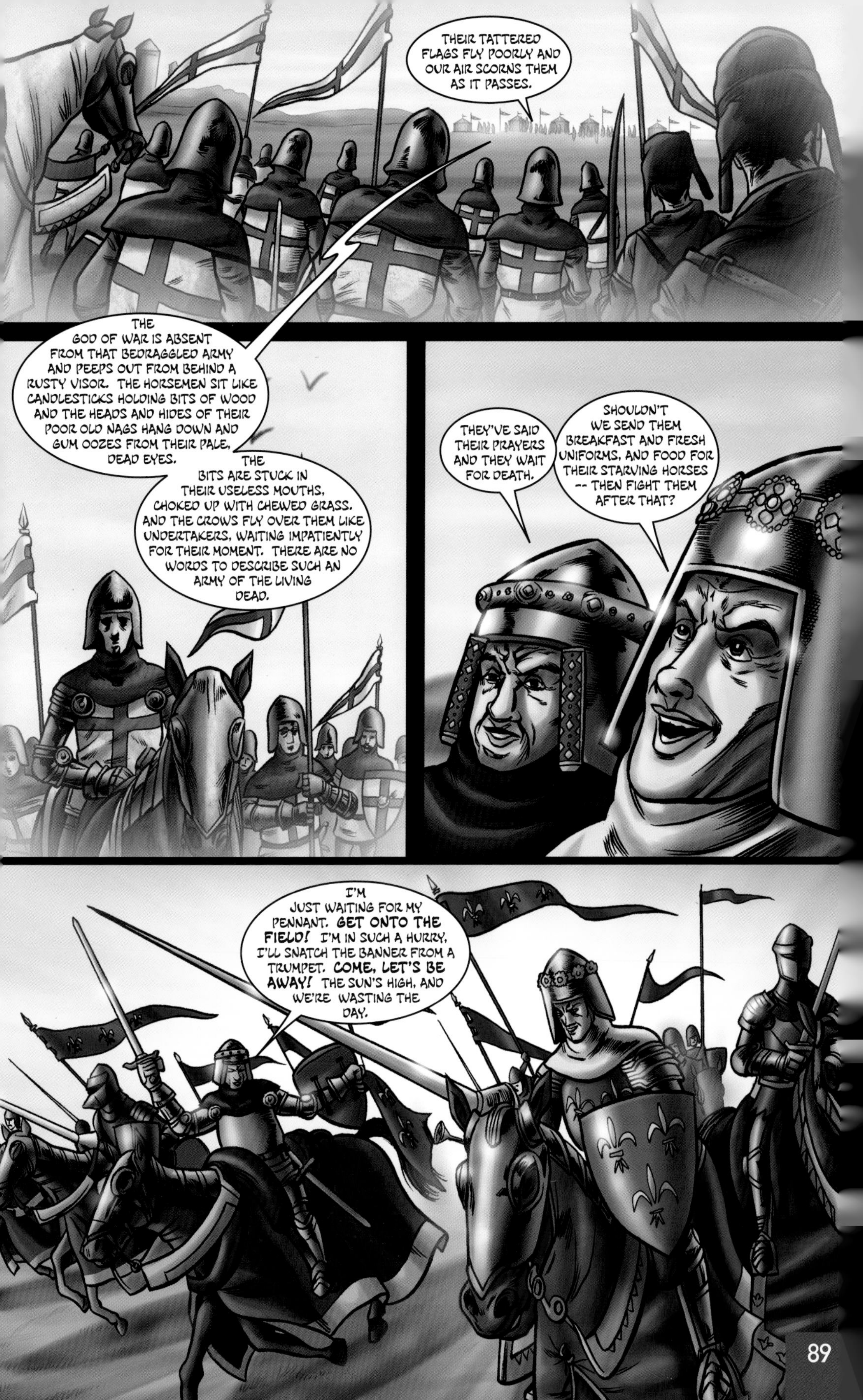
THEIR TATTERED FLAGS FLY POORLY AND OUR AIR SCORNS THEM AS IT PASSES.
THE GOD OF WAR IS ABSENT FROM THAT BEDRAGGLED ARMY AND PEEPS OUT FROM BEHIND A RUSTY VISOR. THE HORSEMEN SIT LIKE CANDLESTICKS HOLDING BITS OF WOOD AND THE HEADS AND HIDES OF THEIR POOR OLD NAGS HANG DOWN AND GUM OOZES FROM THEIR PALE, DEAD EYES.
THE BITS ARE STUCK IN THEIR USELESS MOUTHS, CHOKED UP WITH CHEWED GRASS. AND THE CROWS FLY OVER THEM LIKE UNDERTAKERS, WAITING IMPATIENTLY FOR THEIR MOMENT. THERE ARE NO WORDS TO DESCRIBE SUCH AN ARMY OF THE LIVING DEAD.
THEY'VE SAID THEIR PRAYERS AND THEY WAIT FOR DEATH.
SHOULDN'T WE SEND THEM BREAKFAST AND FRESH UNIFORMS, AND FOOD FOR THEIR STARVING HORSES -- THEN FIGHT THEM AFTER THAT?
I'M JUST WAITING FOR MY PENNANT. GET ONTO THE FIELD! I'M IN SUCH A HURRY, I'LL SNATCH THE BANNER FROM A TRUMPET. COME, LET'S BE AWAY! THE SUN'S HIGH, AND WE'RE WASTING THE DAY.

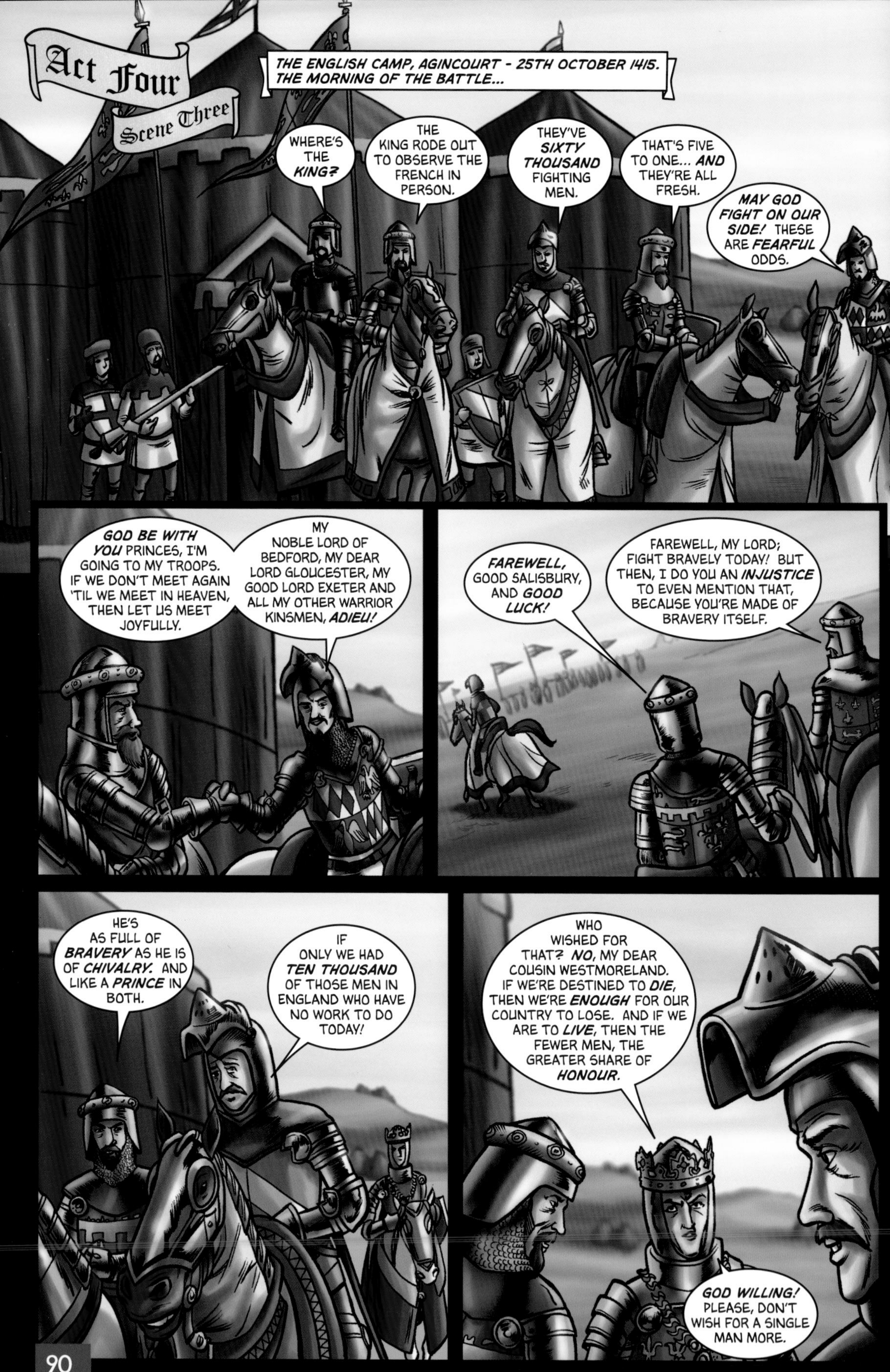
Act Four
Scene Three
THE ENGLISH CAMP, AGINCOURT - 25TH OCTOBER 1415. THE MORNING OF THE BATTLE...
WHERE'S THE KING?
THE KING RODE OUT TO OBSERVE THE FRENCH IN PERSON.
THEY'VE SIXTY THOUSAND FIGHTING MEN.
THAT'S FIVE TO ONE... AND THEY'RE ALL FRESH.
MAY GOD FIGHT ON OUR SIDE! THESE ARE FEARFUL ODDS.
GOD BE WITH YOU PRINCES, I'M GOING TO MY TROOPS. IF WE DON'T MEET AGAIN 'TIL WE MEET IN HEAVEN, THEN LET US MEET JOYFULLY.
MY NOBLE LORD OF BEDFORD, MY DEAR LORD GLOUCESTER, MY GOOD LORD EXETER AND ALL MY OTHER WARRIOR KINSMEN, ADIEU!
FAREWELL, GOOD SALISBURY, AND GOOD LUCK!
FAREWELL, MY LORD; FIGHT BRAVELY TODAY! BUT THEN, I DO YOU AN INJUSTICE TO EVEN MENTION THAT, BECAUSE YOU'RE MADE OF BRAVERY ITSELF.
HE'S AS FULL OF BRAVERY AS HE IS OF CHIVALRY. AND LIKE A PRINCE IN BOTH.
IF ONLY WE HAD TEN THOUSAND OF THOSE MEN IN ENGLAND WHO HAVE NO WORK TO DO TODAY!
WHO WISHED FOR THAT? NO, MY DEAR COUSIN WESTMORELAND. IF WE'RE DESTINED TO DIE, THEN WE'RE ENOUGH FOR OUR COUNTRY TO LOSE. AND IF WE ARE TO LIVE, THEN THE FEWER MEN, THE GREATER SHARE OF HONOUR.
GOD WILLING! PLEASE, DON'T WISH FOR A SINGLE MAN MORE.

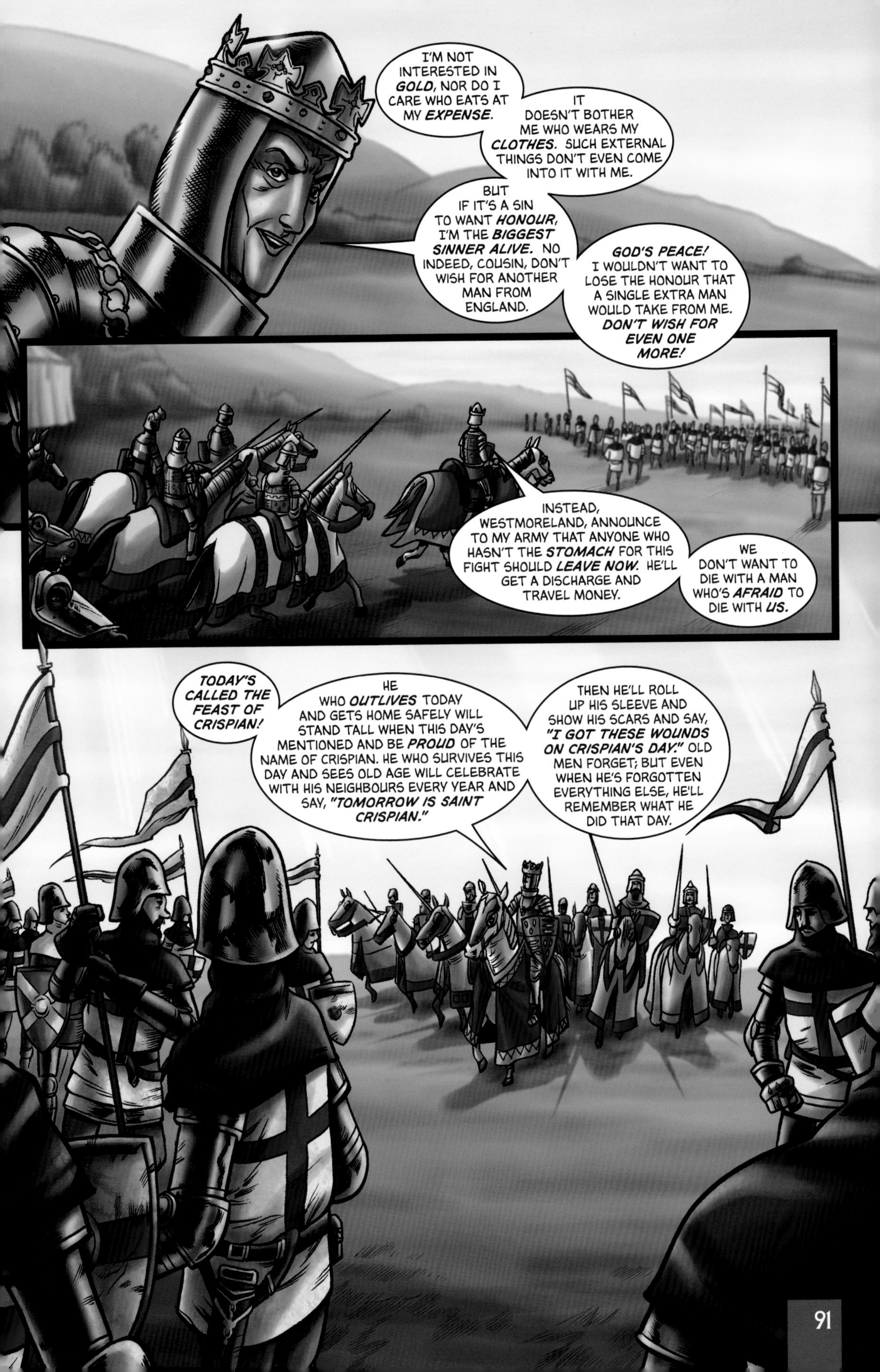

I'M NOT INTERESTED IN GOLD, NOR DO I CARE WHO EATS AT MY EXPENSE.
IT DOESN'T BOTHER ME WHO WEARS MY CLOTHES. SUCH EXTERNAL THINGS DON'T EVEN COME INTO IT WITH ME.
BUT IF IT'S A SIN TO WANT HONOUR, I'M THE BIGGEST SINNER ALIVE. NO INDEED, COUSIN, DON'T WISH FOR ANOTHER MAN FROM ENGLAND.
GOD'S PEACE! I WOULDN'T WANT TO LOSE THE HONOUR THAT A SINGLE EXTRA MAN WOULD TAKE FROM ME. DON'T WISH FOR EVEN ONE MORE!
INSTEAD, WESTMORELAND, ANNOUNCE TO MY ARMY THAT ANYONE WHO HASN'T THE STOMACH FOR THIS FIGHT SHOULD LEAVE NOW. HE'LL GET A DISCHARGE AND TRAVEL MONEY.
WE DON'T WANT TO DIE WITH A MAN WHO'S AFRAID TO DIE WITH US.
TODAY'S CALLED THE FEAST OF CRISPIAN!
HE WHO OUTLIVES TODAY AND GETS HOME SAFELY WILL STAND TALL WHEN THIS DAY'S MENTIONED AND BE PROUD OF THE NAME OF CRISPIAN. HE WHO SURVIVES THIS DAY AND SEES OLD AGE WILL CELEBRATE WITH HIS NEIGHBOURS EVERY YEAR AND SAY, "TOMORROW IS SAINT CRISPIAN."
THEN HE'LL ROLL UP HIS SLEEVE AND SHOW HIS SCARS AND SAY, "I GOT THESE WOUNDS ON CRISPIAN'S DAY." OLD MEN FORGET; BUT EVEN WHEN HE'S FORGOTTEN EVERYTHING ELSE, HE'LL REMEMBER WHAT HE DID THAT DAY.

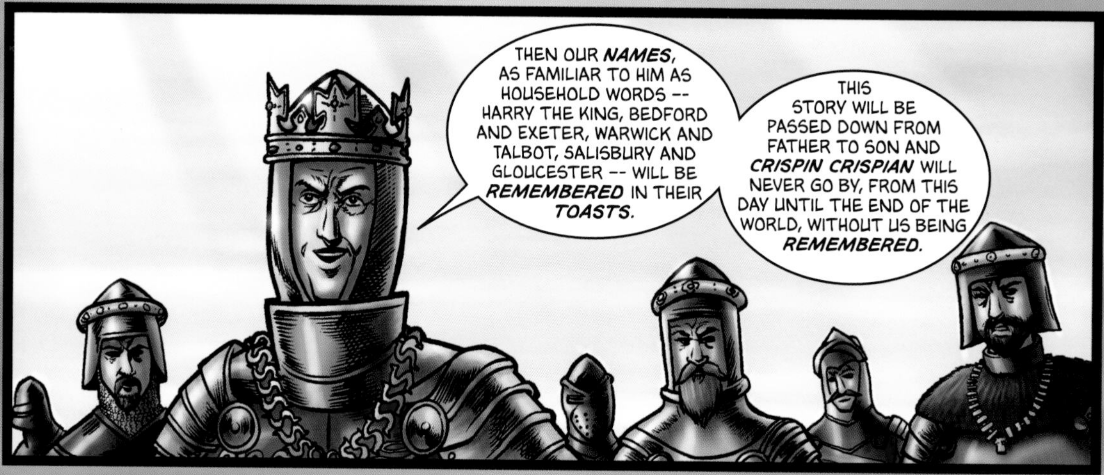
THEN OUR NAMES, AS FAMILIAR TO HIM AS HOUSEHOLD WORDS -- HARRY THE KING, BEDFORD AND EXETER, WARWICK AND TALBOT, SALISBURY AND GLOUCESTER -- WILL BE REMEMBERED IN THEIR TOASTS.
THIS STORY WILL BE PASSED DOWN FROM FATHER TO SON AND CRISPIN CRISPIAN WILL NEVER GO BY, FROM THIS DAY UNTIL THE END OF THE WORLD, WITHOUT US BEING REMEMBERED.

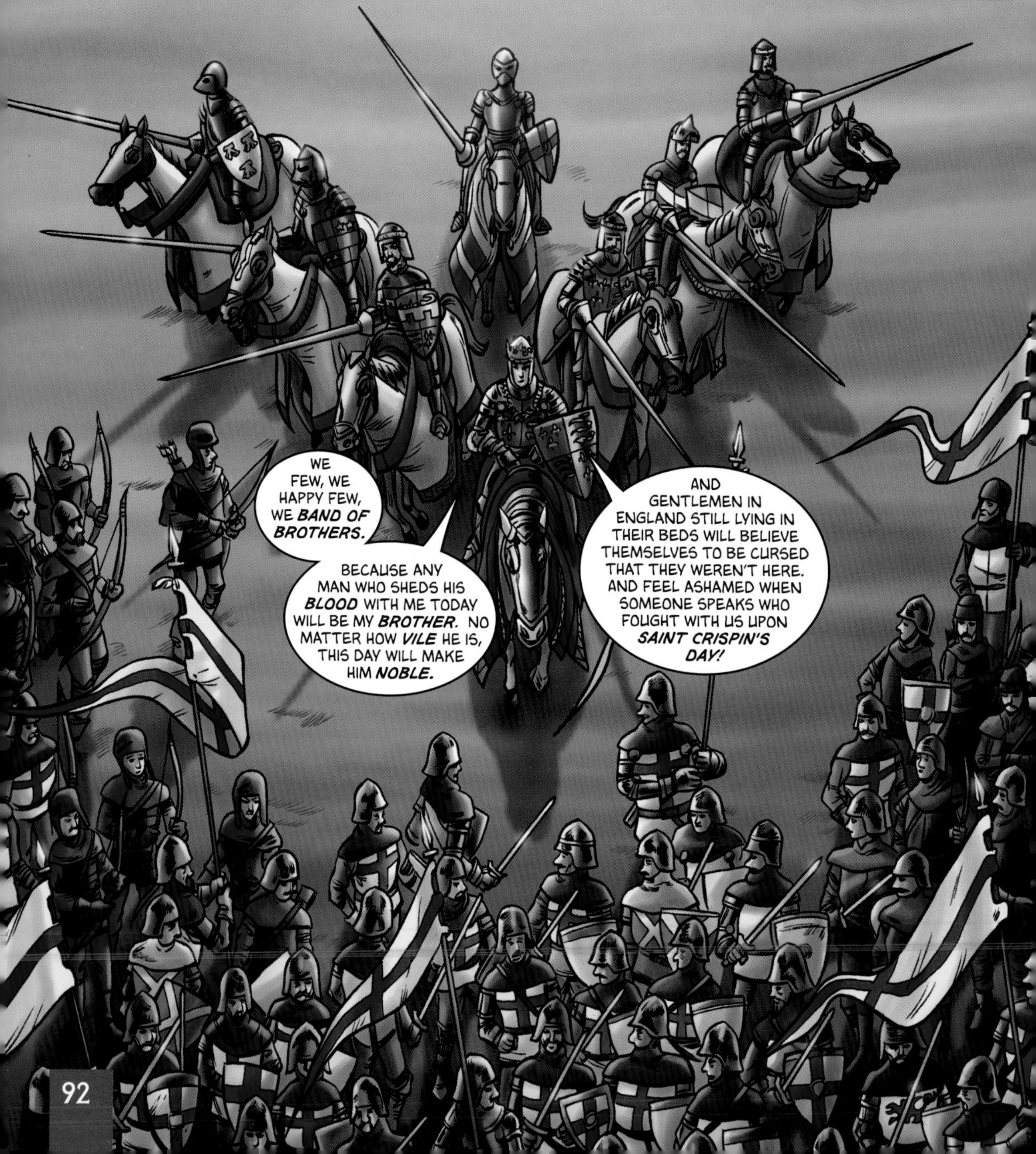
WE FEW, WE HAPPY FEW, WE BAND OF BROTHERS.
BECAUSE ANY MAN WHO SHEDS HIS BLOOD WITH ME TODAY WILL BE MY BROTHER. NO MATTER HOW VILE HE IS, THIS DAY WILL MAKE HIM NOBLE.
AND GENTLEMEN IN ENGLAND STILL LYING IN THEIR BEDS WILL BELIEVE THEMSELVES TO BE CURSED THAT THEY WEREN'T HERE. AND FEEL ASHAMED WHEN SOMEONE SPEAKS WHO FOUGHT WITH US UPON SAINT CRISPIN'S DAY!

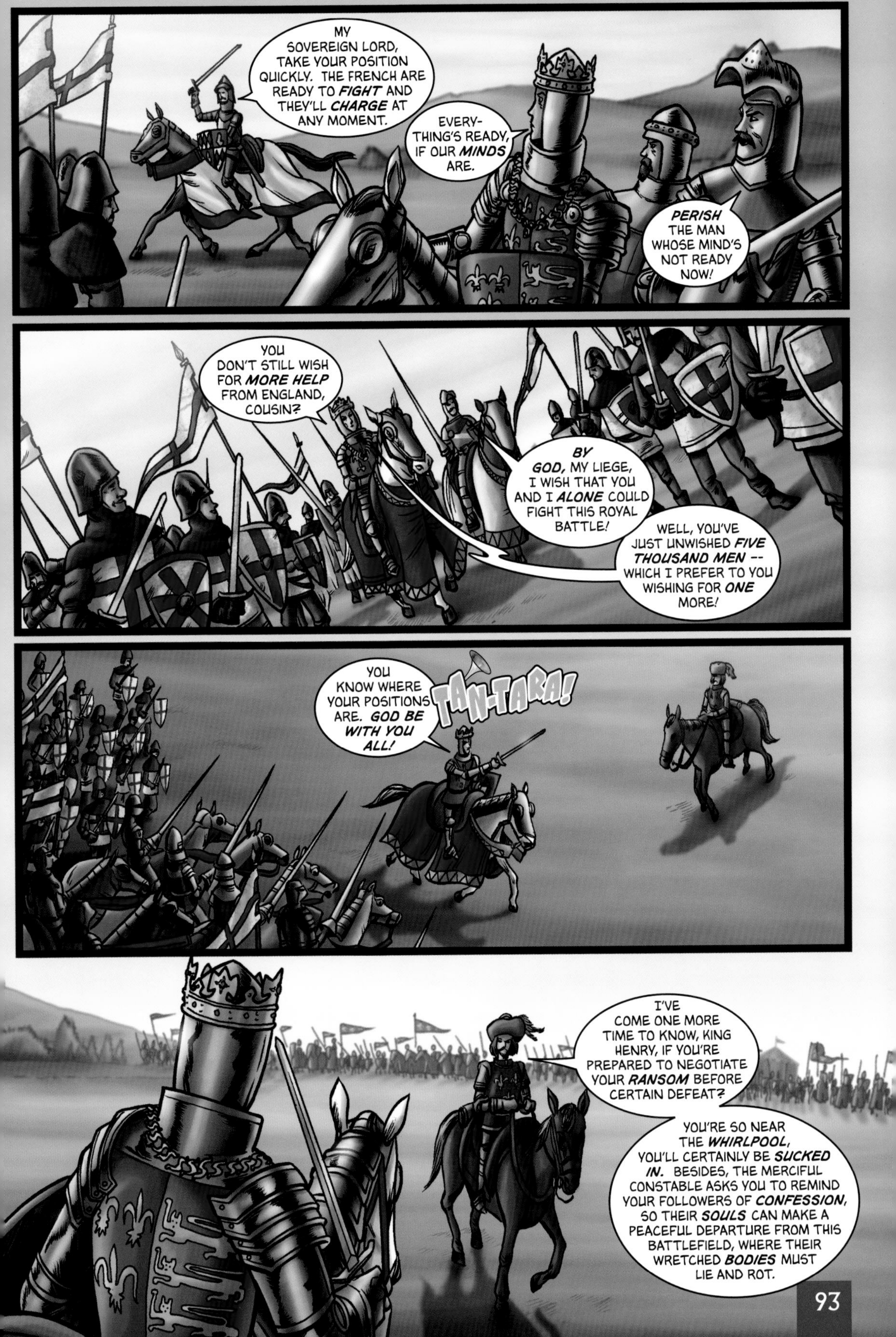
MY SOVEREIGN LORD, TAKE YOUR POSITION QUICKLY. THE FRENCH ARE READY TO FIGHT AND THEY'LL CHARGE AT ANY MOMENT.
EVERY-THING'S READY, IF OUR MINDS ARE.
PERISH THE MAN WHOSE MIND'S NOT READY NOW!
YOU DON'T STILL WISH FOR MORE HELP FROM ENGLAND, COUSIN?
BY GOD, MY LIEGE, I WISH THAT YOU AND I ALONE COULD FIGHT THIS ROYAL BATTLE!
WELL, YOU'VE JUST UNWISHED FIVE THOUSAND MEN -- WHICH I PREFER TO YOU WISHING FOR ONE MORE!
YOU KNOW WHERE YOUR POSITIONS ARE. GOD BE WITH YOU ALL!
TAN-TARA!
I'VE COME ONE MORE TIME TO KNOW, KING HENRY, IF YOU'RE PREPARED TO NEGOTIATE YOUR RANSOM BEFORE CERTAIN DEFEAT?
YOU'RE SO NEAR THE WHIRLPOOL, YOU'LL CERTAINLY BE SUCKED IN. BESIDES, THE MERCIFUL CONSTABLE ASKS YOU TO REMIND YOUR FOLLOWERS OF CONFESSION, SO THEIR SOULS CAN MAKE A PEACEFUL DEPARTURE FROM THIS BATTLEFIELD, WHERE THEIR WRETCHED BODIES MUST LIE AND ROT.

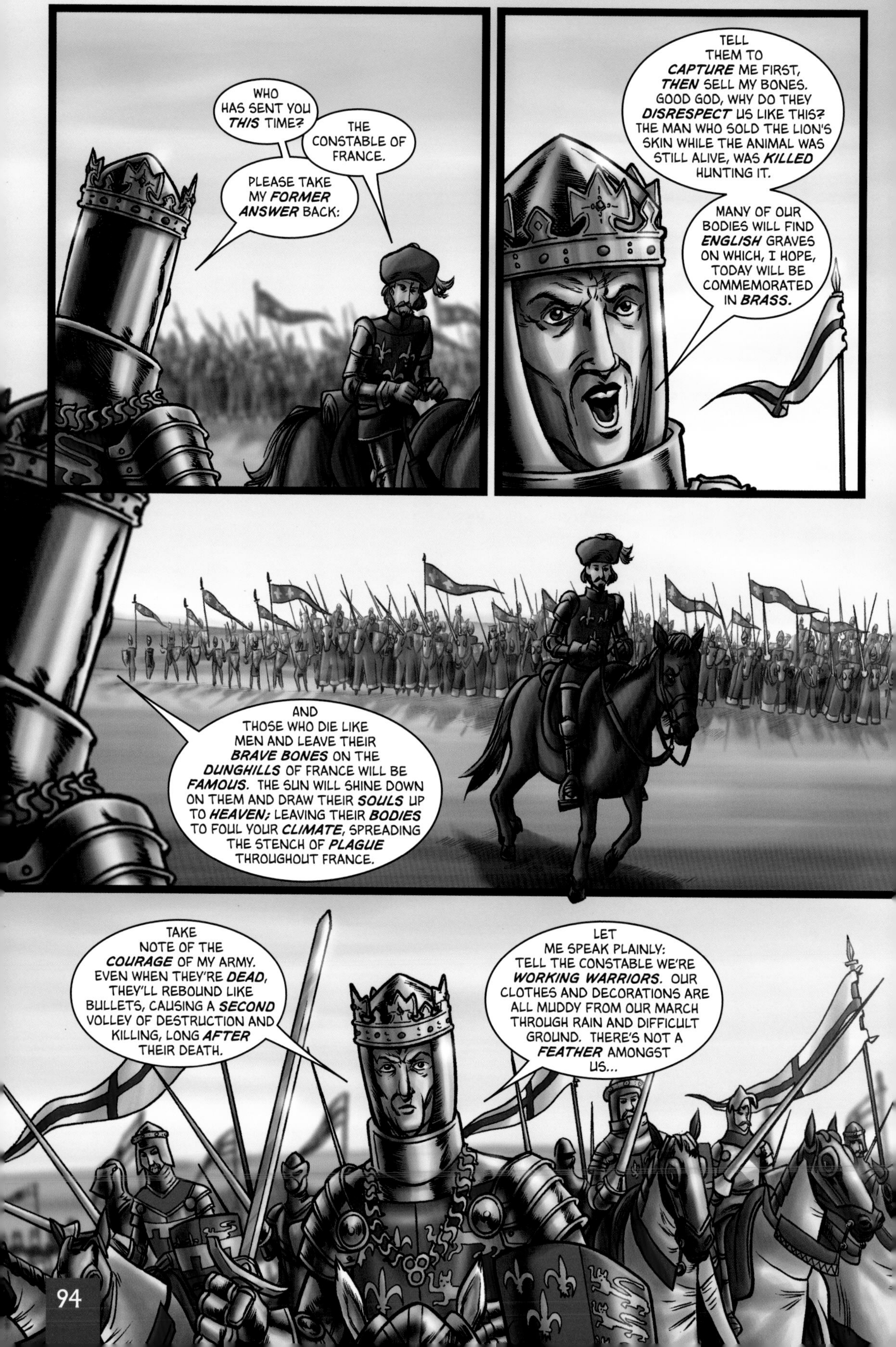
WHO HAS SENT YOU *THIS* TIME?
THE CONSTABLE OF FRANCE.
PLEASE TAKE MY *FORMER ANSWER* BACK:
TELL THEM TO *CAPTURE* ME FIRST, *THEN* SELL MY BONES. GOOD GOD, WHY DO THEY *DISRESPECT* US LIKE THIS? THE MAN WHO SOLD THE LION'S SKIN WHILE THE ANIMAL WAS STILL ALIVE, WAS *KILLED* HUNTING IT.
MANY OF OUR BODIES WILL FIND *ENGLISH* GRAVES ON WHICH, I HOPE, TODAY WILL BE COMMEMORATED IN *BRASS.*
AND THOSE WHO DIE LIKE MEN AND LEAVE THEIR *BRAVE BONES* ON THE *DUNGHILLS* OF FRANCE WILL BE *FAMOUS.* THE SUN WILL SHINE DOWN ON THEM AND DRAW THEIR *SOULS* UP TO *HEAVEN;* LEAVING THEIR *BODIES* TO FOUL YOUR *CLIMATE*, SPREADING THE STENCH OF *PLAGUE* THROUGHOUT FRANCE.
TAKE NOTE OF THE *COURAGE* OF MY ARMY. EVEN WHEN THEY'RE *DEAD*, THEY'LL REBOUND LIKE BULLETS, CAUSING A *SECOND* VOLLEY OF DESTRUCTION AND KILLING, LONG *AFTER* THEIR DEATH.
LET ME SPEAK PLAINLY: TELL THE CONSTABLE WE'RE *WORKING WARRIORS.* OUR CLOTHES AND DECORATIONS ARE ALL MUDDY FROM OUR MARCH THROUGH RAIN AND DIFFICULT GROUND. THERE'S NOT A *FEATHER* AMONGST US...

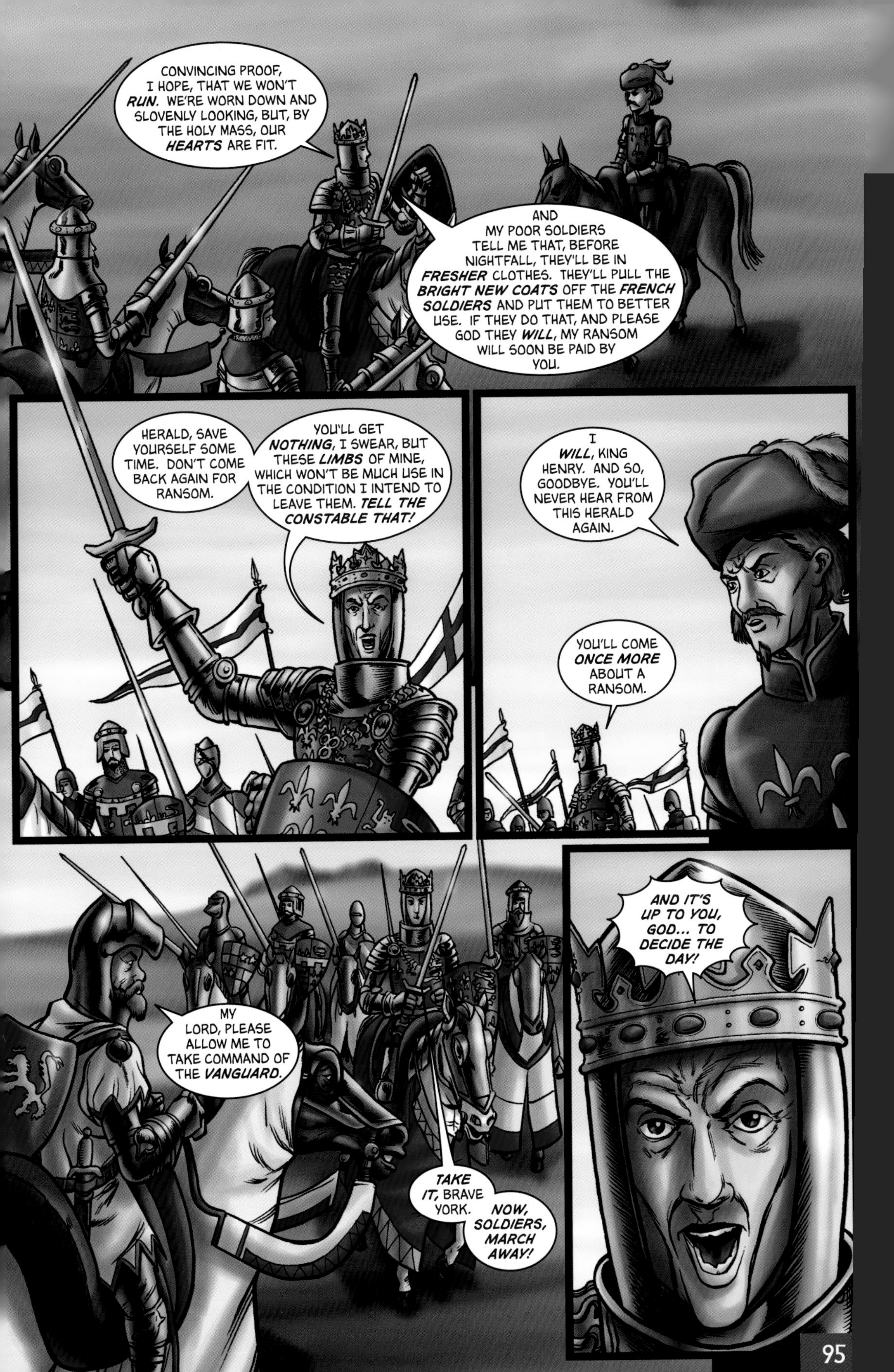

CONVINCING PROOF, I HOPE, THAT WE WON'T RUN. WE'RE WORN DOWN AND SLOVENLY LOOKING, BUT, BY THE HOLY MASS, OUR HEARTS ARE FIT.
AND MY POOR SOLDIERS TELL ME THAT, BEFORE NIGHTFALL, THEY'LL BE IN FRESHER CLOTHES. THEY'LL PULL THE BRIGHT NEW COATS OFF THE FRENCH SOLDIERS AND PUT THEM TO BETTER USE. IF THEY DO THAT, AND PLEASE GOD THEY WILL, MY RANSOM WILL SOON BE PAID BY YOU.
HERALD, SAVE YOURSELF SOME TIME. DON'T COME BACK AGAIN FOR RANSOM.
YOU'LL GET NOTHING, I SWEAR, BUT THESE LIMBS OF MINE, WHICH WON'T BE MUCH USE IN THE CONDITION I INTEND TO LEAVE THEM. TELL THE CONSTABLE THAT!
I WILL, KING HENRY. AND SO, GOODBYE. YOU'LL NEVER HEAR FROM THIS HERALD AGAIN.
YOU'LL COME ONCE MORE ABOUT A RANSOM.
MY LORD, PLEASE ALLOW ME TO TAKE COMMAND OF THE VANGUARD.
TAKE IT, BRAVE YORK.
NOW, SOLDIERS, MARCH AWAY!
AND IT'S UP TO YOU, GOD... TO DECIDE THE DAY!

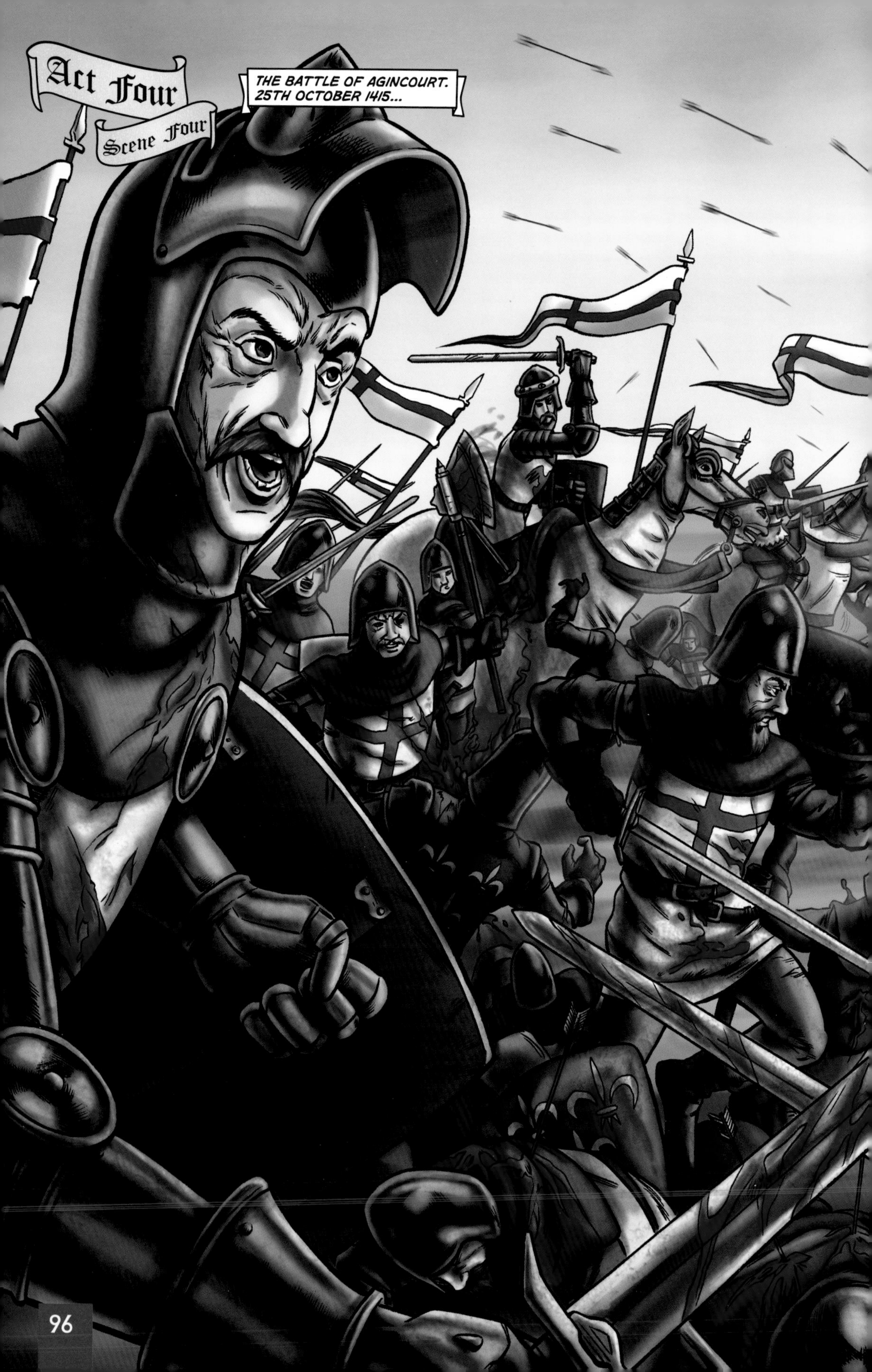
Act Four
Scene Four
THE BATTLE OF AGINCOURT. 25TH OCTOBER 1415...

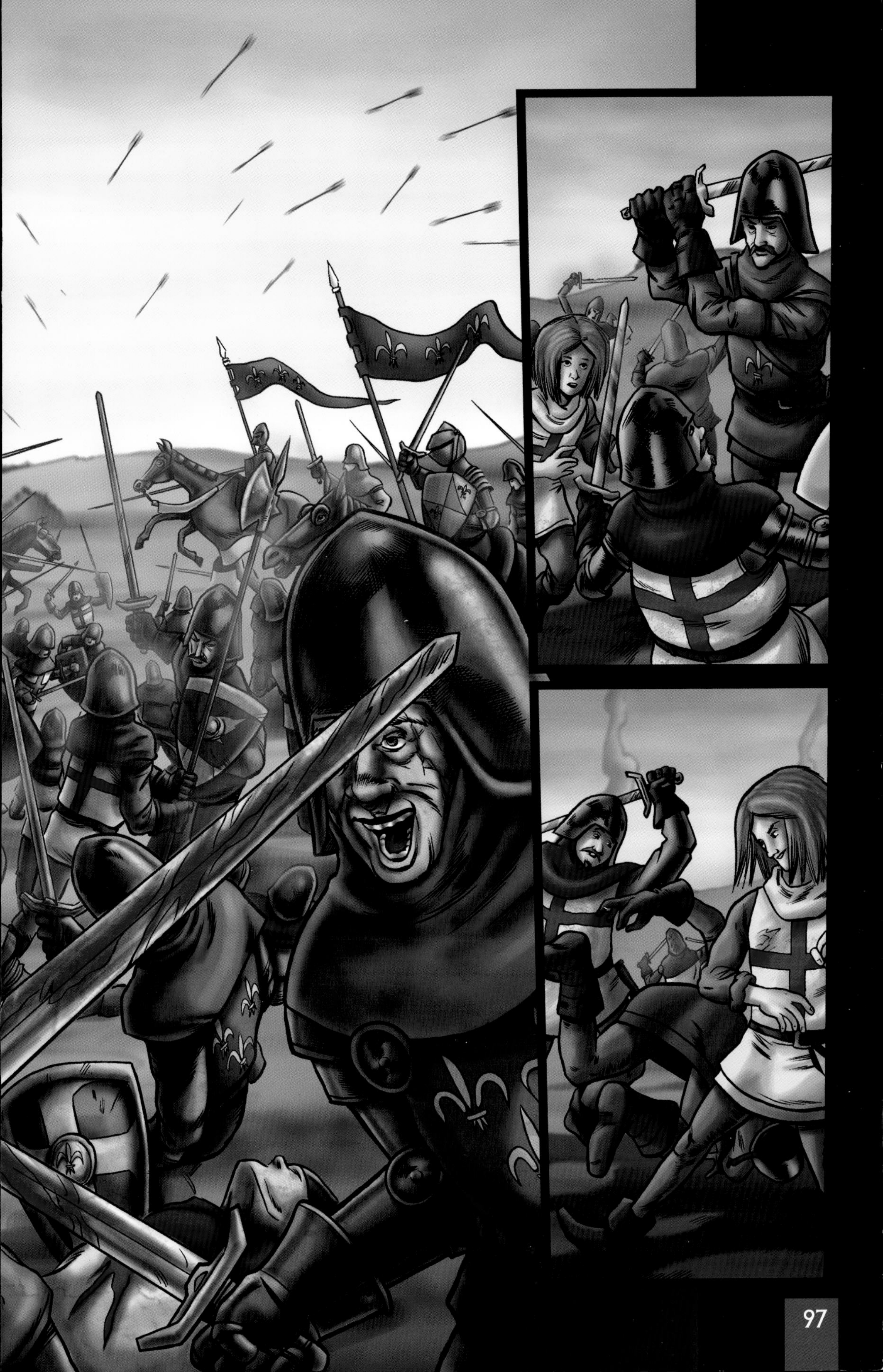

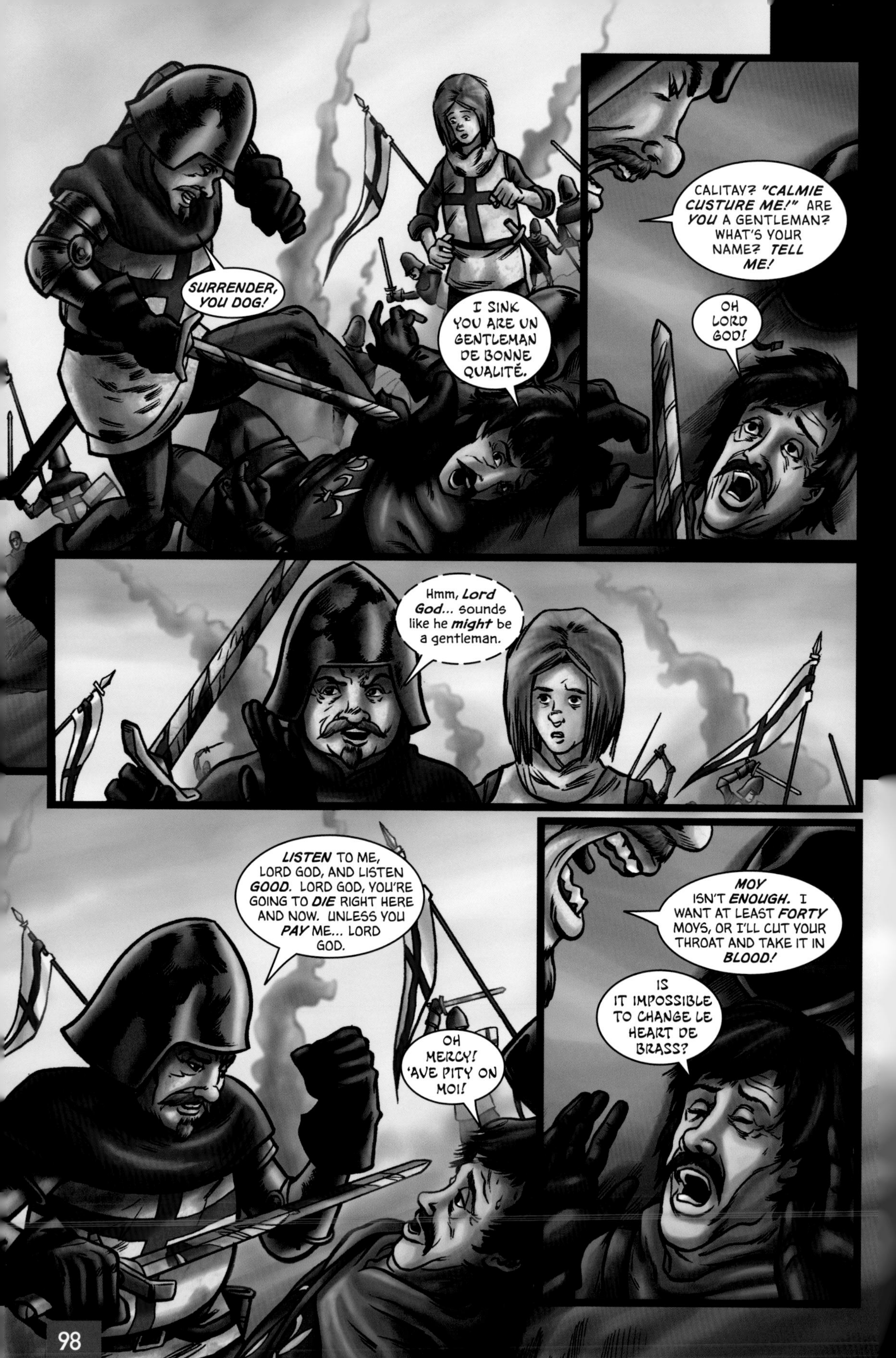

SURRENDER, YOU DOG!
I SINK YOU ARE UN GENTLEMAN DE BONNE QUALITÉ.
CALITAY? "CALMIE CUSTURE ME!" ARE YOU A GENTLEMAN? WHAT'S YOUR NAME? TELL ME!
OH LORD GOD!
Hmm, Lord God... sounds like he might be a gentleman.
LISTEN TO ME, LORD GOD, AND LISTEN GOOD. LORD GOD, YOU'RE GOING TO DIE RIGHT HERE AND NOW. UNLESS YOU PAY ME... LORD GOD.
OH MERCY! 'AVE PITY ON MOI!
MOY ISN'T ENOUGH. I WANT AT LEAST FORTY MOYS, OR I'LL CUT YOUR THROAT AND TAKE IT IN BLOOD!
IS IT IMPOSSIBLE TO CHANGE LE HEART DE BRASS?

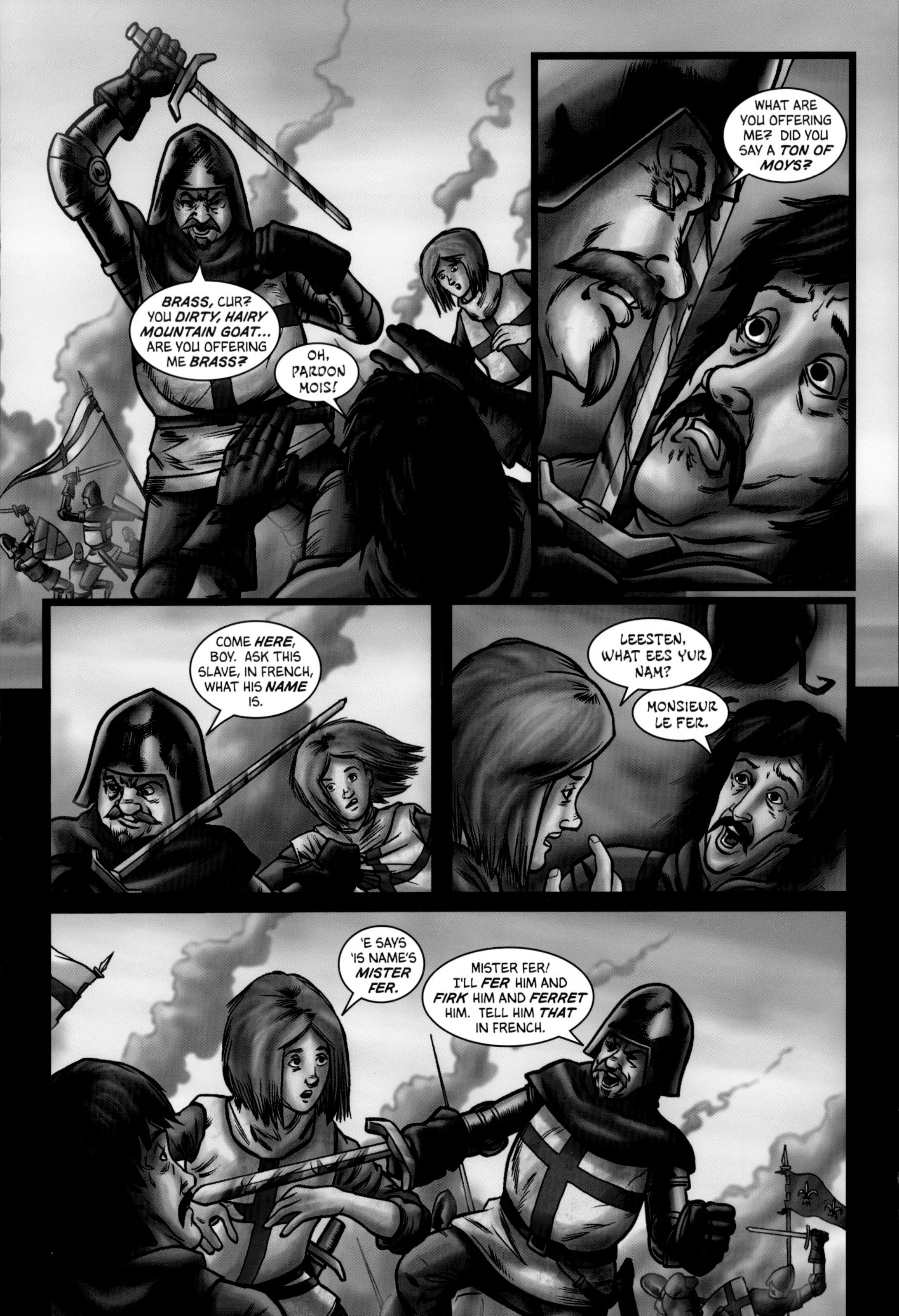

BRASS, CUR? YOU DIRTY, HAIRY MOUNTAIN GOAT... ARE YOU OFFERING ME BRASS?
OH, PARDON MOIS!
WHAT ARE YOU OFFERING ME? DID YOU SAY A TON OF MOYS?
COME HERE, BOY. ASK THIS SLAVE, IN FRENCH, WHAT HIS NAME IS.
LEESTEN, WHAT EES YUR NAM?
MONSIEUR LE FER.
'E SAYS 'IS NAME'S MISTER FER.
MISTER FER! I'LL FER HIM AND FIRK HIM AND FERRET HIM. TELL HIM THAT IN FRENCH.

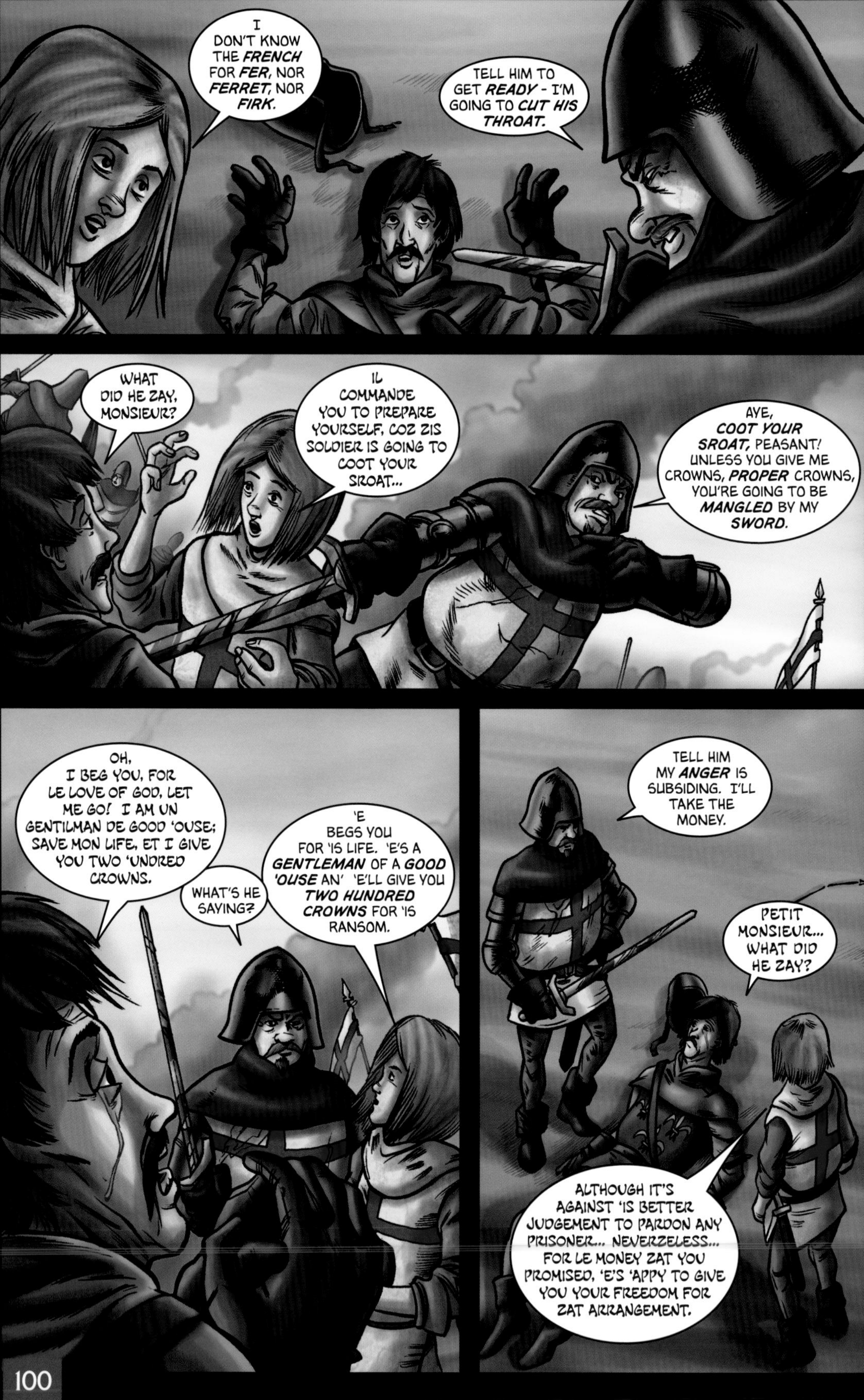

I DON'T KNOW THE FRENCH FOR FER, NOR FERRET, NOR FIRK.
TELL HIM TO GET READY - I'M GOING TO CUT HIS THROAT.
WHAT DID HE ZAY, MONSIEUR?
IL COMMANDE YOU TO PREPARE YOURSELF, COZ ZIS SOLDIER IS GOING TO COOT YOUR SROAT...
AYE, COOT YOUR SROAT, PEASANT! UNLESS YOU GIVE ME CROWNS, PROPER CROWNS, YOU'RE GOING TO BE MANGLED BY MY SWORD.
OH, I BEG YOU, FOR LE LOVE OF GOD, LET ME GO! I AM UN GENTILMAN DE GOOD 'OUSE; SAVE MON LIFE, ET I GIVE YOU TWO 'UNDRED CROWNS.
WHAT'S HE SAYING?
'E BEGS YOU FOR 'IS LIFE. 'E'S A GENTLEMAN OF A GOOD 'OUSE AN' 'E'LL GIVE YOU TWO HUNDRED CROWNS FOR 'IS RANSOM.
TELL HIM MY ANGER IS SUBSIDING. I'LL TAKE THE MONEY.
PETIT MONSIEUR... WHAT DID HE ZAY?
ALTHOUGH IT'S AGAINST 'IS BETTER JUDGEMENT TO PARDON ANY PRISONER... NEVERZELESS... FOR LE MONEY ZAT YOU PROMISED, 'E'S 'APPY TO GIVE YOU YOUR FREEDOM FOR ZAT ARRANGEMENT.

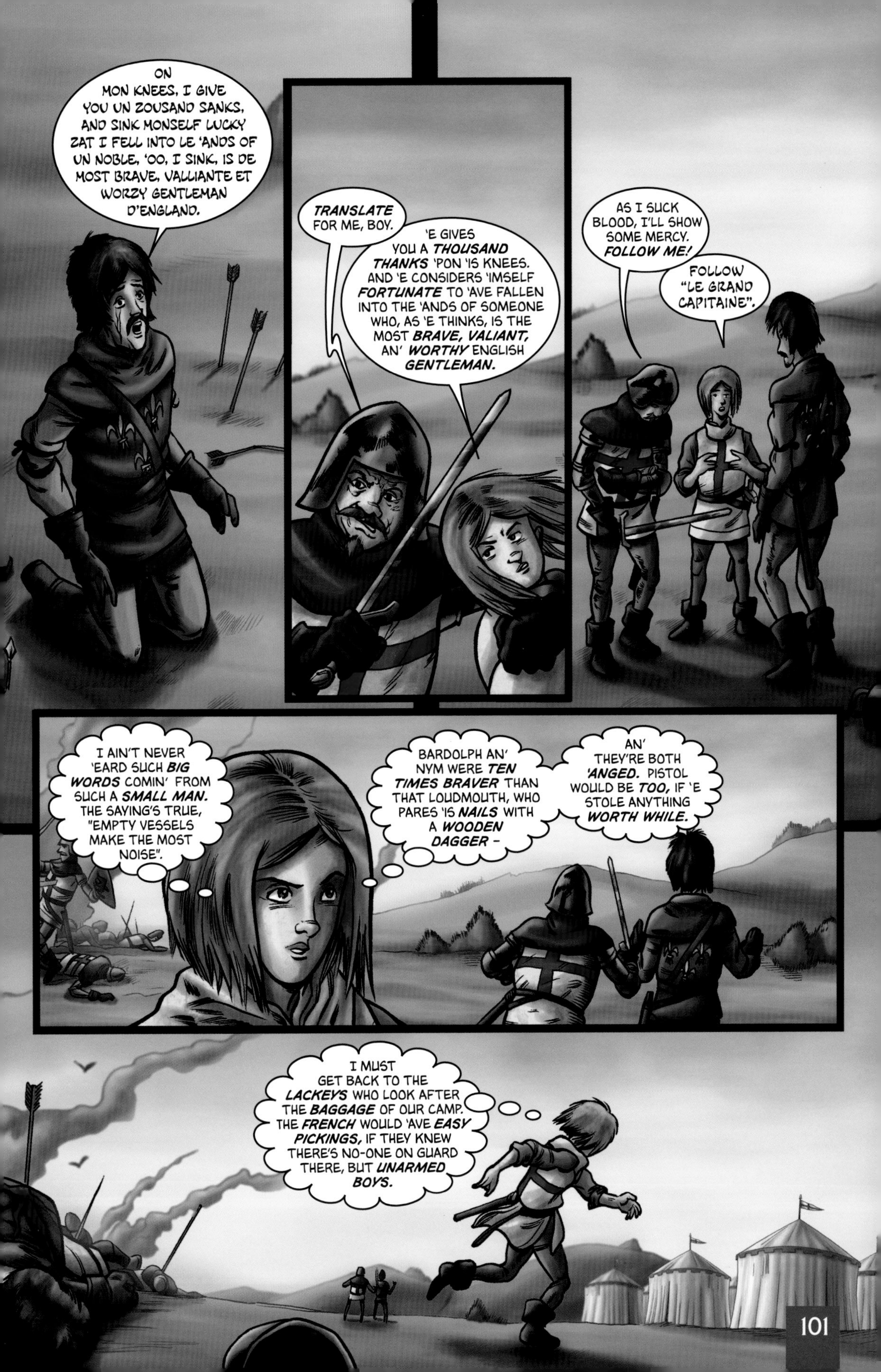
ON MON KNEES, I GIVE YOU UN ZOUSAND SANKS, AND SINK MONSELF LUCKY ZAT I FELL INTO LE 'ANDS OF UN NOBLE, 'OO, I SINK, IS DE MOST BRAVE, VALLIANTE ET WORZY GENTLEMAN D'ENGLAND.
TRANSLATE FOR ME, BOY.
'E GIVES YOU A THOUSAND THANKS 'PON 'IS KNEES. AND 'E CONSIDERS 'IMSELF FORTUNATE TO 'AVE FALLEN INTO THE 'ANDS OF SOMEONE WHO, AS 'E THINKS, IS THE MOST BRAVE, VALIANT, AN' WORTHY ENGLISH GENTLEMAN.
AS I SUCK BLOOD, I'LL SHOW SOME MERCY. FOLLOW ME!
FOLLOW "LE GRAND CAPITAINE".
I AIN'T NEVER 'EARD SUCH BIG WORDS COMIN' FROM SUCH A SMALL MAN. THE SAYING'S TRUE, "EMPTY VESSELS MAKE THE MOST NOISE".
BARDOLPH AN' NYM WERE TEN TIMES BRAVER THAN THAT LOUDMOUTH, WHO PARES 'IS NAILS WITH A WOODEN DAGGER –
AN' THEY'RE BOTH 'ANGED. PISTOL WOULD BE TOO, IF 'E STOLE ANYTHING WORTH WHILE.
I MUST GET BACK TO THE LACKEYS WHO LOOK AFTER THE BAGGAGE OF OUR CAMP. THE FRENCH WOULD 'AVE EASY PICKINGS, IF THEY KNEW THERE'S NO-ONE ON GUARD THERE, BUT UNARMED BOYS.

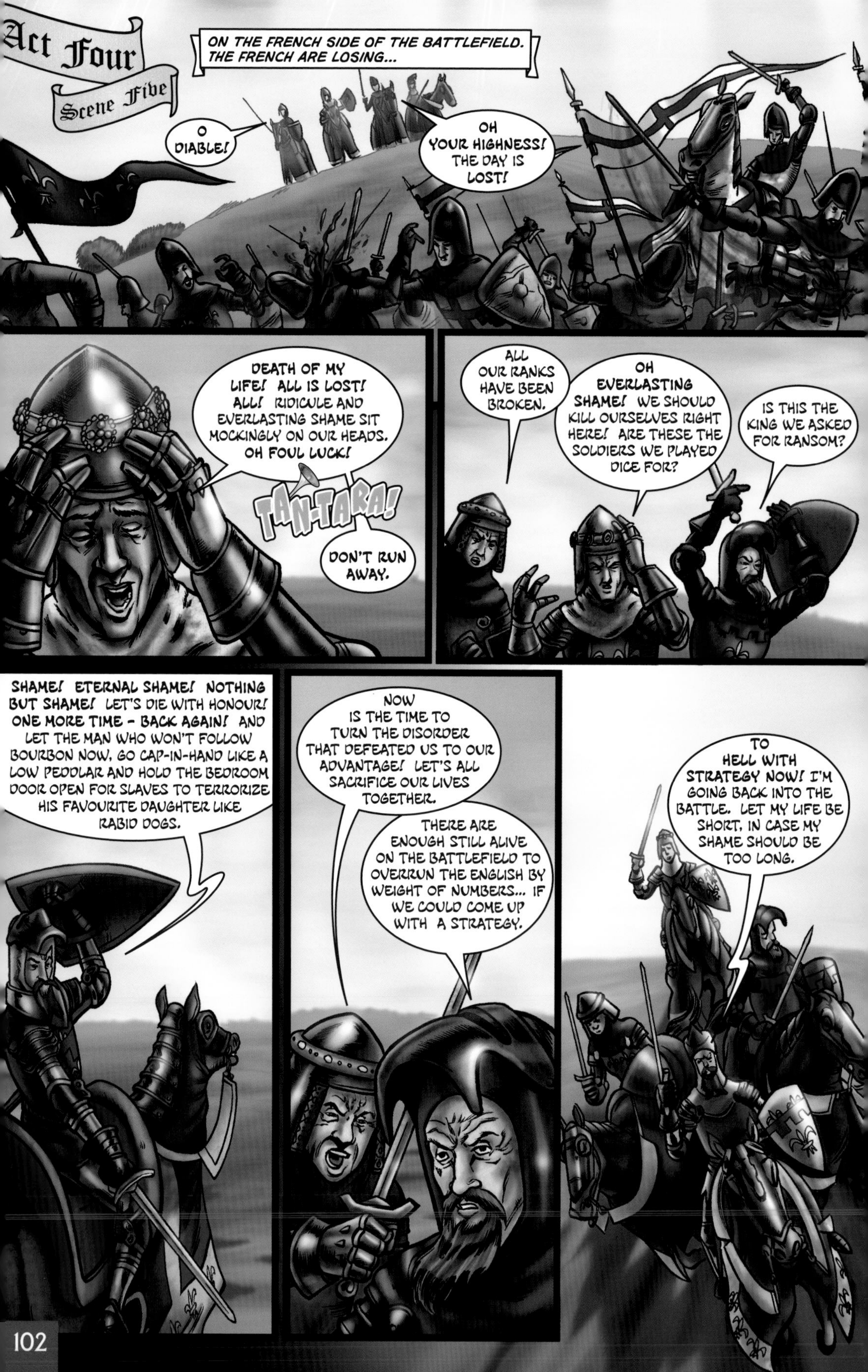

Act Four
Scene Five
ON THE FRENCH SIDE OF THE BATTLEFIELD. THE FRENCH ARE LOSING...
O DIABLE!
OH YOUR HIGHNESS! THE DAY IS LOST!
DEATH OF MY LIFE! ALL IS LOST! ALL! RIDICULE AND EVERLASTING SHAME SIT MOCKINGLY ON OUR HEADS. OH FOUL LUCK!
TAN-TARA!
DON'T RUN AWAY.
ALL OUR RANKS HAVE BEEN BROKEN.
OH EVERLASTING SHAME! WE SHOULD KILL OURSELVES RIGHT HERE! ARE THESE THE SOLDIERS WE PLAYED DICE FOR?
IS THIS THE KING WE ASKED FOR RANSOM?
SHAME! ETERNAL SHAME! NOTHING BUT SHAME! LET'S DIE WITH HONOUR! ONE MORE TIME - BACK AGAIN! AND LET THE MAN WHO WON'T FOLLOW BOURBON NOW, GO CAP-IN-HAND LIKE A LOW PEDDLAR AND HOLD THE BEDROOM DOOR OPEN FOR SLAVES TO TERRORIZE HIS FAVOURITE DAUGHTER LIKE RABID DOGS.
NOW IS THE TIME TO TURN THE DISORDER THAT DEFEATED US TO OUR ADVANTAGE! LET'S ALL SACRIFICE OUR LIVES TOGETHER.
THERE ARE ENOUGH STILL ALIVE ON THE BATTLEFIELD TO OVERRUN THE ENGLISH BY WEIGHT OF NUMBERS... IF WE COULD COME UP WITH A STRATEGY.
TO HELL WITH STRATEGY NOW! I'M GOING BACK INTO THE BATTLE. LET MY LIFE BE SHORT, IN CASE MY SHAME SHOULD BE TOO LONG.

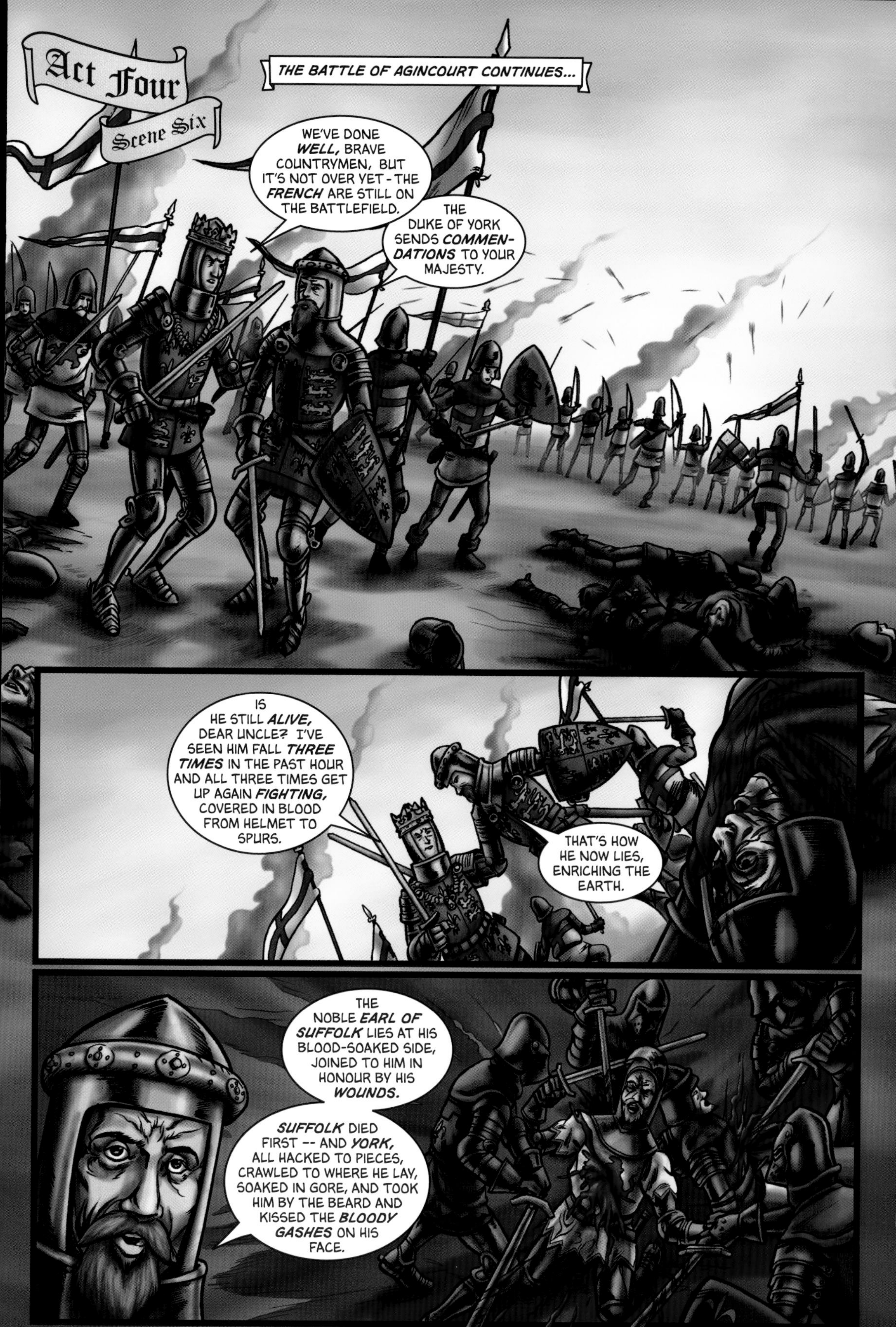
Act Four
Scene Six
THE BATTLE OF AGINCOURT CONTINUES...
WE'VE DONE WELL, BRAVE COUNTRYMEN, BUT IT'S NOT OVER YET - THE FRENCH ARE STILL ON THE BATTLEFIELD.
THE DUKE OF YORK SENDS COMMENDATIONS TO YOUR MAJESTY.
IS HE STILL ALIVE, DEAR UNCLE? I'VE SEEN HIM FALL THREE TIMES IN THE PAST HOUR AND ALL THREE TIMES GET UP AGAIN FIGHTING, COVERED IN BLOOD FROM HELMET TO SPURS.
THAT'S HOW HE NOW LIES, ENRICHING THE EARTH.
THE NOBLE EARL OF SUFFOLK LIES AT HIS BLOOD-SOAKED SIDE, JOINED TO HIM IN HONOUR BY HIS WOUNDS.
SUFFOLK DIED FIRST -- AND YORK, ALL HACKED TO PIECES, CRAWLED TO WHERE HE LAY, SOAKED IN GORE, AND TOOK HIM BY THE BEARD AND KISSED THE BLOODY GASHES ON HIS FACE.

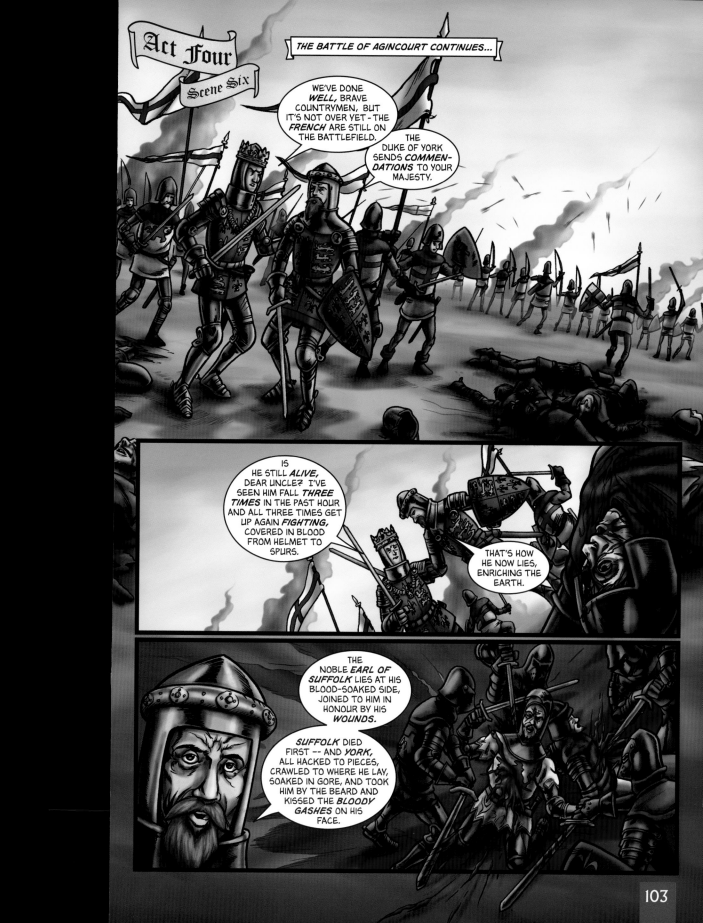

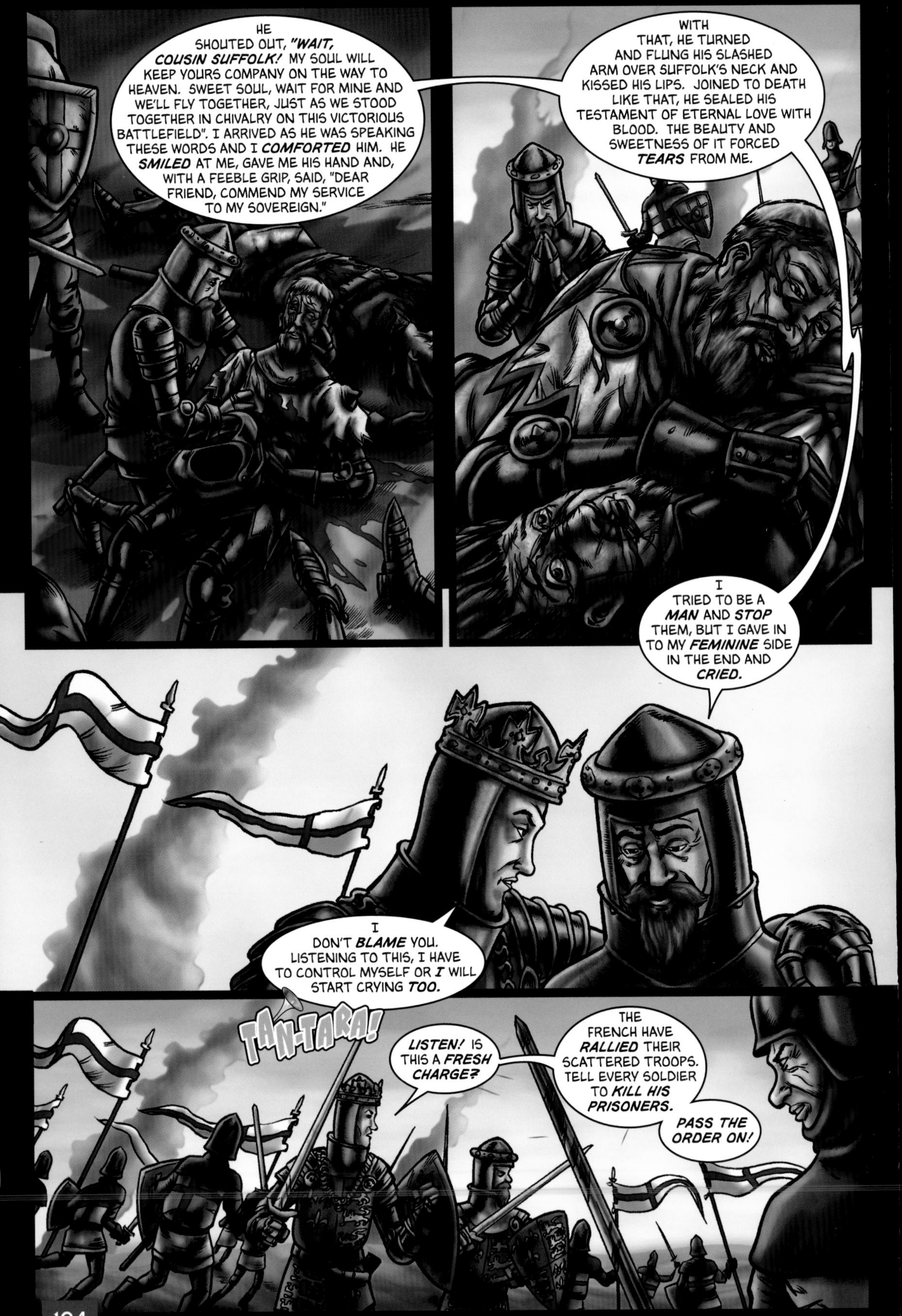
HE SHOUTED OUT, "WAIT, COUSIN SUFFOLK! MY SOUL WILL KEEP YOURS COMPANY ON THE WAY TO HEAVEN. SWEET SOUL, WAIT FOR MINE AND WE'LL FLY TOGETHER, JUST AS WE STOOD TOGETHER IN CHIVALRY ON THIS VICTORIOUS BATTLEFIELD". I ARRIVED AS HE WAS SPEAKING THESE WORDS AND I COMFORTED HIM. HE SMILED AT ME, GAVE ME HIS HAND AND, WITH A FEEBLE GRIP, SAID, "DEAR FRIEND, COMMEND MY SERVICE TO MY SOVEREIGN."
WITH THAT, HE TURNED AND FLUNG HIS SLASHED ARM OVER SUFFOLK'S NECK AND KISSED HIS LIPS. JOINED TO DEATH LIKE THAT, HE SEALED HIS TESTAMENT OF ETERNAL LOVE WITH BLOOD. THE BEAUTY AND SWEETNESS OF IT FORCED TEARS FROM ME.
I TRIED TO BE A MAN AND STOP THEM, BUT I GAVE IN TO MY FEMININE SIDE IN THE END AND CRIED.
I DON'T BLAME YOU. LISTENING TO THIS, I HAVE TO CONTROL MYSELF OR I WILL START CRYING TOO.
TAN-TARA!
LISTEN! IS THIS A FRESH CHARGE?
THE FRENCH HAVE RALLIED THEIR SCATTERED TROOPS. TELL EVERY SOLDIER TO KILL HIS PRISONERS.
PASS THE ORDER ON!

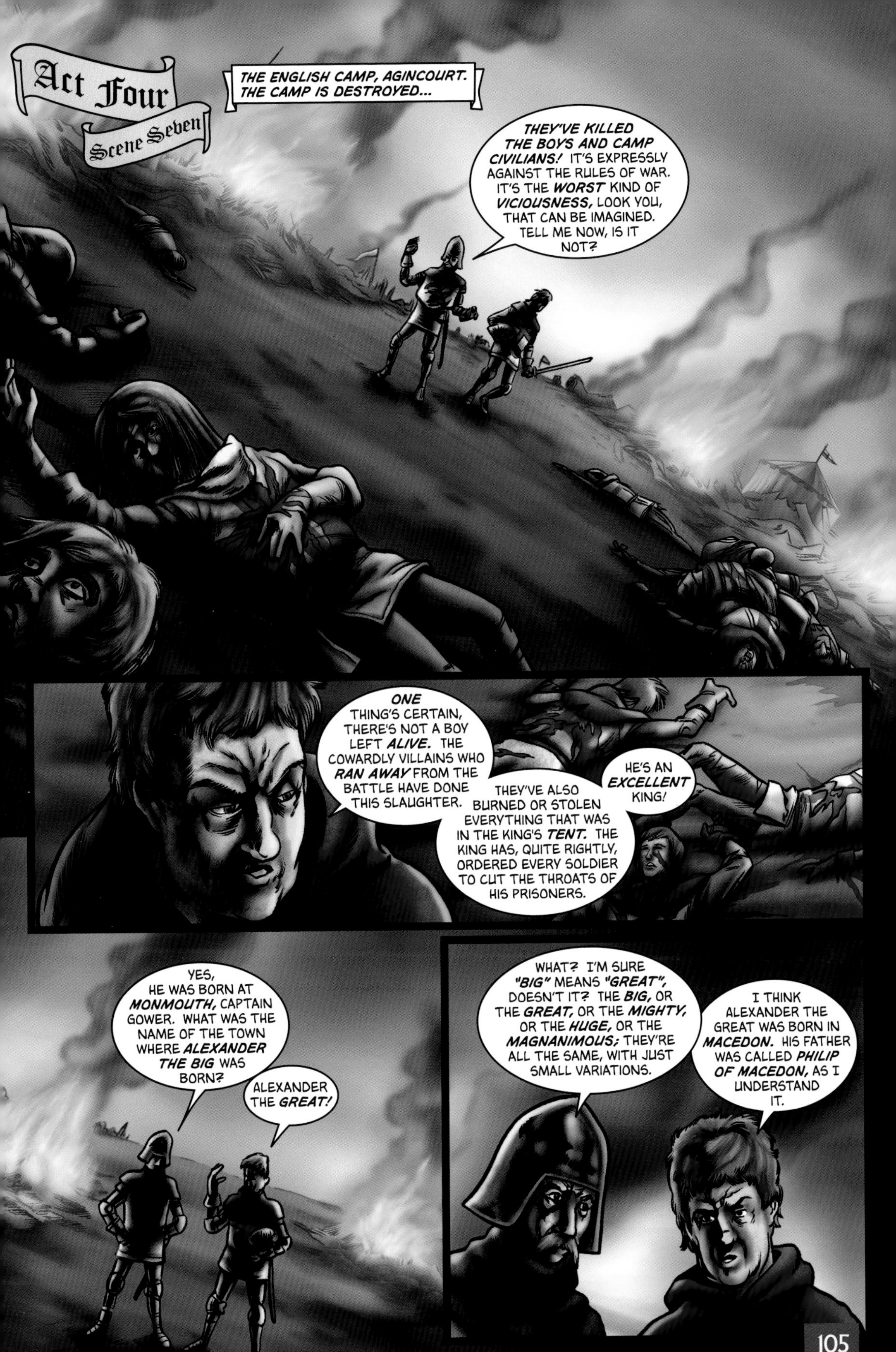
Act Four
Scene Seven
THE ENGLISH CAMP, AGINCOURT. THE CAMP IS DESTROYED...
THEY'VE KILLED THE BOYS AND CAMP CIVILIANS! IT'S EXPRESSLY AGAINST THE RULES OF WAR. IT'S THE WORST KIND OF VICIOUSNESS, LOOK YOU, THAT CAN BE IMAGINED. TELL ME NOW, IS IT NOT?
ONE THING'S CERTAIN, THERE'S NOT A BOY LEFT ALIVE. THE COWARDLY VILLAINS WHO RAN AWAY FROM THE BATTLE HAVE DONE THIS SLAUGHTER.
THEY'VE ALSO BURNED OR STOLEN EVERYTHING THAT WAS IN THE KING'S TENT. THE KING HAS, QUITE RIGHTLY, ORDERED EVERY SOLDIER TO CUT THE THROATS OF HIS PRISONERS.
HE'S AN EXCELLENT KING!
YES, HE WAS BORN AT MONMOUTH, CAPTAIN GOWER. WHAT WAS THE NAME OF THE TOWN WHERE ALEXANDER THE BIG WAS BORN?
ALEXANDER THE GREAT!
WHAT? I'M SURE "BIG" MEANS "GREAT", DOESN'T IT? THE BIG, OR THE GREAT, OR THE MIGHTY, OR THE HUGE, OR THE MAGNANIMOUS; THEY'RE ALL THE SAME, WITH JUST SMALL VARIATIONS.
I THINK ALEXANDER THE GREAT WAS BORN IN MACEDON. HIS FATHER WAS CALLED PHILIP OF MACEDON, AS I UNDERSTAND IT.

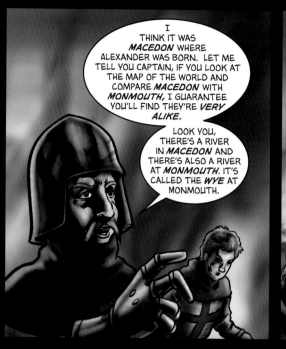

I THINK IT WAS *MACEDON* WHERE ALEXANDER WAS BORN. LET ME TELL YOU CAPTAIN, IF YOU LOOK AT THE MAP OF THE WORLD AND COMPARE *MACEDON* WITH *MONMOUTH*, I GUARANTEE YOU'LL FIND THEY'RE *VERY ALIKE*.

LOOK YOU, THERE'S A RIVER IN *MACEDON* AND THERE'S ALSO A RIVER AT *MONMOUTH*. IT'S CALLED THE *WYE* AT MONMOUTH.

I CAN'T REMEMBER THE *NAME* OF THE OTHER RIVER. IT DOESN'T MATTER, THEY'RE AS ALIKE AS MY *FINGERS* ARE TO EACH OTHER AND THERE'S *SALMON* IN BOTH. IF YOU KNOW ABOUT *ALEXANDER'S* LIFE, *HARRY OF MONMOUTH'S* LIFE RESEMBLES IT *CLOSELY*. YOU SEE, THERE ARE PARALLELS IN EVERYTHING...

ALEXANDER, AS YOU KNOW, *KILLED* HIS FRIEND *CLEITUS*, WHILE IN ONE OF HIS RAGES, OR FURIES, OR ANGERS, OR TEMPERS, OR MOODS, OR IRRITATIONS, OR INDIGNATIONS, OR WHEN HE WAS *DRUNK* OUT OF HIS BRAINS. LOOK YOU, ALES OR ANGERS... WHATEVER.

OUR KING'S NOTHING LIKE HIM! HE NEVER KILLED ANY OF HIS FRIENDS.

YOU'RE OUT OF *LINE*, LOOK YOU, INTERRUPTING MY STORY BEFORE IT'S *FINISHED*.

I'M SPEAKING *FIGURATIVELY* AND *COMPARATIVELY*. IN THE SAME WAY AS ALEXANDER KILLED HIS FRIEND CLEITUS WHILE HE WAS DRUNK; HARRY MONMOUTH GOT RID OF THE *FAT KNIGHT* WITH THE *BIG BELLY*, WHILE HE WAS SOBER AS A JUDGE.

HE WAS FULL OF *JOKES* AND *JIBES* AND *MISCHIEF* AND *MOCKERY*... THE *FAT KNIGHT*. I'VE FORGOTTEN HIS NAME.

SIR JOHN *FALSTAFF*.

THAT'S HIM. I'LL TELL YOU *THIS*, THERE'S *GOOD MEN* BORN AT MONMOUTH.

HERE COMES *HIS MAJESTY*.

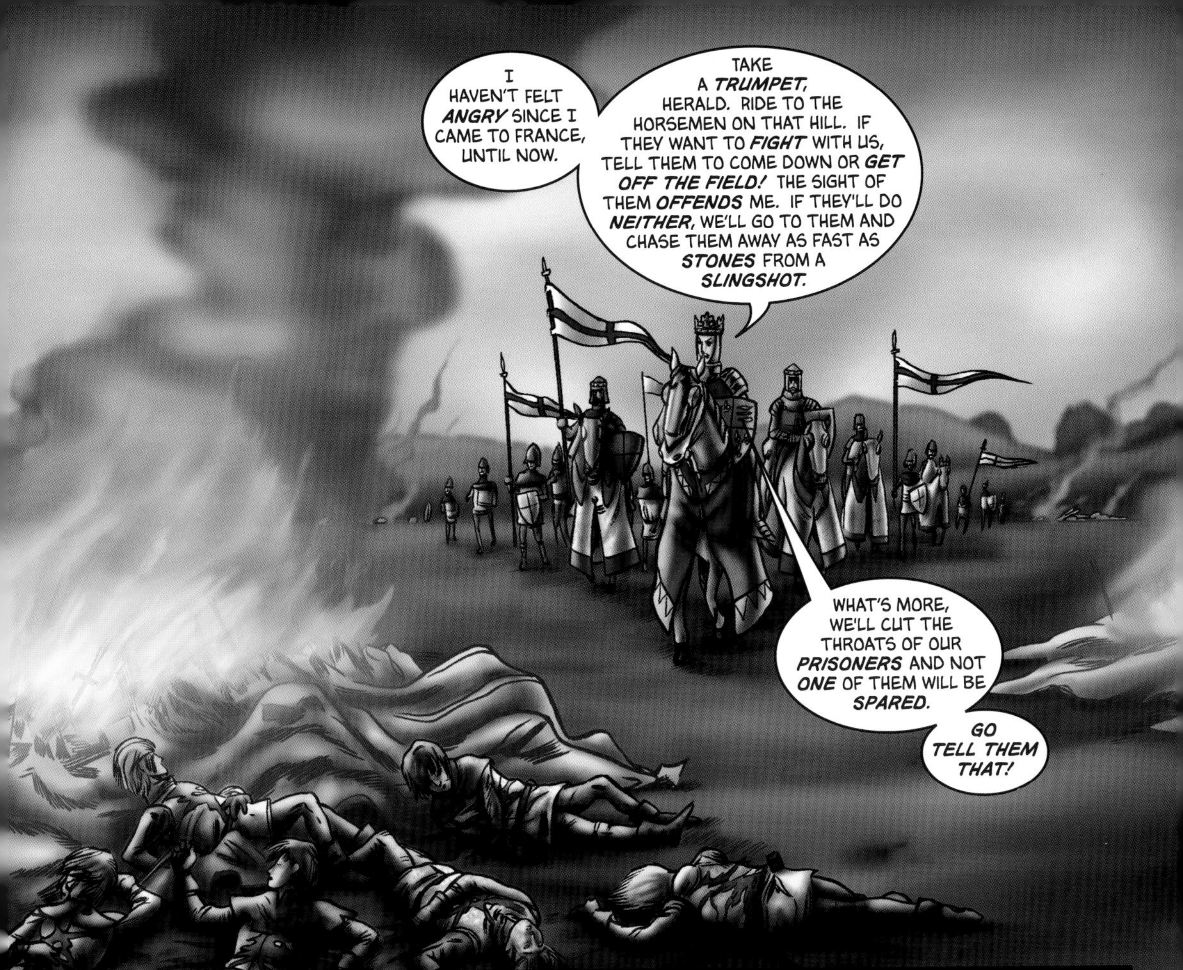
I HAVEN'T FELT ANGRY SINCE I CAME TO FRANCE, UNTIL NOW.
TAKE A TRUMPET, HERALD. RIDE TO THE HORSEMEN ON THAT HILL. IF THEY WANT TO FIGHT WITH US, TELL THEM TO COME DOWN OR GET OFF THE FIELD! THE SIGHT OF THEM OFFENDS ME. IF THEY'LL DO NEITHER, WE'LL GO TO THEM AND CHASE THEM AWAY AS FAST AS STONES FROM A SLINGSHOT.
WHAT'S MORE, WE'LL CUT THE THROATS OF OUR PRISONERS AND NOT ONE OF THEM WILL BE SPARED.
GO TELL THEM THAT!

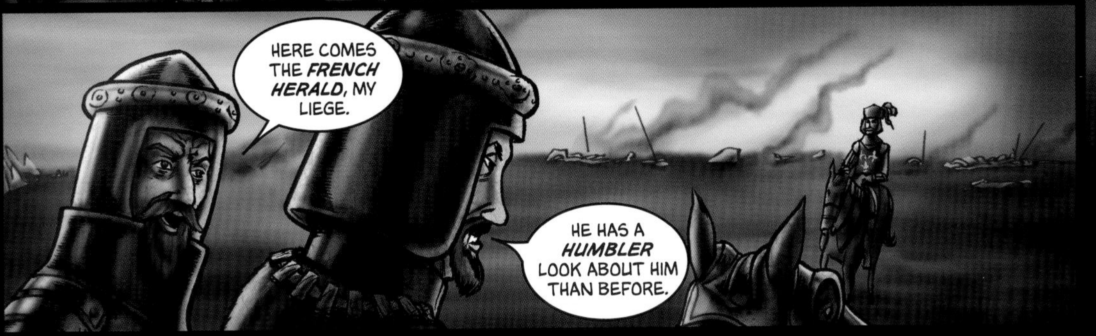
HERE COMES THE FRENCH HERALD, MY LIEGE.
HE HAS A HUMBLER LOOK ABOUT HIM THAN BEFORE.

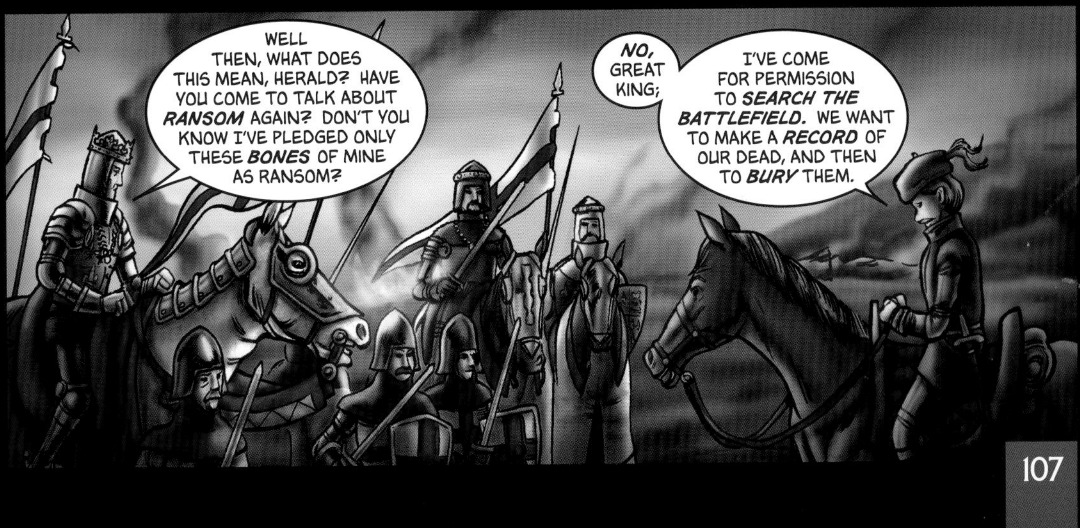
WELL THEN, WHAT DOES THIS MEAN, HERALD? HAVE YOU COME TO TALK ABOUT RANSOM AGAIN? DON'T YOU KNOW I'VE PLEDGED ONLY THESE BONES OF MINE AS RANSOM?
NO, GREAT KING;
I'VE COME FOR PERMISSION TO SEARCH THE BATTLEFIELD. WE WANT TO MAKE A RECORD OF OUR DEAD, AND THEN TO BURY THEM.

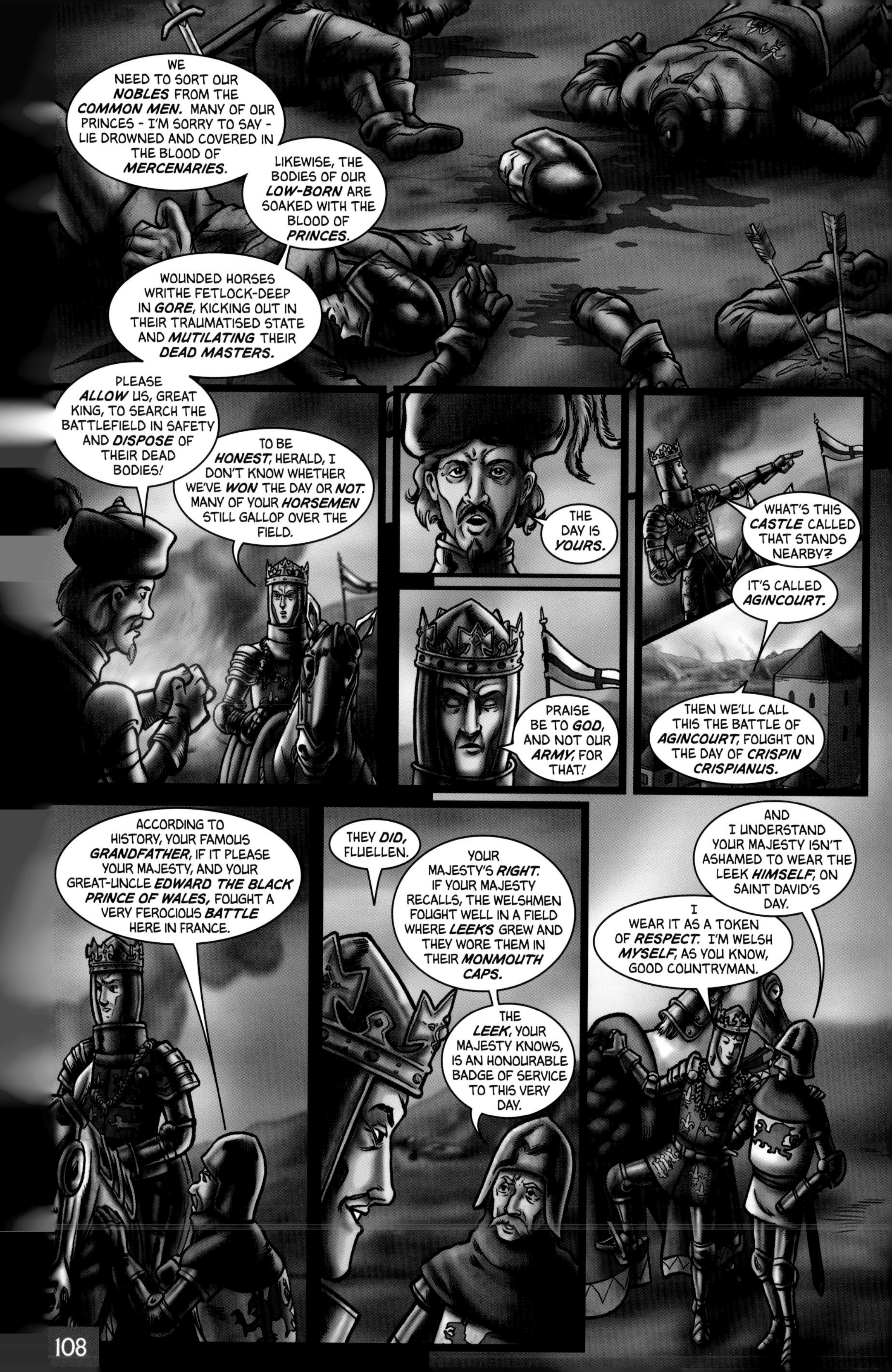
WE NEED TO SORT OUR NOBLES FROM THE COMMON MEN. MANY OF OUR PRINCES - I'M SORRY TO SAY - LIE DROWNED AND COVERED IN THE BLOOD OF MERCENARIES.
LIKEWISE, THE BODIES OF OUR LOW-BORN ARE SOAKED WITH THE BLOOD OF PRINCES.
WOUNDED HORSES WRITHE FETLOCK-DEEP IN GORE, KICKING OUT IN THEIR TRAUMATISED STATE AND MUTILATING THEIR DEAD MASTERS.
PLEASE ALLOW US, GREAT KING, TO SEARCH THE BATTLEFIELD IN SAFETY AND DISPOSE OF THEIR DEAD BODIES!
TO BE HONEST, HERALD, I DON'T KNOW WHETHER WE'VE WON THE DAY OR NOT. MANY OF YOUR HORSEMEN STILL GALLOP OVER THE FIELD.
THE DAY IS YOURS.
PRAISE BE TO GOD, AND NOT OUR ARMY, FOR THAT!
WHAT'S THIS CASTLE CALLED THAT STANDS NEARBY?
IT'S CALLED AGINCOURT.
THEN WE'LL CALL THIS THE BATTLE OF AGINCOURT, FOUGHT ON THE DAY OF CRISPIN CRISPIANUS.
ACCORDING TO HISTORY, YOUR FAMOUS GRANDFATHER, IF IT PLEASE YOUR MAJESTY, AND YOUR GREAT-UNCLE EDWARD THE BLACK PRINCE OF WALES, FOUGHT A VERY FEROCIOUS BATTLE HERE IN FRANCE.
THEY DID, FLUELLEN.
YOUR MAJESTY'S RIGHT. IF YOUR MAJESTY RECALLS, THE WELSHMEN FOUGHT WELL IN A FIELD WHERE LEEKS GREW AND THEY WORE THEM IN THEIR MONMOUTH CAPS.
THE LEEK, YOUR MAJESTY KNOWS, IS AN HONOURABLE BADGE OF SERVICE TO THIS VERY DAY.
AND I UNDERSTAND YOUR MAJESTY ISN'T ASHAMED TO WEAR THE LEEK HIMSELF, ON SAINT DAVID'S DAY.
I WEAR IT AS A TOKEN OF RESPECT. I'M WELSH MYSELF, AS YOU KNOW, GOOD COUNTRYMAN.

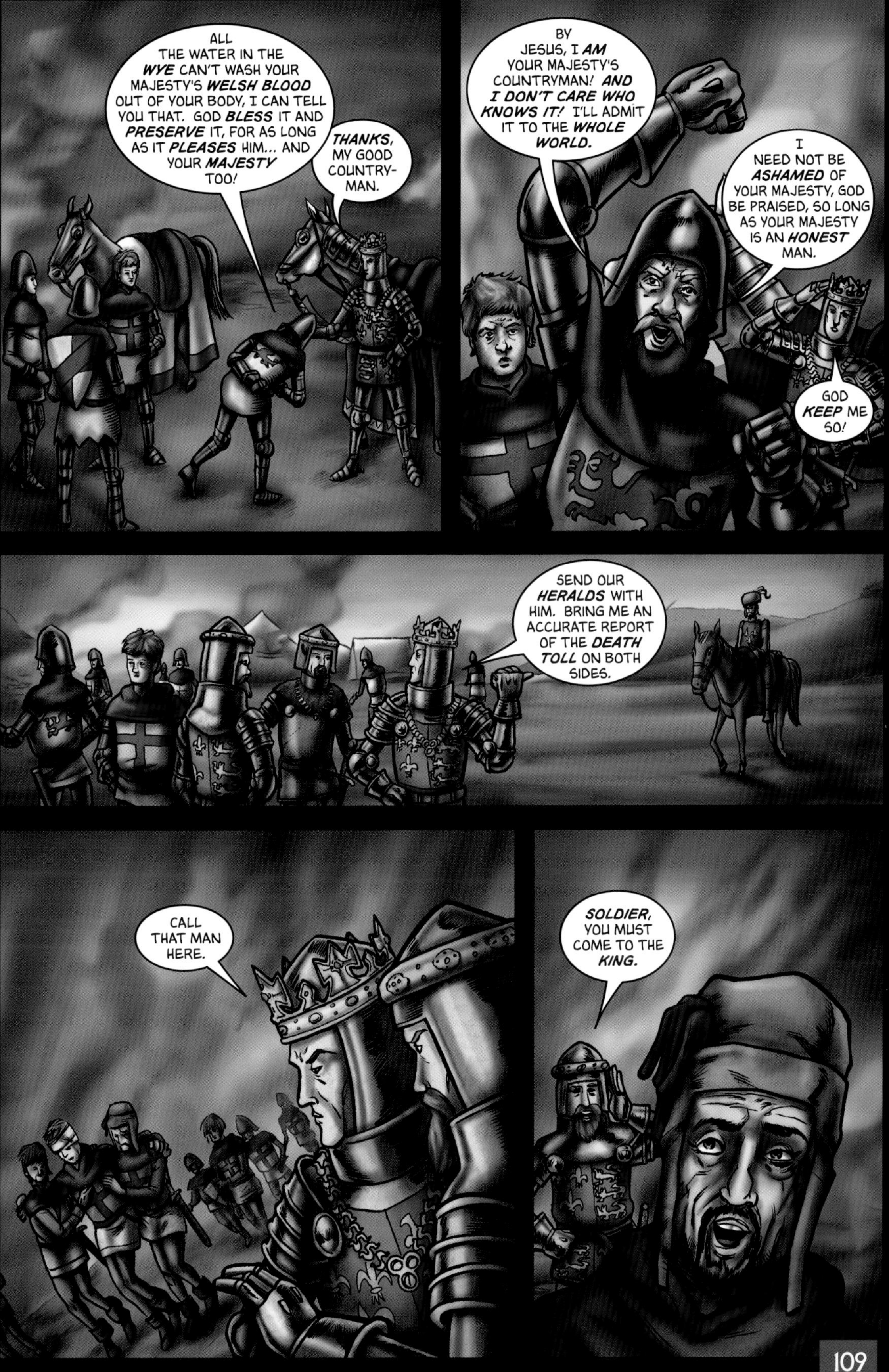
ALL THE WATER IN THE WYE CAN'T WASH YOUR MAJESTY'S WELSH BLOOD OUT OF YOUR BODY, I CAN TELL YOU THAT. GOD BLESS IT AND PRESERVE IT, FOR AS LONG AS IT PLEASES HIM... AND YOUR MAJESTY TOO!
THANKS, MY GOOD COUNTRYMAN.
BY JESUS, I AM YOUR MAJESTY'S COUNTRYMAN! AND I DON'T CARE WHO KNOWS IT! I'LL ADMIT IT TO THE WHOLE WORLD.
I NEED NOT BE ASHAMED OF YOUR MAJESTY, GOD BE PRAISED, SO LONG AS YOUR MAJESTY IS AN HONEST MAN.
GOD KEEP ME SO!
SEND OUR HERALDS WITH HIM. BRING ME AN ACCURATE REPORT OF THE DEATH TOLL ON BOTH SIDES.
CALL THAT MAN HERE.
SOLDIER, YOU MUST COME TO THE KING.

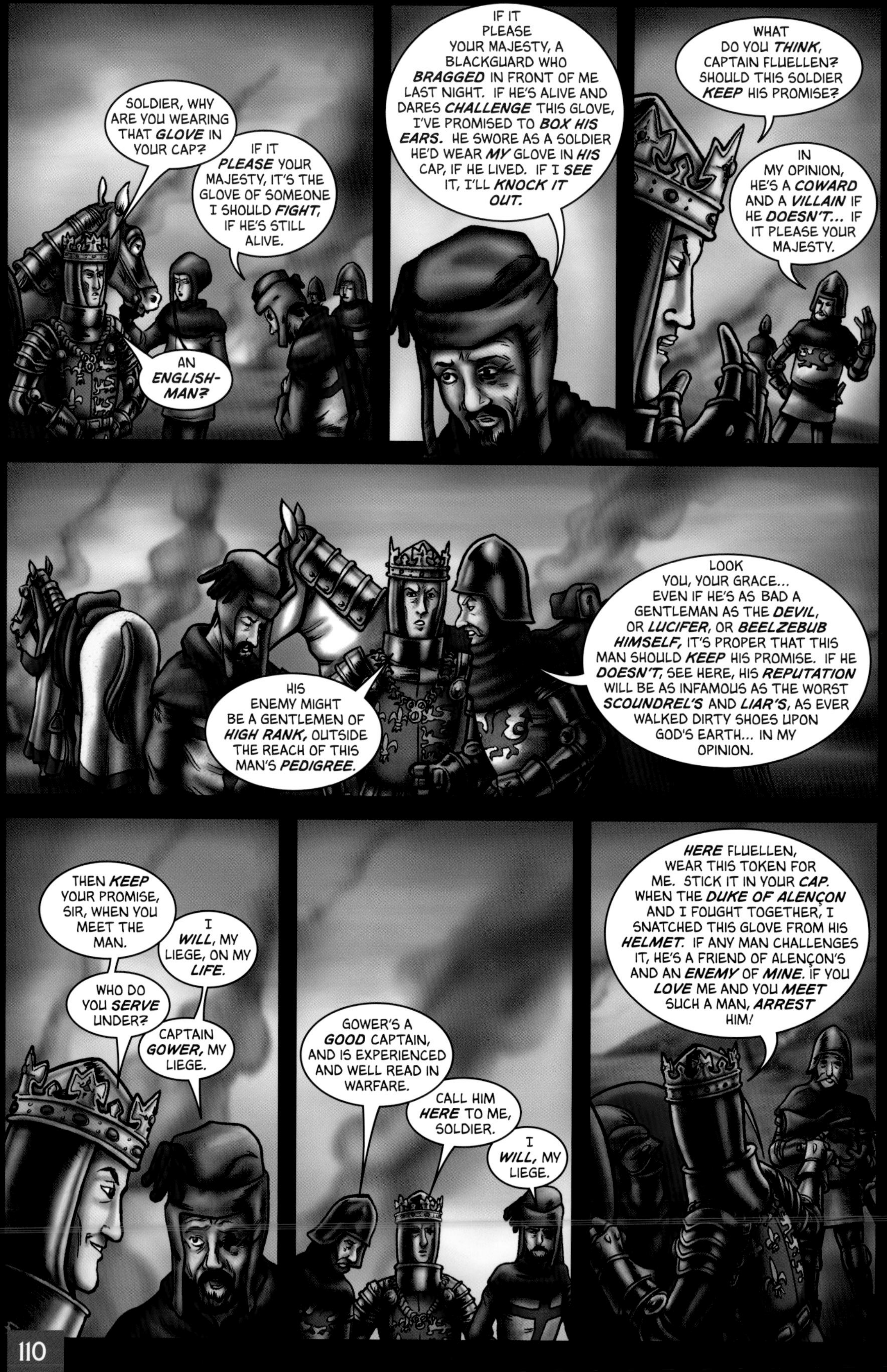

SOLDIER, WHY ARE YOU WEARING THAT GLOVE IN YOUR CAP?
IF IT PLEASE YOUR MAJESTY, IT'S THE GLOVE OF SOMEONE I SHOULD FIGHT, IF HE'S STILL ALIVE.
AN ENGLISH-MAN?
IF IT PLEASE YOUR MAJESTY, A BLACKGUARD WHO BRAGGED IN FRONT OF ME LAST NIGHT. IF HE'S ALIVE AND DARES CHALLENGE THIS GLOVE, I'VE PROMISED TO BOX HIS EARS. HE SWORE AS A SOLDIER HE'D WEAR MY GLOVE IN HIS CAP, IF HE LIVED. IF I SEE IT, I'LL KNOCK IT OUT.
WHAT DO YOU THINK, CAPTAIN FLUELLEN? SHOULD THIS SOLDIER KEEP HIS PROMISE?
IN MY OPINION, HE'S A COWARD AND A VILLAIN IF HE DOESN'T... IF IT PLEASE YOUR MAJESTY.
HIS ENEMY MIGHT BE A GENTLEMEN OF HIGH RANK, OUTSIDE THE REACH OF THIS MAN'S PEDIGREE.
LOOK YOU, YOUR GRACE... EVEN IF HE'S AS BAD A GENTLEMAN AS THE DEVIL, OR LUCIFER, OR BEELZEBUB HIMSELF, IT'S PROPER THAT THIS MAN SHOULD KEEP HIS PROMISE. IF HE DOESN'T, SEE HERE, HIS REPUTATION WILL BE AS INFAMOUS AS THE WORST SCOUNDREL'S AND LIAR'S, AS EVER WALKED DIRTY SHOES UPON GOD'S EARTH... IN MY OPINION.
THEN KEEP YOUR PROMISE, SIR, WHEN YOU MEET THE MAN.
I WILL, MY LIEGE, ON MY LIFE.
WHO DO YOU SERVE UNDER?
CAPTAIN GOWER, MY LIEGE.
GOWER'S A GOOD CAPTAIN, AND IS EXPERIENCED AND WELL READ IN WARFARE.
CALL HIM HERE TO ME, SOLDIER.
I WILL, MY LIEGE.
HERE FLUELLEN, WEAR THIS TOKEN FOR ME. STICK IT IN YOUR CAP. WHEN THE DUKE OF ALENÇON AND I FOUGHT TOGETHER, I SNATCHED THIS GLOVE FROM HIS HELMET. IF ANY MAN CHALLENGES IT, HE'S A FRIEND OF ALENÇON'S AND AN ENEMY OF MINE. IF YOU LOVE ME AND YOU MEET SUCH A MAN, ARREST HIM!

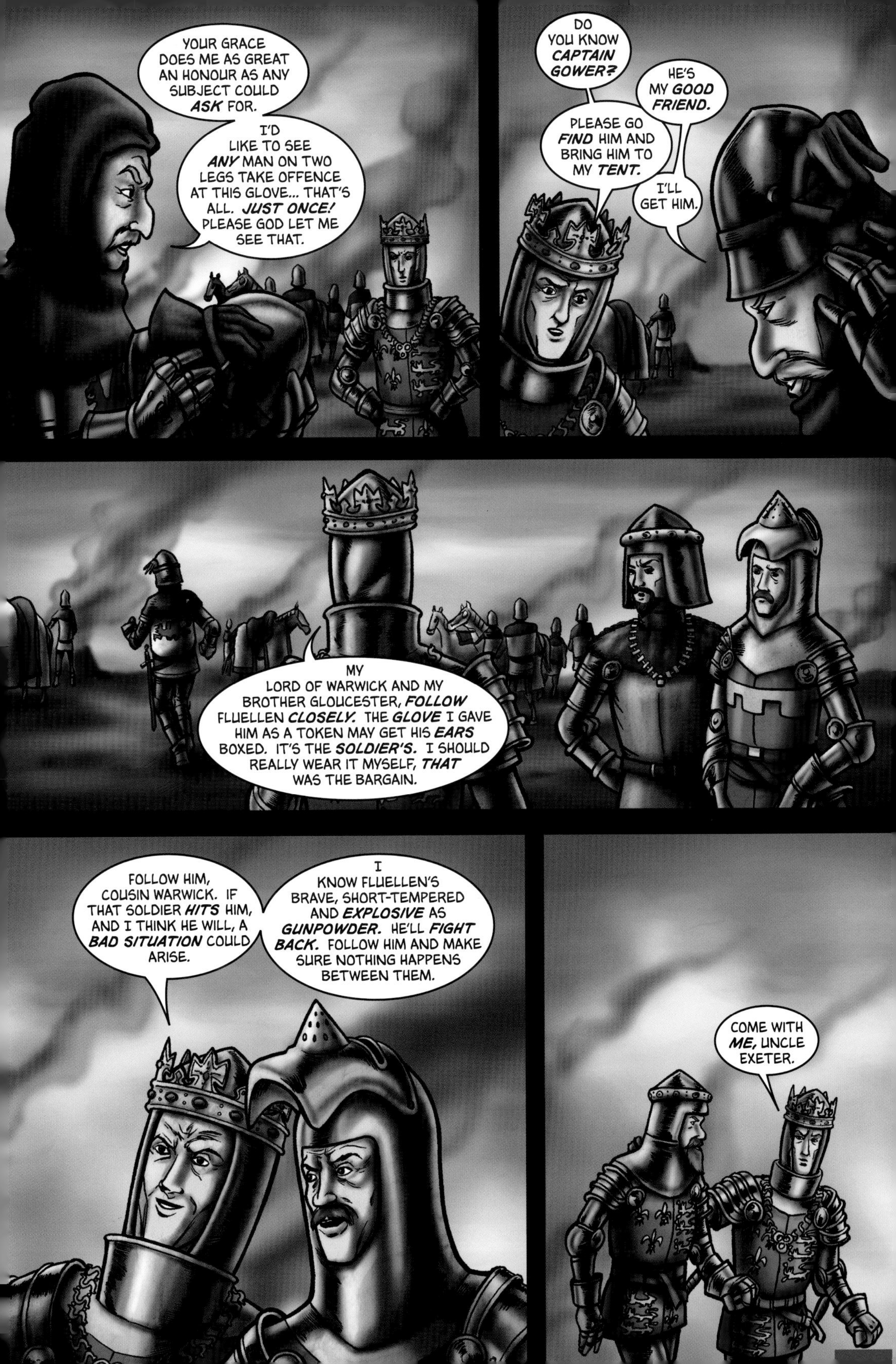
YOUR GRACE DOES ME AS GREAT AN HONOUR AS ANY SUBJECT COULD ASK FOR.
I'D LIKE TO SEE ANY MAN ON TWO LEGS TAKE OFFENCE AT THIS GLOVE... THAT'S ALL. JUST ONCE! PLEASE GOD LET ME SEE THAT.
DO YOU KNOW CAPTAIN GOWER?
HE'S MY GOOD FRIEND.
PLEASE GO FIND HIM AND BRING HIM TO MY TENT.
I'LL GET HIM.
MY LORD OF WARWICK AND MY BROTHER GLOUCESTER, FOLLOW FLUELLEN CLOSELY. THE GLOVE I GAVE HIM AS A TOKEN MAY GET HIS EARS BOXED. IT'S THE SOLDIER'S. I SHOULD REALLY WEAR IT MYSELF, THAT WAS THE BARGAIN.
FOLLOW HIM, COUSIN WARWICK. IF THAT SOLDIER HITS HIM, AND I THINK HE WILL, A BAD SITUATION COULD ARISE.
I KNOW FLUELLEN'S BRAVE, SHORT-TEMPERED AND EXPLOSIVE AS GUNPOWDER. HE'LL FIGHT BACK. FOLLOW HIM AND MAKE SURE NOTHING HAPPENS BETWEEN THEM.
COME WITH ME, UNCLE EXETER.

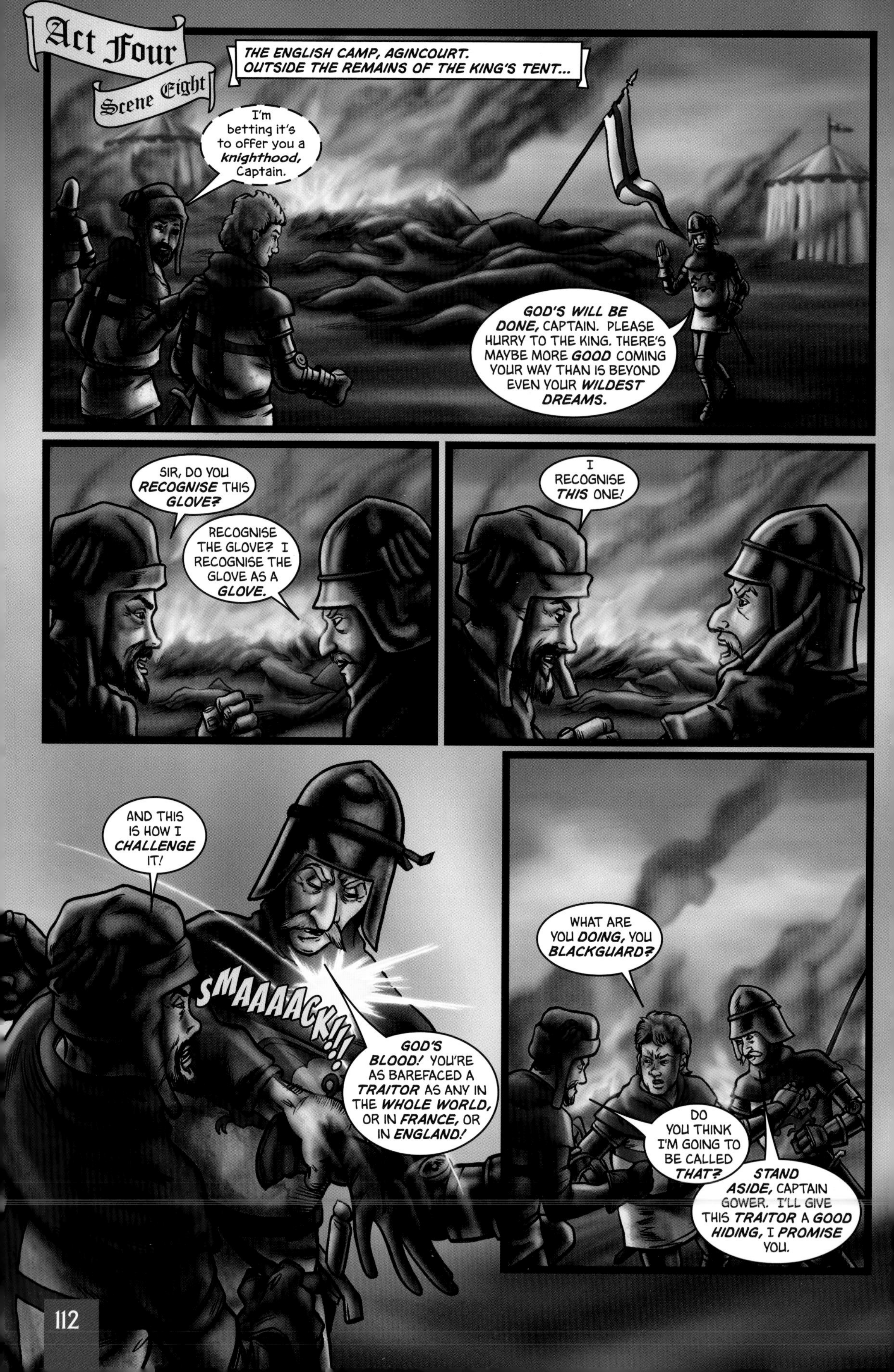
Act Four
Scene Eight
THE ENGLISH CAMP, AGINCOURT. OUTSIDE THE REMAINS OF THE KING'S TENT...
I'm betting it's to offer you a knighthood, Captain.
GOD'S WILL BE DONE, CAPTAIN. PLEASE HURRY TO THE KING. THERE'S MAYBE MORE GOOD COMING YOUR WAY THAN IS BEYOND EVEN YOUR WILDEST DREAMS.
SIR, DO YOU RECOGNISE THIS GLOVE?
RECOGNISE THE GLOVE? I RECOGNISE THE GLOVE AS A GLOVE.
I RECOGNISE THIS ONE!
AND THIS IS HOW I CHALLENGE IT!
SMAAAACK!!!
GOD'S BLOOD! YOU'RE AS BAREFACED A TRAITOR AS ANY IN THE WHOLE WORLD, OR IN FRANCE, OR IN ENGLAND!
WHAT ARE YOU DOING, YOU BLACKGUARD?
DO YOU THINK I'M GOING TO BE CALLED THAT?
STAND ASIDE, CAPTAIN GOWER. I'LL GIVE THIS TRAITOR A GOOD HIDING, I PROMISE YOU.

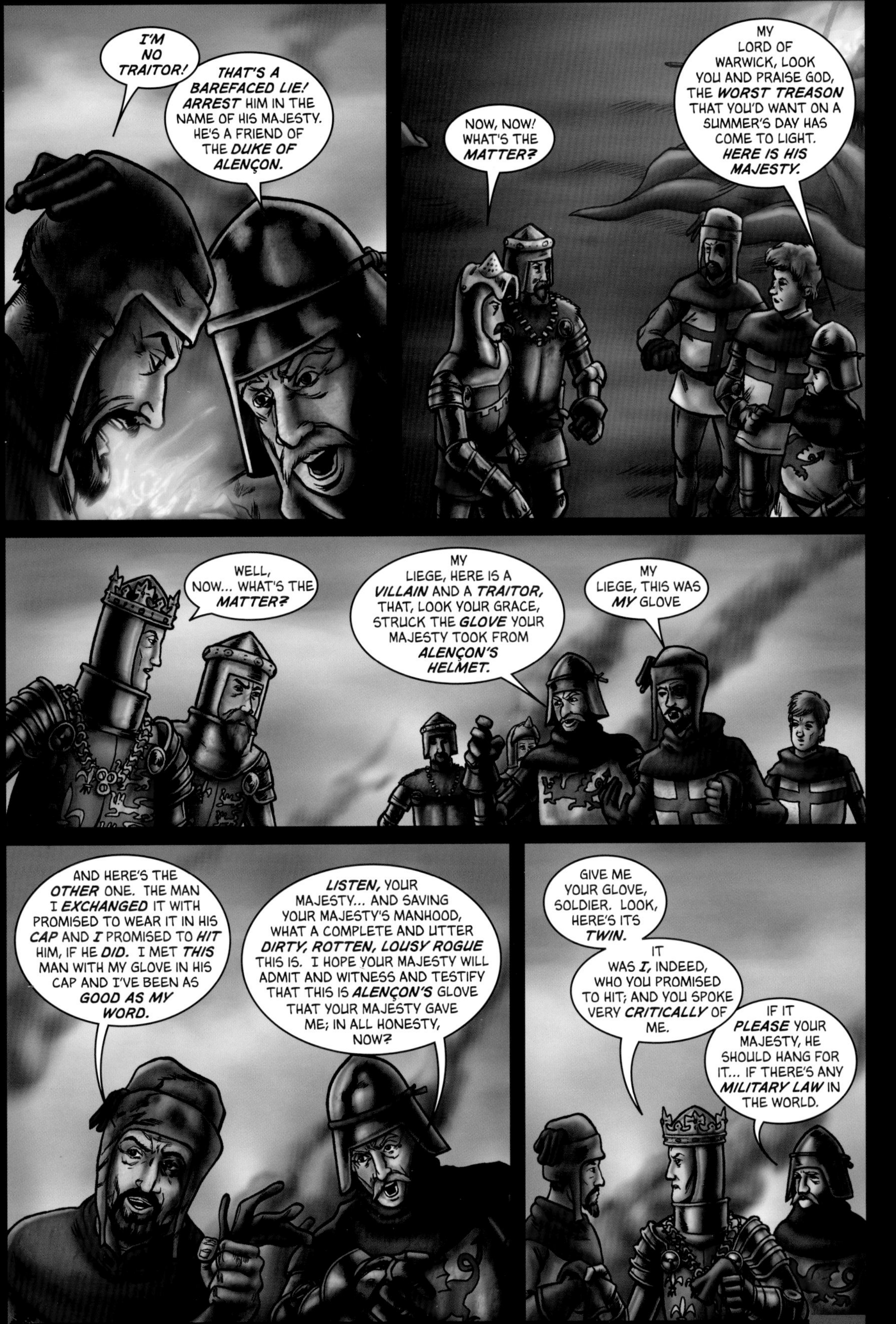
I'M NO TRAITOR!
THAT'S A BAREFACED LIE! ARREST HIM IN THE NAME OF HIS MAJESTY. HE'S A FRIEND OF THE DUKE OF ALENÇON.
NOW, NOW! WHAT'S THE MATTER?
MY LORD OF WARWICK, LOOK YOU AND PRAISE GOD, THE WORST TREASON THAT YOU'D WANT ON A SUMMER'S DAY HAS COME TO LIGHT. HERE IS HIS MAJESTY.
WELL, NOW... WHAT'S THE MATTER?
MY LIEGE, HERE IS A VILLAIN AND A TRAITOR, THAT, LOOK YOUR GRACE, STRUCK THE GLOVE YOUR MAJESTY TOOK FROM ALENÇON'S HELMET.
MY LIEGE, THIS WAS MY GLOVE
AND HERE'S THE OTHER ONE. THE MAN I EXCHANGED IT WITH PROMISED TO WEAR IT IN HIS CAP AND I PROMISED TO HIT HIM, IF HE DID. I MET THIS MAN WITH MY GLOVE IN HIS CAP AND I'VE BEEN AS GOOD AS MY WORD.
LISTEN, YOUR MAJESTY... AND SAVING YOUR MAJESTY'S MANHOOD, WHAT A COMPLETE AND UTTER DIRTY, ROTTEN, LOUSY ROGUE THIS IS. I HOPE YOUR MAJESTY WILL ADMIT AND WITNESS AND TESTIFY THAT THIS IS ALENÇON'S GLOVE THAT YOUR MAJESTY GAVE ME; IN ALL HONESTY, NOW?
GIVE ME YOUR GLOVE, SOLDIER. LOOK, HERE'S ITS TWIN.
IT WAS I, INDEED, WHO YOU PROMISED TO HIT; AND YOU SPOKE VERY CRITICALLY OF ME.
IF IT PLEASE YOUR MAJESTY, HE SHOULD HANG FOR IT... IF THERE'S ANY MILITARY LAW IN THE WORLD.

HOW CAN YOU GIVE ME *SATISFACTION?*

ALL OFFENCES, MY LORD, COME FROM THE *HEART.* NONE EVER CAME FROM *MINE,* THAT MIGHT *OFFEND* YOUR MAJESTY.

IT WAS *ME, PERSONALLY,* WHO YOU ABUSED.

YOUR MAJESTY CAME IN *DISGUISE.* YOU LOOKED TO ME LIKE A *COMMON MAN.* IT WAS *NIGHT,* YOUR CLOTHES, YOUR HUMBLE MANNER... WHATEVER ABUSE YOUR HIGHNESS SUFFERED IN *THAT* DISGUISE, YOU SHOULD CONSIDER IT TO BE YOUR *OWN* FAULT AND NOT *MINE.*

IF YOU'D BEEN WHO I *TOOK* YOU FOR, THERE WAS *NO OFFENCE.* SO, UNDER THE CIRCUMSTANCES, I ASK YOUR HIGHNESS TO *PARDON* ME.

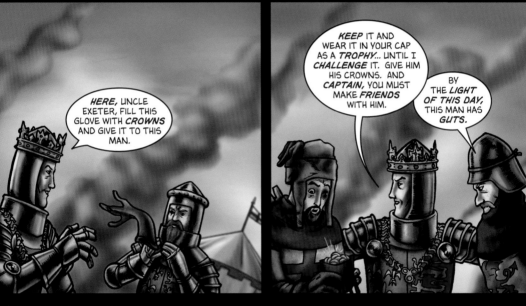

HERE, UNCLE EXETER, FILL THIS GLOVE WITH *CROWNS* AND GIVE IT TO THIS MAN.

KEEP IT AND WEAR IT IN YOUR CAP AS A *TROPHY...* UNTIL I *CHALLENGE* IT. GIVE HIM HIS CROWNS. AND *CAPTAIN,* YOU MUST MAKE *FRIENDS* WITH HIM.

BY THE *LIGHT OF THIS DAY,* THIS MAN HAS *GUTS.*

WAIT! HERE'S *TWELVE PENCE* FOR YOU; AND I HOPE YOU'LL SERVE GOD AND KEEP OUT OF *FIGHTS* AND *SQUABBLES* AND *QUARRELS* AND *ARGUMENTS.* I PROMISE THAT'S THE *BEST THING* FOR YOU.

I DON'T WANT *YOUR* MONEY.

IT'S IN *GOOD FAITH,* I CAN TELL YOU. YOU CAN USE IT TO *MEND YOUR SHOES.* COME ON, DON'T BE SHY. YOUR *SHOES* ARE IN A *STATE.* IF IT'S NOT A *GENUINE* SHILLING, I PROMISE YOU, I'LL *CHANGE* IT.

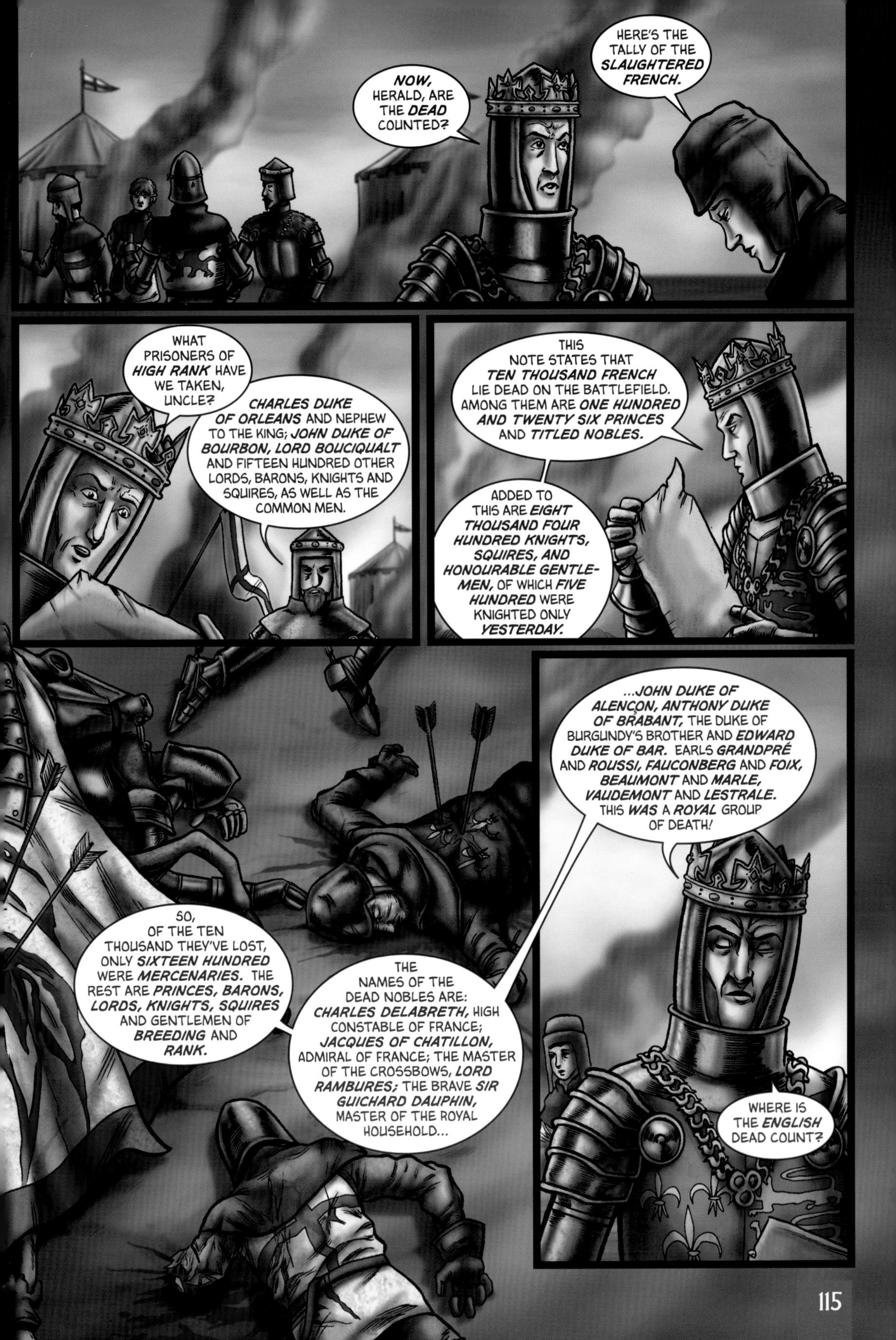
NOW, HERALD, ARE THE DEAD COUNTED?
HERE'S THE TALLY OF THE SLAUGHTERED FRENCH.
WHAT PRISONERS OF HIGH RANK HAVE WE TAKEN, UNCLE?
CHARLES DUKE OF ORLEANS AND NEPHEW TO THE KING; JOHN DUKE OF BOURBON, LORD BOUCIQUALT AND FIFTEEN HUNDRED OTHER LORDS, BARONS, KNIGHTS AND SQUIRES, AS WELL AS THE COMMON MEN.
THIS NOTE STATES THAT TEN THOUSAND FRENCH LIE DEAD ON THE BATTLEFIELD. AMONG THEM ARE ONE HUNDRED AND TWENTY SIX PRINCES AND TITLED NOBLES.
ADDED TO THIS ARE EIGHT THOUSAND FOUR HUNDRED KNIGHTS, SQUIRES, AND HONOURABLE GENTLEMEN, OF WHICH FIVE HUNDRED WERE KNIGHTED ONLY YESTERDAY.
SO, OF THE TEN THOUSAND THEY'VE LOST, ONLY SIXTEEN HUNDRED WERE MERCENARIES. THE REST ARE PRINCES, BARONS, LORDS, KNIGHTS, SQUIRES AND GENTLEMEN OF BREEDING AND RANK.
THE NAMES OF THE DEAD NOBLES ARE: CHARLES DELABRETH, HIGH CONSTABLE OF FRANCE; JACQUES OF CHATILLON, ADMIRAL OF FRANCE; THE MASTER OF THE CROSSBOWS, LORD RAMBURES; THE BRAVE SIR GUICHARD DAUPHIN, MASTER OF THE ROYAL HOUSEHOLD...
...JOHN DUKE OF ALENÇON, ANTHONY DUKE OF BRABANT, THE DUKE OF BURGUNDY'S BROTHER AND EDWARD DUKE OF BAR. EARLS GRANDPRÉ AND ROUSSI, FAUCONBERG AND FOIX, BEAUMONT AND MARLE, VAUDEMONT AND LESTRALE. THIS WAS A ROYAL GROUP OF DEATH!
WHERE IS THE ENGLISH DEAD COUNT?

EDWARD, DUKE OF YORK; THE EARL OF SUFFOLK; SIR RICHARD KETLY; DAVY GAM ESQUIRE. NOBODY ELSE OF NOBLE BIRTH AND ONLY TWENTY FIVE OTHER MEN. OH GOD, YOUR POWER WAS WITH US!

WE MUST THANK YOU ALONE FOR OUR VICTORY! WHEN WERE SUCH LARGE AND SUCH SMALL LOSSES EVER KNOWN IN REGULAR BATTLE, THAT IS, NOT COUNTING AMBUSHES OR SKIRMISHES? TAKE CREDIT FOR IT GOD, FOR IT IS YOURS ALONE!

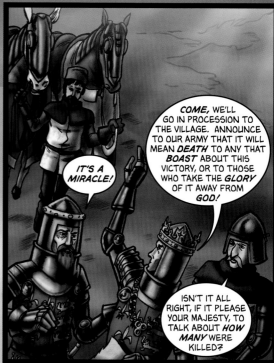

IT'S A MIRACLE!

COME, WE'LL GO IN PROCESSION TO THE VILLAGE. ANNOUNCE TO OUR ARMY THAT IT WILL MEAN DEATH TO ANY THAT BOAST ABOUT THIS VICTORY, OR TO THOSE WHO TAKE THE GLORY OF IT AWAY FROM GOD!

ISN'T IT ALL RIGHT, IF IT PLEASE YOUR MAJESTY, TO TALK ABOUT HOW MANY WERE KILLED?

YES, CAPTAIN; BUT YOU MUST ACKNOWLEDGE THAT GOD FOUGHT WITH US.

YES. HE GAVE US GREAT HELP.

WE'LL CELEBRATE ALL THE HOLY RITES. LET THE 'NON NOBIS' AND THE 'TE DEUM' BE SUNG. THE DEAD WILL BE BURIED WITH HONOUR. THEN WE'LL GO TO CALAIS; AND FROM THERE ON TO ENGLAND -- WE'LL BE THE HAPPIEST MEN TO EVER ARRIVE THERE FROM FRANCE.

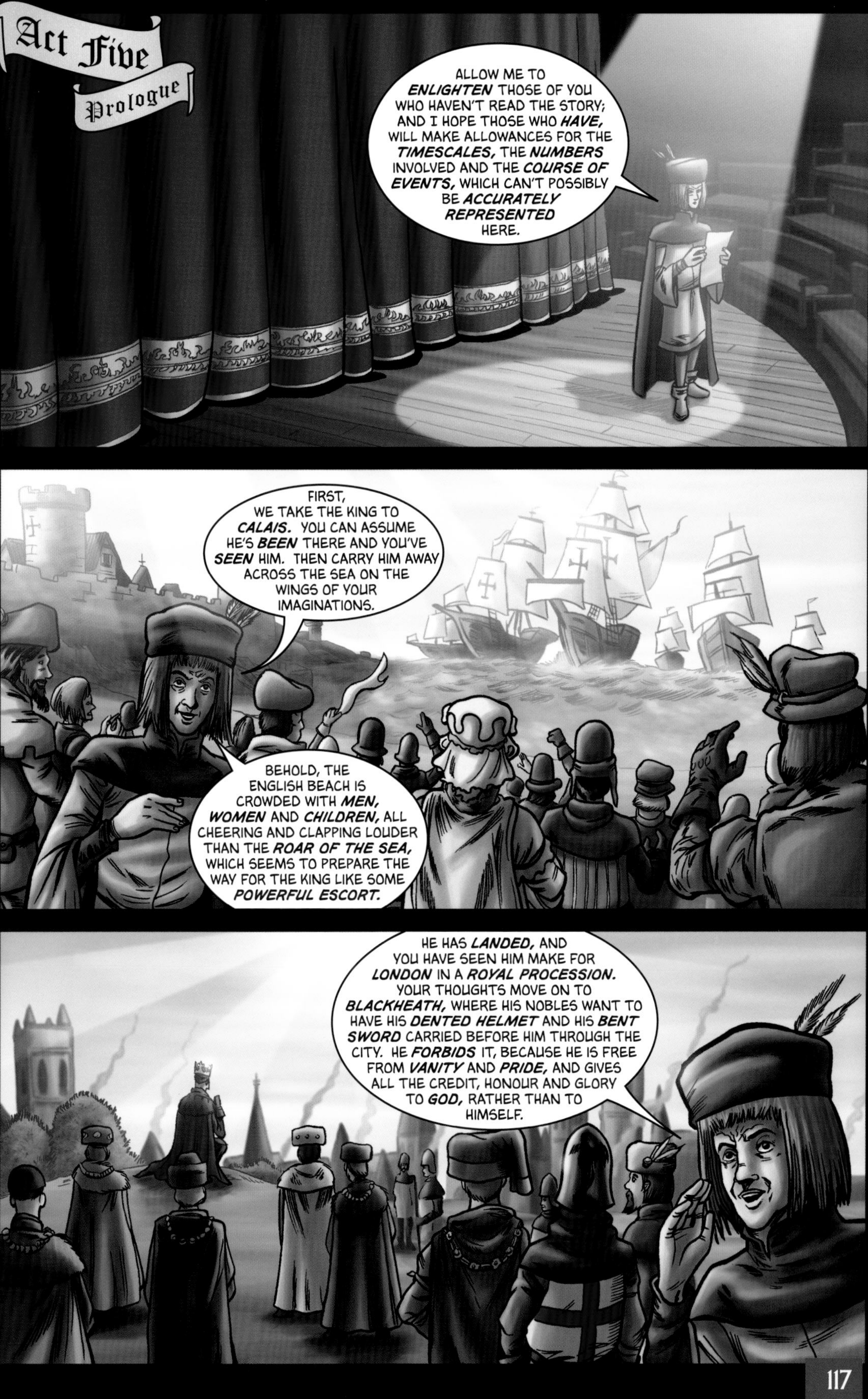
Act Five
Prologue
ALLOW ME TO ENLIGHTEN THOSE OF YOU WHO HAVEN'T READ THE STORY; AND I HOPE THOSE WHO HAVE, WILL MAKE ALLOWANCES FOR THE TIMESCALES, THE NUMBERS INVOLVED AND THE COURSE OF EVENTS, WHICH CAN'T POSSIBLY BE ACCURATELY REPRESENTED HERE.
FIRST, WE TAKE THE KING TO CALAIS. YOU CAN ASSUME HE'S BEEN THERE AND YOU'VE SEEN HIM. THEN CARRY HIM AWAY ACROSS THE SEA ON THE WINGS OF YOUR IMAGINATIONS.
BEHOLD, THE ENGLISH BEACH IS CROWDED WITH MEN, WOMEN AND CHILDREN, ALL CHEERING AND CLAPPING LOUDER THAN THE ROAR OF THE SEA, WHICH SEEMS TO PREPARE THE WAY FOR THE KING LIKE SOME POWERFUL ESCORT.
HE HAS LANDED, AND YOU HAVE SEEN HIM MAKE FOR LONDON IN A ROYAL PROCESSION. YOUR THOUGHTS MOVE ON TO BLACKHEATH, WHERE HIS NOBLES WANT TO HAVE HIS DENTED HELMET AND HIS BENT SWORD CARRIED BEFORE HIM THROUGH THE CITY. HE FORBIDS IT, BECAUSE HE IS FREE FROM VANITY AND PRIDE, AND GIVES ALL THE CREDIT, HONOUR AND GLORY TO GOD, RATHER THAN TO HIMSELF.

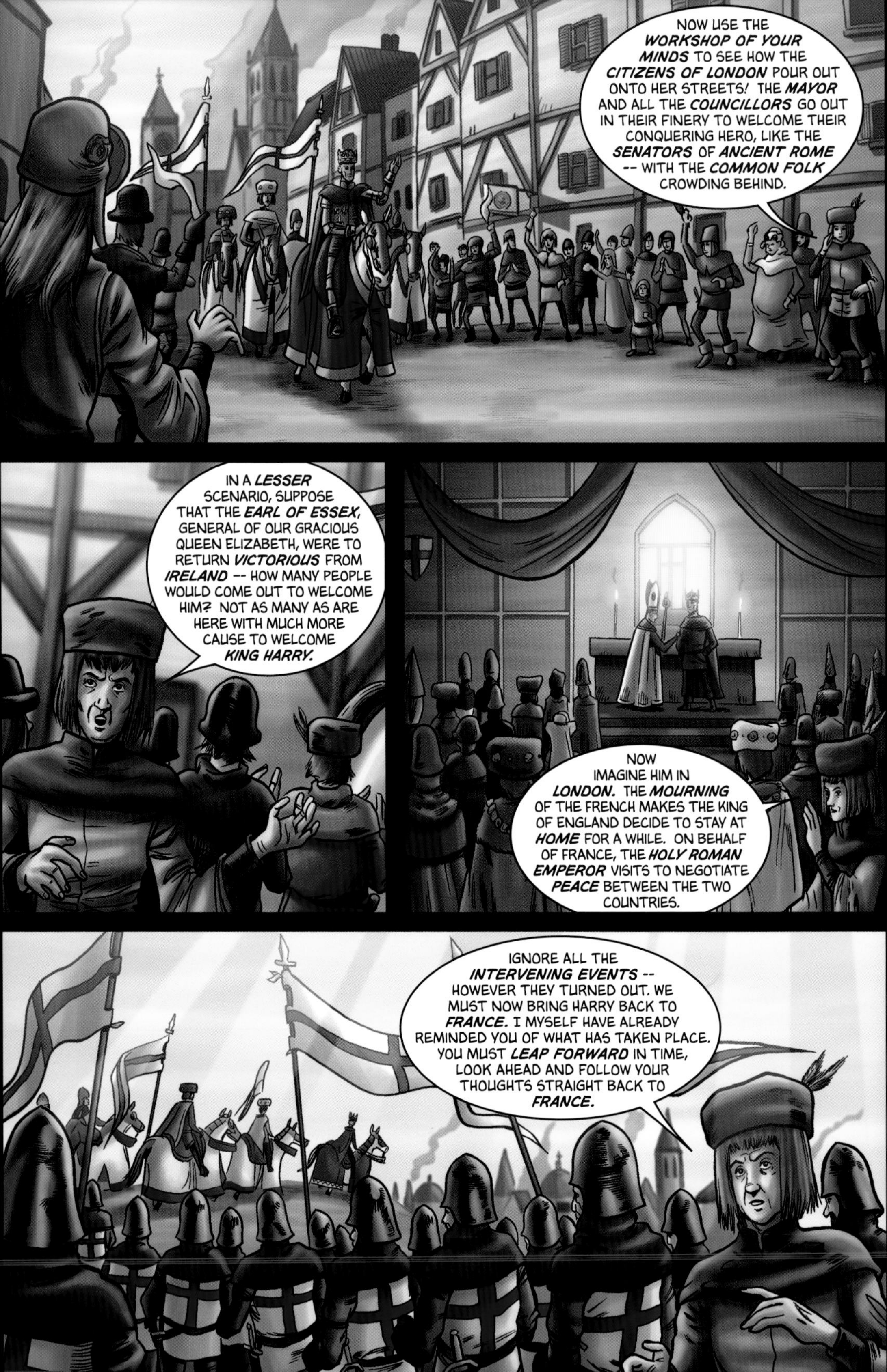
NOW USE THE WORKSHOP OF YOUR MINDS TO SEE HOW THE CITIZENS OF LONDON POUR OUT ONTO HER STREETS! THE MAYOR AND ALL THE COUNCILLORS GO OUT IN THEIR FINERY TO WELCOME THEIR CONQUERING HERO, LIKE THE SENATORS OF ANCIENT ROME -- WITH THE COMMON FOLK CROWDING BEHIND.
IN A LESSER SCENARIO, SUPPOSE THAT THE EARL OF ESSEX, GENERAL OF OUR GRACIOUS QUEEN ELIZABETH, WERE TO RETURN VICTORIOUS FROM IRELAND -- HOW MANY PEOPLE WOULD COME OUT TO WELCOME HIM? NOT AS MANY AS ARE HERE WITH MUCH MORE CAUSE TO WELCOME KING HARRY.
NOW IMAGINE HIM IN LONDON. THE MOURNING OF THE FRENCH MAKES THE KING OF ENGLAND DECIDE TO STAY AT HOME FOR A WHILE. ON BEHALF OF FRANCE, THE HOLY ROMAN EMPEROR VISITS TO NEGOTIATE PEACE BETWEEN THE TWO COUNTRIES.
IGNORE ALL THE INTERVENING EVENTS -- HOWEVER THEY TURNED OUT. WE MUST NOW BRING HARRY BACK TO FRANCE. I MYSELF HAVE ALREADY REMINDED YOU OF WHAT HAS TAKEN PLACE. YOU MUST LEAP FORWARD IN TIME, LOOK AHEAD AND FOLLOW YOUR THOUGHTS STRAIGHT BACK TO FRANCE.

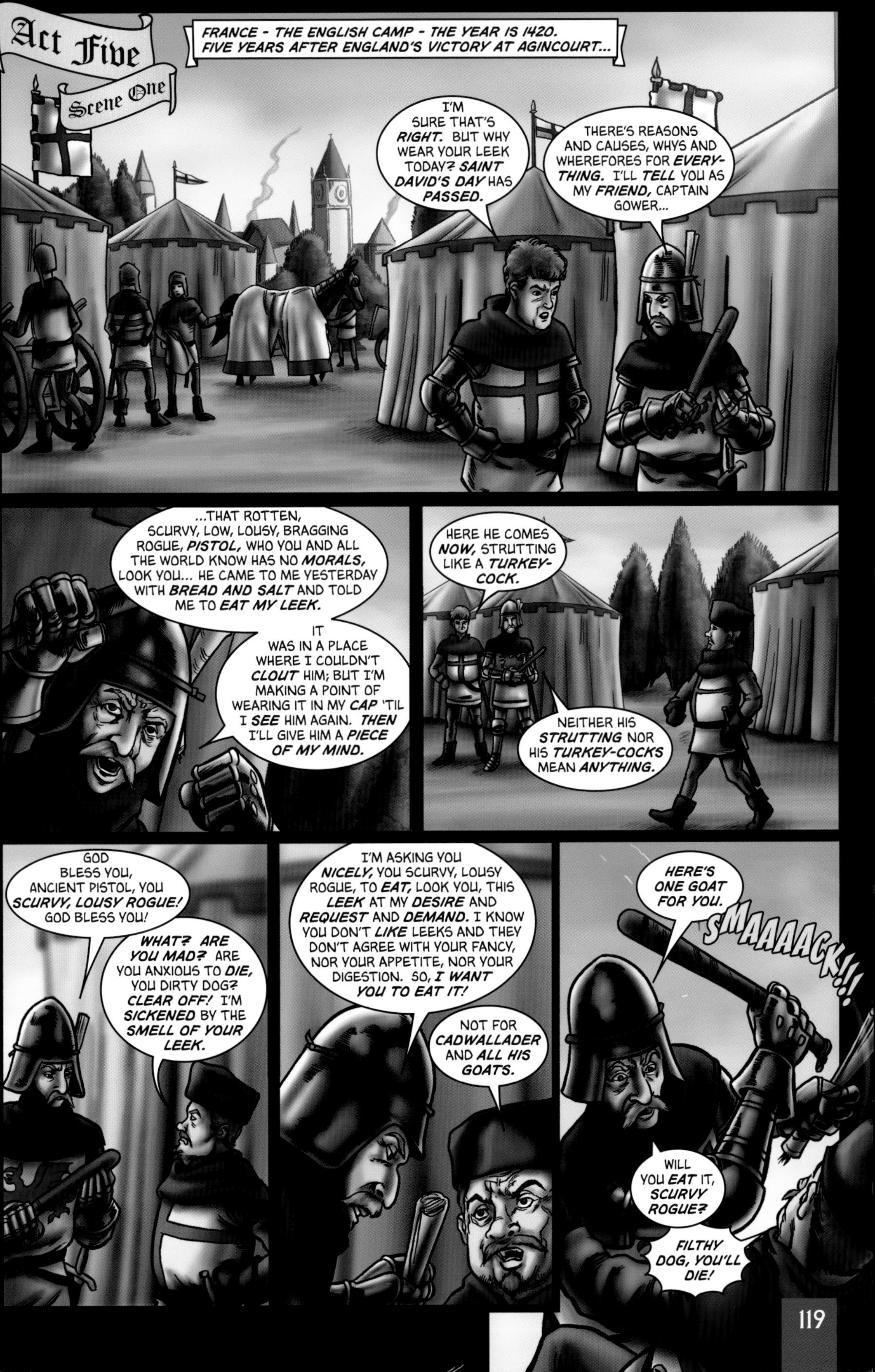
Act Five
Scene One
FRANCE - THE ENGLISH CAMP - THE YEAR IS 1420. FIVE YEARS AFTER ENGLAND'S VICTORY AT AGINCOURT...
I'M SURE THAT'S RIGHT. BUT WHY WEAR YOUR LEEK TODAY? SAINT DAVID'S DAY HAS PASSED.
THERE'S REASONS AND CAUSES, WHYS AND WHEREFORES FOR EVERYTHING. I'LL TELL YOU AS MY FRIEND, CAPTAIN GOWER...
...THAT ROTTEN, SCURVY, LOW, LOUSY, BRAGGING ROGUE, PISTOL, WHO YOU AND ALL THE WORLD KNOW HAS NO MORALS, LOOK YOU... HE CAME TO ME YESTERDAY WITH BREAD AND SALT AND TOLD ME TO EAT MY LEEK.
IT WAS IN A PLACE WHERE I COULDN'T CLOUT HIM; BUT I'M MAKING A POINT OF WEARING IT IN MY CAP 'TIL I SEE HIM AGAIN. THEN I'LL GIVE HIM A PIECE OF MY MIND.
HERE HE COMES NOW, STRUTTING LIKE A TURKEY-COCK.
NEITHER HIS STRUTTING NOR HIS TURKEY-COCKS MEAN ANYTHING.
GOD BLESS YOU, ANCIENT PISTOL, YOU SCURVY, LOUSY ROGUE! GOD BLESS YOU!
WHAT? ARE YOU MAD? ARE YOU ANXIOUS TO DIE, YOU DIRTY DOG? CLEAR OFF! I'M SICKENED BY THE SMELL OF YOUR LEEK.
I'M ASKING YOU NICELY, YOU SCURVY, LOUSY ROGUE, TO EAT, LOOK YOU, THIS LEEK AT MY DESIRE AND REQUEST AND DEMAND. I KNOW YOU DON'T LIKE LEEKS AND THEY DON'T AGREE WITH YOUR FANCY, NOR YOUR APPETITE, NOR YOUR DIGESTION. SO, I WANT YOU TO EAT IT!
NOT FOR CADWALLADER AND ALL HIS GOATS.
HERE'S ONE GOAT FOR YOU.
SMAAAACK!!!
WILL YOU EAT IT, SCURVY ROGUE?
FILTHY DOG, YOU'LL DIE!

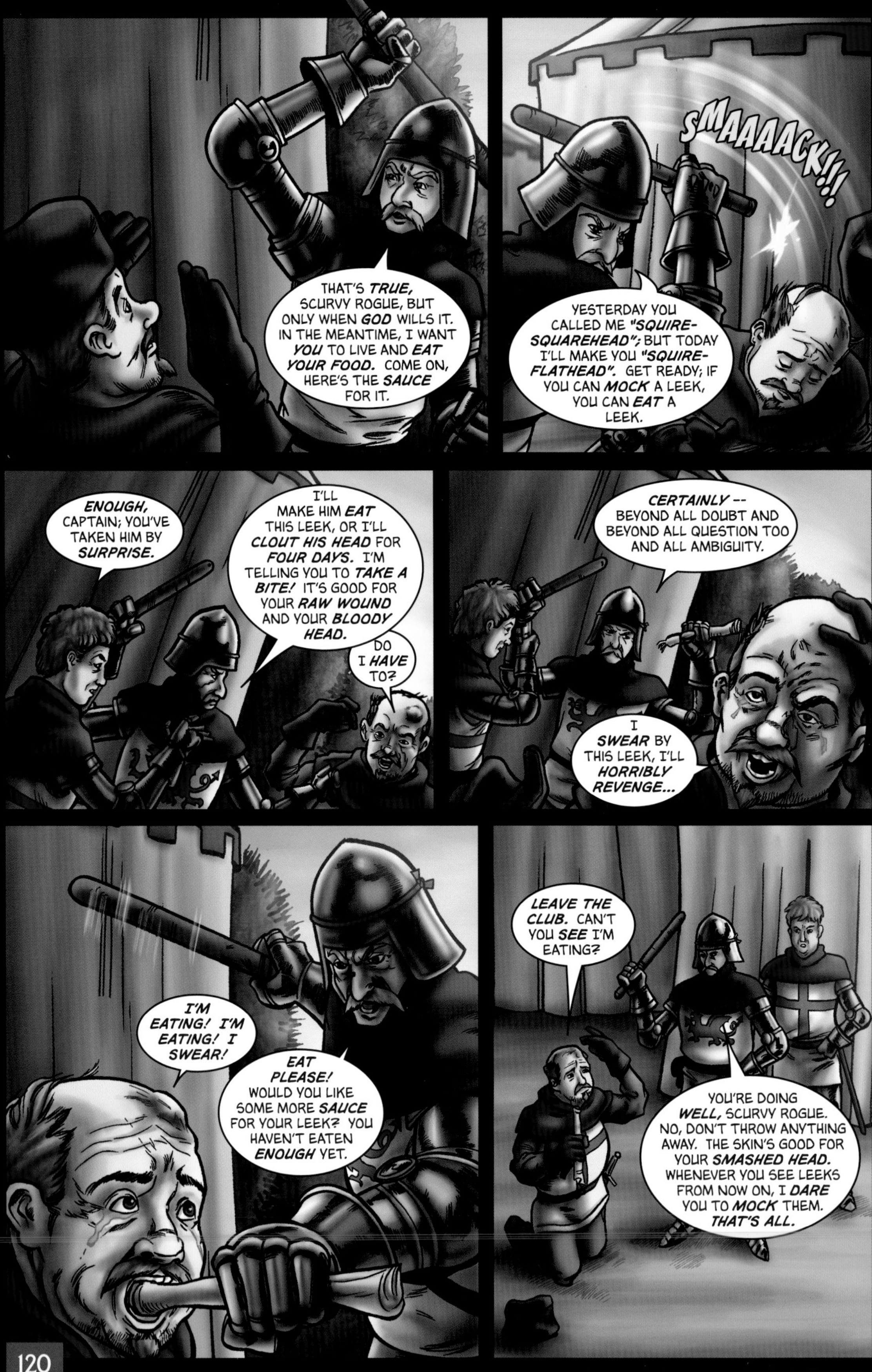
THAT'S TRUE, SCURVY ROGUE, BUT ONLY WHEN GOD WILLS IT. IN THE MEANTIME, I WANT YOU TO LIVE AND EAT YOUR FOOD. COME ON, HERE'S THE SAUCE FOR IT.
SMAAAACK!!!
YESTERDAY YOU CALLED ME "SQUIRE-SQUAREHEAD"; BUT TODAY I'LL MAKE YOU "SQUIRE-FLATHEAD". GET READY; IF YOU CAN MOCK A LEEK, YOU CAN EAT A LEEK.
ENOUGH, CAPTAIN; YOU'VE TAKEN HIM BY SURPRISE.
I'LL MAKE HIM EAT THIS LEEK, OR I'LL CLOUT HIS HEAD FOR FOUR DAYS. I'M TELLING YOU TO TAKE A BITE! IT'S GOOD FOR YOUR RAW WOUND AND YOUR BLOODY HEAD.
DO I HAVE TO?
CERTAINLY -- BEYOND ALL DOUBT AND BEYOND ALL QUESTION TOO AND ALL AMBIGUITY.
I SWEAR BY THIS LEEK, I'LL HORRIBLY REVENGE...
I'M EATING! I'M EATING! I SWEAR!
EAT PLEASE! WOULD YOU LIKE SOME MORE SAUCE FOR YOUR LEEK? YOU HAVEN'T EATEN ENOUGH YET.
LEAVE THE CLUB. CAN'T YOU SEE I'M EATING?
YOU'RE DOING WELL, SCURVY ROGUE. NO, DON'T THROW ANYTHING AWAY. THE SKIN'S GOOD FOR YOUR SMASHED HEAD. WHENEVER YOU SEE LEEKS FROM NOW ON, I DARE YOU TO MOCK THEM. THAT'S ALL.

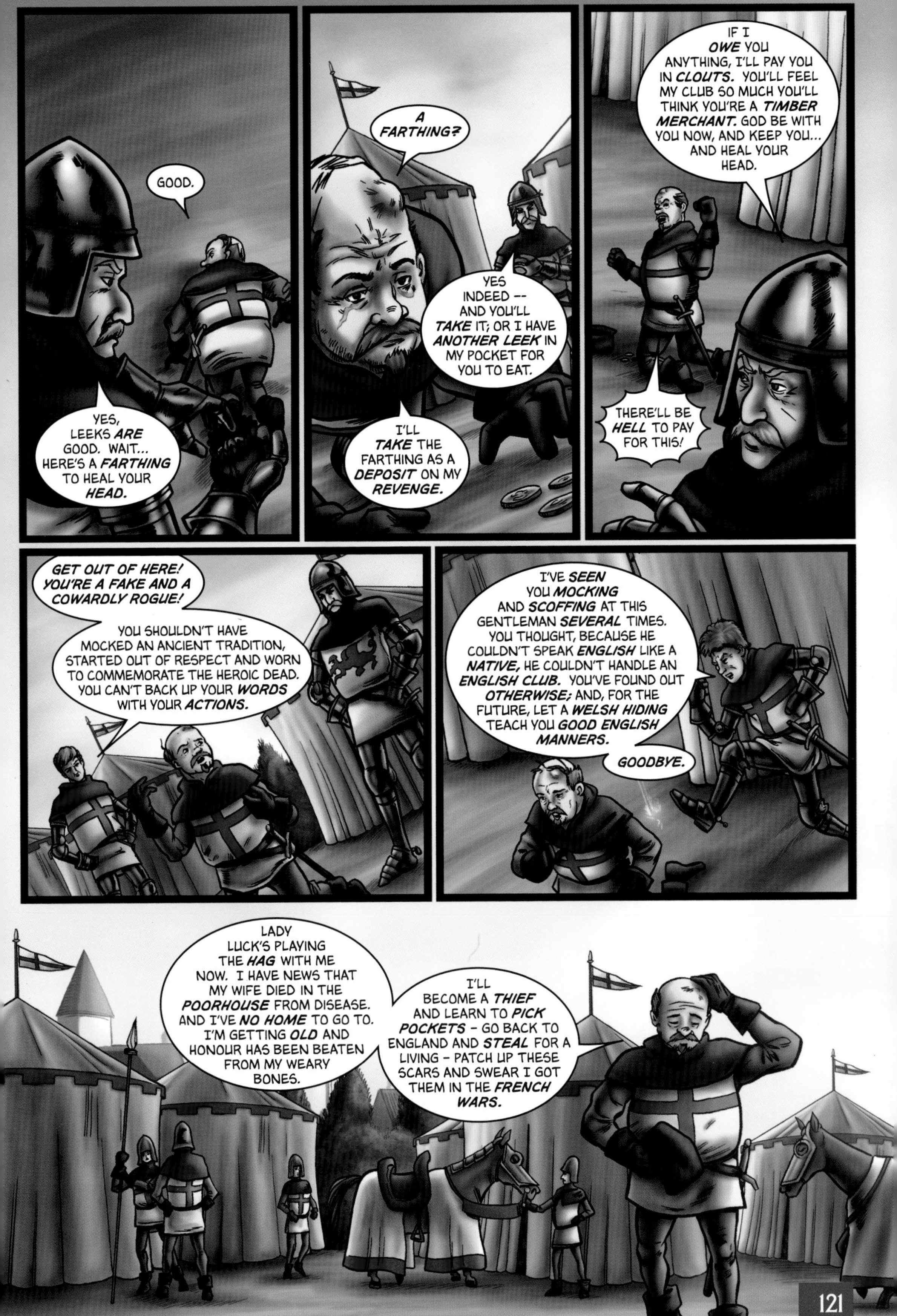
GOOD.
YES, LEEKS ARE GOOD. WAIT... HERE'S A FARTHING TO HEAL YOUR HEAD.
A FARTHING?
YES INDEED -- AND YOU'LL TAKE IT; OR I HAVE ANOTHER LEEK IN MY POCKET FOR YOU TO EAT.
I'LL TAKE THE FARTHING AS A DEPOSIT ON MY REVENGE.
IF I OWE YOU ANYTHING, I'LL PAY YOU IN CLOUTS. YOU'LL FEEL MY CLUB SO MUCH YOU'LL THINK YOU'RE A TIMBER MERCHANT. GOD BE WITH YOU NOW, AND KEEP YOU... AND HEAL YOUR HEAD.
THERE'LL BE HELL TO PAY FOR THIS!
GET OUT OF HERE! YOU'RE A FAKE AND A COWARDLY ROGUE!
YOU SHOULDN'T HAVE MOCKED AN ANCIENT TRADITION, STARTED OUT OF RESPECT AND WORN TO COMMEMORATE THE HEROIC DEAD. YOU CAN'T BACK UP YOUR WORDS WITH YOUR ACTIONS.
I'VE SEEN YOU MOCKING AND SCOFFING AT THIS GENTLEMAN SEVERAL TIMES. YOU THOUGHT, BECAUSE HE COULDN'T SPEAK ENGLISH LIKE A NATIVE, HE COULDN'T HANDLE AN ENGLISH CLUB. YOU'VE FOUND OUT OTHERWISE; AND, FOR THE FUTURE, LET A WELSH HIDING TEACH YOU GOOD ENGLISH MANNERS.
GOODBYE.
LADY LUCK'S PLAYING THE HAG WITH ME NOW. I HAVE NEWS THAT MY WIFE DIED IN THE POORHOUSE FROM DISEASE. AND I'VE NO HOME TO GO TO. I'M GETTING OLD AND HONOUR HAS BEEN BEATEN FROM MY WEARY BONES.
I'LL BECOME A THIEF AND LEARN TO PICK POCKETS – GO BACK TO ENGLAND AND STEAL FOR A LIVING – PATCH UP THESE SCARS AND SWEAR I GOT THEM IN THE FRENCH WARS.

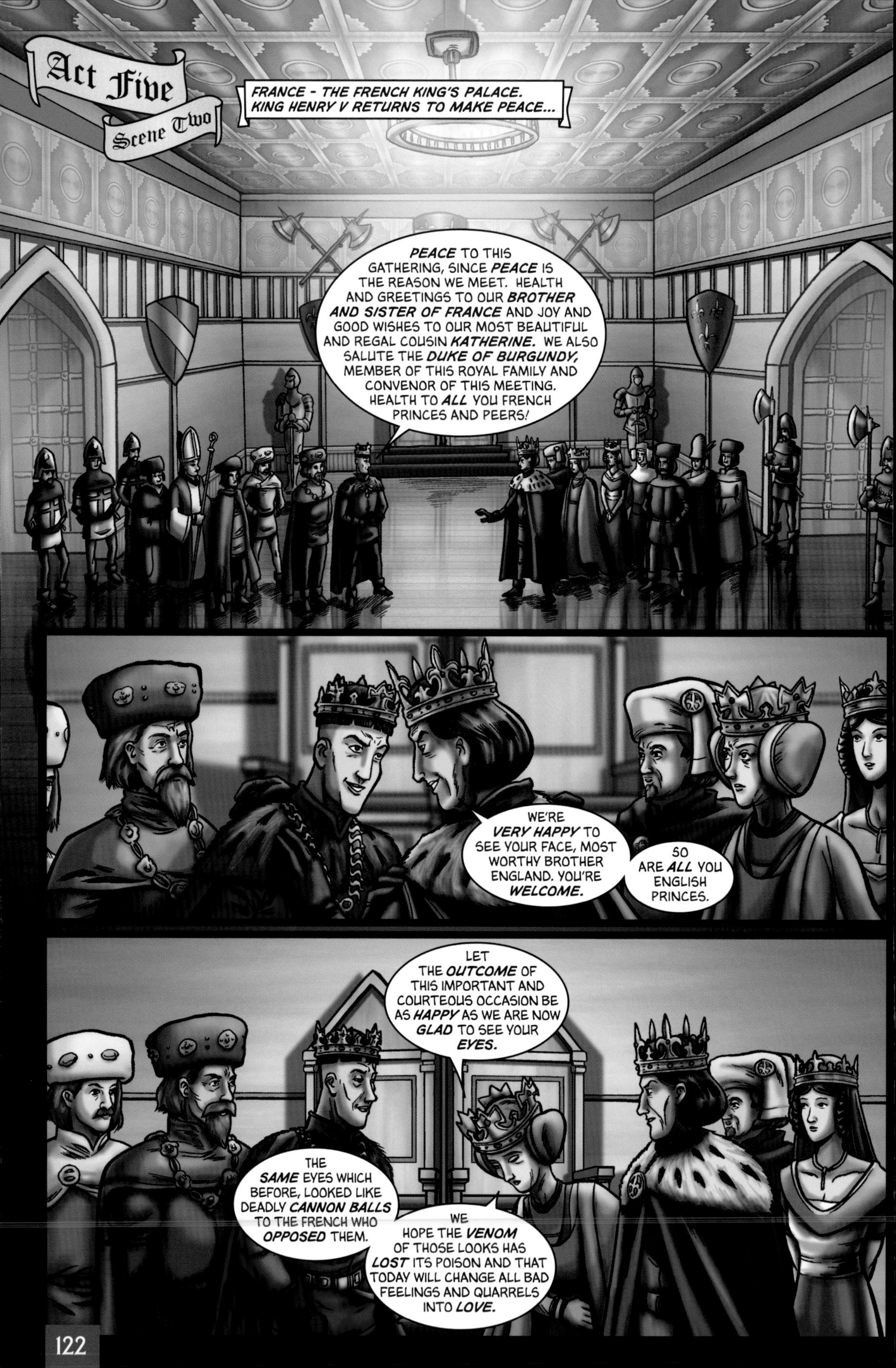
Act Five
Scene Two
FRANCE - THE FRENCH KING'S PALACE. KING HENRY V RETURNS TO MAKE PEACE...
PEACE TO THIS GATHERING, SINCE PEACE IS THE REASON WE MEET. HEALTH AND GREETINGS TO OUR BROTHER AND SISTER OF FRANCE AND JOY AND GOOD WISHES TO OUR MOST BEAUTIFUL AND REGAL COUSIN KATHERINE. WE ALSO SALUTE THE DUKE OF BURGUNDY, MEMBER OF THIS ROYAL FAMILY AND CONVENOR OF THIS MEETING. HEALTH TO ALL YOU FRENCH PRINCES AND PEERS!
WE'RE VERY HAPPY TO SEE YOUR FACE, MOST WORTHY BROTHER ENGLAND. YOU'RE WELCOME.
SO ARE ALL YOU ENGLISH PRINCES.
LET THE OUTCOME OF THIS IMPORTANT AND COURTEOUS OCCASION BE AS HAPPY AS WE ARE NOW GLAD TO SEE YOUR EYES.
THE SAME EYES WHICH BEFORE, LOOKED LIKE DEADLY CANNON BALLS TO THE FRENCH WHO OPPOSED THEM.
WE HOPE THE VENOM OF THOSE LOOKS HAS LOST ITS POISON AND THAT TODAY WILL CHANGE ALL BAD FEELINGS AND QUARRELS INTO LOVE.

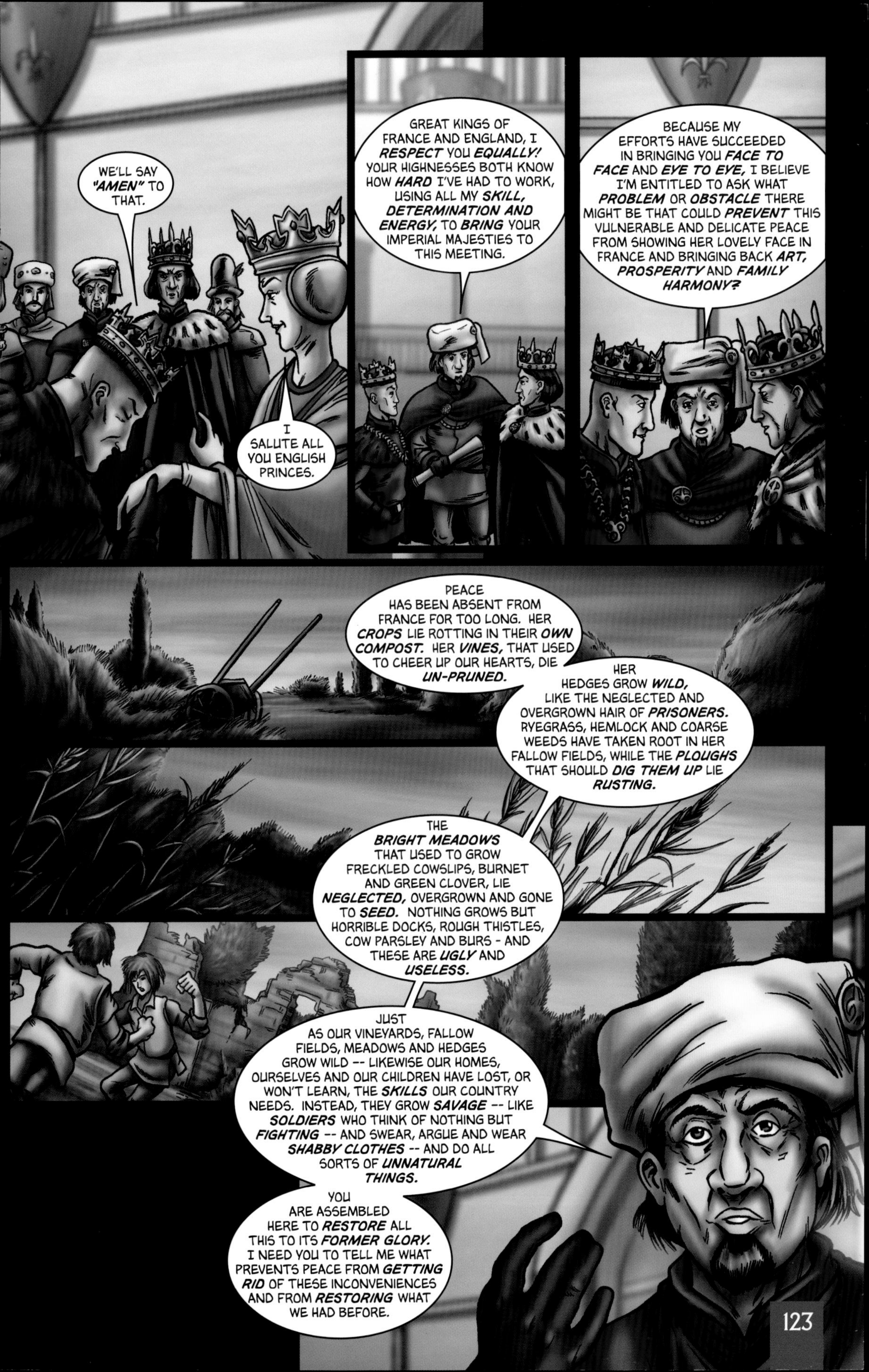
WE'LL SAY "AMEN" TO THAT.
I SALUTE ALL YOU ENGLISH PRINCES.
GREAT KINGS OF FRANCE AND ENGLAND, I RESPECT YOU EQUALLY! YOUR HIGHNESSES BOTH KNOW HOW HARD I'VE HAD TO WORK, USING ALL MY SKILL, DETERMINATION AND ENERGY, TO BRING YOUR IMPERIAL MAJESTIES TO THIS MEETING.
BECAUSE MY EFFORTS HAVE SUCCEEDED IN BRINGING YOU FACE TO FACE AND EYE TO EYE, I BELIEVE I'M ENTITLED TO ASK WHAT PROBLEM OR OBSTACLE THERE MIGHT BE THAT COULD PREVENT THIS VULNERABLE AND DELICATE PEACE FROM SHOWING HER LOVELY FACE IN FRANCE AND BRINGING BACK ART, PROSPERITY AND FAMILY HARMONY?
PEACE HAS BEEN ABSENT FROM FRANCE FOR TOO LONG. HER CROPS LIE ROTTING IN THEIR OWN COMPOST. HER VINES, THAT USED TO CHEER UP OUR HEARTS, DIE UN-PRUNED.
HER HEDGES GROW WILD, LIKE THE NEGLECTED AND OVERGROWN HAIR OF PRISONERS. RYEGRASS, HEMLOCK AND COARSE WEEDS HAVE TAKEN ROOT IN HER FALLOW FIELDS, WHILE THE PLOUGHS THAT SHOULD DIG THEM UP LIE RUSTING.
THE BRIGHT MEADOWS THAT USED TO GROW FRECKLED COWSLIPS, BURNET AND GREEN CLOVER, LIE NEGLECTED, OVERGROWN AND GONE TO SEED. NOTHING GROWS BUT HORRIBLE DOCKS, ROUGH THISTLES, COW PARSLEY AND BURS - AND THESE ARE UGLY AND USELESS.
JUST AS OUR VINEYARDS, FALLOW FIELDS, MEADOWS AND HEDGES GROW WILD -- LIKEWISE OUR HOMES, OURSELVES AND OUR CHILDREN HAVE LOST, OR WON'T LEARN, THE SKILLS OUR COUNTRY NEEDS. INSTEAD, THEY GROW SAVAGE -- LIKE SOLDIERS WHO THINK OF NOTHING BUT FIGHTING -- AND SWEAR, ARGUE AND WEAR SHABBY CLOTHES -- AND DO ALL SORTS OF UNNATURAL THINGS.
YOU ARE ASSEMBLED HERE TO RESTORE ALL THIS TO ITS FORMER GLORY. I NEED YOU TO TELL ME WHAT PREVENTS PEACE FROM GETTING RID OF THESE INCONVENIENCES AND FROM RESTORING WHAT WE HAD BEFORE.

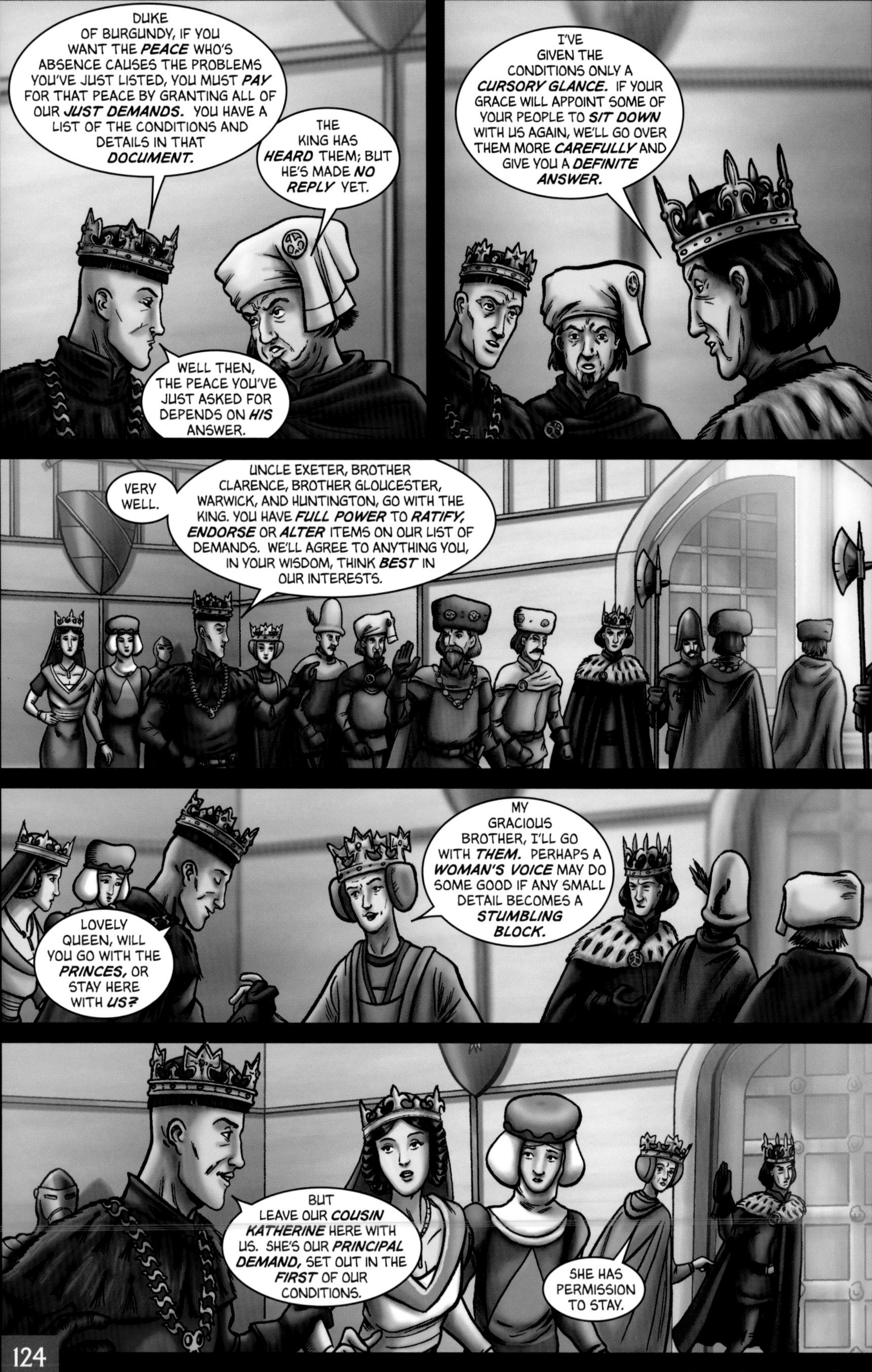
DUKE OF BURGUNDY, IF YOU WANT THE PEACE WHO'S ABSENCE CAUSES THE PROBLEMS YOU'VE JUST LISTED, YOU MUST PAY FOR THAT PEACE BY GRANTING ALL OF OUR JUST DEMANDS. YOU HAVE A LIST OF THE CONDITIONS AND DETAILS IN THAT DOCUMENT.
THE KING HAS HEARD THEM; BUT HE'S MADE NO REPLY YET.
WELL THEN, THE PEACE YOU'VE JUST ASKED FOR DEPENDS ON HIS ANSWER.
I'VE GIVEN THE CONDITIONS ONLY A CURSORY GLANCE. IF YOUR GRACE WILL APPOINT SOME OF YOUR PEOPLE TO SIT DOWN WITH US AGAIN, WE'LL GO OVER THEM MORE CAREFULLY AND GIVE YOU A DEFINITE ANSWER.
VERY WELL.
UNCLE EXETER, BROTHER CLARENCE, BROTHER GLOUCESTER, WARWICK, AND HUNTINGTON, GO WITH THE KING. YOU HAVE FULL POWER TO RATIFY, ENDORSE OR ALTER ITEMS ON OUR LIST OF DEMANDS. WE'LL AGREE TO ANYTHING YOU, IN YOUR WISDOM, THINK BEST IN OUR INTERESTS.
LOVELY QUEEN, WILL YOU GO WITH THE PRINCES, OR STAY HERE WITH US?
MY GRACIOUS BROTHER, I'LL GO WITH THEM. PERHAPS A WOMAN'S VOICE MAY DO SOME GOOD IF ANY SMALL DETAIL BECOMES A STUMBLING BLOCK.
BUT LEAVE OUR COUSIN KATHERINE HERE WITH US. SHE'S OUR PRINCIPAL DEMAND, SET OUT IN THE FIRST OF OUR CONDITIONS.
SHE HAS PERMISSION TO STAY.

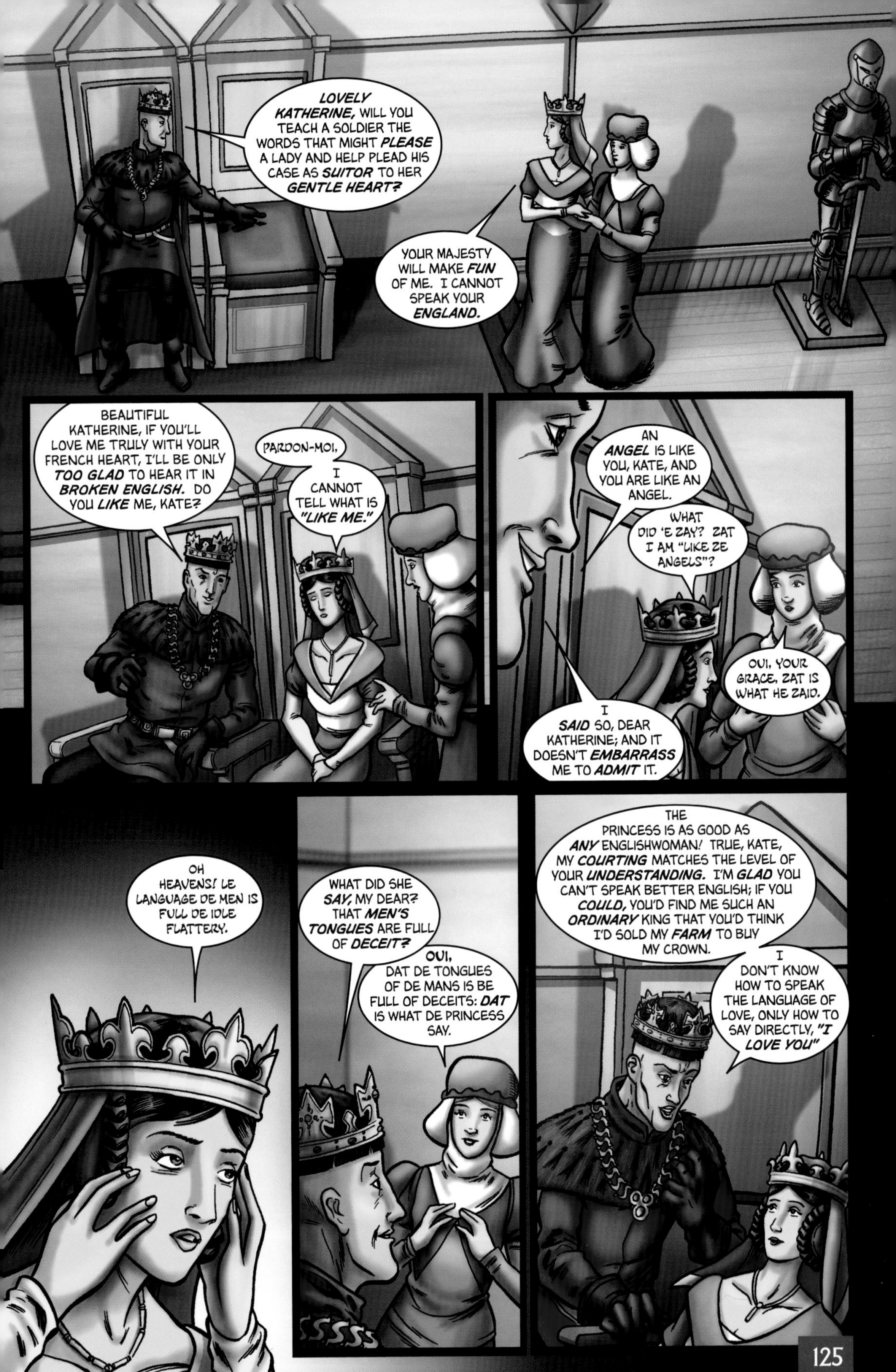
LOVELY KATHERINE, WILL YOU TEACH A SOLDIER THE WORDS THAT MIGHT PLEASE A LADY AND HELP PLEAD HIS CASE AS SUITOR TO HER GENTLE HEART?
YOUR MAJESTY WILL MAKE FUN OF ME. I CANNOT SPEAK YOUR ENGLAND.
BEAUTIFUL KATHERINE, IF YOU'LL LOVE ME TRULY WITH YOUR FRENCH HEART, I'LL BE ONLY TOO GLAD TO HEAR IT IN BROKEN ENGLISH. DO YOU LIKE ME, KATE?
PARDON-MOI,
I CANNOT TELL WHAT IS "LIKE ME."
AN ANGEL IS LIKE YOU, KATE, AND YOU ARE LIKE AN ANGEL.
WHAT DID 'E ZAY? ZAT I AM "LIKE ZE ANGELS"?
OUI, YOUR GRACE, ZAT IS WHAT HE ZAID.
I SAID SO, DEAR KATHERINE; AND IT DOESN'T EMBARRASS ME TO ADMIT IT.
OH HEAVENS! LE LANGUAGE DE MEN IS FULL DE IDLE FLATTERY.
WHAT DID SHE SAY, MY DEAR? THAT MEN'S TONGUES ARE FULL OF DECEIT?
OUI, DAT DE TONGUES OF DE MANS IS BE FULL OF DECEITS: DAT IS WHAT DE PRINCESS SAY.
THE PRINCESS IS AS GOOD AS ANY ENGLISHWOMAN! TRUE, KATE, MY COURTING MATCHES THE LEVEL OF YOUR UNDERSTANDING. I'M GLAD YOU CAN'T SPEAK BETTER ENGLISH; IF YOU COULD, YOU'D FIND ME SUCH AN ORDINARY KING THAT YOU'D THINK I'D SOLD MY FARM TO BUY MY CROWN.
I DON'T KNOW HOW TO SPEAK THE LANGUAGE OF LOVE, ONLY HOW TO SAY DIRECTLY, "I LOVE YOU"

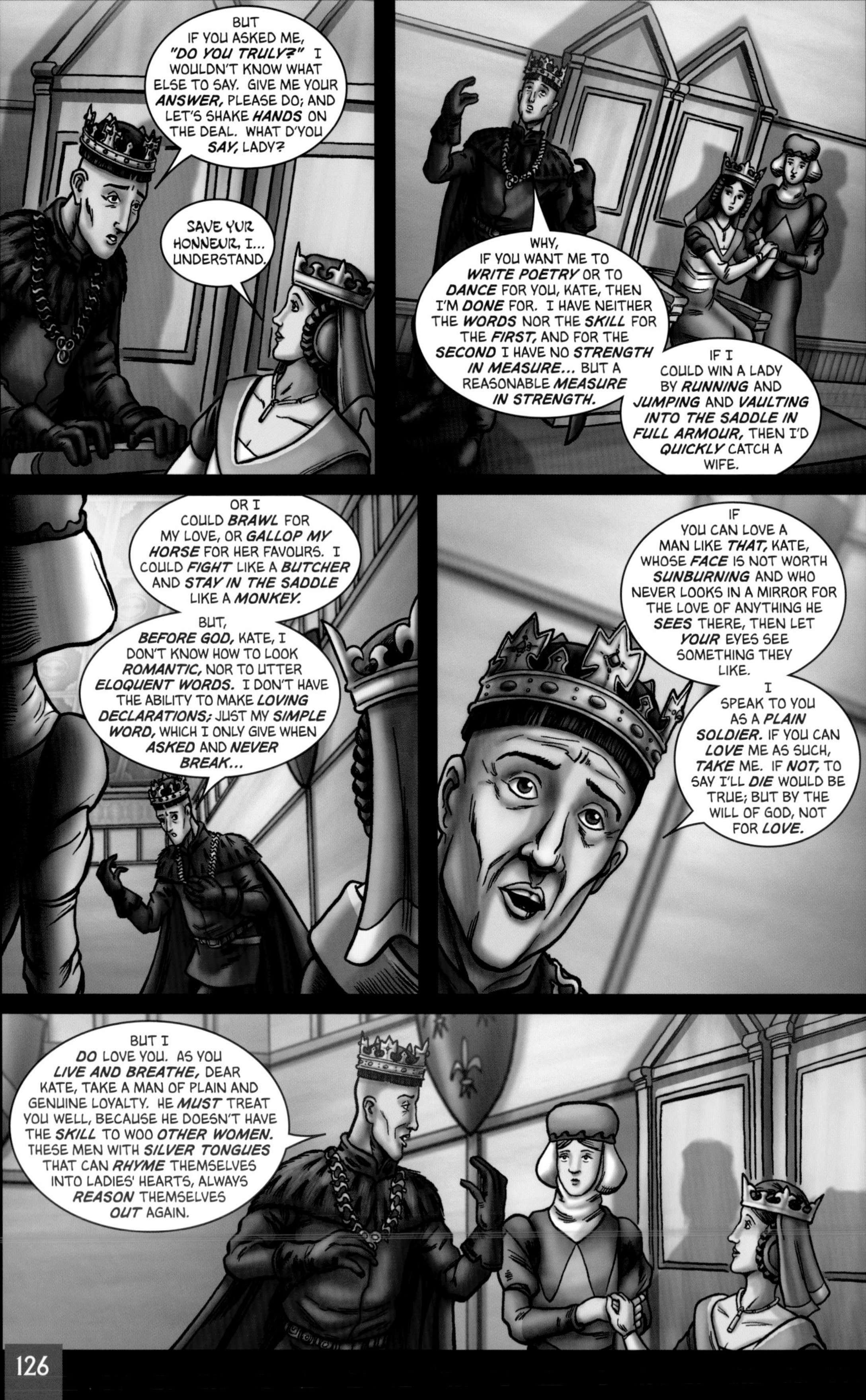

BUT IF YOU ASKED ME, "DO YOU TRULY?" I WOULDN'T KNOW WHAT ELSE TO SAY. GIVE ME YOUR ANSWER, PLEASE DO; AND LET'S SHAKE HANDS ON THE DEAL. WHAT D'YOU SAY, LADY?
SAVE YUR HONNEUR, I... UNDERSTAND.
WHY, IF YOU WANT ME TO WRITE POETRY OR TO DANCE FOR YOU, KATE, THEN I'M DONE FOR. I HAVE NEITHER THE WORDS NOR THE SKILL FOR THE FIRST, AND FOR THE SECOND I HAVE NO STRENGTH IN MEASURE... BUT A REASONABLE MEASURE IN STRENGTH.
IF I COULD WIN A LADY BY RUNNING AND JUMPING AND VAULTING INTO THE SADDLE IN FULL ARMOUR, THEN I'D QUICKLY CATCH A WIFE.
OR I COULD BRAWL FOR MY LOVE, OR GALLOP MY HORSE FOR HER FAVOURS. I COULD FIGHT LIKE A BUTCHER AND STAY IN THE SADDLE LIKE A MONKEY.
BUT, BEFORE GOD, KATE, I DON'T KNOW HOW TO LOOK ROMANTIC, NOR TO UTTER ELOQUENT WORDS. I DON'T HAVE THE ABILITY TO MAKE LOVING DECLARATIONS; JUST MY SIMPLE WORD, WHICH I ONLY GIVE WHEN ASKED AND NEVER BREAK...
IF YOU CAN LOVE A MAN LIKE THAT, KATE, WHOSE FACE IS NOT WORTH SUNBURNING AND WHO NEVER LOOKS IN A MIRROR FOR THE LOVE OF ANYTHING HE SEES THERE, THEN LET YOUR EYES SEE SOMETHING THEY LIKE.
I SPEAK TO YOU AS A PLAIN SOLDIER. IF YOU CAN LOVE ME AS SUCH, TAKE ME. IF NOT, TO SAY I'LL DIE WOULD BE TRUE; BUT BY THE WILL OF GOD, NOT FOR LOVE.
BUT I DO LOVE YOU. AS YOU LIVE AND BREATHE, DEAR KATE, TAKE A MAN OF PLAIN AND GENUINE LOYALTY. HE MUST TREAT YOU WELL, BECAUSE HE DOESN'T HAVE THE SKILL TO WOO OTHER WOMEN. THESE MEN WITH SILVER TONGUES THAT CAN RHYME THEMSELVES INTO LADIES' HEARTS, ALWAYS REASON THEMSELVES OUT AGAIN.

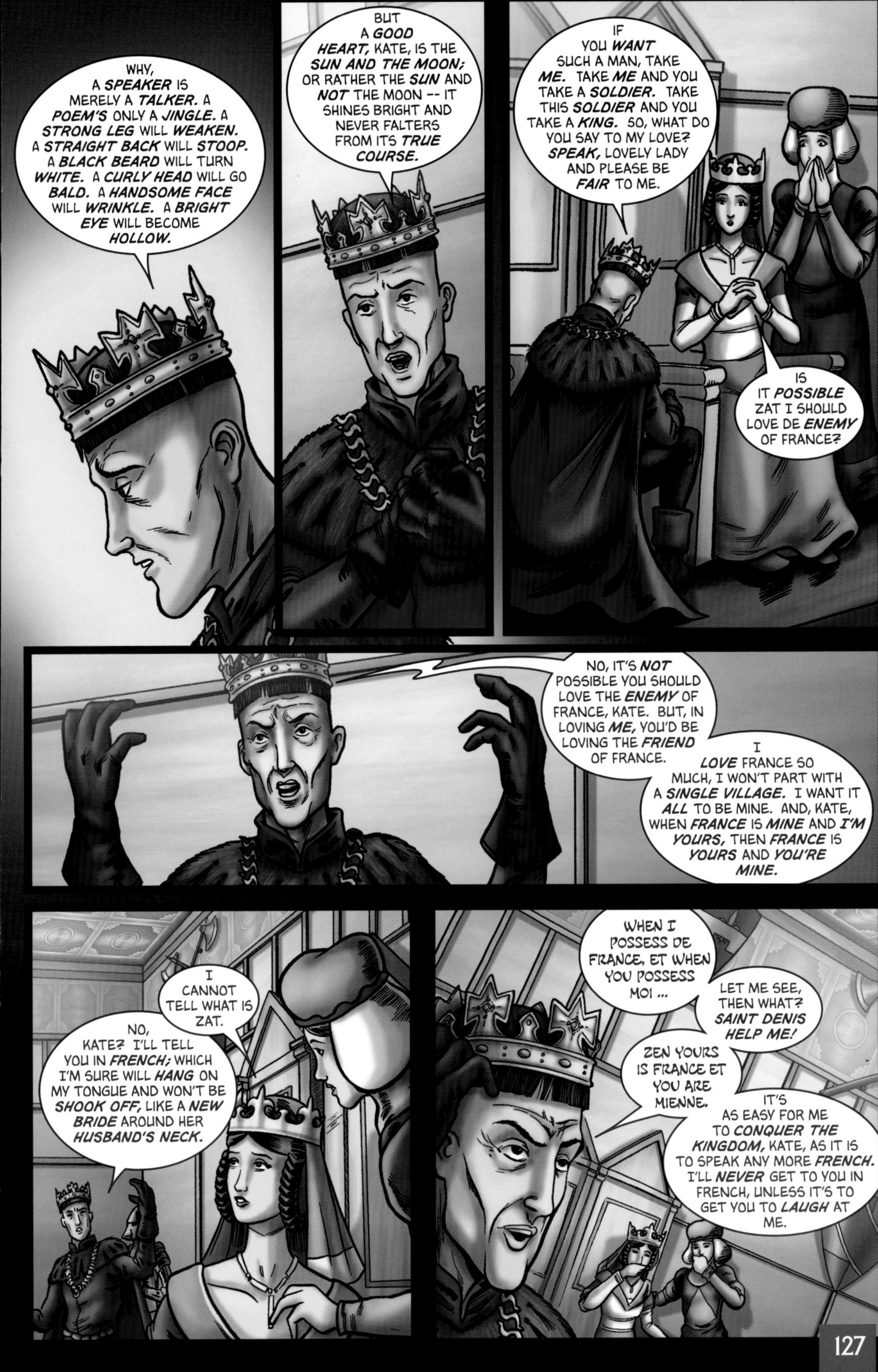
WHY, A SPEAKER IS MERELY A TALKER. A POEM'S ONLY A JINGLE. A STRONG LEG WILL WEAKEN. A STRAIGHT BACK WILL STOOP. A BLACK BEARD WILL TURN WHITE. A CURLY HEAD WILL GO BALD. A HANDSOME FACE WILL WRINKLE. A BRIGHT EYE WILL BECOME HOLLOW.
BUT A GOOD HEART, KATE, IS THE SUN AND THE MOON; OR RATHER THE SUN AND NOT THE MOON -- IT SHINES BRIGHT AND NEVER FALTERS FROM ITS TRUE COURSE.
IF YOU WANT SUCH A MAN, TAKE ME. TAKE ME AND YOU TAKE A SOLDIER. TAKE THIS SOLDIER AND YOU TAKE A KING. SO, WHAT DO YOU SAY TO MY LOVE? SPEAK, LOVELY LADY AND PLEASE BE FAIR TO ME.
IS IT POSSIBLE ZAT I SHOULD LOVE DE ENEMY OF FRANCE?
NO, IT'S NOT POSSIBLE YOU SHOULD LOVE THE ENEMY OF FRANCE, KATE. BUT, IN LOVING ME, YOU'D BE LOVING THE FRIEND OF FRANCE.
I LOVE FRANCE SO MUCH, I WON'T PART WITH A SINGLE VILLAGE. I WANT IT ALL TO BE MINE. AND, KATE, WHEN FRANCE IS MINE AND I'M YOURS, THEN FRANCE IS YOURS AND YOU'RE MINE.
I CANNOT TELL WHAT IS ZAT.
NO, KATE? I'LL TELL YOU IN FRENCH; WHICH I'M SURE WILL HANG ON MY TONGUE AND WON'T BE SHOOK OFF, LIKE A NEW BRIDE AROUND HER HUSBAND'S NECK.
WHEN I POSSESS DE FRANCE, ET WHEN YOU POSSESS MOI ...
LET ME SEE, THEN WHAT? SAINT DENIS HELP ME!
ZEN YOURS IS FRANCE ET YOU ARE MIENNE.
IT'S AS EASY FOR ME TO CONQUER THE KINGDOM, KATE, AS IT IS TO SPEAK ANY MORE FRENCH. I'LL NEVER GET TO YOU IN FRENCH, UNLESS IT'S TO GET YOU TO LAUGH AT ME.

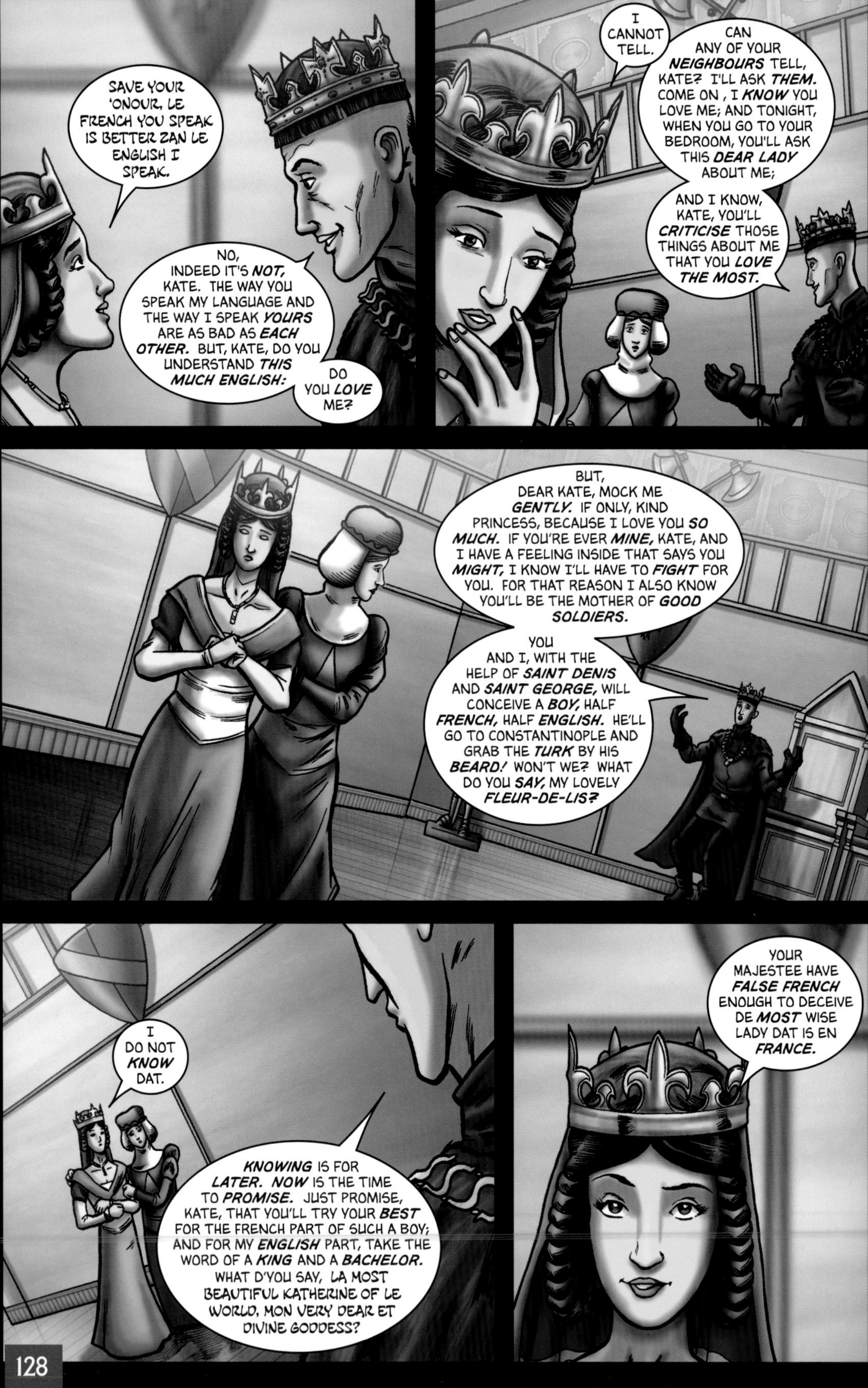
SAVE YOUR 'ONOUR, LE FRENCH YOU SPEAK IS BETTER ZAN LE ENGLISH I SPEAK.
NO, INDEED IT'S *NOT,* KATE. THE WAY YOU SPEAK MY LANGUAGE AND THE WAY I SPEAK *YOURS* ARE AS BAD AS *EACH OTHER.* BUT, KATE, DO YOU UNDERSTAND *THIS MUCH ENGLISH:*
DO YOU *LOVE* ME?
I CANNOT TELL.
CAN ANY OF YOUR *NEIGHBOURS* TELL, KATE? I'LL ASK *THEM.* COME ON , I *KNOW* YOU LOVE ME; AND TONIGHT, WHEN YOU GO TO YOUR BEDROOM, YOU'LL ASK THIS *DEAR LADY* ABOUT ME;
AND I KNOW, KATE, YOU'LL *CRITICISE* THOSE THINGS ABOUT ME THAT YOU *LOVE THE MOST.*
BUT, DEAR KATE, MOCK ME *GENTLY.* IF ONLY, KIND PRINCESS, BECAUSE I LOVE YOU *SO MUCH.* IF YOU'RE EVER *MINE,* KATE, AND I HAVE A FEELING INSIDE THAT SAYS YOU *MIGHT,* I KNOW I'LL HAVE TO *FIGHT* FOR YOU. FOR THAT REASON I ALSO KNOW YOU'LL BE THE MOTHER OF *GOOD SOLDIERS.*
YOU AND I, WITH THE HELP OF *SAINT DENIS* AND *SAINT GEORGE,* WILL CONCEIVE A *BOY,* HALF *FRENCH,* HALF *ENGLISH.* HE'LL GO TO CONSTANTINOPLE AND GRAB THE *TURK* BY HIS *BEARD!* WON'T WE? WHAT DO YOU *SAY,* MY LOVELY *FLEUR-DE-LIS?*
I DO NOT *KNOW* DAT.
KNOWING IS FOR *LATER. NOW* IS THE TIME TO *PROMISE.* JUST PROMISE, KATE, THAT YOU'LL TRY YOUR *BEST* FOR THE FRENCH PART OF SUCH A BOY; AND FOR MY *ENGLISH* PART, TAKE THE WORD OF A *KING* AND A *BACHELOR.* WHAT D'YOU SAY, LA MOST BEAUTIFUL KATHERINE OF LE WORLD, MON VERY DEAR ET DIVINE GODDESS?
YOUR MAJESTEE HAVE *FALSE FRENCH* ENOUGH TO DECEIVE DE *MOST* WISE LADY DAT IS EN *FRANCE.*

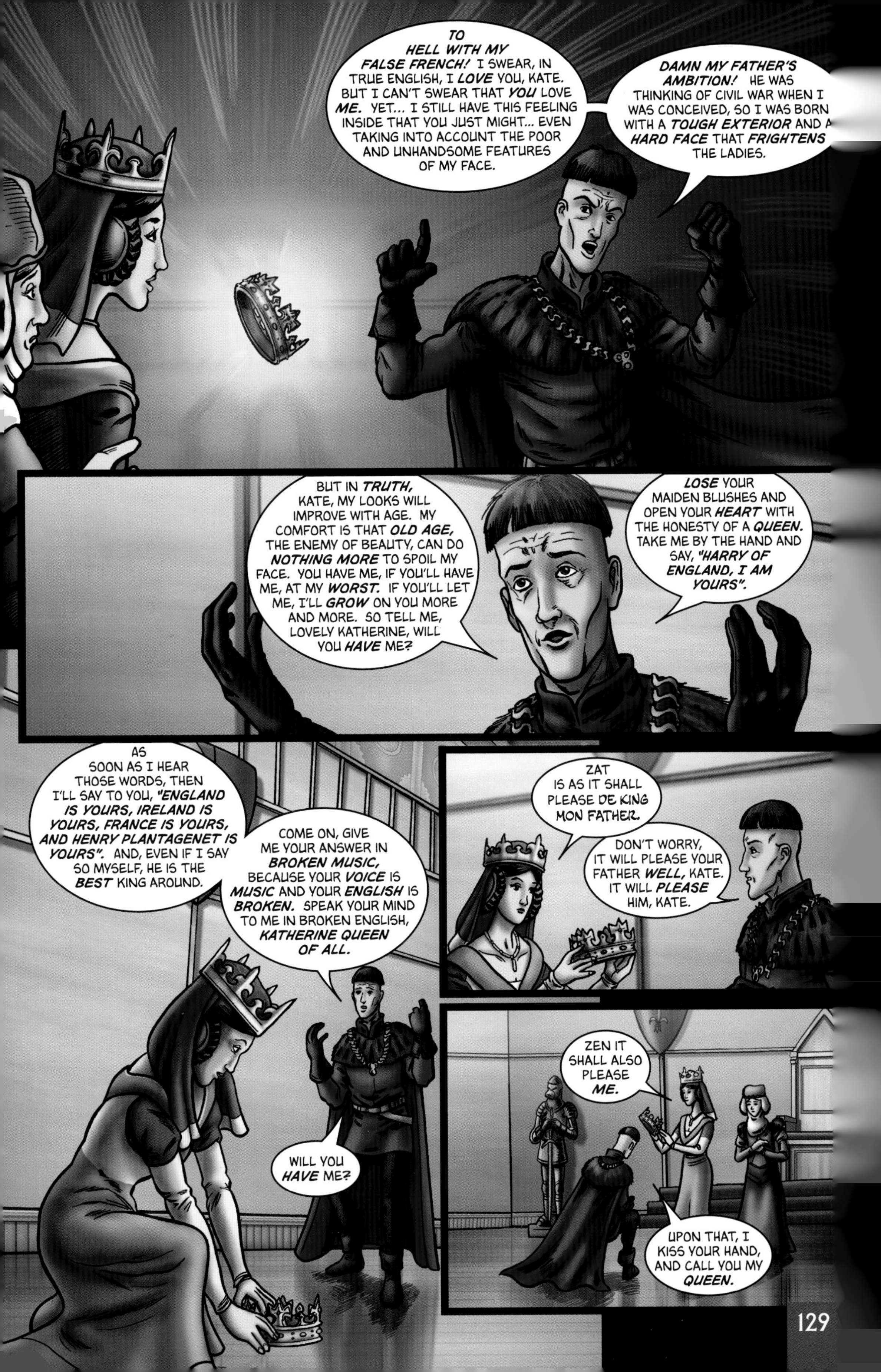
TO HELL WITH MY FALSE FRENCH! I SWEAR, IN TRUE ENGLISH, I LOVE YOU, KATE. BUT I CAN'T SWEAR THAT YOU LOVE ME. YET... I STILL HAVE THIS FEELING INSIDE THAT YOU JUST MIGHT... EVEN TAKING INTO ACCOUNT THE POOR AND UNHANDSOME FEATURES OF MY FACE.
DAMN MY FATHER'S AMBITION! HE WAS THINKING OF CIVIL WAR WHEN I WAS CONCEIVED, SO I WAS BORN WITH A TOUGH EXTERIOR AND A HARD FACE THAT FRIGHTENS THE LADIES.
BUT IN TRUTH, KATE, MY LOOKS WILL IMPROVE WITH AGE. MY COMFORT IS THAT OLD AGE, THE ENEMY OF BEAUTY, CAN DO NOTHING MORE TO SPOIL MY FACE. YOU HAVE ME, IF YOU'LL HAVE ME, AT MY WORST. IF YOU'LL LET ME, I'LL GROW ON YOU MORE AND MORE. SO TELL ME, LOVELY KATHERINE, WILL YOU HAVE ME?
LOSE YOUR MAIDEN BLUSHES AND OPEN YOUR HEART WITH THE HONESTY OF A QUEEN. TAKE ME BY THE HAND AND SAY, "HARRY OF ENGLAND, I AM YOURS".
AS SOON AS I HEAR THOSE WORDS, THEN I'LL SAY TO YOU, "ENGLAND IS YOURS, IRELAND IS YOURS, FRANCE IS YOURS, AND HENRY PLANTAGENET IS YOURS". AND, EVEN IF I SAY SO MYSELF, HE IS THE BEST KING AROUND.
COME ON, GIVE ME YOUR ANSWER IN BROKEN MUSIC, BECAUSE YOUR VOICE IS MUSIC AND YOUR ENGLISH IS BROKEN. SPEAK YOUR MIND TO ME IN BROKEN ENGLISH, KATHERINE QUEEN OF ALL.
WILL YOU HAVE ME?
ZAT IS AS IT SHALL PLEASE DE KING MON FATHER.
DON'T WORRY, IT WILL PLEASE YOUR FATHER WELL, KATE. IT WILL PLEASE HIM, KATE.
ZEN IT SHALL ALSO PLEASE ME.
UPON THAT, I KISS YOUR HAND, AND CALL YOU MY QUEEN.

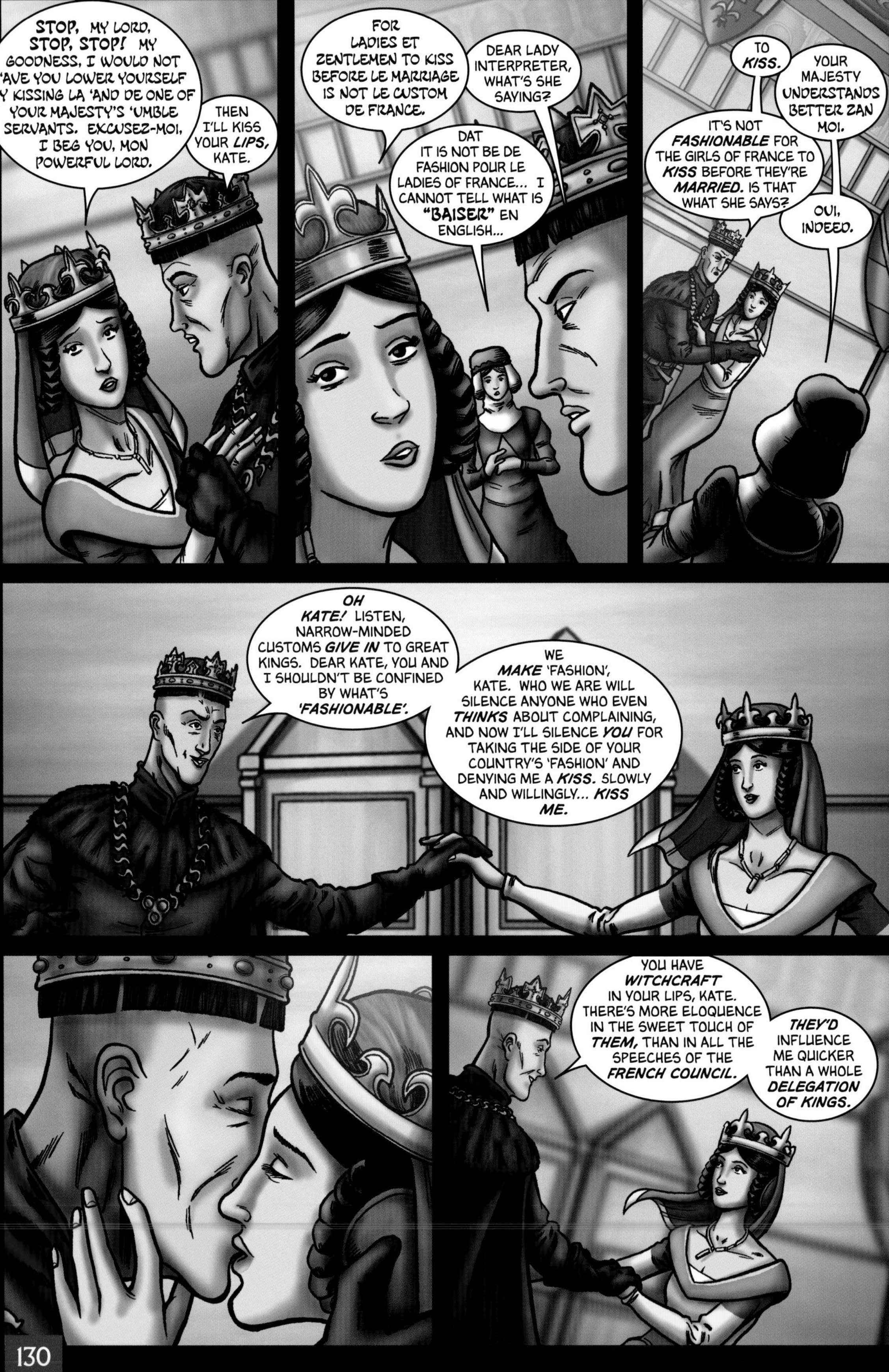
STOP, MY LORD, STOP, STOP! MY GOODNESS, I WOULD NOT 'AVE YOU LOWER YOURSELF BY KISSING LA 'AND DE ONE OF YOUR MAJESTY'S 'UMBLE SERVANTS. EXCUSEZ-MOI, I BEG YOU, MON POWERFUL LORD.
THEN I'LL KISS YOUR LIPS, KATE.
FOR LADIES ET ZENTLEMEN TO KISS BEFORE LE MARRIAGE IS NOT LE CUSTOM DE FRANCE.
DEAR LADY INTERPRETER, WHAT'S SHE SAYING?
DAT IT IS NOT BE DE FASHION POUR LE LADIES OF FRANCE... I CANNOT TELL WHAT IS "BAISER" EN ENGLISH...
TO KISS.
YOUR MAJESTY UNDERSTANDS BETTER ZAN MOI.
IT'S NOT FASHIONABLE FOR THE GIRLS OF FRANCE TO KISS BEFORE THEY'RE MARRIED. IS THAT WHAT SHE SAYS?
OUI, INDEED.
OH KATE! LISTEN, NARROW-MINDED CUSTOMS GIVE IN TO GREAT KINGS. DEAR KATE, YOU AND I SHOULDN'T BE CONFINED BY WHAT'S 'FASHIONABLE'.
WE MAKE 'FASHION', KATE. WHO WE ARE WILL SILENCE ANYONE WHO EVEN THINKS ABOUT COMPLAINING, AND NOW I'LL SILENCE YOU FOR TAKING THE SIDE OF YOUR COUNTRY'S 'FASHION' AND DENYING ME A KISS. SLOWLY AND WILLINGLY... KISS ME.
YOU HAVE WITCHCRAFT IN YOUR LIPS, KATE. THERE'S MORE ELOQUENCE IN THE SWEET TOUCH OF THEM, THAN IN ALL THE SPEECHES OF THE FRENCH COUNCIL.
THEY'D INFLUENCE ME QUICKER THAN A WHOLE DELEGATION OF KINGS.

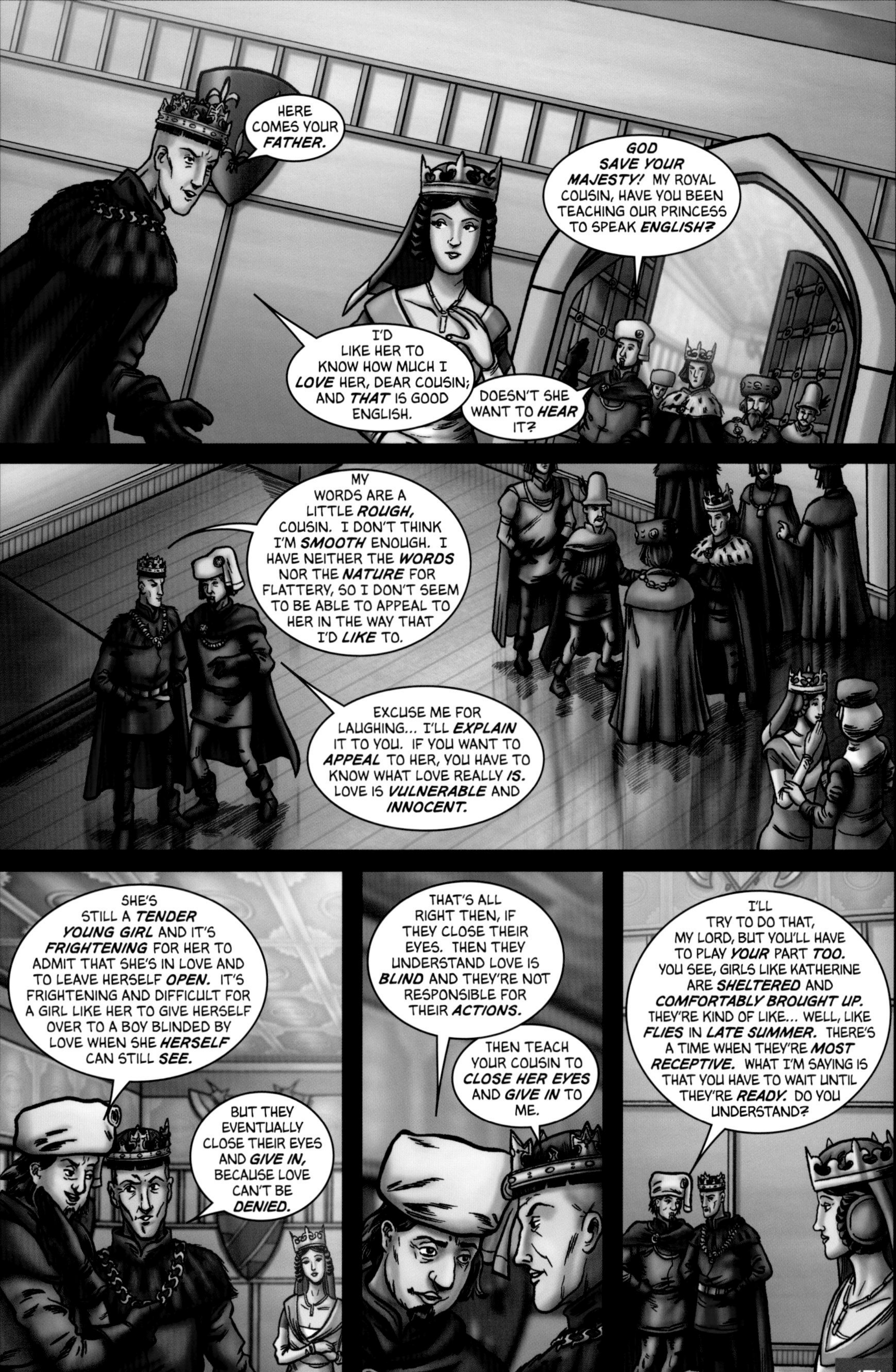
HERE COMES YOUR FATHER.
GOD SAVE YOUR MAJESTY! MY ROYAL COUSIN, HAVE YOU BEEN TEACHING OUR PRINCESS TO SPEAK ENGLISH?
I'D LIKE HER TO KNOW HOW MUCH I LOVE HER, DEAR COUSIN; AND THAT IS GOOD ENGLISH.
DOESN'T SHE WANT TO HEAR IT?
MY WORDS ARE A LITTLE ROUGH, COUSIN. I DON'T THINK I'M SMOOTH ENOUGH. I HAVE NEITHER THE WORDS NOR THE NATURE FOR FLATTERY, SO I DON'T SEEM TO BE ABLE TO APPEAL TO HER IN THE WAY THAT I'D LIKE TO.
EXCUSE ME FOR LAUGHING... I'LL EXPLAIN IT TO YOU. IF YOU WANT TO APPEAL TO HER, YOU HAVE TO KNOW WHAT LOVE REALLY IS. LOVE IS VULNERABLE AND INNOCENT.
SHE'S STILL A TENDER YOUNG GIRL AND IT'S FRIGHTENING FOR HER TO ADMIT THAT SHE'S IN LOVE AND TO LEAVE HERSELF OPEN. IT'S FRIGHTENING AND DIFFICULT FOR A GIRL LIKE HER TO GIVE HERSELF OVER TO A BOY BLINDED BY LOVE WHEN SHE HERSELF CAN STILL SEE.
BUT THEY EVENTUALLY CLOSE THEIR EYES AND GIVE IN, BECAUSE LOVE CAN'T BE DENIED.
THAT'S ALL RIGHT THEN, IF THEY CLOSE THEIR EYES. THEN THEY UNDERSTAND LOVE IS BLIND AND THEY'RE NOT RESPONSIBLE FOR THEIR ACTIONS.
THEN TEACH YOUR COUSIN TO CLOSE HER EYES AND GIVE IN TO ME.
I'LL TRY TO DO THAT, MY LORD, BUT YOU'LL HAVE TO PLAY YOUR PART TOO. YOU SEE, GIRLS LIKE KATHERINE ARE SHELTERED AND COMFORTABLY BROUGHT UP. THEY'RE KIND OF LIKE... WELL, LIKE FLIES IN LATE SUMMER. THERE'S A TIME WHEN THEY'RE MOST RECEPTIVE. WHAT I'M SAYING IS THAT YOU HAVE TO WAIT UNTIL THEY'RE READY. DO YOU UNDERSTAND?

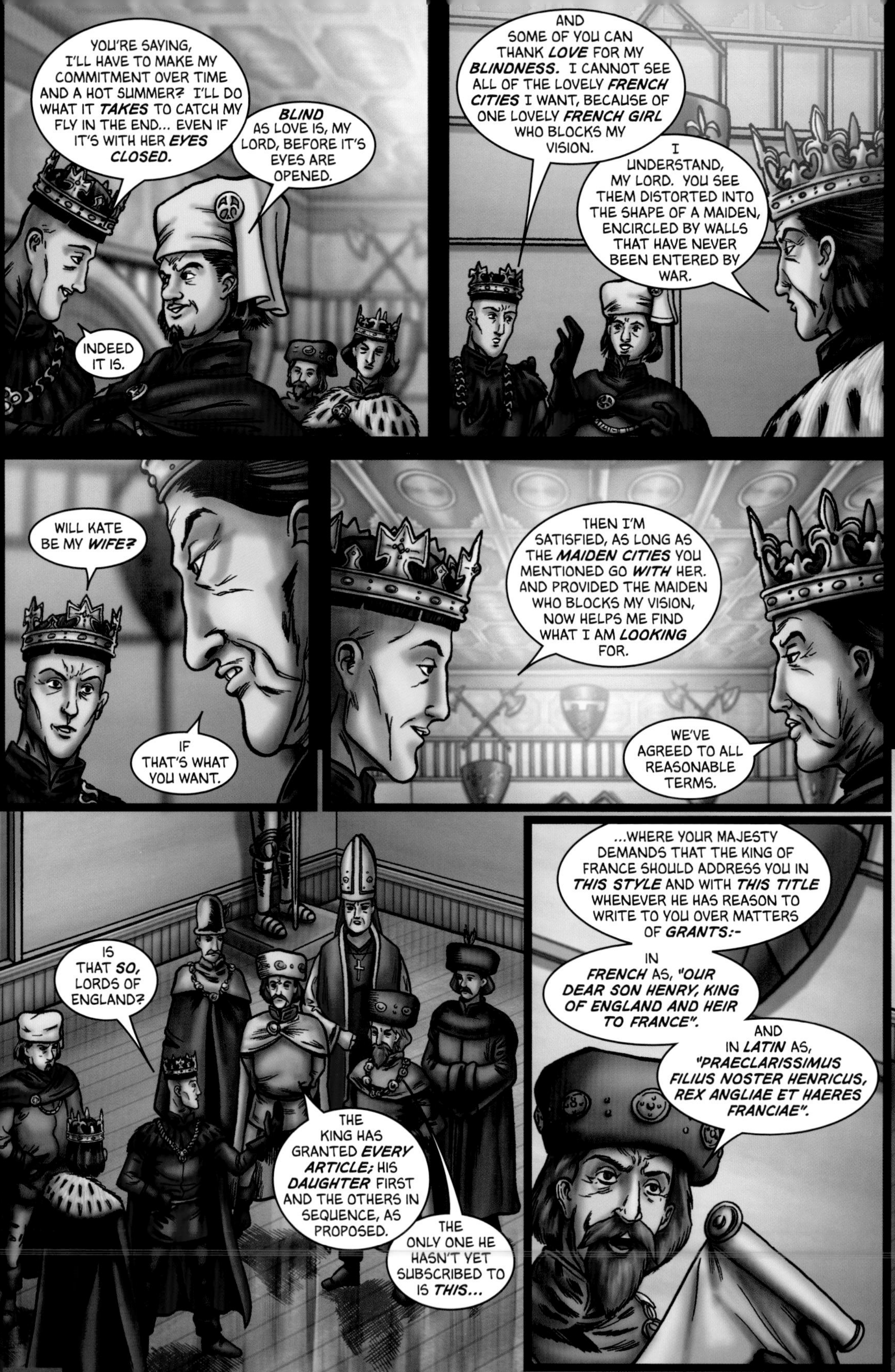
YOU'RE SAYING, I'LL HAVE TO MAKE MY COMMITMENT OVER TIME AND A HOT SUMMER? I'LL DO WHAT IT TAKES TO CATCH MY FLY IN THE END... EVEN IF IT'S WITH HER EYES CLOSED.
BLIND AS LOVE IS, MY LORD, BEFORE IT'S EYES ARE OPENED.
INDEED IT IS.
AND SOME OF YOU CAN THANK LOVE FOR MY BLINDNESS. I CANNOT SEE ALL OF THE LOVELY FRENCH CITIES I WANT, BECAUSE OF ONE LOVELY FRENCH GIRL WHO BLOCKS MY VISION.
I UNDERSTAND, MY LORD. YOU SEE THEM DISTORTED INTO THE SHAPE OF A MAIDEN, ENCIRCLED BY WALLS THAT HAVE NEVER BEEN ENTERED BY WAR.
WILL KATE BE MY WIFE?
IF THAT'S WHAT YOU WANT.
THEN I'M SATISFIED, AS LONG AS THE MAIDEN CITIES YOU MENTIONED GO WITH HER. AND PROVIDED THE MAIDEN WHO BLOCKS MY VISION, NOW HELPS ME FIND WHAT I AM LOOKING FOR.
WE'VE AGREED TO ALL REASONABLE TERMS.
IS THAT SO, LORDS OF ENGLAND?
THE KING HAS GRANTED EVERY ARTICLE; HIS DAUGHTER FIRST AND THE OTHERS IN SEQUENCE, AS PROPOSED.
THE ONLY ONE HE HASN'T YET SUBSCRIBED TO IS THIS...
...WHERE YOUR MAJESTY DEMANDS THAT THE KING OF FRANCE SHOULD ADDRESS YOU IN THIS STYLE AND WITH THIS TITLE WHENEVER HE HAS REASON TO WRITE TO YOU OVER MATTERS OF GRANTS:-
IN FRENCH AS, "OUR DEAR SON HENRY, KING OF ENGLAND AND HEIR TO FRANCE".
AND IN LATIN AS, "PRAECLARISSIMUS FILIUS NOSTER HENRICUS, REX ANGLIAE ET HAERES FRANCIAE".

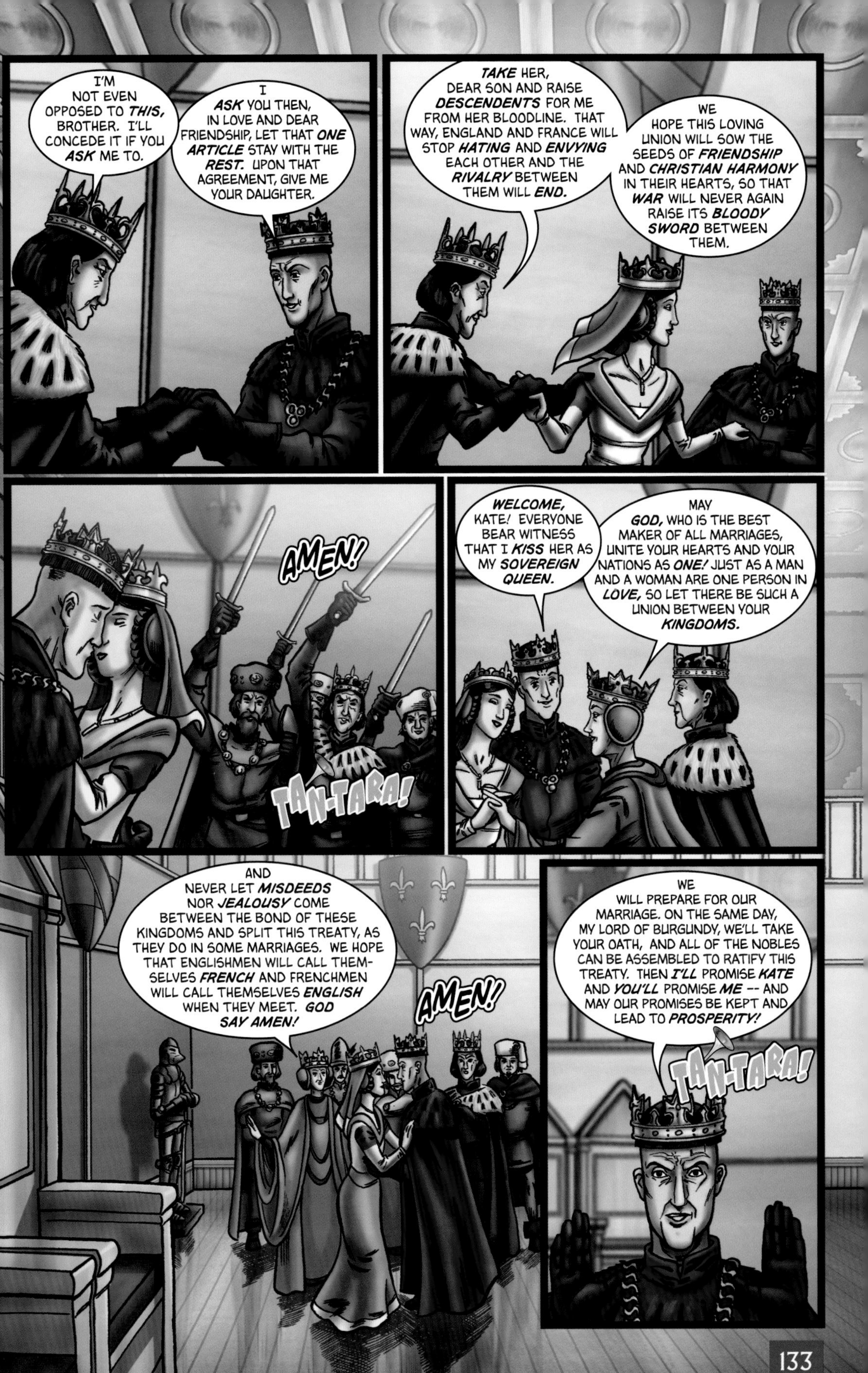
I'M NOT EVEN OPPOSED TO THIS, BROTHER. I'LL CONCEDE IT IF YOU ASK ME TO.
I ASK YOU THEN, IN LOVE AND DEAR FRIENDSHIP, LET THAT ONE ARTICLE STAY WITH THE REST. UPON THAT AGREEMENT, GIVE ME YOUR DAUGHTER.
TAKE HER, DEAR SON AND RAISE DESCENDENTS FOR ME FROM HER BLOODLINE. THAT WAY, ENGLAND AND FRANCE WILL STOP HATING AND ENVYING EACH OTHER AND THE RIVALRY BETWEEN THEM WILL END.
WE HOPE THIS LOVING UNION WILL SOW THE SEEDS OF FRIENDSHIP AND CHRISTIAN HARMONY IN THEIR HEARTS, SO THAT WAR WILL NEVER AGAIN RAISE ITS BLOODY SWORD BETWEEN THEM.
AMEN!
TAN-TARA!
WELCOME, KATE! EVERYONE BEAR WITNESS THAT I KISS HER AS MY SOVEREIGN QUEEN.
MAY GOD, WHO IS THE BEST MAKER OF ALL MARRIAGES, UNITE YOUR HEARTS AND YOUR NATIONS AS ONE! JUST AS A MAN AND A WOMAN ARE ONE PERSON IN LOVE, SO LET THERE BE SUCH A UNION BETWEEN YOUR KINGDOMS.
AND NEVER LET MISDEEDS NOR JEALOUSY COME BETWEEN THE BOND OF THESE KINGDOMS AND SPLIT THIS TREATY, AS THEY DO IN SOME MARRIAGES. WE HOPE THAT ENGLISHMEN WILL CALL THEMSELVES FRENCH AND FRENCHMEN WILL CALL THEMSELVES ENGLISH WHEN THEY MEET. GOD SAY AMEN!
AMEN!
WE WILL PREPARE FOR OUR MARRIAGE. ON THE SAME DAY, MY LORD OF BURGUNDY, WE'LL TAKE YOUR OATH, AND ALL OF THE NOBLES CAN BE ASSEMBLED TO RATIFY THIS TREATY. THEN I'LL PROMISE KATE AND YOU'LL PROMISE ME -- AND MAY OUR PROMISES BE KEPT AND LEAD TO PROSPERITY!
TAN-TARA!

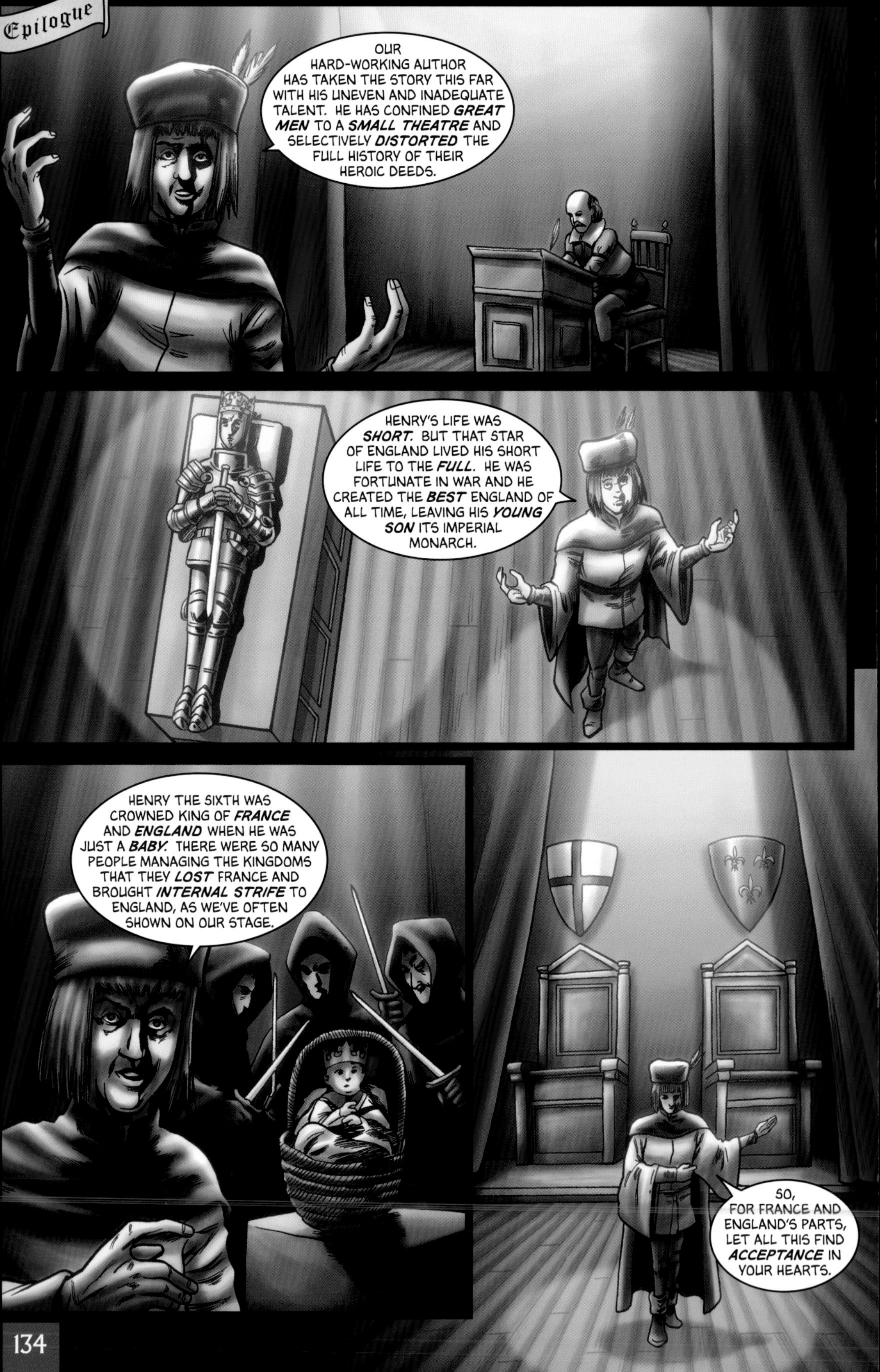
OUR HARD-WORKING AUTHOR HAS TAKEN THE STORY THIS FAR WITH HIS UNEVEN AND INADEQUATE TALENT. HE HAS CONFINED GREAT MEN TO A SMALL THEATRE AND SELECTIVELY DISTORTED THE FULL HISTORY OF THEIR HEROIC DEEDS.
HENRY'S LIFE WAS SHORT. BUT THAT STAR OF ENGLAND LIVED HIS SHORT LIFE TO THE FULL. HE WAS FORTUNATE IN WAR AND HE CREATED THE BEST ENGLAND OF ALL TIME, LEAVING HIS YOUNG SON ITS IMPERIAL MONARCH.
HENRY THE SIXTH WAS CROWNED KING OF FRANCE AND ENGLAND WHEN HE WAS JUST A BABY. THERE WERE SO MANY PEOPLE MANAGING THE KINGDOMS THAT THEY LOST FRANCE AND BROUGHT INTERNAL STRIFE TO ENGLAND, AS WE'VE OFTEN SHOWN ON OUR STAGE.
SO, FOR FRANCE AND ENGLAND'S PARTS, LET ALL THIS FIND ACCEPTANCE IN YOUR HEARTS.

Henry V

End

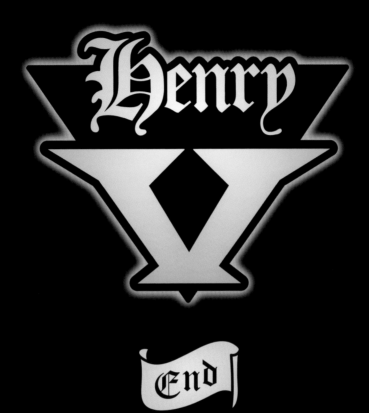

William Shakespeare

(c.1564 - 1616 AD)

National Portrait Gallery, London

William Shakespeare is one of the most widely read authors and possibly the best dramatist ever to live. The actual date of his birth is not known, but traditionally April 23rd 1564 (St George's Day) has been his accepted birthday, as this was three days before his baptism. He died on the same date in 1616, aged 52.

The life of William Shakespeare can be divided into three acts. The first 20 years of his life were spent in Stratford-upon-Avon where he grew up, went to school, got married and became a father. The next 25 years he spent as an actor and playwright in London; and he spent his last few years back in Stratford-upon-Avon, where he enjoyed his retirement in moderate wealth gained from his successful years in the theatre.

William was the eldest son of tradesman John Shakespeare and Mary Arden, and the third of eight children. His father was later elected mayor of Stratford, which was the highest post a man in civic politics could attain. In sixteenth-century England, William was lucky to survive into adulthood; syphilis, scurvy, smallpox, tuberculosis, typhus and dysentery shortened life expectancy at the time to approximately 35 years. The Bubonic Plague took the lives of many and was believed to have

been the cause of death for three of William's seven siblings.

Little is known of William's childhood, other than it is thought that he attended the local grammar school, where he studied Latin and English Literature. In 1582, at the age of 18, William married a local farmer's daughter, Anne Hathaway, who was eight years his senior and three months pregnant. During their marriage they had three children: Susanna, born on May 26th 1583 and twins, Hamnet and Judith, born on February 2nd 1585. Hamnet, William's only son, caught Bubonic Plague and died aged just 11.

Five years into his marriage William moved to London and appeared in many small parts at

The Globe Theatre, then one of the biggest theatres in England. His first appearance in public as a poet was in 1593 with "Venus and Adonis" and again in the following year with "The Rape of Lucrece". Later on, in 1599, he became joint proprietor of The Globe.

When Queen Elizabeth died in 1603, she was succeeded by her cousin King James of Scotland. King James supported William and his band of actors and gave them license to call themselves the "King's Men" in return for entertaining the court.

In just 23 years, between approximately 1590 and 1613, William Shakespeare is attributed with writing 38 plays, 154 sonnets and 5 poems. "Love's Labour's Lost" and "The Comedy of

Errors" are thought to be among Shakespeare's earliest plays, followed by, "The Two Gentlemen of Verona" and "Romeo and Juliet". His final play was "Henry VIII", written two years before he died. The cause of his death remains unknown.

He was buried on April 25th 1616, two days after his death, at the Church of the Holy Trinity (the same Church where he had been baptised 52 years earlier). His gravestone bears these words (believed to have been written by William himself):-

"Good friend for Jesus sake forbear,
To dig the dust enclosed here!
Blest be the man that spares these stones,
And curst be he that moves my bones"

At the time of his death, William had substantial properties, which he bestowed on his family and associates from the theatre.

In his will he left his wife, the former Anne Hathaway, his second best bed!

William Shakespeare's last direct descendant died in 1670. She was his granddaughter, Elizabeth.

Henry V, King of England

(c.1387 - 1422 AD)

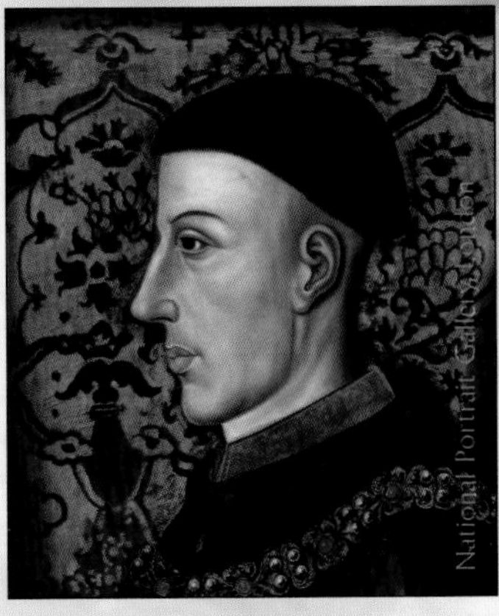
National Portrait Gallery, London

One of the great warrior kings of medieval England, Henry is most famous for his victory against the French at the Battle of Agincourt.

Henry V, the eldest son of Henry IV and Mary Bohun, was born in 1387. He became Prince of Wales at his father's coronation in 1399. Henry was an accomplished soldier: at 14 he fought the Welsh forces of Owain Glyndwr; in 1403, aged 16, he commanded his father's forces at the battle of Shrewsbury. He was also keen to have a role in government, leading to many disagreements with his father. Henry became king in 1413.

In 1415, he successfully crushed an uprising designed to put Edmund Mortimer, Earl of March, on the throne. Shortly afterwards he sailed for France, which was to be the focus of his attentions for most of his reign. Henry was determined to regain the lands in France previously held by his ancestors and so laid his claim to the French throne. The French war served two purposes - to gain lands lost in previous battles and to focus attention away from any of his cousins' royal ambitions.

He first captured the port of Harfleur and then on October 25th 1415 defeated the French at the Battle of Agincourt. Between 1417 and 1419 Henry followed up this success with the conquest of Normandy. Rouen surrendered in January 1419 and his successes forced the French to agree to the Treaty of Troyes in May 1420.

Henry was recognised as heir to the French throne and married Katherine, the daughter of the French king. In February 1421, Henry returned to England for the first time in three and half years, and he and Katherine undertook a royal progress round the country. In June, he returned to France and died suddenly, probably of dysentery, on August 31st 1422. His nine-month-old son succeeded him (Henry never saw his child). Had Henry lived a mere two months longer, he would have been king of both England and France.

The historian Rafael Holinshed, in the Chronicles of England, summed up Henry's reign as such: "This Henry was a king, of life without spot, a prince whom all men loved, and of none disdained, a captain against whom fortune never frowned, nor mischance once spurned, whose people him so severe a justicer both loved and obeyed (and so humane withal) that he left no offence unpunished, nor friendship unrewarded; a terror to rebels, and suppressor of sedition, his virtues notable, his qualities most praiseworthy."

The Battle of Agincourt October 25th, 1415 (St. Crispin's Day)

'From the thirteenth until the sixteenth century, the national weapon of the English army was the longbow. It was this weapon which conquered Wales and Scotland, gave the English their victories in the Hundred Years War, and permitted England to replace France as the foremost military power in Medieval Europe. The longbow was the machine gun of the Middle Ages: accurate, deadly, possessed of a long-range and rapid rate of fire, the flight of its missiles was liken to a storm. Cheap and simple enough for the yeoman to own and master, it made him superior to a knight on the field of battle.'

The Medieval English Longbow
by Robert E. Kaiser, M.A.

Henry V, King of England, and (according to him and his advisors), parts of France, invaded France on August 13th, 1415 to claim by force his French Kingdom. He first laid siege to the port of Harfleur, in the classic medieval style using primitive cannons (bombards), trenches and ramparts encircling the town's walls. Harfleur finally fell on September 22nd and on October 8th Henry's by now smaller, starving and weary army of some 5,000 archers and 1,000 men-at-arms began a 260-mile march to Calais, hoping to reach England before winter set in.

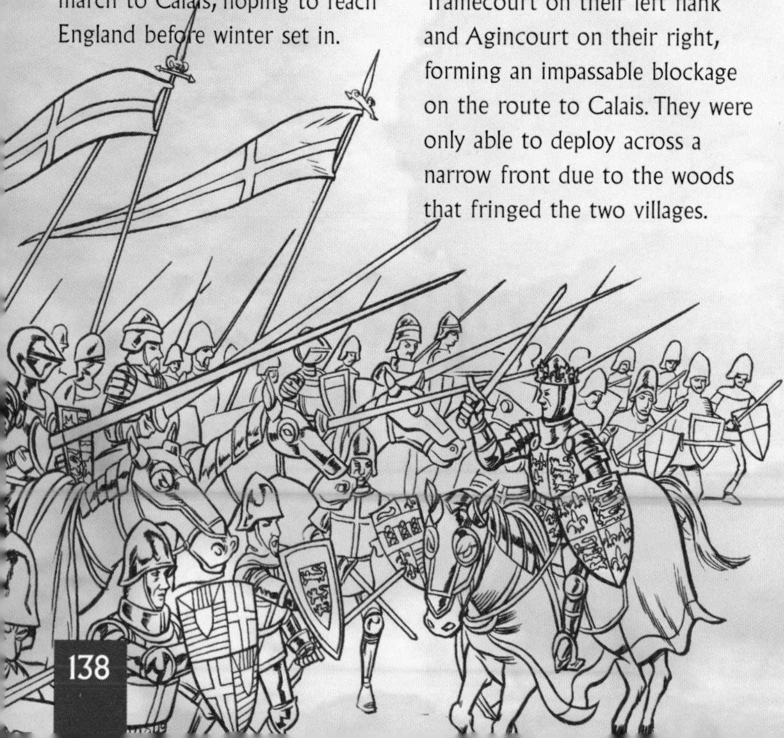

The main French army started from Rouen in pursuit of the English. On October 24th Henry's scouts spotted the French army near the little river Ternoise, completely blocking the path to Calais. Henry now had no choice but to give battle to the far larger French army of some 15,000-36,000 men (as accurate an estimate as can be given!)

October 25th dawned cold and wet, with the French army drawn up between the villages of Tramecourt on their left flank and Agincourt on their right, forming an impassable blockage on the route to Calais. They were only able to deploy across a narrow front due to the woods that fringed the two villages.

The English army was gathered in between the woods at the other end of the field, roughly a kilometre from the French.

This meant that the battle took place on recently ploughed fields between the woods - a decisive factor in the final outcome.

The French formed three massive divisions (called battles), with the first two consisting of dismounted men-at-arms with cavalry on their flanks, and a third division consisting entirely of cavalry. Crossbowmen and archers were to take up position at the front of the divisions.

The French planned to shower the English with arrows, then move in with the flanking cavalry to take out the bowmen of the English army, as the French men-at-arms moved in to dispatch the English infantry.

By 11am the English could wait no longer for a French advance. Henry's troops were tired and weak from hunger, dysentery and the long, wet march; so they advanced to within 200 metres of the French troops. At this point the English archers halted and pounded in pointed wooden stakes (palings) in front of their positions to keep the French cavalry at bay.

Charles d'Albret
Agincourt
Tramecourt
Archers
Archers
Camoys
Henry V
York

The English advance threw the French into confusion and precipitated the premature charge of the French heavy cavalry. The cavalry advanced slowly in the mud and under a hail of arrows. They tried to outflank the English but were hemmed in by the woods and forced to continue with a frontal assault. They quickly found themselves and their horses impaled upon the stakes and under unremitting fire from the English archers. The English line held and what was left of the French cavalry was forced to withdraw.

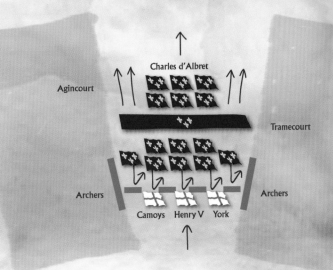

The first French division of men-at-arms lumbered forward after the failure of the cavalry assault. The English arrows took their toll but the French finally closed with the English men-at-arms. Many French nobles had already been killed by arrows and, as the line pushed forward, many more men fell and were trampled to death, hampered by their heavy armour.

Initially the impact of the French advance drove the English line back, but they quickly recovered; and the English men-at-arms and archers joined the fray with mallets, axes and swords, easily dispatching the tightly packed and heavily armoured columns of French knights. As the first French division was being decimated, the remaining English archers kept up a heavy hail of arrows on the advancing second French division of men-at-arms. The knights in this second division saw what was happening to their comrades and began leaving the field without engaging the English. This left the mounted French third division as the last hope for the French to snatch a victory from defeat. However, attacking the English longbowmen was more than those troops wished to contemplate and they too began drifting away through the Tramecourt Woods.

The English interpreted this movement as a potential threat, with the French moving through the woods and possibly threatening the English rear. This news, coupled with reports that the English baggage train had been attacked, led Henry to order the deaths of all the prisoners, as there were not enough soldiers left to guard the prisoners and fend off another attack.

Many prisoners were killed but some English knights who were horrified by this order saved their prisoners. It is believed that more French deaths took place during this slaughter, than during the battle itself.

By the end of the day it is estimated that between 7,000 and 10,000 French had perished but only 500 English. Henry and his army went on to Calais and then back to England, with a number of French nobles held to ransom.

It was an incredible English victory that would go down in the annals of warfare.

Arguably, the deciding factor for the outcome was the terrain. The narrow field of battle, of recently ploughed land hemmed in by dense woodland, favoured the English.

However, Shakespeare appears to have favoured a rather different rationale, basing the victory on the will of God, given that Henry's cause was just.

Page Creation

In order to create three versions of the same book, the play is first adapted into three scripts: Original Text, Plain Text and Quick Text. While the degree of complexity changes for each script, the artwork remains the same for all three books.

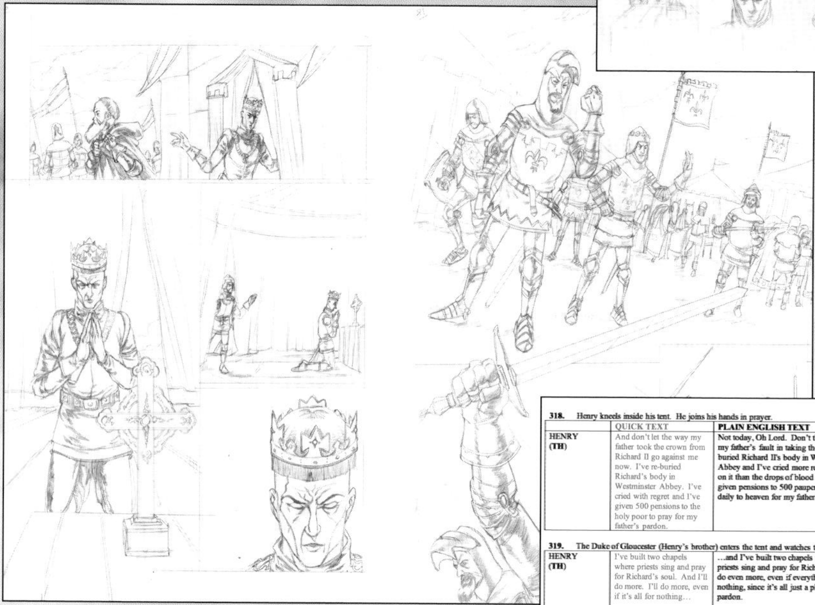

Above is a rough thumbnail sketch of pages 86 and 87 created from the script. Once the rough sketch is approved it is redrawn as a clean finished pencil sketch (left).

318.	Henry kneels inside his tent. He joins his hands in prayer.		
	QUICK TEXT	PLAIN ENGLISH TEXT	ORIGINAL TEXT
HENRY (TH)	And don't let the way my father took the crown from Richard II go against me now. I've re-buried Richard's body in Westminster Abbey. I've cried with regret and I've given 500 pensions to the holy poor to pray for my father's pardon.	Not today, Oh Lord. Don't think today about my father's fault in taking the crown! I've re-buried Richard II's body in Westminster Abbey and I've cried more remorseful tears on it than the drops of blood it spilled. I've given pensions to 500 paupers to pray twice daily to heaven for my father's pardon…	Not to-day, O Lord! O! not to-day, think not upon the fault My father made in compassing the crown. I Richard's body have interred new, And on it have bestow'd more contrite tears Than from it issued forced drops of blood. Five hundred poor I have in yearly pay, Who twice a day their wither'd hands hold up Toward heaven, to pardon blood;
319.	The Duke of Gloucester (Henry's brother) enters the tent and watches the King in prayer.		
HENRY (TH)	I've built two chapels where priests sing and pray for Richard's soul. And I'll do more. I'll do more, even if it's all for nothing…	…and I've built two chapels where devout priests sing and pray for Richard's soul. I'll do even more, even if everything I do means nothing, since it's all just a plea for personal pardon.	and I have built Two chantries, where the sad and solemn priests Sing still for Richard's soul. More will I do; Though all that I can do is nothing worth, Since that my penitence comes after all, Imploring pardon.
GLOUCESTER	My lord!	My liege!	My liege!
320.	Henry doesn't look up.		
HENRY	That's my brother Gloucester's voice. I know what you want. I'll go with you, because everything waits for me.	My brother Gloucester's voice? Yes, I know what you want. I'll go with you. The day, my friends, and all other things wait for me.	My brother Gloucester's voice? —Ay; I know thy errand, I will go with thee: — The day, my friends, and all things stay for me.

From the pencil sketch we can now create an inked version of the same page (below).

Inking is not simply tracing over the pencil sketch, it is the process of using black ink to fill in the shaded areas and to add clarity and cohesion to the "pencils".

The "inks" give us the final outline and the next stage is to add colour to the inked image.

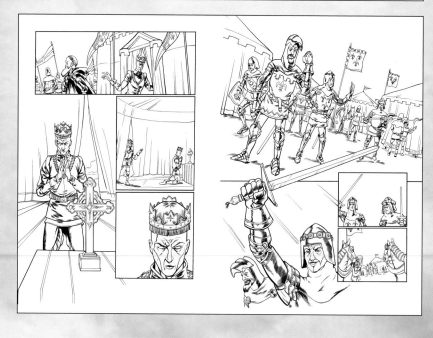

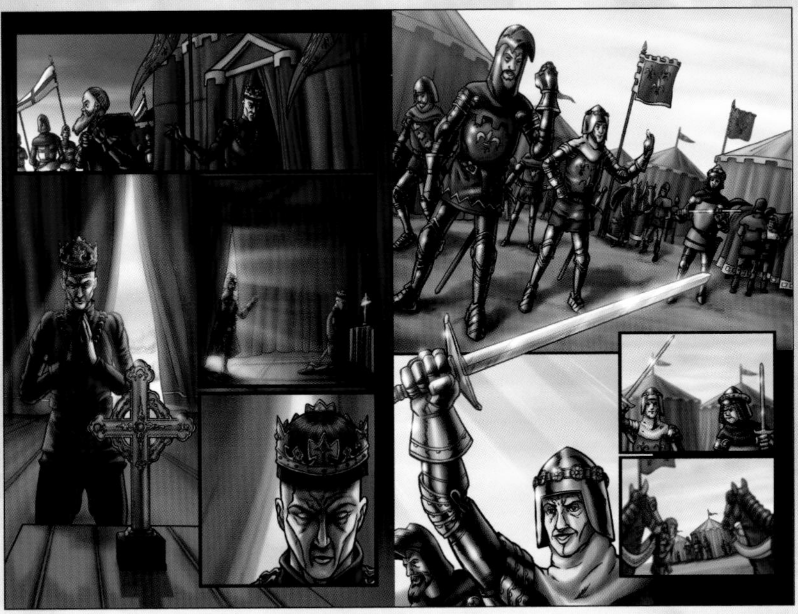

Adding colour brings the page and its characters to life.

Each character has a detailed Character Study drawn. This is useful for the inkers and the colourists to refer to and ensures continuity throughout the book.

The last stage of page creation is to add the speech and any sound effects.

Speech bubbles are created from the script and are laid over the finished coloured pages.

Three versions of lettered pages are produced for the three different versions of Henry V. These are then saved as final artwork pages and compiled into books.

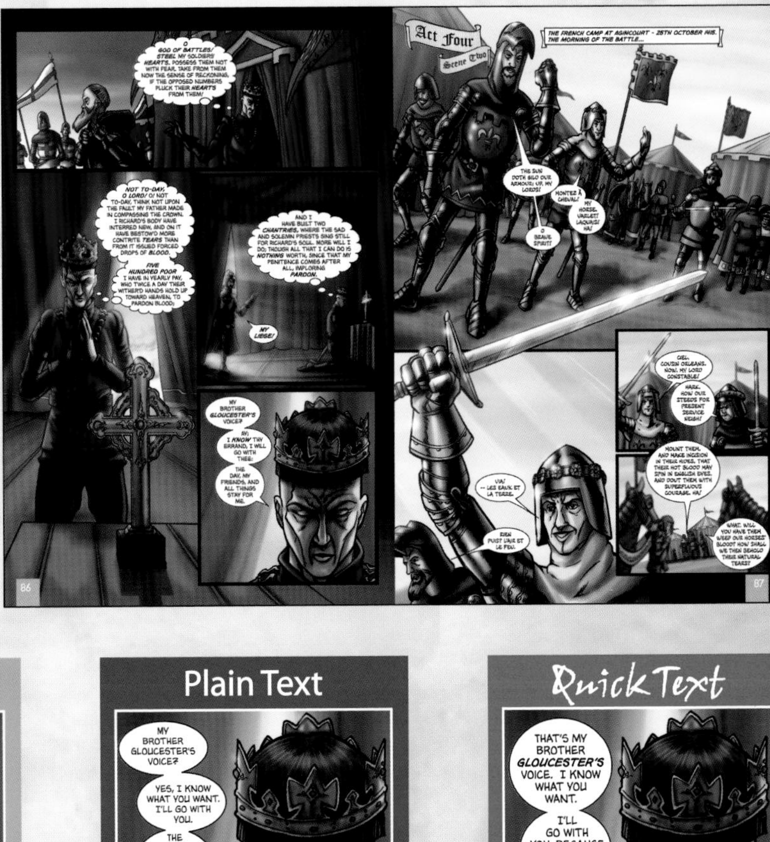
O GOD OF BATTLES! STEEL MY SOLDIERS' HEARTS. POSSESS THEM NOT WITH FEAR. TAKE FROM THEM NOW THE SENSE OF RECKONING, IF THE OPPOSED NUMBERS PLUCK THEIR HEARTS FROM THEM!
NOT TO-DAY, O LORD! O! NOT TO-DAY, THINK NOT UPON THE FAULT MY FATHER MADE IN COMPASSING THE CROWN. I RICHARD'S BODY HAVE INTERRED NEW, AND ON IT HAVE BESTOW'D MORE CONTRITE TEARS THAN FROM IT ISSUED FORCED DROPS OF BLOOD.
FIVE HUNDRED POOR I HAVE IN YEARLY PAY, WHO TWICE A DAY THEIR WITHER'D HANDS HOLD UP TOWARD HEAVEN, TO PARDON BLOOD;
AND I HAVE BUILT TWO CHANTRIES, WHERE THE SAD AND SOLEMN PRIESTS SING STILL FOR RICHARD'S SOUL. MORE WILL I DO; THOUGH ALL THAT I CAN DO IS NOTHING WORTH, SINCE THAT MY PENITENCE COMES AFTER ALL, IMPLORING PARDON.
MY LIEGE!
MY BROTHER GLOUCESTER'S VOICE?
AY; I KNOW THY ERRAND, I WILL GO WITH THEE:
THE DAY, MY FRIENDS, AND ALL THINGS STAY FOR ME.
86
Act Four
Scene Two
THE FRENCH CAMP AT AGINCOURT - 25TH OCTOBER 1415. THE MORNING OF THE BATTLE...
THE SUN DOTH GILD OUR ARMOUR; UP, MY LORDS!
MONTEZ À CHEVAL!
MY HORSE. VARLET! LAQUAIS! HA!
O BRAVE SPIRIT!
CIEL. COUSIN ORLEANS. NOW, MY LORD CONSTABLE!
HARK. HOW OUR STEEDS FOR PRESENT SERVICE NEIGH!
MOUNT THEM, AND MAKE INCISION IN THEIR HIDES, THAT THEIR HOT BLOOD MAY SPIN IN ENGLISH EYES, AND DOUT THEM WITH SUPERFLUOUS COURAGE. HA!
VIA! -- LES EAUX ET LA TERRE.
RIEN PUIST L'AIR ET LE FEU.
WHAT. WILL YOU HAVE THEM WEEP OUR HORSES' BLOOD? HOW SHALL WE THEN BEHOLD THEIR NATURAL TEARS?
87

Original Text

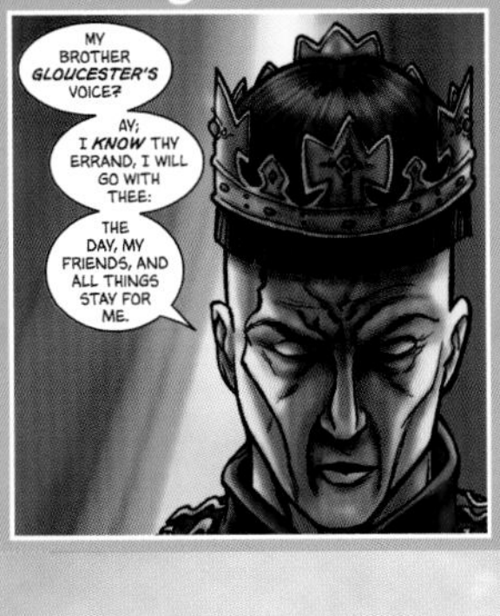
MY BROTHER GLOUCESTER'S VOICE?
AY; I KNOW THY ERRAND, I WILL GO WITH THEE:
THE DAY, MY FRIENDS, AND ALL THINGS STAY FOR ME.

Plain Text

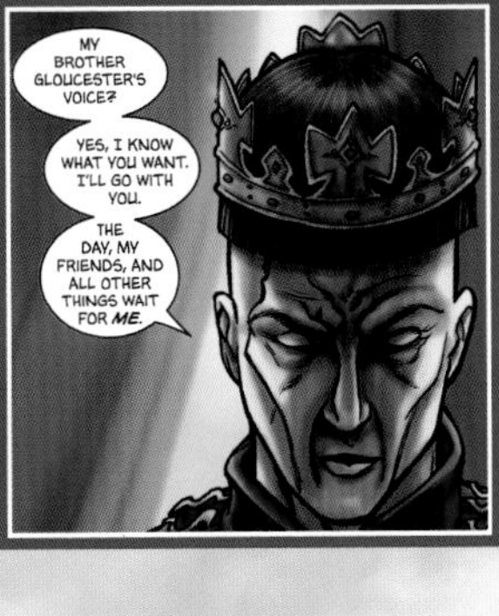
MY BROTHER GLOUCESTER'S VOICE?
YES, I KNOW WHAT YOU WANT. I'LL GO WITH YOU.
THE DAY, MY FRIENDS, AND ALL OTHER THINGS WAIT FOR ME.

Quick Text

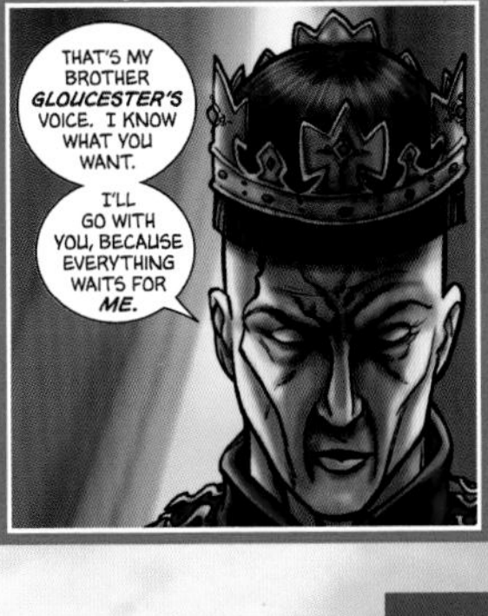
THAT'S MY BROTHER GLOUCESTER'S VOICE. I KNOW WHAT YOU WANT.
I'LL GO WITH YOU, BECAUSE EVERYTHING WAITS FOR ME.

Shakespeare Around the Globe

The Globe Theatre and Shakespeare

Although it's hard to appreciate today, theatres were actually a new idea in William Shakespeare's time. The very first theatre in Elizabethan London to only show plays, aptly called 'The Theatre', was introduced by an entrepreneur called James Burbage. In fact, 'The Globe Theatre', possibly the most famous theatre of that era, was built from the timbers of 'The Theatre'. The landlord of 'The Theatre' was Giles Allen, who was a Puritan that disapproved of theatrical entertainment. When he decided to enforce a huge rent increase in the winter of 1598, the theatre members dismantled the building piece by piece and shipped it across the Thames to Southwark for reassembly. Allen was powerless to do anything, as the company owned the wood (although he spent three years in court trying to sue the perpetrators)!

The report of the dismantling party (written by Schoenbaum) says: *"ryotous... armed... with divers and manye unlawfull and offensive weapons... in verye ryotous outragious and forcyble manner and contrarye to the lawes of your highnes Realme... and there pulling breaking and throwing downe the sayd Theater in verye outragious violent and riotous sort to the great disturbance and terrefyeing not onlye of your subjectes... but of divers others of your majesties loving subjectes there neere inhabitinge."*

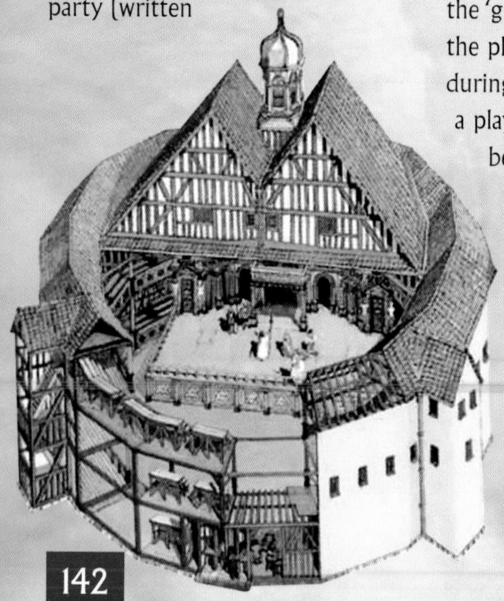

William Shakespeare became a part owner of this new Globe Theatre in 1599. It was one of four major theatres in the area, along with the Swan, the Rose, and the Hope. The exact physical structure of the Globe is unknown, although scholars are fairly sure of some details through drawings from the period. The theatre itself was a closed structure with an open courtyard where the stage stood. Tiered galleries around the open area accommodated the wealthier patrons who could afford seats, and those of the lower classes - the 'groundlings' - stood around the platform or 'thrust' stage during the performance of a play. The space under and behind the stage was used for special effects, storage and costume changes. Surprisingly, although the entire structure was not very big by modern standards, it is known to have accommodated fairly large crowds - as many as 3,000 people - during a single performance.

The Globe II

In 1613, the original Globe Theatre burned to the ground when a cannon shot during a performance of "Henry VIII" set fire to the thatched roof of the gallery. Undeterred, the company completed a new Globe (this time with a tiled roof) on the foundations of its predecessor. Opened in 1614, Shakespeare didn't write any new plays for this theatre. He retired to Stratford-Upon-Avon that year, and died two years later. Despite that, performances continued until 1642, when the Puritans closed down all theatres and places of entertainment. Two years later, the Puritans razed the building to the ground in order to build tenements upon the site. No more was to be seen of the Globe for 352 years.

Shakespeare's Globe

Led by the vision of the late Sam Wanamaker, work began on the construction of a new Globe in 1993, close to the site of the original theatre. It was completed three years later, and Queen Elizabeth II officially opened the New Globe Theatre on June 12th, 1997 with a production of "Henry V".

The New Globe Theatre is as faithful a reproduction as possible to the Elizabethan theatre, given that the details of the original are only known from sketches of the time. The building can accommodate 1,500 people between the galleries and the 'groundlings.'

www.shakespeares-globe.org

There are also replica Globe theatres in Rome and Berlin, The Old Globe in San Diego, and even an 'Ice Globe' in Sweden. In New York, ambitious plans are underway to convert a decaying military fortification, built to defend America against the British in the War of 1812, into a New Globe – and amazingly, the existing structure has an identical footprint to Shakespeare's Globe Theatre in London.

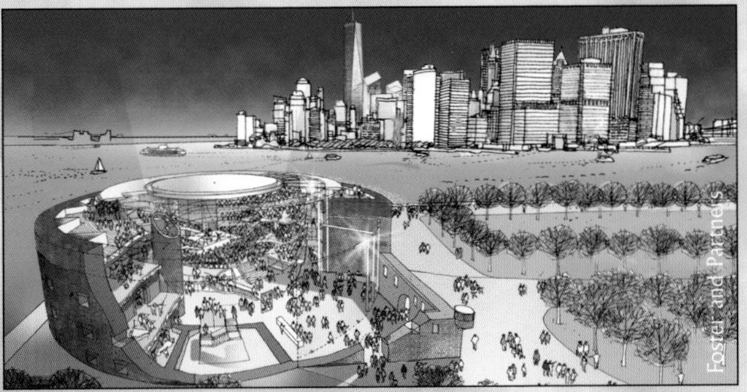
Foster and Partners

New York: **www.newglobe.org**
Rome: **www.globetheatreroma.com**
San Diego: **www.oldglobe.org**
Berlin: **www.shakespeare-company.de**
Sweden: **www.athropolis.com**

Shakespeare Today

Our fascination with William Shakespeare has not diminished over the centuries. Despite being written over 400 years ago, his plays are still read in schools, adapted into graphic novels(!), made into films, performed in theatres the world over, and are still taken to the public by acting troupes, such as the **British Shakespeare Company**. The tradition of open-air theatre is deeply rooted in British culture. For over a thousand years companies have created theatres in the centre of towns, erecting a pageant wagon or scaffolding stage from which to perform great historical and classical drama for a mass audience. These open-air acting troupes, which weathered the theatrical shifts from medieval Mystery and Morality plays towards the sophisticated characterisation of Elizabethan drama, were the inspiration behind the British Shakespeare Company. The pageant wagons, and later inn-yards and amphitheatres outside London, were for centuries the only means by which Shakespeare and others could communicate with audiences beyond the capital. Today, more than 100,000 people watch BSC performances each year. With a full company of players and performances that feature original live music and songs, beautiful period costumes and the magic of a summer's evening, the BSC is fulfilling that primary aim of all performers throughout the years: to enchant and delight audiences of all classes and ages. **www.britishshakespearecompany.com**

On the other side of the Atlantic, New York has **Shakespeare in the Park**. Since 1962, The Public Theater has staged productions of Shakespeare at The Delacorte Theater in Central Park. These performances are seen by approximately 80,000 New Yorkers and visitors each summer. In fact, since its inception, many of today's most acclaimed actors have taken part, including Morgan Freeman, Meryl Streep, Denzel Washington, Christopher Walken, Kevin Kline, Natalie Portman, Marcia Gay Harden, Philip Seymour Hoffman, Patrick Stewart, Jeff Goldblum and Billy Crudup, as well as dozens of directors and designers. **www.publictheater.org**

Another groundbreaking scheme belongs to the **Canadian Adaptations of Shakespeare Project.** CASP aims to be the largest collection of teaching and learning resources related to Shakespeare on the Internet. They are continuing to develop resources that use adaptation theory to study and teach about Shakespeare's works and their cultural effects, drawing on multimedia presentations and even including an arcade-style game to promote learning.

www.canadianshakespeares.ca

It seems that whatever time brings to our global society, and whatever developments take place within our cultures, William Shakespeare continues to have a place in our hearts and in our lives.

A UK publisher creating graphic novel adaptations of literary classics. True to the original vision of the authors, our books have been further enhanced by using only the finest artists - giving you a truly wonderful reading experience that you'll return to again and again.

Henry V is available in three text formats, all using the same high quality artwork:

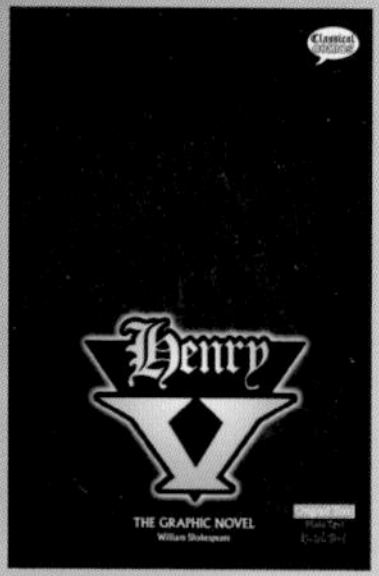
Henry V
THE GRAPHIC NOVEL
William Shakespeare

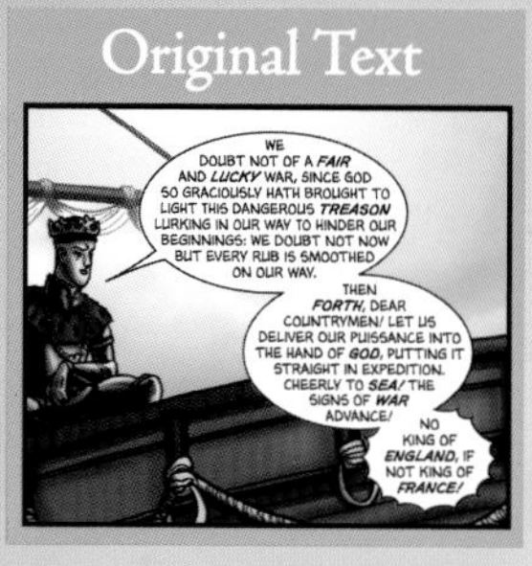
Original Text
WE DOUBT NOT OF A FAIR AND LUCKY WAR, SINCE GOD SO GRACIOUSLY HATH BROUGHT TO LIGHT THIS DANGEROUS TREASON LURKING IN OUR WAY TO HINDER OUR BEGINNINGS: WE DOUBT NOT NOW BUT EVERY RUB IS SMOOTHED ON OUR WAY.
THEN FORTH, DEAR COUNTRYMEN! LET US DELIVER OUR PUISSANCE INTO THE HAND OF GOD, PUTTING IT STRAIGHT IN EXPEDITION. CHEERLY TO SEA! THE SIGNS OF WAR ADVANCE!
NO KING OF ENGLAND, IF NOT KING OF FRANCE!

Original Text

This is the full, original script - just as The Bard intended. This version is ideal for purists, students and for readers who want to experience the unaltered text; but unlike a cold script, our beautiful artwork turns reading the play into a much more fulfilling experience. All of the text, all of the excitement!

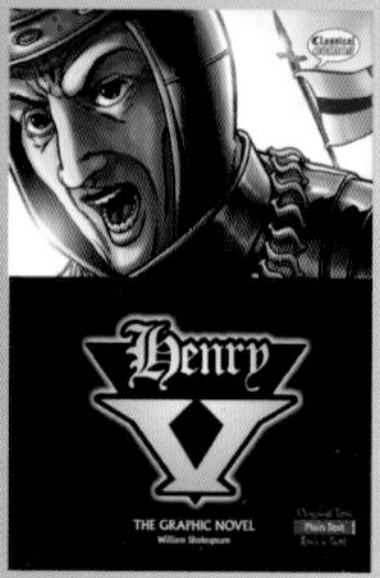
Henry V
THE GRAPHIC NOVEL
William Shakespeare

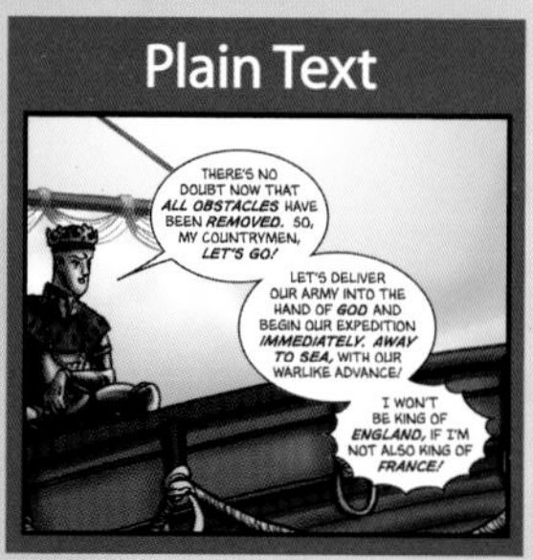
Plain Text
THERE'S NO DOUBT NOW THAT ALL OBSTACLES HAVE BEEN REMOVED. SO, MY COUNTRYMEN, LET'S GO!
LET'S DELIVER OUR ARMY INTO THE HAND OF GOD AND BEGIN OUR EXPEDITION IMMEDIATELY. AWAY TO SEA, WITH OUR WARLIKE ADVANCE!
I WON'T BE KING OF ENGLAND, IF I'M NOT ALSO KING OF FRANCE!

Plain Text

We take the original script and "convert" it into modern English, verse-for-verse. If you've ever wanted to fully appreciate the works of Shakespeare, but find the original language rather cryptic, then this is the version for you! This adaptation is ideal to help you fully understand the original text.

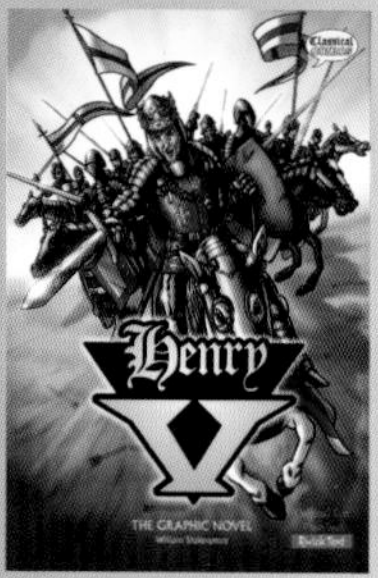
Henry V
THE GRAPHIC NOVEL
William Shakespeare

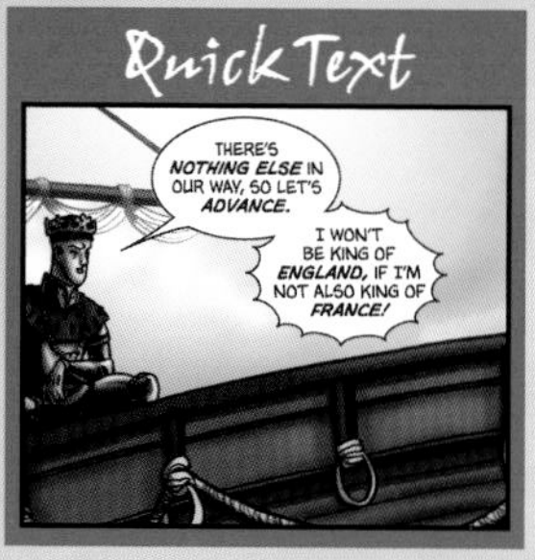
Quick Text
THERE'S NOTHING ELSE IN OUR WAY, SO LET'S ADVANCE.
I WON'T BE KING OF ENGLAND, IF I'M NOT ALSO KING OF FRANCE!

Quick Text

A revolution in graphic novels! We take the dialogue and reduce it to as few words as possible, but still retain the full essence of the story. This version allows readers to enter into and enjoy the stories quickly; and because the word balloons are smaller than in the other text versions, it also allows the fullest appreciation of our stunning artwork.

Classical Comics – Bringing classics to life!

OTHER CLASSICAL COMICS TITLES:

Macbeth

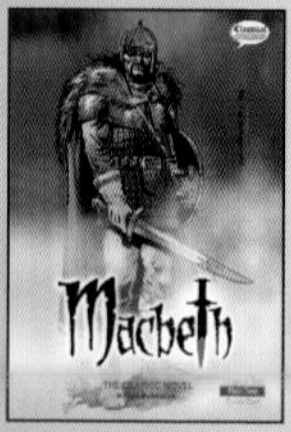
Macbeth

Published February 2008

Jane Eyre

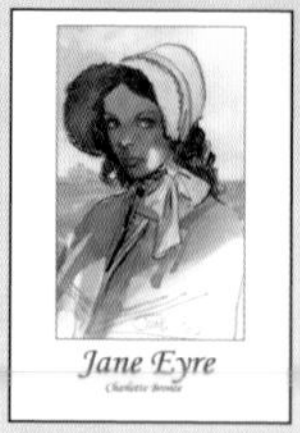
Jane Eyre

Published Spring 2008

Great Expectations

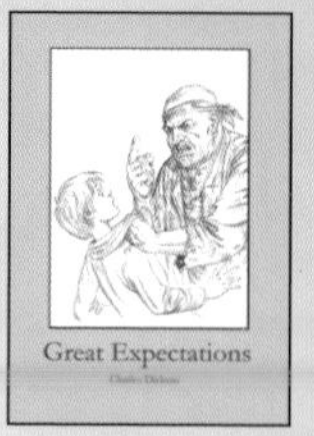
Great Expectations

Published Spring 2008

Frankenstein

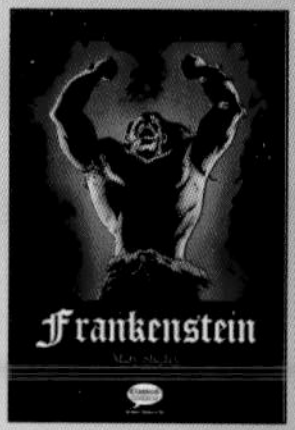
Frankenstein

Published Summer 2008

Cover designs for illustration purposes only.